SERENGETI

J.B. ROCKWELL

SEVERED PRESS
HOBART TASMANIA

SERENGETI

ONE

Serengeti dropped out of hyperspace into a quiet, empty section of the cosmos.

Too quiet. Too empty.

Sensors drank in data, feeding it to *Serengeti's* AI brain.

"Something's not right," she said

Henricksen cocked his head, looking up at the camera. "Because *we're* here or because the ships we came after *aren't?*"

Serengeti shunted the sensors' feeds to the bridge. "Take a look for yourself."

Henricksen frowned and stabbed at a panel, parsing through the information it displayed. "Nothing." He shook his head. "Doesn't make sense. There should be *something* here."

"There should," *Serengeti* agreed, studying him through the camera's electronic eye. "That's what has me worried."

Brutus—Bastion class, commander of their fleet—sent three scouts ahead, but none of them came back. Needless to say, *Brutus* was *not* happy. In his inimitable wisdom, he decided to send yet one *more* ship after those missing three. That's how *Serengeti* ended up here, in this oh-so-quiet, oh-so-empty section of space. She and Henricksen, the rest of their crew.

Drew the short straw. Lucky us.

She scanned the area around them and found nothing. No marker buoys or distress beacons. No radiation signatures, none of the electronic noise interstellar vessels endlessly squawked out. Not one sign of their scouts or the enemy warships they'd been tracking. Just an unsettling silence

Not good. Not good at all.

Space was many things, but it was seldom quiet.

"Nothing." Henricksen pounded the panel in frustration. "Not a goddamned thing." He straightened, looking out the huge windows wrapping the front of the bridge. "Where the hell are they, *Serengeti?*"

Gone, she thought, drifting in the darkness, the stars keeping her company. *Destroyed like all the other ships before them.*

Three ships—*Osage, Barlow, Veil of Tears*—lost with all their crew. Hundreds lives—AI and human both—wiped out in an instant. Hundreds added to the thousands already spent in this decades-long war between the Dark Star Revolution and the Meridian Alliance government.

"Bastard." Henricksen punched the panel in front of him. "*Brutus* already had intel on the DSR ships. He never should've sent *Barlow* and the others here. Or you after them," he added, turning his eyes back to the camera.

Serengeti considered him a moment, deciding how to answer. Henricksen was captain—her fourth captain in as many decades and by far her favorite. Solid man. Smart. Good instincts. Cool under pressure, when so many of his kind ran hot. More importantly, he knew his place. Knew he was captain of *Serengeti's* crew, but not of *Serengeti* herself.

His predecessor never quite figured that out.

"Bastion says go, we go," she said simply. "He leads this fleet, whether we like it or not."

Henricksen grimaced, obviously *not* liking it. Not one bit.

Serengeti didn't blame him. As AIs went, *Brutus* was kind of a prick.

"There won't *be* a fleet if he keeps throwing away ships like this." Henricksen stared at the camera, waiting for *Serengeti* to respond, dropped his eyes to the display in front of him when she didn't and toggled the feed, swapping one view for another and another. And when the electronic displays didn't give him what he wanted, Henricksen turned to the bridge's windows, searching the stars outside for answers.

Serengeti found that amusing. As if human eyes could ever compete with AI sensors.

"Dammit." Henricksen curled his hands into fists, smacking the panel in frustration. "What the hell's going on, *Serengeti*?" He looked up at a camera. "They should be here. *Something* should be here."

"There should," she said again, having nothing better to offer.

Henricksen grimaced, obviously hoping for more. "Two weeks, *Serengeti*. Two goddamn weeks we've been chasing those DSR bastards, and now they're just gone. Ghosted away."

"And our scouts gone with them."

"Yeah." Henricksen sighed and rubbed his face, scrubbed fingers through his short-clipped hair.

Dark hair. Black as coal, once. Peppered with grey now, after so many years travelling the dark and stars.

"*Brutus* is gonna be pissed," he said, eyeing the camera.

"Probably right." *Serengeti* paused, choosing her words carefully. "This mission—"

"Mission." Kusikov—Communications Officer, a slim, bookish-looking young man in an ill-fitting uniform—snorted in disdain. "More like wild goose chase," he said, throwing a sullen look at the nearest camera.

Henricksen folded his arms, glowering at his comms officer. "You got a problem, Kusikov?"

Kusikov flushed and cut his eyes away, taking a sudden interest in the station in front of him. He was overly smart for a human, and well aware of it—a fact *Serengeti* found amusing at times, and flat-out annoying at others—but even Kusikov knew better than to lock horns with Henricksen. Especially on the bridge.

"No, sir," Kusikov muttered. "No problem."

"Good," Henricksen grunted, turning away.

"Waste of time," Kusikov mumbled.

Henricksen froze, back rigid, head turning slowly toward Comms. "Is that what you think? Really?"

"I wasn't—"

"'Cause I don't think the relatives of those people on Tissolo do."

Ice in Henricksen's voice, an arctic tundra in his grey eyes.

"I didn't—I wasn't—" Shock drained the color from Kusikov's face, shame sparked two bright blooms on his cheeks. "I'm sorry, sir."

"Damn right, you are. Tissolo started all this, Kusikov. Not the war maybe—that's been going on as long as anyone can remember—but that's why we're here now," Henricksen jerked a thumb at the windows, "taking census of this backwater section of space."

Kusikov ducked his head, flushing more brightly.

They all knew about Tissolo now, and the mining colony the Dark Star Revolution destroyed a few weeks back. No one paid much attention to the planet before then, but after what the DSR did...uproar. Demands for retaliation, blood for blood.

That's how things went these days.

And so, to appease the people on Tissolo, and address the fears of the twenty-eight other planets under Meridian Alliance rule, the Citadel sent *Brutus* and a small armada after them. Three hundred and forty-two heavily armed AI warships sent after a rag-tag fleet of DSR vessels.

Brutus, being *Brutus,* was only too happy to take on the challenge. After all, it was a big operation—an *important* operation—and a chance to get noticed by the Citadel, who was admiral in charge of the fleet. Two weeks they'd been searching, chasing the DSR ships that attached Tissolo across light years of space. Two weeks of failure and missed chances.

Brutus was starting to feel the pressure. *Serengeti* almost felt bad for him. Almost.

"Tissolo was a massacre." Henricksen took a step towards Comms.

Kusikov blanched and moved a step away.

"Our job, Kusikov, is to hunt down every last one of those DSR bastards and destroy them."

Cold words. Simple, brutal orders passed down from the highest levels. No trial this time. No second chances. No benefit of the doubt or consideration of the DSR's intentions. Just death and vengeance. That's the point they'd gotten to in this war.

Henricksen moved another step closer. "Bastion says find those ships and chew them into tiny metallic bits, then that's what we're gonna do. Savvy?"

"Yes, sir," Kusikov said quietly.

"Good. Now stop complaining and find something useful to do."

"Aye, sir." Kusikov stared at his feet—head bowed, shoulders slumped, looking like a contrite schoolboy. A quick look at the camera above him, shoulders shrugging apologetically, and Kusikov stabbed at the panel in front of him, carefully avoiding his captain's eyes, never quite looking him in the face.

Henricksen gave him a long look, eyeing Kusikov suspiciously as he puttered about, trying to appear busy. "I said *useful*, Kusikov. That's just randomly poking buttons."

"Yes, sir." A hint of sullenness crept back into Kusikov's voice, but he grabbed up his comms visor, fiddling with the settings before slipping it over his head.

Henricksen grunted, shaking his head as he turned away from Comms and looked up at the nearest camera. "So whaddaya wanna do?"

Serengeti thought a moment before answering. "Empty this place may be, but there's more here, I think, than meets the eye."

Or sensors in her case. *Serengeti* didn't really have eyes, just her systems and her sensors, the cameras throughout her body. But then, those were better than human eyes, weren't they?

Infinitely better. Far more exact.

She studied the stars outside through those sensors, activated a dozen different cameras set in the plating of her hull and peered through those too, AI mind processing, parsing through reams of streaming data.

Not much there. Not much to go on at all.

"I say we take a closer look."

Henricksen dropped his eyes to the bridge's front windows, taking a look himself. "Good idea," he said, nodding slowly.

"Initiating active scans." *Serengeti* reached for systems, sending a deluge of muons and other elementary particles into the emptiness around them.

"Short range is coming up empty," a woman's crisp voice said.

That was Finlay at the Scan station—late to the party and trying to make up for it. She was a tiny thing, even for a human. Petite and red-headed with a spray of freckles across her cheeks and nose, bright—though not the genius Kusikov claimed to be, nor a tenth as annoying—eager and just the tiniest bit naive.

Serengeti liked her. Liked her a lot. In fact, she liked *most* of the crew she'd been given this time around. Even Kusikov when he wasn't being a smart-ass know-it-all. Not as many veterans on board as there once were, but she enjoyed this crew's youthful exuberance. Their idealistic approach to a war that had raged for half a century and more.

A little *too* idealistic sometimes, *Serengeti* admitted, but Henricksen kept them grounded. Henricksen and Sikuuku, the handful of other veterans throughout the ship. They'd seen it all—the worst war had to offer—and adapted. Overcame. Kept on fighting.

Serengeti respected that, and them. Youthful exuberance was one thing. Youthful exuberance *unfettered* could get them all killed.

She let the scans run, processed the data they returned and then waited, holding her tongue, letting Finlay work through the information in her slow, methodical way.

Finlay cycled her panel, swapping one data screen for another. "Long-range scan's picking something up."

Good girl.

"What?" Henricksen demanded. "What's out there?"

"Hard to tell." Finlay frowned in confusion, shaking her head. "Few pings, that's it." She tapped at the panel in front of her, scrolling through the sensors' data streams one after the other. Lot of information there. Hard for a human mind—even a bright one like Finlay's—to make sense of it all. "Dammit." Finlay swiped at the panel in frustration, starting over from the beginning.

Serengeti parsed a few strings, ran a quick correlation, and pushed the results to the Scan station to help Finlay out. She'd get it eventually, but *Serengeti* needed to move this along. An AI only had so much patience for the slowing processing of a human mind, after all.

Finlay pulled the new data over to her central screen and leaned close, brow furrowed as her eyes devoured the information. "Looks like...metal? Some kind of alloy? Or composite, maybe." A few more taps at her screen, another shake of her head. "Whatever's out there, it's *not* a ship."

"At least not anymore," Henricksen said softly. Far too softly for Finlay or the rest of the bridge crew to hear, just loud enough for *Serengeti's* microphones to pick his words up. He raised his eyes to the camera in front of him, mounted high up on the wall. "Could've been, once upon a time."

He stared into the camera's lens a second or two and then flicked his eyes back to the front windows, looking out at the stars.

Serengeti looked with him, studying the emptiness outside with one fraction of her consciousness while the bulk of her processing power sifted through the wealth of data her systems collected.

Definitely metal out there. Metal and composite both. But whether it was the remains of a ship or not…

Hard to tell. Finlay's right in that.

Serengeti amped up the sensors, reaching farther out with her scans, stretching to the very edge of her systems' range to suck in more data.

Information poured in, but it didn't really offer anything more than what Finlay had already reported. There wasn't much out there—that's just about all the scan data said.

But those pings…

Distant as they were, *scattered* as they were, those pings merited further investigation.

"Launching probes," *Serengeti* said, voice soft and serene, infinitely confident.

Flares erupted along her port and starboard sides, rounded metallic shapes shooting off into space, ion drives glowing cobalt blue in the darkness.

"Finlay. Bring the probes' cameras up on the main screen," Henricksen ordered.

Finlay stared at the console a moment, lips pressed tight, looking like she'd eaten a lemon.

"Finlay!"

"Aye, sir." Finlay threw an irritated look at the closest camera as she set her hands on the panels in front of her. She was mad—that was clear—and her fingers fairly flew across the Scan station as she called up the feeds from the twelve probes *Serengeti* had sent out. A few seconds of processing and she shunted the video to the front windows—thick panes stretching from the floor to ceiling, curving with the outside wall of the bridge—so the rest of the command crew could see.

Odd, those windows, and that state of the art vessels like *Serengeti*, still came equipped with them. Once upon a time, those reinforced panes were necessary, back in the days when ships' scans were limited and line of sight still mattered. But now…modern ships' systems provided far more information than human eyes could ever discern.

And yet human designers clung to the idea of windows anyway, inserting them into every new ship that rolled off the line. *Serengeti* asked Henricksen about that once, wondering why humans insisted on keeping such a silly, useless thing. Henricksen just shrugged and said they liked them. That they liked to look *through* them at the stars…

An error message appeared, flashing until *Serengeti* gave it her attention. She spotted the problem right away and started to fix it.

Finlay belatedly noticed and jumped in to help. "Number Ten's malfunctioning." She frowned at the blank window where the data from the Number Ten feed should have been. Number Ten had always been buggy—a manufacturing defect, or maybe just a quirk of its programming. The probes were AI, after all, and designed by humans. "Running diagnostics."

Faster if *Serengeti* ran the diagnostics herself, but she left Finlay to it to appease her, and cast her eyes about the bridge while she waited for the results.

Five stations on the bridge—plus the captain's chair—with a single crewman manning each. The Captain's Command Post sat dead center in the middle with the other stations—Scan, Communications, Navigation, Engineering, Artillery—arranged in a ring around it.

Circular stations, circular bridge, circular camera eyes watching over it all. The ship designers certainly do like circles, *Serengeti* thought idly.

She checked in on Finlay, working away at her circular station, found her still working furiously away.

This was taking too long. Ten was a puzzle *Serengeti* figured out long ago, no sense having Finlay try to recover that ground. She reached for the probe herself, bypassing Finlay entirely to dip directly into Number Ten's systems.

"Repairs complete," *Serengeti* said, making a last few adjustments before bringing the probe's feed online.

"I had it," Finlay muttered, stabbing angrily at the console in front of her.

"Stow it, Finlay," Henricksen barked.

Finlay flushed brightly. "Aye, sir. Sorry, sir." She raised her eyes to the camera in front of her, looking angry and contrite at the same time. She nodded stiffly to the camera and then bowed her head, focusing all of her attention on the Scan station in front of her.

Finlay was a hard charger and didn't like being shown up. By anyone. Not even a Valkyrie class starship. *Serengeti* filed that away, adding it to the library of information she'd collected from her human crews over the years. She was AI, her mind a thousand times more powerful than a human's organic brain, but she forgot sometimes how important it was for humans to feel needed.

Need. Such a strange concept. So difficult for an AI to understand. Truth be told, *Serengeti* didn't really *need* her human crew. It was slower—infinitely slower—to let them run basic ship's operations. She could manage everything on her own and *still* have enough processing power to monitor the hundreds of cameras and relays, circuits and networks and every other thing wired into her body.

But I like having them about, Serengeti thought to herself.

Crew was…comforting. For herself *and* the humans who'd made her. Truth be told, humans still didn't quite trust AIs. Funny, considering human engineers designed every last one of them, making them stronger, more capable with each generation. Humans built AIs and wrapped them inside armored shells they launched into the stars, but they still wanted human crews on board those space-faring ships. Human minds and human judgment as a counter—or perhaps a foil—to ship's intelligence. Because most AIs couldn't *feel* in the way humans did.

Maybe there's something to that, Serengeti mused. *We've learned emotion—some of us anyway—but it's not organic. Not innate.*

She cast her eyes across the bridge, looking from Henricksen to the stations behind him, circling around to Finlay at Scan. Need was important—*Serengeti* learned that over the years. Next time, she'd let Finlay run the scans and argue with Number Ten.

Good luck with that *one, sister.*

Two

"What's the displacement variation for this one?" Henricksen glanced at the camera, nodded to the dark and stars showing outside the bridge's windows. "Jump's not exactly a precise operation. Could be *Barlow* and the others are here somewhere, just out of range of our scans."

"Possible," *Serengeti* agreed. *Though not likely.*

She kept that last part to herself.

Jump coordinates approximated an area covering nearly a thousand square kilometers of space. They'd sent themselves to the same coordinates as the advance scouts and found nothing. But it was possible those three ships had jumped through to one extreme of the jump displacement and *Serengeti* and her crew to the other.

A slim hope, but better than no hope at all. Hope was a different kind of need. Humans died when they ran out of hope.

Serengeti ran the calculations, factoring in distance and the time that had elapsed since the three scouts left the fleet. "Forty-eight hundred."

Henricksen chewed at his lip, thinking that over. He leaned over, tapping at one of a half dozen consoles bolted to his chair—one panel for each of the bridge's stations and a mash-up screen that showed everything at once—making the Captain's Command Post look like some kind of mutated octopus. He worked at the Scan screen a minute, switched to the console for Nav, then transferred the data from both to the mashup-screen in front of him.

"Damn," he said softly. "Debris falls within the displacement zone."

Grim look on Henricksen's face. Angry, weary tone in his voice.

The bridge crew went silent, staring at their captain before quickly looking away.

"It could be them. But it could just as easily be one of the DSR ships," *Serengeti* told him. "Or nothing at all. Just ancient space junk transiting through the area."

"Maybe." But from the way he shook his head, the way his hands gripped the edge of his console, knuckles showing white against the skin, Henricksen didn't believe it. "Damn," he growled, angry, frustrated. "Damn, damn, damn."

Believe it or not, she knew how he felt. *Serengeti's* designers would be appalled if they knew the depths of the anger that seethed inside her. AIs were never *meant* to feel—not anything, just the concept of emotions—but AIs never stopped learning, and war...war taught *Serengeti* many things. Damn right she understood anger. She'd learned what *true* anger meant in her fifty-three years of service to the Meridian Alliance, fighting the DSA on the front lines. Fifty-three years, three lost crews, and two complete refits, *Serengeti's* crystal-matrix mind transferred from one twisted, shredded metal shell to another, exchanging her battered form for a sparkling new Valkyrie skin, complete with an arsenal of the latest weapons, and a shiny new crew. Fifty-three years of brothers and sisters dying, their AI containment pods cracked, brilliant minds destroyed with the metal composite hull around them. Fifty-three years, and each loss still hurt. Each one added to the load of anger churning deep within her crystal-matrix mind. *Serengeti* was tenth generation AI, her body armed and armored, a carapace built for war, but the losses were hard to handle. Even for her.

Too much dying. Too much loss, human and AI both.

Stop being so melancholy, Serengeti.

She pushed those thoughts away and focused on the mission at hand. "We need to clear the area before we send word back to the armada. I don't want them coming through until I'm sure it's safe."

Henricksen nodded and looked to the camera, waiting for her orders. For *her* orders, because *Serengeti* was ship, and ultimately in charge.

"Probes are sitting idle," she said, offering that much, let him work out the rest for himself.

"Run 'em in a grid pattern?" he suggested.

"Makes sense."

"Right. Finlay. Get Ten and Six in there to investigate those debris clouds and find out what they are."

"Aye, sir." Finlay set to work.

Henricksen watched her for a moment and then turned his eyes to the front windows, brow creasing in a frown of worry.

"Henricksen." *Serengeti* waited until Henricksen looked up at the camera. "*Osage* and *Veil of Tears* came here. *Barlow* was right behind them. They're not here now and I want to know why. I want to know where they went. I want to know what happened to them."

She dropped the calm, serene tones and let the anger show through in her voice. Henricksen cocked his head to one side, giving the camera a considering look. And then he nodded—just once—and looked away, barking orders at Comms.

"Kusikov!"

"Aye, sir!" Kusikov's muffled response came from somewhere beneath the Comms station. He extracted himself and climbed to his feet, slipping a multi-tool surreptitiously into his pocket. He'd obviously been fiddling with something—he always was in his spare time, insisting *Serengeti's* comms package and language routines needed improvement.

Serengeti didn't like people messing with her systems, and Henricksen knew it. "For the luvva god, Kusikov, stop messing with the equipment!"

"Yes, sir. Sorry, sir."

Automatic response accompanied by a mischievous, most-definitely-not-sorry smile.

"Cut the shit, Kusikov."

Kusikov's smile withered, sobering up quickly under Henricksen's withering gaze. "Sorry, sir," he said, doing his best to sound sincere.

"You are that, Kusikov. Now if you're done screwin' with *Serengeti's* systems, *maybe* you could actually do your fucking job."

Henricksen didn't swear often—well, he used 'damn' a lot but that really didn't count—so when he did it got the crew's attention. Fast.

"Aye, sir." Kusikov saluted smartly, all business now. He reached for the cables dangling from his station, jacking relays into the ports in his wrists and neck, grabbing the comms visor from the panel where he'd set it and slipping it over his eyes.

He was…interesting, this one. Arrogant. Cocky as hell. And yet, one of the brightest human minds *Serengeti* had come across in her travels. She wasn't quite sure if she *liked* Kusikov, but she respected him. She just hoped he never figured it out. If he did, she'd never heard the end of it.

"Send a comms buoy back to the fleet," Henricksen ordered. "Tell them the scouts aren't here. Advise them to hold back while we figure out what's going on."

"Aye, sir." Kusikov went still for a few seconds, fingers splayed out on the console in front of him, eyes flicking rapid-fire from one piece of data to another, drinking in the information the visor displayed. A twitch of his fingers sent instructions back out, delivering the orders as fast as his human brain could process them. "Buoy away, sir."

"Right."

Henricksen turned to one side, staring out the windows, waiting for the buoy to appear. It took a few seconds—the buoys were simple things and not equipped with the probes' ion drives—but once it appeared, the buoy quickly moved away. Henricksen watched it, tracking the little buoy with his eyes until it flashed and jumped away, returning to the fleet of ships waiting light years away.

"How we doing, Finlay?" he asked, staring at the back of Finlay's red head.

Finlay was having a tough time of it—the look on her face made that clear. Probes One through Five were in place and patiently working their way through the grid pattern she'd laid out, Six had reached the edge of the huge cloud of drifting debris and started sending data back, but she'd just barely gotten the others into place when good old Number Ten started to act up again.

Serengeti had seen it coming, knew the warning signs that meant Ten was up to his old shenanigans but—true to her word—she'd left it for Finlay to figure out this time. In retrospect, that might not have been such a good idea.

"Probes are working their way through, Captain, but Ten's being a bit balky again. I can't—it won't—" Finlay huffed in frustration, hands curling into fists on the console in front of her. "I'm sorry, sir. I know *Serengeti*—"

"Finlay."

Finlay stiffened and then bowed her head.

Serengeti watched her, flipping from one camera to another, cycling through the many views of the bridge her electronics eyes offered. Movement from Henricksen—a slight shake of his head, eyes locked onto the front camera as he stepped away from his Command Post and walked over to the Scan station.

"Don't take it personally." Henricksen leaned close to Finlay, pitching his voice low so the other bridge crew wouldn't hear.

Serengeti zoomed in, studying the two of them together, enjoying the moment—this rare glimpse at was scarred, grizzled, oh-so-very-military Henricksen's softer side. Dark and imposing—that was Henricksen. Tough as old leather and about as cuddly as a brick, everything planes and angles and muscles stretched taut across tendon and bone. In military fashion, he kept his dark hair clipped short and buzzed tight against his head, uniform crisp and clean, snugged close and fitted perfectly to his rangy frame. Henricksen loomed over tiny, red-haired Finlay, a dark shadow wrapped in a jet black uniform, the silver stars of Command flashing brightly at his throat while Finlay sat her station, looking tiny and girlish, her own dark uniform somehow making her look tinier still.

Black and silver—those were *Serengeti's* colors. *All* the uniforms were black here, the crew themselves thin shadows half-hidden in the sparse light of the ship's bridge.

"Can't compete with an AI, Finlay. No one can. No *person*," Henricksen amended, lips quirking in a rueful smile. His eyes lifted, looking directly into the camera in front of him.

Henricksen knew she was watching. *Serengeti's* eyes were everywhere, her mind split into a hundred sub-minds keeping tabs on everything and everyone in the ship, but unlike her other captains, Henricksen didn't seem to mind. That was another reason *Serengeti* liked him. Trust, respect—not all humans felt them toward AI.

A wink at the camera and Henricksen focused back on Finlay, hand settling on her shoulder, squeezing gently. "A mind like *Serengeti's*…hell, even the other AIs feel inferior compared to a Valkyrie like her. Crystal matrix, Finlay. Hundred times the processing power of that piece-a grey matter you got in your head," he said, giving her a playful tap on the temple. "Makes the likes of you and me look like idiots." Another smile, this one for Finlay.

She turned her head and looked up at her captain, face surprised, hopeful, infinitely grateful. "Yes, sir." Finlay dipped her head. "Thank you, sir."

Henricksen straightened, returning to gruff captain mode. "Alright. Eyes up front now, Finlay. Let's see what those probes have to show us."

"Yes, sir." Finlay faced around, sucked in a breath and then started tapping away at her console, adding a scrolling readout of data to each of the video feeds.

Ten's feed was garbled—*Serengeti* slipped in and fixed it when Finlay wasn't looking—and the other feeds from most of the other probes were empty, just twinkles and black and line after line of data that basically said the universe was stardust and moonbeams and could *Serengeti* please keep it down a bit because she was ever so noisy.

Cheeky, she sent.

The probes sent protests and AI laughter back.

Serengeti flipped to the probes' cameras, tapping into them directly so she could gaze upon the stars through their electronic eyes. She loved the stars—not really surprising since she'd been born to the darkness and the distant, twinkling lights—and the freedom that came with floating in that endless black, jumping through hyperspace from one star cluster to another, witnessing the miracles the universe had to offer.

Humans craved planets, fought endless wars over rock and dirt and vegetation, but *Serengeti* cared nothing for those balls of water and soil. All she'd ever wanted was the stars. All she wanted was to explore the universe and drink in the endless black.

"Probes have reached the debris cloud." Finlay nodded to the feeds from Ten and Six showing on the front windows, adjusted the probes' cameras from her station and zoomed in.

Ten and Six entered the collection of junk from opposite directions, working their way through the cloud, dodging this bit and that, sensor arrays reaching out, scanning everything in their path and sending it back to *Serengeti*. Their feeds—now that they were both working properly—were *quite* interesting.

"Carbon, titanium, cadmium—that's metal composite out there, alright. Maybe some plastics as well. Zoom in on that, would you?" Henricksen pointed to something at the edge of Number Ten's video feed.

Finlay nodded and sent instructions to the probe, turning it to one side and then moving it closer to one of the larger bits of debris. The space junk tumbled round and round, making it hard for the little probe to get a fix on it, so Finlay extruded a metal arm from the probe's side, catching the hunk of scrap with grasping, finger-like appendages and then pulling it close to the camera so they could get a better look.

"Huh," Henricksen grunted. "Whatever it was, it's been shredded."

"You think it's one of the scouts, sir?" Finlay asked him.

"Hard to tell. Could be. Could just be some old clunker got blown up decades ago," he added with a nod to *Serengeti's* forward-facing camera. "Only one way to be sure. Send the probe in to get a reading on the mass of that debris cloud. Collect some samples while it's at it. See if that can't tell us anything."

"Aye, sir."

Finlay sent a stream of instructions to the probe, eyes focused on the screen, watching its movements, making adjustments on the fly. Scan picked up an incoming ship, but she was so busy with the probe that she didn't notice. *Serengeti* nudged the data to the edge of Finlay's screen, nudged it again when she brushed it aside. Oh well, no time to wait for her.

Sorry, Finlay. Breaking my promise already.

Serengeti sounded the proximity alarm, setting klaxons to scream all over the ship.

THREE

"Perimeter alert."

Serengeti's calm, clear voice cut clean through the sirens sounding on the bridge.

Finlay's panel lit up like a Christmas tree, warning lights flashing all over her screen. "Incoming vessel," she cried, abandoning the probes outside to pour through the new data coming in.

"Where?" Henricksen barked.

"Dropping out of hyperspace."

"Obviously, but where, Finlay. Goddammit *where*?"

"Aft. Starboard side," *Serengeti* told him, throwing that feed onto the screen along with all the others. A cluttered mess of data streams and video feeds filled the front windows. She shoved the probes' feeds to the side for now, letting this newest one take front and center. "Hundred and fifty kilometers, give or take."

"Too close," Henricksen growled. "Way too close." He stared at the feed for a moment, seeming to think something over, and then spun to the side, barking orders at the blocky specimen of humanity stuffed into the Artillery station. "Sikuuku! Fire up the aft turrets. Alert the port and starboard batteries we've got company."

"Aye, sir," Sikuuku called back. He grabbed his targeting helmet and stuffed it over his head as he called down to the ancillary stations, telling them to bring all of *Serengeti's* batteries on-line. Sikuuku was a veteran like his captain—a squat, square man with a swirling pattern of tattoos on his face and burn scars running up and down his arms. He ran the main gun from the Artillery station—a gimbaled pod set on the far side of the bridge—while simultaneously coordinating the preparations of the forty odd batteries sticking out of Serengeti's hull. "Firing solution plotted. Armaments are primed and ready, Captain."

"Good. Finlay. Talk to me. What's out there?"

"Can't tell. Still coming in."

"Is it ours?" Henricksen asked her, throwing Finlay's screens onto the panel beside him.

Serengeti tapped into the Scan feed and parsed the information looking for data tags, electronic signatures, anything to tell them what was coming in. But it was all just noise—shredded information distorted by hyperspace, impossible to interpret until the ship out there dropped in.

"Finlay!"

"Trying, sir."

"*Is it ours, Finlay?*" Henricksen demanded.

"Not sure," she said, fingers flying across the panel, eyes flicking everywhere, devouring the data it displayed.

A wrinkle in space, starlight bending one side and the other revealing a gaping black hole that tunneled into hyperspace. A squirt of data hit them—names, call signs, beacon markers loudly proclaiming the identity of the vessels coming through. *Serengeti* drank it in and then waited, wasting precious seconds while Finlay's slower human brain worked its way through that same data.

"C'mon, Finlay," Henricksen growled.

"*Brutus!*" she cried. "*Brutus* in-bound, sir."

Serengeti killed the klaxons, sounded the all clear.

"Artillery stations. Power down and stand by," Sikuuku called, sending the message to all the batteries at once.

Kusikov opened the ship-wide channel and sent a message to the rest of the crew. "Friendlies," he said in his crisp, business-like, this-is-the-comms-officer-speaking voice. "*Brutus* in-bound. Family's all here."

Okay. Maybe *not* so business-like.

A sigh of relief spread across the bridge, crewmen smiling at one another, laughing nervously as they worked at screens with trembling, adrenaline-hyped fingers. Henricksen flicked his eyes across them and then glared out the front windows, looking completely pissed off as the dark void outside sucked inward, becoming negative light, not just black, and then seemed to pull the stars into it, eating them up. The void bent and swirled, an angry, writhing, hungry beast, and then the darkness shredded, bathing the bridge in a blinding flash of silver-white light.

The glare blinded *Serengeti's* cameras. She waited an eternity, internal chronometer counting each endless second until the light finally faded, leaving a monster behind—a hulking, grey-skinned shape hovering right where the void had been.

The Number Five probe went offline—run over by the lumpen vessel that unexpectedly parked itself right on top of it. Five's feed cut off, AI sub-mind dead in an instant—another minor casualty of this decades-long war.

Careless, Serengeti thought, eyeing *Brutus's* hulking, malformed shape across the kilometers of space separating them.

More flashes, a coordinated series of silver-white flares as *Brutus's* entourage appeared—twenty grey-skinned Dreadnoughts arrayed in a protective ring around the monstrous Bastion at their center.

Brutus was impressive, in a monstrous, misshapen sort of way, the Bastion's design born of drunken nightmares, or so the old joke went. And the Dreadnoughts...the Dreadnoughts were ugly but daunting, newer than the Valkyries—the latest and greatest in interstellar warships, dwarfed only by the Bastion that led them—and yet built on the same chassis. A chassis the designers lengthened and bulked up, adding more weapons and more armor, turning the Valkyries' smooth, sleek, torpedo shape into a warped and twisted horror. A warrior's design, sacrificing aesthetics for armor, beauty for sheer firepower.

Not that *Serengeti* was a slouch, mind you. The Valkyrie design included plasma cannons and missile batteries at bow and stern, and ranks of high-powered turret guns up and down either side. But the Dreadnoughts had guns *everywhere*, packed into every last quadrant of their bodies. In their quest to create the perfect machine of war, the engineers had even sacrificed comms arrays to make more room for still *more* weapons—as many as they could cram into the Dreadnoughts body. But what *truly* set the Dreadnoughts apart was their skin. *Serengeti's* twinkled into the darkness, her composite metal hull laced with photovoltaic cells that gathered up moonbeams and starlight, drawing their energy inside her as she drifted close and feeding it in to the power cells in her belly. An ingenious design, if she did say so herself, and one that allowed the Valkyries to recharge while travelling. One that gave her enough internal power to run her basic systems, if not her engines. Those were anti-matter—fueled by swirling chaos.

The engineers dropped the photovoltaic skin from the Dreadnought specs for some reason and added reinforced nanofiber panels instead—a complex binding of carbon weave, titanium and heat-dispersing glass forming a thin skin over the Dreadnoughts' four-tiered hull. They kept the drive system, outfitting the Dreadnoughts with the same quasi-stable, antimatter power solution that *Serengeti* and her sisters used, but the loss of photovoltaic skin turned the Dreadnoughts dark and dull, ominous-looking as they stalked between the stars. Still, the engineers claimed they were superior. Pointed to the design specs to prove it, proudly proclaiming to anyone who'd listen that the ship they'd created and the AI inside it were the epitome of what a warship should aspire to be.

That was a human opinion. Ask *Serengeti* and the other Valkyries—ask *any* of the AIs travelling in this fleet that *weren't* Dreadnought or Bastion—and you'd get a different view on the matter. They'd tell you the Dreadnoughts were thugs. Brutish, unthinking, heavily armed hooligans serving the Bastion without question.

The Bastion, not the fleet. Not the Meridian Alliance. Certainly not humanity. That too was key.

Brutus and his brethren wanted soldiers that fell in line, and *Serengeti* and her sisters asked just a few too many questions. Challenged their leadership a bit too much. So when it came time to design the Dreadnoughts—eleventh generation AI, more advanced, in theory, than the Valkyries—the Bastions subtly influenced the programming of their crystal-matrix AI brains. Encouraged the engineers to tinker a bit. Think outside the box.

Good idea, poor execution. The engineers tinkered with the Dreadnoughts' design just a little *too* much, in *Serengeti's* opinion. The Dreadnoughts were larger than the Valkyries, and more powerful, but they lost something along the way. Something important. A sense of community, of *being* that was essential to an AI's mind.

Brutus loves them, Serengeti thought, watching *Homunculus* and *Gorgon*—the last two Dreadnoughts—slide into position. *He loves the Dreadnoughts for their loyalty, their durability, their unflinching devotion. But the Dreadnoughts are cold, hard, almost indifferent to the other ships. They don't seem to care about anything, even their own crews. To the Dreadnoughts, everyone but* Brutus *is expendable. The Bastion and the mission—that's all that matters to them.*

The Dreadnoughts tightened up their formation, circling *Brutus* close about. And as they did, the rest of the armada began to appear—dozens upon dozens of hyperspace breaches forming and then dissipating in bright flares of silver-white brilliance, leaving trails of radiation behind.

No Dreadnoughts here, nor Valkyries either. The bulk of the fleet were grey-skinned Titans with bodies like four-pointed spearheads, and disc-shaped Auroras, rounded bridge pods bulging bulbously at their middle, engines arranged in double rows at their hind ends. They were smaller ships—half the size of the Dreadnoughts that preceded them, tiny compared to *Brutus* at their center, far less powerful than any of them, including *Serengeti* and her sisters—but they formed the heart of the armada. The Auroras were sixth generation AI, the Titans eighth, both mind sets known for being quirky, cheeky, often argumentative. Not their fault, really—that was part of their programming, the result of building more and more human characteristics into an AI mind. They'd dialed it back a bit when they designed the Valkyries, and even more so with the Dreadnoughts. And with the Bastions like *Brutus,* they dialed it back even more. *Too* far back, some would say, though that was a topic of endless debate.

Serengeti watched the smaller vessels appear one by one, drinking in ships' names, sifting through the data their beacons squawked out. But her eyes kept returning to the Bastion. To the hulking ship at the armada's center.

Brutus looked nothing like *Serengeti,* nor the Dreadnoughts either. Nothing like *any* of the ships it commanded. The Valkyries were smooth and sleek, warships built to kick ass and look pretty while doing it. The Dreadnoughts…well, even they had a certain flare about them, ominous as they might be. But *Brutus…Brutus* was massive. Monstrous. More fortress than warship, blocky and brutal-looking, bristling with armaments, comms towers, and sensor arrays that stuck out at every angle.

If Frankenstein ever designed a warship, its name would be *Brutus.*

"God that thing's ugly." Kusikov grimaced, studying the Bastion outside. "Ya know, they say the engineers were drunk when they came up with the Bastion design."

"Son of a bitch," Henricksen swore, punching the panel in front of him.

Kusikov jumped, instantly looked repentant. "Sorry, sir."

"Not you, Kusikov. Him. That AI piece-a shit out there." Henricksen mashed at a comms panel with his hand. "Dammit, *Brutus,* thought we told you to stay put."

Not exactly the best way to talk to the flagship, but Henricksen was a Valkyrie captain, and the Valkyrie captains were allowed a few more liberties than the Titans and Auroras. And they were known for being a bit bolder than the captains the Dreadnoughts chose.

"I've had enough of waiting, Captain."

"*Brutus,*" Kusikov breathed, staring in horror at his captain. "That was *Brutus* himself, not Comms."

Or the Captain. Surprising that the Bastion would answer himself, and probably not good, but Henricksen didn't seem to care *who* did the talking. He just looked ticked off at the entire situation. He opened his mouth, ready to volley something equally pithy back. *Serengeti* decided it was time for her to intervene.

"May I?"

She didn't need Henricksen's permission, but she respected him. And when his blood was up, the captain could be somewhat…unpredictable.

Henricksen frowned in annoyance and then glanced outside, considering *Brutus*'s far-off bulk. "Have at it," he said, waving his hand angrily.

"*Brutus,* this is *Serengeti.* Request you hold position while we finish our sweep of the area."

Silence. Absolutely silence for a full five seconds. *Brutus's* way of showing his displeasure.

"Acknowledged," he sent back. And after a short pause, "Hurry up about it."

Annoying.

"That's the plan," *Serengeti* said brightly and then closed the comms, all but cutting the Bastion off.

Seychelles sent a message—private channel, one Valkyrie saying hello to another, trading messages faster than a human blinked an eye.

Sorry for the intrusion, her message read. *Our fearless leader was in a hurry.*

Smiley face appended to the end. *Serengeti* couldn't help but laugh.

He's grumpier than usual, Serengeti sent back.

Yeah. Well. Cerberus called while you were away.

The Citadel himself. Wow. That can't be good.

Nope. Seems the masses aren't very happy that this is taking so long. Cerberus is thinking of replacing him, Seychelles confided.

Really.

Uh-huh.

This was a private message I assume. Ship-to-ship, not meant for other ears?

Mm-hmm.

And how, pray-tell, did you *come by this message?*

Seychelles sent a winky smiley face. *Refit crew owed me a favor.*

You bugged him. You bugged Brutus's comms system during an upgrade. Unbelievable!

You're just mad you didn't think of it first. Another smiley face, then, *Ciao, sister. Stay out of trouble.*

Serengeti wiped the messages—best not to keep that kind of thing around—and returned her attention to the bridge.

"Hurry up he says." Henricksen snorted in derision. "What's he think we've been doing? Sitting here with our thumbs up our asses?"

"Brutus is under pressure," *Serengeti* told him. "We've been chasing those DSR ships for almost three weeks now and *Cerberus* wants this over and done with so he can call the rest of us back to the fleet."

Cerberus, Citadel class—the one and only, the AI Admiral in charge of the entire Meridian Alliance fleet. *Brutus* was one of five Bastions, *Serengeti* one of four hundred and ninety-eight Valkyries, the twenty Dreadnoughts out there a small subset of a nearly seven hundred ship contingent, and the Titans and Auroras numbered almost eight *thousand.* All those ships, and just one *Cerberus.* Just one Citadel in all the galaxy, because that's all the Meridian Alliance could afford to build. *Serengeti* wasn't sure if that was a good or a bad thing.

"*Cerberus* will take his command if he fails," *Serengeti* noted.

"Yeah? Well, boo-hoo. We're all sick of chasing those bastards around the galaxy." Henricksen folded his arms over his chest, grey eyes glaring out the windows. "Shouldn't be here," he growled. "Armada's got no goddamn business being here until we've swept the area and called them through."

"*Brutus* leads the fleet," *Serengeti* reminded him.

"Not all of it," he told her, eyes shifting, staring angrily at a camera. "Just this piece. Last I checked, it was *Cerberus* who called the shots."

"*Cerberus* is the flagship of the fleet," *Serengeti* agreed, "and it was *Cerberus* that put *Brutus* in charge of this armada."

"And it was *Brutus* that sent you on this scouting mission," Henricksen thundered. "You tell him to wait, that arrogant AI prick needs to wait!"

Serengeti's laughter caught Henricksen off-guard. He flushed darkly, thinking she laughed *at* him, but truth was, she found his righteous anger amusing. And she had to admit, she was the tiniest bit pleased that Henricksen—proud, protective Henricksen—was angry on her behalf.

"I'll relay your message," *Serengeti* said.

Henricksen froze, eyes wide, mouth hanging open. "Wait. What?"

"You're right. We were sent ahead for a reason. It was stupid and careless of *Brutus* to come barreling through without knowing what was waiting on the other side. I'll let him know."

"Umm...alright..." Henricksen glanced over at Sikuuku, but the gunner just shrugged.

Serengeti tapped into comms, bypassing the normal ship-to-ship channel to send a message directly to *Brutus*. And then she copied the message, sending it via an encoded channel to the Valkyries in the armada, trusting them to relay it to the rest of their small fleet.

"*Brutus* has been notified."

"Notified? Notified of what?" Henricksen asked suspiciously. "What the hell did you say to him, *Serengeti*?"

"I told the arrogant AI prick he needs to wait next time." That wasn't *quite* what she'd said, but it was close enough. And the look on Henricksen's face was priceless.

"You told him..." Henricksen blinked and stared, eyes wide with disbelief. He turned his head, looking to where the hulking monstrosity that was *Brutus* floated outside, and started laughing.

"Finlay," *Serengeti* called. "Please proceed with the sample capture. Have Six and Ten siphon up as much of the debris as they can and bring it back here for the robots to go over."

The robots were her other crew—three hundred and sixteen configurable electronic minions charged with maintenance and repairs, among other things. If there were ship parts inside that debris cloud, they'd know it. And if those parts belonged to a Meridian Alliance ship, the robots would know that too. They were clever little things, and every bit as loyal as Henricksen and the others.

A message came back from *Brutus*. *Serengeti* didn't bother opening it. She was pretty sure she knew what it said. "And Finlay. Tell them to hurry up about it," she said, letting a hint of amusement creep into her voice.

"Yes, ma'am. I mean, ship. Valkyrie," Finlay corrected quickly, cheeks flushing furiously as she stumbled over the honorifics.

The etiquette for addressing AI warships was a bit...vague to say the least, but they were used to taking orders from the captain, and he from *Serengeti,* not having to address her themselves.

Serengeti slipped into Finlay's console, flashing a smiling kitty face on her screen. "*Serengeti,*" she said. "*Serengeti* will do just fine, Finlay."

"Yes, ma'am." A shy glance at the camera as Finlay tapped at her station, sending a little cartoon owl back.

"*Serengeti,*" she corrected with a laugh.

"*Serengeti,*" Finlay repeated, flushing even brighter. She ducked her head, smiling happily as she relayed *Serengeti's* instructions to the probes. "Six and Ten heading in. Grid mapping...thirty-two percent complete. Nothing yet."

"Thank you, Finlay."

Silence after that brief exchange, all of them waiting, studying the feeds Ten and Six sent back as they worked their way through the debris field, sucking up the drifting space junk and storing it in the compartments at their middles. Lot of debris out there, no way they could get it all—the probes were small, after all, and the cloud of debris diffuse and massive—but they only needed enough for the robots to analyze.

Serengeti tracked the probes' progress as they passed through the mass of floating bits, ran some calculations—measuring the width of the debris field, the density of the pieces—and made a disturbing discovery.

Not just big, she thought. *Huge. Large enough to be a ship.*

She looked to Henricksen, wondering if he saw what she did. But Henricksen seemed distracted. He watched the probes' operation for a while, but his eyes kept returning to *Brutus* and the other ships.

"They're keeping their distance," he noted, looking to the camera, quirking an eyebrow in question. "Your doing I assume?"

"I advised the Bastion that it would be best if the armada stayed put until the probes complete their scans and we've had a chance to analyze the debris."

"And he listened?"

"He may be an arrogant AI prick but he knows sense when he hears it," Serengeti said dryly. That got another laugh from Henricksen.

"Collection complete, Captain," Finlay announced.

"Alright then, Finlay. Bring the boys back. Let's see what we've got."

Finlay nodded and ordered Six and Ten back to the ship.

Serengeti checked the Chron and found the entire operation—from the launching of the probes to the order to return—had taken just a little under twenty minutes. Not bad, considering they had a human running the operation.

"Finlay. How much longer do the rest of the probes need to complete the grid sweep?"

"Pattern is…sixty-eight percent complete, Captain. Chron estimates ten minutes, twenty-eight seconds. Give or take."

"You suppose that'll be quick enough for him?" Henricksen nodded to the video feed showing *Brutus* lurking behind them.

Serengeti was about to answer when a message arrived. A message sent directly to her, bypassing the comms station entirely. She opened it, read quickly and then flashed the message to Henricksen's Command Post.

"Apparently not," she said, and then deleted the message in a fit of pique.

FOUR

Six and Ten were back on board in a little under five minutes. *Serengeti* flipped her attention to the cargo hold, watching the huge outer doors slide open and the two collection probes slip inside. The hold was a huge space, empty and echoing, but the probes—silly, mischievous things that they were—seemed not to know it. They skittered around like frightened moths, making wandering loops of the hold's frigid confines before dropping down to the floor.

The outer doors slid closed as the probes settled. Atmosphere systems kicked in, repressurizing the cargo bay, banishing the worst of the vacuum's chill before an inner hatch opened, letting six little robots into the cargo area. The robots were cute little things and walked on long, spidery legs, oval bodies gleaming dully, round, chromed faces lit with brilliant cobalt eyes. They stepped into the hold and squatted down, dropping onto triangular tank treads set in their bellies, trundling across the open space with their jointed legs tucked tight against their bodies, blue eyes glowing brightly in moon-shaped faces, pin lights flashing in pre-programmed patterns across their cheeks and foreheads as they communicated in their shared robot language—a strange combination of *beeps* and *borps* and other electronic noises that filtered through *Serengeti's* microphone pick-ups.

The robots rolled to the middle of the cargo bay and then divided— three of them heading over to the Number Six probe while the other three trundled in the opposite direction, clustering around balky, oft-capricious Ten. Out came those long, spidery legs, unfurling from the robots' sides, metal tips tapping at the decking as they lifted themselves up and tucked their tank treads tight against their bellies. No trundling like tiny tanks now. The robots *crawled* across the probes like the metal arachnids they were, poking at hidden panels, entering coded sequences to get access to the probes' insides.

Six slid open with a puff of air, hinged doors releasing on either side of its ovoid body, revealing a space packed tight with scorched metal, melted plastics and every other thing the probe had collected. Ten, on the other hand, had to be a bit more difficult. Ten flat out rejected the first set of codes the robots entered, and then balked at opening its doors when they tried to use a back-up set of codes.

"Ten. Behave," *Serengeti* ordered, speaking through a comms panel set in the hold's wall.

Ten *beeped* loudly and then flashed a series of error messages, insisting its door controls weren't working properly.

"Fine. You want to do it the hard way, we'll do it the hard way."

Part of her was tempted to shut the probe down completely. The controls were there, an integrated part of her systems, and all it would take was a single command. *Serengeti* considered it and then tapped into the robots' comms channel instead, calling in the cavalry.

"TIG. Cargo bay."

A maintenance door opened at the far end of the huge space and another, even smaller robot rolled out. It paused just a few feet in and assessed the situation, face lights flashing, front legs lifting, scraping together in a gesture of worry that was peculiar to all the TIGs. The TIGs were smaller than the TSDs gathered around probes Six and Ten—repair robot, not analysis like their larger cousins—and came equipped with eight legs instead of the usual six, but other than that, the two robot models were nearly identical.

The TIG *beeped* softly and raised its head, staring at the camera as it waited for orders.

"Come here." *Serengeti* flashed the light above a camera and then waited while the little robot extended its legs and tippy-tapped over.

It stopped just below the camera, neck craned backward, chromed face looking up. *Serengeti* zoomed in on its side, reading the numbers and letters stenciled there to get its designation.

TIG-442.

"I want that probe open, 442," *Serengeti* said sternly. "Repair the doors and then run a full diagnostic so we don't have any more problems. A *full* diagnostic," she added, emphasizing that one word, "inside and out."

A strange, strangled sound from Ten and his compartment doors magically sighed open.

Too late, you little pain in the ass.

"Run the diagnostics anyway."

TIG-442 nodded, face lights ticking up one side and down the other, and then he flailed his legs excitedly and scurried away.

Serengeti turned the camera, addressing the TSDs around Ten. "Go through its hold," she said, pointedly ignoring the probe's protests. "Run a broad spectrum analysis on everything in there and then clear all that junk out."

Beeps and *borps* all around. Flashes of swirling face lights as the TSDs communicated with one another, figuring out who was going to do what. *Serengeti* left them to it.

"TIG-442." *Serengeti* swung the camera away, pointed it at the little repair droid again. "I want you to wipe Ten's software when you're done. Wipe it and reinstall, then run the diagnostics again to make sure there are no bugs left behind."

Ten *beeped* in complaint, insisting he was fine now. Really. Just a temporary malfunction and hardly worth all the fuss.

Serengeti really didn't care. It was high time Ten learned how to behave.

A message popped up, flashing insistently, clamoring for attention. A message from *Brutus*—no surprise there—demanding to know when they'd be done so the armada could move in.

Patience is a virtue, she started to send back, and then deleted it, querying her systems instead, checking on the progress of the other probes. *Ten minutes,* she wrote. *Stand by.*

Serengeti sent the message and closed the channel, patently ignoring the indignant response *Brutus* sent back. "Go," she told the TIG. "Be quick about it."

TIG-442 nodded, face lights flashing, cobalt eyes blinking slowly as he opened a panel beside Ten's hatch and stuck the end of one leg into a socket inside.

The TSDs, meanwhile, had crawled inside Number Ten's compartment and were busy sifting through its contents, using the sensors, diagnostic equipment and other specialized electronics built into the ends of their long, metal legs to analyze each and every piece of space junk the probe had gathered before chucking it outside, adding it to a growing mound on the cargo bay floor. *Serengeti* watched the operation closely, switching from one camera to another, eager to see what the probes had brought back. She even tapped into the TSDs themselves after a while so she could sort through the analytical data in real time rather than waiting for them to feed it to her.

And all the while, the messages kept coming. More messages from *Brutus,* each one angrier, more impatient than the one before. And a single query from Henricksen on the bridge.

Wait, she told them all. That and nothing more while the robots went through the last few pieces of space junk and closed the two probes back up.

She tarried a moment longer, making sure Number Ten didn't give TIG-442 any problems before switching her primary consciousness back to the bridge, flashing an indicator on the Command Post's mash-up panel to let Henricksen know she was there.

"Well?" he asked her.

"*Barlow*," she said. "The debris the probes brought in is from *Barlow*. That's all that's left of him." She cut off Number Ten's video feed, shunted the TSDs' data to the front windows so the crew could see for themselves.

"Shit," Sikuuku swore.

Kusikov stood up and leaned forward, hands pressed flat against the comms panel as he read through the data. Finlay just sat there, eyes wide and staring, head moving from one side to the other.

"Any chance we can salvage the AI?" Henricksen asked her.

"No." A single word, filled with sadness and anger. "*Barlow* died with his crew."

"And the others?" Henricksen asked softly. "*Osage? Veil of Tears*? Is there—are they…" He frowned and glanced at the crew around him. "Was there anything from them?"

"No. Just *Barlow*. If *Osage* and *Veil of Tears* were here—" A perimeter breach warning flashed through *Serengeti's* systems, cutting her off. "Proximity alarm," she announced, voice calm and cool as ever. She reached out with her sensors, searching for whatever was out there.

"Shit-shit-shit-shit-*shit*!" from the Artillery station. Henricksen might not swear often, but Sikuuku had no such qualms.

Finlay leaned forward, working desperately at her station, looking for the black void of displacement that marked a ship coming in. It was there, *Serengeti* could feel it through her sensor arrays, but from the way she shook her head, Finlay obviously hadn't found it yet.

Serengeti tapped into the Scan station, scrolling the detection grid to one side until the jump breach showed at the center.

"Buckle forming one thousand kilometers off the starboard bow," Finlay called.

Good girl.

Brutus sent a message, using the main comms channel this time rather than the direct line to *Serengeti* herself. *Serengeti* read it and then waited, letting Kusikov relay the communication to Henricksen.

"*Brutus* is asking for details, sir. Wants to know what's coming in."

"As if we have any more idea than he does," Henricksen growled. "Tell that son-of-a-bitch—"

Flare of cobalt blue light in the video feed tracking *Brutus* and the other ships in the armada. More flares, bright spots of color popping up everywhere as the fleet of ships fired up their engines and closed in on *Serengeti's* location.

"*Brutus* in-bound, sir!" Kusikov called, a hint of alarm creeping into his voice.

"In-bound? What the hell does he think he's doing? Kusikov—forget it." Henricksen mashed at the comms panel attached to his Command Post, opening a ship-to-ship channel to *Brutus.* "*Brutus,* this is *Serengeti.* Maintain position. Repeat. Maintain position until we know what's coming in." Henricksen closed the channel and turned to Finlay. "Anything?"

"Not yet, sir. Breach is still forming. Chatter coming through but it's indecipherable at this point."

"Recall the probes."

"But they're not done—"

"*I said recall the goddamn probes, Finlay!*"

"Yes, sir." Finlay tapped furiously at her panel, sending recall instructions to the probes outside.

"Sikuuku! Bring the forward artillery stations back online."

"Already did. Forward stations are hot, sir. Port and starboard in stand-by."

"Good." Henricksen looked to the aft feed, swore softly when he saw *Brutus* and the rest of the armada still moving. "*Serengeti.* Any chance you can use your AI wiles to talk some sense into that bastard?"

"I'll try."

Brutus and the rest of the armada were just two minutes out now. *Serengeti* sent a coded request directly to the Bastion using a private channel, received a squeal of static in response.

Prick.

"Any luck?" Henricksen asked her. He didn't sound all that hopeful. He could see for himself that the fleet was still moving toward them.

"None. Apparently *Brutus* isn't in the mood for AI wiles."

"Prick."

"My thoughts exactly."

"Finlay—"

"Almost! Breach is forming."

A flash outside, bathing the bridge in silver-white radiance. Finlay hunched forward, shading her eyes as she searched through the reams of information scrolling across her Scan station.

"It's a ship," she said slowly, frowning in concentration. "Signal's garbled though. Not squawking like it should." She fiddled with something, scrolled through a screen of data, fed it into a secondary panel. More fiddling and a muttered curse as she shook her head in frustration. "Can't seem to get the call sign."

Serengeti slipped in behind her, parsing through the data, finding gaps and errors, mangled translations the Scan systems couldn't deal with. "Something's wrong." She grabbed the Number Two probe and reversed its course, sending it out toward the breach.

"What's happening?" Henricksen asked her. "What's out there, *Serengeti*?"

"I don't know."

A chilling admission coming from an AI. The mood on the bridge turned decidedly tense.

The Number Two probe drifted closer, camera picking up an object just exiting the breach, sending the video feed back to *Serengeti's* bridge.

"That's a ship, alright," Henricksen said, studying the feed. "Hard to tell from here but it looks like…Titan class? You suppose that's—"

"*Osage! Osage! Osage!*" an electronic voice yelled, screaming through the ship's speakers.

Not good. Not good at all.

"*Osage! Osage! Osage!*"

"Goddammit, Kusikov! Cut that thing off."

"Aye, sir. Sorry, sir." Kusikov mashed at his panel until the artificial voice finally shut up.

"*Osage,*" Henricksen grunted, staring at Number Two's feed. "But that wasn't *Osage* herself, was it?"

"No," *Serengeti* said quietly.

The AI should have announced the ship's arrival. Or the captain or comms officer if the AI was disabled. But the voice that poured through her speakers sounded pre-recorded. *Serengeti* tapped into the comms channel, listened to the voice for a few seconds, analyzing the speech patterns until she confirmed her suspicions.

"So. Is it?" Henricksen asked her.

Serengeti cut the comms. "Is what what?"

"The ship out there. Is it *Osage*?"

Hard to tell, honestly. The ship was Titan class—the data the Number Two probe sent back made that much clear—but its electronic beacon was badly scrambled, the information it put out so garbled that *Serengeti* couldn't make heads or tails of it. And when she reached out, searching for *Osage's* AI mind, she found nothing. Just a blank space and a wall.

"Number Two's coming in visual range," Finlay announced. She reached for the camera controls, panned the lens around as Number Two came head-on to the intruder and then slipped around to its side, and the letters written in bold, slanting font.

"*Osage*," Henricksen breathed. "Dammit. Dammit all to hell."

Osage had found them, but *Osage* was dead. Well and truly dead. Holes showed in the grey-skin of her hull, rents scored along both sides, tearing through her triple-walled hull, exposing her skeleton and the corridors underneath to the vacuum of space. And the damage didn't stop there. The ship's back end was gone. Just gone—ripped away entirely, leaving snaking lines of cables, circuitry and shredded hull material trailing behind her, and a cloud of metallic debris floating long in her wake.

"What happened to her?" Sikuuku whispered. "What the *hell* happened to her?"

"And where's she been?" Henricksen added. "Shredded as she is, how'd she manage to make jump?"

"Where's *Veil of Tears*?" *Serengeti* wondered.

She saw something—a bright red sparkle just inside *Osage's* hull—and took the controls from Finlay without asking, steering the Number Two probe inside the damaged ship and then panning its cameras left and right.

"*Osage* is accelerating!" Finlay called, voice filled with alarm.

"Accelerating? *How?*" Henricksen demanded. "Thing's a wreck! Half the bloody engines are gone!"

"Don't know, sir, but she's moving. Looks like she's got one engine that's still operational and she's using that to push herself along."

"Goddammit. What the hell's going on?" Henricksen growled.

Good question. *Serengeti* studied *Osage* a moment, watching the dead ship drift closer, wondering where she'd gone, and how she'd gotten back.

A perimeter alert popped up, flashing brightly, screaming for her attention.

"Breach forming off the starboard bow." *Serengeti* pulled back, refocusing on a patch of inky darkness swirling to one side.

"Distance?" Henricksen asked.

"Five hundred kilometers."

A last look at *Osage*—sister ship and companion. A last moment to wonder where the ghost ship had come from, how anything was still operating when the AI inside was dead.

Where were you, sister? What happened to you? Serengeti wondered.

She considered a moment and then tapped into the Number Two probe, streaming its position in real time to her AI brain so she could track *Osage's* location.

More alarms, proximity alerts lighting up faster than *Serengeti* could address them. She abandoned the probe, letting one of her sub-minds monitor the feed as she swiveled electronic eyes to the darkness outside.

Multiple breach signatures now, buckles forming, creating black voids that sucked inward before blowing back out. She threw a schematic on the bridge windows, marking each new breach as it formed, waiting for ships to appear as they exited jump. One breach became ten, then twenty, then fifty, with more and more forming every minute. *Serengeti* added each new contact to the schematic and, slowly but surely, a pattern began to emerge: A thick crescent of buckles arcing around the armada's port side.

"Talk to me, Finlay!" Henricksen called. "What's going on out there?"

"*Osage* is closing."

"Forget *Osage*. How many, Finlay? How many breach signatures are out there?"

Finlay worked at her panel a moment and then froze, staring hard as the stars lit up outside and the first of the ships appeared. Data came through—a name and call sign, all the electronic information an interstellar vessel endlessly squawked out. More flashes—a dozen on either side of that first arrival—accompanied by more data, more information for *Serengeti* to pour through. She processed it in a moment, found nothing but bad news. And then she waited, watching Finlay chew at her lip, taking it all in.

"I count...a hundred. Hundred and three. Hundred and five. Hundred and—holy," Finlay breathed, eyes widening, looking surprised, and worried, and a little bit scared as more and more ships popped into existence. "It's them, sir." Finlay half-turned, looking behind her. "I think we found them. I think we found the DSR fleet."

"Fuck," Henricksen swore. "This is all going backward."

"But we *found* them—"

"*They* found *us*, Finlay."

"Oh," she said in a small voice.

The whole idea of sending the scouts ahead—and *Serengeti* after them—was so they could get the drop on the Dark Star Revolution. Scan their capabilities and see what they were up against before it all went sideways. Instead, it was the DSR who'd gotten the drop on them. They had *Brutus* to thank for that. *Brutus* who'd so foolishly brought the rest of the fleet in.

"Must've been watching this place. Left a probe or a beacon somewhere. Something too small for the scans to pick up. Something cloaked maybe. Hidden." Henricksen frowned at the schematic, muttering curses as ship after ship flashed into existence, completing the crescent walling them in on one side. "What's the count, Finlay?" he asked again.

"Twenty-three ships transited from jump so far. Looks like…another hundred and three buckles resolving. Hundred and thirty vessels in total, sir. Most of those yet to transit."

"Hundred and thirty," he muttered. "Thought there were more." He reached to one side, querying the system, frowning at the information it brought back. Henricksen looked up at the camera, pointing a finger at the screen and then tapping at a single piece of data. "Two hundred sixty-three," he said softly. He flicked his eyes to the windows, then back to the camera. "System said a fleet of two hundred sixty-three ships attacked Tissolo. Satellites around the planets confirmed that information. So where are the rest of them?"

Serengeti checked the data, confirming the scan results and Finlay's count. "Scans are empty. Perhaps they divided. Left this group to play rear guard while the rest slipped away."

"Or the rest of the DSR ships are waiting out there somewhere, just outside our scans' range."

"Or that," *Serengeti* acknowledged.

"I don't like this." Henricksen stared at the camera a moment longer, then glanced out the windows, watching the gap between the Meridian Alliance fleet and the DSR vessels slowly close. And far out—port side and still several hundred kilometers distant—was the lonely blip of *Osage*, tracking ever so slowly toward the fleet that once claimed her. "I don't like this at all," he said, eyes flicking between the DSR ships and *Osage's* beacon. "Something's not right. Kusikov—send word to the fleet. Tell them to take up defensive positions and ready themselves for jump."

"*Brutus* won't retreat," *Serengeti* warned him. "Not now. Not after two weeks of fruitless chasing."

"A hundred and thirty ships against a force nearly three times that size. This is wrong and you know it," Henricksen said quietly. "The DSR's desperate but they're not *that* desperate. And they're certainly not that stupid."

He was right, of course, and from the objections pouring in—peppering *Serengeti* and the other Valkyries, bypassing the Dreadnoughts who they knew wouldn't care—the Titans and Auroras weren't liking *Brutus'* orders any better.

Serengeti sent a message to the Bastion and received a response in return reminding her of her place, ordering her to form up with the others and mind her own business.

So much for that idea.

"*Brutus* has ordered the fleet to come about."

Serengeti sent instructions to Nav and Engineering, fired up her maneuvering thrusters and turned her bulk hard to port. The rest of the fleet turned with her, forming a wedge shape with *Brutus* at its middle and the Dreadnoughts ringing him about. The Titans and Auroras shifted and drifted, some moving forward, others back, creating a spearhead in front of *Brutus* and the Dreadnoughts and a thick shield wall behind.

Serengeti and the five other Valkyries moved to the outside of the wedge, spacing themselves widely so they could guard the armada's edges and still bring all their guns to bear. Six Valkyries. Just six to watch over this armada, and twenty Dreadnought bruisers to guard *Brutus* himself. Not something to sneeze at normally, but deep down, *Serengeti* wondered if it was enough.

Have to be. Cerberus *himself has spoken.* And in his AI wisdom, deemed six and twenty to be 'sufficient' for dealing with the DSR rabble that attacked Tissolo. *Hope he's right, Serengeti* thought.

She fired her maneuvering jets and assumed her assigned position on the starboard side of the fleet. *Marianas* and *Atacama* followed suit, maneuvering around the smaller ships so they could slot in behind her, while *Antigone* cruised over to the port side with *Seychelles* and *Sechura* in tow. And when it was all done—when the last ship was finally in place—the Meridian Alliance turned their eyes forward and waited for the DSR ships to come into range.

"God I hate this part." Henricksen stared at the bridge windows, lips twisting sourly as he studied the schematic showing the Meridian Alliance ships and the approaching DSR fleet. "So, this is his grand plan? We punch through the middle of their blockade and then circle around and hunt the remaining ships down?"

"The theory is sound." *Serengeti* hated that answer but it was the best she could offer.

"Theory," Henricksen snarled, hands slamming hard against the panel in front of him. "The *theory* is crap! Stupid, arrogant, son-of-a-bitch. He knows there's more to this than meets the eye but he just won't back down. Bastard shouldn't even be here. *Fleet* shouldn't be here. Smartest thing we could do is retreat and regroup. Come at them another time."

Serengeti thought a minute, recognizing the sense in what Henricksen said. She relayed a message to *Brutus,* urging caution, asking the Bastion to rethink this whole matter and consider pulling the fleet back.

Silence from *Brutus*. Nothing at all in response.

A surreptitious communication to the other Valkyries then. A quick back and forth between the half dozen ships, all of whom advised the same caution.

But *Brutus* wasn't listening—not to any of them—and *Serengeti* was pretty sure she knew why. AIs had their pride, after all, and *Brutus'* pride was hurting. After weeks of chasing the DSR, he finally had them in sight—had them outnumbered and outgunned to boot—and nothing she or the other Valkyries said was going to convince him to back down.

Mutiny was out of the question—Henricksen would never ask it of her and *Serengeti* would never turn on her own. Besides, she couldn't abandon the fleet. Not to save herself.

"If he'd held position like he was supposed to, none of us would be in this mess," Henricksen growled.

"And yet, here we are," *Serengeti* said simply.

"Yeah. Here we are." Henricksen glared a moment longer, watching the dark voids outside suck inward and then spit dull-skinned vessels out. "Sikuuku," he called, turning toward the Artillery station. "I want all batteries online. Target the closest breach and take out whatever comes through."

"And *Osage*?" Sikuuku asked.

Henricksen glanced out the windows, then to Number Two's feed. The probe was stuck inside *Osage's* damaged hull—dragged along as the wrecked ship advanced—but it was far out. Still a good nine hundred kilometers from *Serengeti's* location and moving slow as a turtle. The DSR ships were closer—a hell of a lot closer—and a much more immediate problem. Henricksen grimaced, eyes flicking to the forward camera and then back to Sikuuku. "Forget her for now. We've got bigger fish to fry."

"Roger!" Sikuuku opened a channel to the artillery stations and relayed the captain's orders to the other batteries.

Henricksen stared at the schematic on the front windows, watching the jump breaches form, throwing worried glances at Number Two's feed now and then. An anguished, agonized look on Henricksen's face as he considered the probe's feed. *Osage* was a companion once. An ally. And now...

What happened to you, sister?

Serengeti opened a channel, tried to make contact with *Osage* one last time. But there was nothing there. Just that electronic voice screaming out the ship's name.

Damn. Time the others knew.

"*Osage* is gone," she said, speaking to Henricksen, knowing the rest of the crew listened in. "The AI is gone and the crew with her from the looks of that hull."

"You don't know for sure—"

"The ship is a ghost, Captain."

Henricksen flinched as if she'd hit him. *Serengeti* never called him captain. It was Henricksen, always Henricksen when it was just she and the crew.

"*Osage* is gone, Henricksen," *Serengeti* said more softly.

Henricksen stared out the window a moment, lips pressed tightly together. "Sikuuku."

"Aye, sir?"

"If she comes in range, blow her."

"Aye, sir." Sikuuku's eyes drifted to *Osage's* blinking dot. He laid his hands on the firing mechanism for the main gun, flexing his fingers as he prepared to fire.

"*Brutus* reports all batteries, online. Fleet is primed and ready, Captain," Kusikov said.

"Good."

"Last of the breaches are resolving, sir. Weapons signatures detected." Movement at the front of the DSR fleet, an oversized object at the crescent's center pushing forward, bringing the rest of the line with it. "They're coming in!" Finlay called.

"God help us," Henricksen whispered.

FIVE

Serengeti sucked in the feeds from all the ships out there, taking an inventory of the force they were up against. The DSR fleet was close enough for her scans to detect each ship and mark them on the perimeter for display, but distant still—far enough away that her hull cameras showed little more than a spreading sea of dark blobs. A bit of fiddling and *Serengeti* zoomed in, enhancing the magnification of her electronic eyes until the shapes of individual ships became clear, but she still wanted more—more input, more data, more details about those vessels out there. So she cancelled the Number Four probe's recall and turned it around, sending its electronic eyes back out into the dark.

The probe sped away—invisible on her screens but for the video feed it sent back, tiny in comparison to the mass of ships out there. *Serengeti* slowed Number Four once it was close enough and zoomed in, using the probe's eyes to get a close-up view of the enemy that had come among them.

A hulking bruiser led the DSR fleet—a wallowing, zeppelin-shaped cruiser bristling with turret guns and comms towers, with something massive and deadly-looking bolted to its front end. *Serengeti* stared at it, studying the ship's design, trying to figure out what it was, but the class and designation eluded her at the moment.

"Interesting," she murmured.

"Interesting?" Henricksen grunted. "Weird's more like it. Looks like a god damn puffer fish. What is that anyway? Some kinda hack job?"

"Not sure," *Serengeti* admitted. "But I know how I can find out."

She tapped into Comms and Scan, drinking in the wealth of data the vessel poured out, found a name—*Trinidad*—and a ream of information about the ship's pedigree and construction, every planet and space station it had visited in the decades since its AI was born. And all that information came to her in the clear, trickling across an unsecured line.

Unencrypted data—that told her something. *Old* ship out there. Fourth generation at best. Anything newer came equipped with data protection—encryption and decryption, keys and permissions required to access the more sensitive areas of a ship's history. After all, the days of open data sharing were over. A smart AI learned to protect its past, and only divulge the information she absolutely *had* to provide.

So what are you? Serengeti wondered, digging deeper.

Lots of information in *Trinidad's* archive. *Serengeti* bypassed most of it and burrowed down to the ship's root directory where its commissioning information was stored.

"Heliotrope," *Serengeti* announced to the bridge crew. "Beacon names it *Trinidad* and its records mark it as Heliotrope. Older class of vessel. Haven't run across one of them in years."

And the last one she'd seen hadn't looked anything like the monster outside.

"Heliotrope?" Henricksen stared at Number Four's feed, arms folded, one finger tapping at his lips. "That's a science vessel, right? What the hell's a science vessel doing with a bunch of plasma cannons and rail guns strapped to its hull?"

She'd been wondering that herself. *Serengeti* set a sub-mind to do a bit more digging and figure that out while the bulk of her consciousness focused on the rest of the DSR fleet.

"Scan shows twenty-three ships through breach, sir," Finlay called out. "Twenty-eight. Thirty-two."

"Captain." Kusikov. Voice dreaming, body rigid as he sorted through the chaos of communications flying through space. "*Brutus* has ordered the fleet forward."

"Well, bully for him," Henricksen growled.

He leaned forward, staring out the forward windows as *Serengeti* turned with rest of the Meridian Alliance fleet, the spearhead of vessels turning until the tip pointed at the arc of DSR ships, and *Trinidad's* huge shape sitting at its center.

Brutus ordered the advance, and *Serengeti* went with them

"We're going through?" Sikuuku turned his head, eyes hidden behind the targeting advisor covering the top half of his face.

Henricksen nodded shortly. "Looks that way. Punch through, come about, form up so we're in a better position to take them on. Not the best plan," he said, looking pointedly at the camera, "but it's better than sitting here getting pounded from all sides."

"If you say so, boss." Sikuuku shrugged his shoulders and then cracked his fingers. "Just tell me what to shoot."

Henricksen grimaced, staring hard at the front windows, pouring over the schematic showing the arc of DSR ships on one side, and the Meridian Alliance wedge on the other, two fleets slowly converging, the space between them growing thinner and thinner.

"Alright!" Henricksen raised his voice, addressing the entire bridge crew. "That's our way out." He tapped at one of the panels in front of him, highlighting the center of the DSR crescent, and *Trinidad's* prickling shape at its middle, pushing it to the front windows for everyone to see. "Looks like *Brutus* is sending our boys after the mutated Heliotrope. Let's see if we can't help them out a bit. Sikuuku—I want you to focus the main gun on that spiny ship out there. Have the forward batteries do the same while the port and starboard cannons pound away at the smaller vessels to either side."

"Aye, sir!" Sikuuku touched two fingers to the side of his visor, opening a channel to the other Artillery stations and pass Henricksen's orders to the gunner crews. "All stations ready, Captain." He reached for the panel in front of him, throwing a series of switches that brought targeting displays to life, pivoted the gimbaled pod to reorient the main gun and set the Heliotrope in its crosshairs. "We'll be in firing range in…four minutes, fifty-three seconds," he said, sinking into the combat system's virtual world.

"Right. Tsu! Evans!" Henricksen barked, turning to the dark-haired, almond-eyed beauty sitting station at Engineering, the dark-skinned, earnest-looking young man manning Navigation beside her. "Maintain course and speed. I don't want us drifting out of line." He hooked a thumb toward Kusikov. "Hot-shot over there will monitor communications, let you know if *Brutus* changes tactics. Until then you keep her straight and steady, you hear?"

"Aye, sir!" they answered in unison, Tsu's voice crisp and clean, Evans' response softer, more muted.

Interesting duo there. Tsu was solid as they came: level-headed, dependable, cool under pressure. Not entirely surprising considering her upbringing—the Hideo-Nippon colony on Sosholo had a first rate military academy and Tsu had graduated top of her class. Not the friendliest person, despite her looks, or perhaps because of it, but Henricksen thought highly of her. Thought she had command potential. In fact, he'd already forwarded her package to the captain's board for consideration, though Tsu didn't know it. Nor the rest of the crew either. Certainly not Finlay.

Finlay. She'd be gutted if she knew.

Serengeti tapped into Finlay's screen, watching the private messages flash back and forth between Finlay at Scan and Tsu at Engineering. They were close, those two. Close as sisters. Close as lovers. That's what Finlay wanted—*Serengeti* read that in the messages Finlay sent from Scan—but Tsu already had a lover. Anoosheh—that name kept repeating in the messages Tsu received from home. Finlay knew about her, of course—how could she not when she and Tsu had grown so close—but that didn't stop her from dreaming. The heart wanted what it wants, after all.

Poor Finlay. Serengeti backed out of the text-based conversation passing between Scan and Engineering. *All your longing will only end in heartache.*

She considered Tsu a moment, studying her profile, the long line of her nose, the tilted brown eyes, and turned the camera a bit, taking a long look at Evans at Navigation.

Tsu was good—damn good—but Evans...*Serengeti* honestly wasn't quite sure about Evans. He'd trained in Nav and done well in the position—not great, not horrible, just...well. 'Competent,' was how Henricksen described him, and that fit too. Fit everything about Evans, in fact. Truth was, *Serengeti* didn't really have a good read on Evans. He was new to her crew—a recent replacement for Santiago who'd been killed in an unfortunate accident in one of her cargo bays—and he mostly kept to himself.

Need to fix that, she thought. *When this is over, I need to look into the mystery that is Evans. Make sure he gets integrated with the rest of the crew.*

Because crew was family while the ship was underway. And family didn't stomach outsiders. Either Evans integrated or he'd been transferred. Or demoted. Either way, he'd be on his way out, and *Serengeti* didn't want that. Not for *any* of her crew, even the ones she hardly knew.

She pulled back a bit, casting the camera's lens wide, watching the crewmen go about their various tasks on the bridge with one sliver of her consciousness—dipping into their consoles now and then to monitoring their activity—while another sub-mind looked outward, measuring the ever-diminishing gap between the Meridian Alliance armada and the DSR fleet. And in the background, a third sub-mind kept processing, chugging its way through *Trinidad's* records.

Something about that ship bothered her. Something just wasn't right.

The sub-mind flashed a message to get *Serengeti's* attention, and then pointed to a single bit of information—the ship's original design specs, and a series of addendums detailing changes and upgrades, a long list of modifications made over the course of the last twenty years.

"He's a refit."

"What is?" Henricksen asked distractedly.

"*Trinidad.*" *Serengeti* highlighted the Heliotrope's marker on the front viewing screen.

"Well, obviously. I mean, *look* at him!" Henricksen waved at hand at the porcupine-shaped vessel showing in Number Four's feed.

"Not that. Well, yes, that too, but I was talking about the AI. The AI is a refit. They ripped the advanced sciences AI out and replaced it with a combat model. Second generation."

Henricksen stared at the camera in disbelief. "*Second*? That's a fucking Neanderthal compared to the AI that was in there. Why the hell would they do that? Why would the AI *agree* to that?"

"I'm betting he didn't. No AI would. *Trinidad*—the original *Trinidad*—probably objected to the vessel changes so they ripped him out and threw him away. A science ship would never allow itself to be converted to a ship of war. Just as a combat AI would never concede to being turned into a miner ship, or hospice vessel, or any other, non-military refit."

Henricksen eyed the Heliotrope darkly and then looked back to the camera. "The AI swap. That in the logs?" he asked softly.

"Some of it. Some of its guesswork. But one thing's for sure—the AI in that Heliotrope is *not* the original."

Henricksen chewed his lip, watching the DSR fleet inch closer, studying the Heliotrope's shape at its center. "Second generation. That's pretty desperate."

"Indeed," *Serengeti* murmured. "Indeed it is."

But they'd seen that, hadn't they? The DSR was every bit the outsider, rebel-resistance force its name implied. Which meant shoestring budgets and salvaged equipment—retrofits of older models rather than shiny new designs. Even their damned name was a retread, the original Dark Star Revolution having died out centuries ago. Henricksen called them a bunch of terrorists—a bunch of up-jumped opportunists with a grandiose name—and, in truth, that's how things started out.

The second coming of the DSR spawned from unrest on just a single planet—a backwater named Isikatamaharu—and from there it spread like wildfire. Like a plague hopping from one planet to another, infecting hundreds of colonies along the way, pulling in the people at the fringes—the angry and disenfranchised, the desperate and destitute. There'd been a point to it all once, way back when. A dream of separation, of an independent planet, separate from Meridian Alliance rule that the DSR could call home. But that dream got lost along the way—forgotten or just given up long ago. Now the DSR was all about guerrilla warfare and quasi-terrorist tactics. About surgical strikes to secure resources and keep themselves going.

Anything they captured—ships included—got pressed into service. That's what happened to *Trinidad.* That much was in his records. And as for the other ships out there…

Serengeti ran a quick analysis of the data she'd gathered, found other ships of *Trinidad's* vintage, some newer models, others that were even older than the Heliotrope. *Desperate,* she thought, reading the signs, knowing the ancient fleet out there meant DSR was almost at an end. This fleet, this cobbled together collection of ships driven far out into unsettled space…it felt like a last stand. A last suicidal act of defiance.

"Pointless," *Serengeti* said. "All of it."

"No argument here." Kusikov studied the information scrolling across the bridge's windows, shaking his head. "Look at 'em. It's like a museum out there. The greatest hits of junk transport." He leaned forward, squinting his eyes as he focused on one shape in particular. "Is that an *Aphelion*?" he asked, pointing at an elongated vessel with a forking metal rod protruding from its nose.

"Can't be," Finlay told him. "Aphelion's are ancient. First generation AI. Minds are based on chip sets rather than the crystal matrix standard they introduced with the fifth generation AI. Totally inefficient. They retired the last of that class a decade ago."

Kusikov gave her a haughty look. "Oh, so you're an AI mindset expert now, huh?"

Finlay glared at him across the bridge and then pointedly turned away, adjusting the settings on the Scan station to add yet more data to the front displays.

Serengeti almost laughed, watching the two of them. Kusikov's know-it-all attitude got under most people's skin, but he and Finlay has a special relation. Those two were forever arguing and never quite seemed to get along. Today was worse, though. The arrival of those DSR ships made everyone nervous and snappish, Finlay and Kusikov included.

Finlay fiddled with her display for a few seconds, pointedly ignoring Kusikov at Comms. Curious, *Serengeti* tapped into her station, found she'd focused in on the ship in question and pulled its data feed onto her screen so she could parse through the ocean of information it had to offer.

"See? Like I said—not an—" Finlay blinked and leaned forward, taking another look. "Ho-lee-shit," she breathed. "He's right, Captain. That's an Aphelion out there, alright."

Kusikov smiled in victory. "Told you."

Finlay gave him a dirty look.

"Focus, Finlay," Henricksen growled.

"Yes, sir."

Finlay flushed and faced around, tapping busily at her station, sneaking glances now and then at the windows in front of her.

Quite the collection out there—a hodge-podge of vessels of various classes and designations that bore only a passing resemblance to a military fleet. Oh the Aphelion—*Parallax,* its beacon named it—had been built as a ship of war. An ancient one admittedly, and severely outclassed by the Valkyries and Dreadnoughts the Meridian Alliance brought with them. Even the Titans and Auroras were better equipped, their guns more powerful, their AIs several generations newer than what the Aphelion had on board. And *Serengeti* spotted Sunstorms and Scimitars scattered throughout the fleet, even a few Cyclone-class cruisers sprinkled here and there, but the bulk of the fleet had never been designed for combat. Merchant ships and retrofitted passenger vessels floated alongside ore haulers, canister containers, and other working-class ships.

"Jesus," Finlay breathed, panning Number Four's camera around. "Look at 'em." She zoomed in on a slab-sided rectangle off *Serengeti's* port side. "Where'd they find *that* hunk of junk?" She frowned at her panel, tapped in a few places and then looked up at the schematic showing in the window. "Huh. No name."

Just a series of numbers and letters repeating over and over again in the feed it threw at the stars.

"What do you suppose it is?" Finlay wondered, pulling the camera in tighter. "I've never even *seen* a ship like that."

"Golem," Kusikov told her, nodding at Number Four's feed. "Major throwback. Long-range hauler, probably built a couple of centuries ago. Thought they were myth, honestly." Kusikov rubbed his chin, devouring the Golem with his eyes. "It's got jump drives, though. Looks like early plasma burners—buggy as hell."

They were also pre-AI. The Aphelion was a wonder of modern technology compared to that Golem out there.

"Heard rumors the DSR was running cloned copies of those glitchy, gen seven AIs. But *pre*-AI?" Kusikov shook his head in disbelief. "Never imagined they'd resort to something like that."

"Scrounging up non-AI ships to fill out their ranks. Foregoing ship's intelligence entirely and relying solely on human crews." Finlay shuddered. "Scary. Truly scary."

"Finlay!" Henricksen smacked the panel in front of him. "What did I say?"

Finlay flinched and whirled around, eyes wide, a spot of color blooming on each cheek. "I—I—I—"

"What did I say?"

"I—Focus. Sir."

"Right. Focus. Do your damn job. But instead you and your boyfriend over there are mooning over that collection of scrap heaps the DSR calls a fleet."

"I didn't—He's not—" Finlay stammered.

"Look. We're not dating, we just—"

"Shut it, Kusikov!"

Kusikov froze, mouth hanging open beneath the comms visor covering his eyes. A flush of anger crept across his cheeks, suffusing his face. "Like I'd waste my time—"

"You wanna think *real* hard before you finish that sentence," Henricksen said quietly. "*Real* hard."

Kusikov ignored the warning. Either that or he just didn't get it. "I'm just trying to explain—"

"I can relieve you if you want," Henricksen interrupted. He cocked his head to one side, giving Kusikov an icy-eyed look. "I can bring someone else up here who can take this situation seriously if you can't. Someone who'll treat this crew with the respect they deserve."

Kusikov licked his lips, eyes flicking to Finlay. "No, sir," he muttered, stabbing surlily at his station. "I'm on it."

"Yeah. Yeah, I can see that," Henricksen grunted. "Alright. Everyone—eyes front. Things are about to get nasty and I need my bridge crew focused and dialed in tight, you hear me?"

A chorus of 'ayes' spread across the bridge.

"Good. Sikuuku—"

"Weapons signature," *Serengeti* cut in.

Sikuuku swore softly and yanked hard on the joystick in his left hand. The gimbaled artillery pod swiveled, motors whirring softly as the gunner reoriented, data scrolling in long strings across the targeting visor obscuring his face. "*Parallax,*" he called. "The Aphelion's powered up that big gun stuck to its nose."

Serengeti turned the Number Four probe toward the Aphelion to get a better look. A cobalt blue charge crackled up and down the length of metal rod sticking out from its bow. A ball formed at the end closest to the ship's hull and quickly spread outward, expanding until it measured nearly a meter across. It hovered there, sparking wildly and then crept forward, growing larger, brighter as it went.

"What the hell is that?" Henricksen asked.

"Forced ion cannon," Sikuuku told him. "All the rage a hundred years ago. Awful thing. Massive amounts of damage. Slow as hell, though. Takes a good three minutes to recharge between shots. And from what I hear, they have tendency to overload. Design's all wrong," he explained.

"See that?" He released one of the pod's joysticks and pointed to where the charging gun connected to the Aphelion's nose. "Too much energy too soon and the charge arcs backward. Take the whole ship out, neat as you please. That's why we stopped using 'em. Too chancy. Not worth the risk. Give me one of these babies any day," he said, patting the Artillery station's seat. "Bertha never back talks."

"Bertha?" Kusikov snorted. "You named it *Bertha*?"

"Shut it, Kusikov." Henricksen flashed a look of warning. Kusikov subsided into surly silence. Henricksen watched him a moment and then went back to studying the Aphelion, rubbing at his chin as he considered the crackling blue orb making its slow way down the length of its protruding gun. "So we've got...what? Two minutes give or take before that thing fires?"

Sikuuku checked the Chron and then nodded. "Right bastard of a weapon, that is. When it goes off...well, let's just say you *really* don't wanna get in its way."

"Can you take it out?"

"Not in range yet, but..." Sikuuku pivoted in his Artillery pod, motors whirring as he adjusted the main cannon, nudging the controls up and down, a bit left then right. "Damn. Smaller ships are blocking it. Can't get a clear line of fire. Pound away long enough and I might be able to get through. Might," he said meaningfully. "No guarantees."

"Forget it then. I want you focused on *Trinidad*. I *know* you can hit that. Tell the starboard-side batteries to focus on the Aphelion."

"Aye, sir." Sikuuku muttered something into the comms unit attached to his targeting helmet and then pivoted away, refocusing on *Trinidad's* mutated Heliotrope shape.

Henricksen left him to it and spun back toward Scan. "Finlay. Keep an eye on the Aphelion. Not sure there's much we can do about it, but I'd at least like a little advance warning before that thing goes off."

Finlay nodded and split the view on her Scan station screen, devoting one panel to *Parallax,* another to the wide crescent of DSR vessels ahead of them, and a third to *Trinidad* at its center. *Serengeti* watched with her, leaving one sub-mind to monitor the Scan feeds while her primary consciousness focused on the Meridian Fleet around them, and the DSR ships ahead.

More energy signatures appeared—weapons firing up all across the DSR fleet as the Meridian Alliance closed in. They'd halved the distance to *Trinidad* by now, and from the looks of things, the DSR seemed to be on to what *Brutus* had planned. Ships' engines fired, DSR vessels sliding forward, tightening the crescent up a bit, diverting more ships to the center where the tip of the Meridian Alliance spear pointed.

"Targets are coming in range." Sikuuku flexed his fingers, wrapping them tight around the pod's firing mechanisms. "*Brutus's* main batteries are on-line. He's firing!" he warned.

Flare of blue outside as *Brutus* opened fire with his cannons—massive, powerful weapons whose range outclassed anything else in the Meridian Alliance fleet. Bright bars marched in a straight line through space, slicing through the darkness as they tracked toward *Trinidad* and its entourage. Everyone waited, holding their breath, counting the seconds as *Brutus's* shots crossed the gap between the two fleets and finally connected.

Trinidad's prickling hull lit up, charged energy munitions arcing wildly as they connected with the Heliotrope front end, crawling in spidering tendrils across his composite metal skin.

Cheers erupted on *Serengeti's* bridge. Kusikov opened up comms, broadcasting the yells and screams of victory issuing from the other ships in the fleet.

"Targets coming into range," *Serengeti* said calmly, cutting through all that noise.

The cheers faded. Kusikov cut the comms as everyone got down to business.

"Main gun primed and ready," Sikuuku called. The gimbaled pod ticked to one side and then the other as he made a last few adjustments. Nervous movements. Nervous and excited—both came with the territory. Sikuuku was a veteran like Henricksen—the scars he wore, marks of pride and shame, earned in encounters just like this one. He knew what was coming and wanted it to come, because the sooner the battle began, the sooner the dying would be done. "Sir?" he prompted, awaiting the order to fire.

"Wait," Henricksen told him.

He glanced over to the Artillery station and then returned his gaze to the front windows, locking onto the schematic showing the Meridian Alliance fleet and the DSR ships. A counter glowed next to it, spiraling steadily downward as *Brutus* pounded away at *Trinidad*. The fleet moved closer, bringing the Titans and Auroras into range. They opened up as well, adding their smaller weapons fire to the mix.

Trinidad fired back, spitting out old-fashioned torpedoes of all things, tips glowing blood-red as the contents inside them swirled angrily. 'Liquid laser' they dubbed that weapon, but the torpedoes' contents were chemical, not light-based—a toxic, corrosive substance that chewed through composite metal like a hot knife cutting through butter.

Highly effective, that concoction, and extremely deadly. Once the torpedo connected, the chemical containment pod shattered, releasing the deadly contents inside, creating an outer layer of insulation to protect an inner layer of acid that dissolved the ship's hull and worked its way to the vessel's softer, more vulnerable insides.

The Meridian Alliance had experimented with something similar, once upon a time, but ultimately given up. See, the thing was, the chemicals in that weapon weren't only toxic, they were highly unstable. The Meridian Alliance had outfitted a dozen or so vessels with weapons like *Trinidad's*, and all but four of them imploded when the gun's chemical containers ruptured, spilling toxic goo inside the ship. Ships ended up being a total loss, and their crews were killed instantly by the fumes that worked their way into the atmosphere generators. The Meridian Alliance almost kept the damned things anyway, but the powers-that-be had run the numbers and worked their way through several cost-benefit scenarios before deciding the risk the guns posed outweighed the reward they offered. That's why they'd scrapped them, and went through all the trouble and expense to rip the guns back out the ship that carried them.

Apparently, the DSR had done the same calculations and come to a different conclusion. Or else they'd found a way around the weapons flaws. Developed some sort of shielding, maybe, to prevent a similar tragic event.

Or maybe they just don't care, Serengeti thought to herself. *Maybe they're willing to risk their crews for the firepower the gun offers.*

Trinidad's liquid laser rounds smashed into the leading edge of the Meridian Alliance spearhead, splattering themselves across the Titans and Auroras at its tip. A few swirling red globes passed through the front line and slammed into the next wave of ships. At first it looked like nothing happened, then damage reports started flowing in.

Intrafleet comms erupted with communications, ships slowed and skipped aside, trying to dodge *Trinidad's* fire. Those near the edges were successful but the center of the ships at the center of the spearhead were packed in tight with almost nowhere to go, no room to maneuver. A bright flare erupted at the front of the spearhead—an Aurora named *Sorrow,* drifting off line, breaking formation. She veered hard to starboard, scraping against *Percival,* obliterating two side cannons, taking out the plating around them for good measure, leaving *Percival* with a sparking, gaping wound.

Percival recovered and brought himself back in line. *Sorrow* wasn't so lucky.

"Breach," Finlay called. "*Sorrow's* got a breach!"

"Dammit," Henricksen swore.

A yellow-white plume puffed from the Aurora's side, flickering, flaring as it licked at empty space. The plume burned brightly for a few seconds and then abruptly died. And a half second later, *Sorrow* exploded.

Shocked silence engulfed the bridge, everyone staring as *Sorrow's* hull cracked and cracked again, shredded into half a dozen large pieces. Bits of metal flew outward, peppering the ships around her as the remains of *Sorrow's* body spun lazily, drifting off into darkness.

The fleet moved, leaving *Sorrow's* dead carcass behind.

"God speed, *Sorrow,*" Henricksen whispered as *Serengeti* passed her by. "God speed."

"*Trinidad* in range," *Serengeti* announced. "*Brutus* sends word: All ships are to fire at will."

"Right." Henricksen scrubbed a hand through his short-cropped hair. "You heard the man, Sikuuku. Destroy that bastard. And get the starboard batteries on *Parallax* and its damned gun."

"Aye, sir!" Sikuuku relayed the second half of Henricksen's message to the other batteries and then hunkered down in the Artillery pod. His fingers squeezed the triggers, sending bright blue orbs of death spinning into the darkness.

Henricksen slammed his hand against a panel, sounding the ship's alarm. "Kusikov! Comms! Wide open. Ship-wide address."

Kusikov twiddled his fingers. "Floor's yours, sir!"

"All hands," Henricksen called, addressing his crew. "All hands to stations. We've engaged the enemy fleet. We're going in."

Six

Chaos erupted, plasma bolts and fractal laser cannons lighting up the darkness outside. Rail guns sputtered and spat, obsidian fire streaking in dark lines interrupted at regular intervals by the tracer rounds the gunners loaded to help them aim. *Serengeti* cruised along just a few kilometers off *Brutus's* starboard side, and fired with the others, adding the full power of her forward guns to the attack.

Death poured from a thousand different guns ranged across the Meridian Alliance fleet, all of them aimed at *Trinidad* and the thirty or so small ships unlucky enough to be positioned around him.

Shots landed on both sides of the confrontation, scoring across the metal skins of the Meridian Alliance vessels, tearing at the hulls of the DSR ships. A Sunstorm named *Daedalus* exploded spectacularly, sides blowing outward, smashing into the DSR ships on either side. But the cheers on *Serengeti's* bridge turned to angry swearing when *Trinidad's* chemical cannon zeroed in on an Aurora named *Bliss*—*Sorrow's* sister ship. *Bliss* was one of the advance ships, positioned near the tip of the spearhead with twenty or so Auroras and Titans. *Trinidad's* gun pounded away at her, chemical rounds coating *Bliss's* bow, chewing mercilessly through her composite metal shell. She held on for a while, and kept going, kept firing away, but the liquid laser was insatiable. It ate through *Bliss's* skin and tore through her bulkheads, dissolving girders beneath until *Bliss's* front end buckled and finally gave way.

There was no explosion this time—not like *Sorrow*. Just a puff of metal and fast cooling air as the atmosphere inside *Bliss* vented. The Aurora shuddered and slewed to one side, drifting aimlessly. Ships veered around her, banking hard to avoid a collision, and then moved on, leaving *Bliss* behind.

Henricksen pounded the panel in front of him. "God damn that thing! Sikuuku. Target *Trinidad's* main gun and take it out."

"Trying!" Sikuuku's pod pivoted, lights flashing furiously across his face as he searched the Heliotrope's prickle-faced surface. "C-mon, c-mon, c-mon. Ha! There it is. Got you, you bastard." Sikuuku squeezed both triggers, lobbing glowing orbs of plasma across the stars. Some hit, some missed, *Trinidad* kept coming regardless. He was a tough old

48

thing—his body wrapped in endless layers of plasmetal, his main gun heavily shielded—and took the hits without slowing, seeming completely unfazed. "Goddammit, just die!" Sikuuku shouted, venting his frustration.

Serengeti thought about taking over and subsuming all of her primary systems now that the battle had begun, but Sikuuku was a first class gunner and seemed to have things under control. *Serengeti* left him to it and settled for just Nav and Engineering, tracking everything around her—every ship, every gun, every round and missile flying in either direction—working her way through the worst of the chaff, taking hits now and then when they simply couldn't be avoided.

And all the while Sikuuku kept firing, crosshairs trained on *Trinidad's* puffer fish shape, landing shot after shot on the area around that big gun. Damage appeared—comms towers destroyed, turret guns crippled, chunks of hull plating ripped away—but *Trinidad's* gun kept right on firing.

"I could use some help here!" Sikuuku called.

Serengeti sent a message to *Atacama* and *Marianas* behind her asking them to divert a few of their turret guns to help Sikuuku out.

Tracer fire reoriented, pounding away at the Heliotrope's liquid laser gun.

"Finlay," Henricksen barked. "Status report on the Aphelion."

"Still charging." Finlay cycled the data on her screen, moving the window showing the ship in question to the center of her panel. "Hard to tell, though, with those smaller ships in the way."

Serengeti switched to the feed from the Number Four probe, saw a silver-blue orb eject itself from the metal rod at the end of the Aphelion's nose. Tendrils of electricity reached backward, clinging to the ship for a second or two, and then the orb broke contact and shot toward the fleet.

"*Parallax* firing!" Finlay yelled, fingers flying across the screen.

Serengeti threw the feed from the Number Four probe onto the windows at the front of the bridge for everyone to see. A check of the Chron showed the time from inception to firing for that round to be three minutes, forty-three seconds. She started the counter and set it on the front screen next to Number Four's feed as *Parallax* reloaded, waiting only for the electric payload from the last round to dissipate before spawning another of those tiny, cobalt blue spheres. It crackled against the Aphelion's hull and then surged forward, tracking slowly along the forking metal rod's length.

The crew worked away at their stations, marking the counter, watching it slowly count down. Hands froze as the next silver-blue sphere wobbled away from *Parallax's* nose. It carved its way through the DSR fleet, forcing the enemy ships to haul over to clear a path for the orb to follow. Some failed to move quickly enough and got side-swiped, or hit directly. Two Sunstorms accidentally blocked in a Scimitar named *Runabout,* shoving him directly into the forced ion orb's path. The orb slammed into him, entering port side aft and exiting *Runabout's* starboard side bow, coring the vessel neatly, leaving him a shredded hulk. Two more DSR ships took glancing blows that peeled hull panels away, exposing the metal composite frameworks beneath. Two more had guns sheered away, comms towers melted, and then the energy orb pushed through and shot out into the open space between the DSR fleet and the Meridian Alliance.

"Look at it," Kusikov breathed, staring wide-eyed at Number Four's feed. The orb picked up speed, continuing to expand as it streaked toward the Meridian Alliance ships. "It's *huge.*"

And growing by the second, tendrils of cobalt fire sparking wildly as the globe reached a size nearly as wide as *Parallax* itself. All that mass, all that forced ion energy headed straight for the fleet, and *Brutus* looming at its center, and there was nothing they could do to stop it.

Serengeti sent a warning to *Brutus*—wonder of wonders, he actually acknowledged her this time and passed a sub-space transmission to the other AIs—but the fleet kept going, not a single ship slowing or straying off line. She added the orb's path to her schematic, running a projection of when and where it would intercept the fleet before calculating probable damages.

It was going to be bad. Very bad.

She sent the calculations to *Brutus* and waited an eternity for his answer.

Acceptable, he sent back—cold, chilling answer, and so very, very AI.

Serengeti saw nothing at all acceptable in a dozen ships lost simply because their pig-headed leader simply refused to move. *Break formation,* she sent, but *Brutus* ignored her this time. She repeated the message with no better result.

Damn you, Brutus.

She reached out to the Valkyries directly, bypassing the Bastion to relay her message to the smaller ships, sending her schematic with it, and the estimate of damages. *Serengeti's* calculations showed a dozen ships lost, but *Atacama* ran the same scenario and doubled that figure. Then again, *Atacama* always *had* been a pessimist...

We should get out of here, Seychelles sent back. *Jump away and regroup to put ourselves in a better tactical position.*

Serengeti whole-heartedly agreed. This was all going wrong—very, very wrong—but *Brutus* wouldn't retreat. She knew that without asking. *Brutus* wouldn't even break formation much less jump away.

Messages flew back and forth as the fleet advanced, ships querying *Brutus*, questioning his orders. Querying *Serengeti* when *Brutus* wouldn't answer, wanting her to speak for them.

I tried, she told them. *I tried and failed.* Brutus *isn't listening.*

"Shit." Henricksen balled up his fist and pounded the panel in front of him. "Shit. Shit. Shit. He doesn't see it. Bastard honestly doesn't see it." He studied the schematic in front of him, eyes flicking across the data screens on the front windows. "We can't do this," he said, raising his eyes, looking directly at the camera. "I can't let this happen."

"Henricksen. You can't—"

"Watch me." Henricksen turned away from the camera and shouted at Comms. "Kusikov! Contact *Brutus* and tell him—"

"*Brutus* is aware," *Serengeti* cut in. "He's notified the fleet."

"Notified," Henricksen repeated. "Fat lotta good that's gonna do 'em. That sphere out there is gonna carve a trench through the forward vessels but they won't goddamn move unless he orders them to break formation and get the hell outta the way!"

She tried again—for Henricksen's sake—knowing it a waste of time. *Brutus* was as obstinate as ever and refused to respond until the other Valkyries added their voices. Then and only then did he deem it worth his while to make concessions.

"*Brutus* advises we maintain course and adjust speed to match his. He's ordered the ships in the orb's path to take evasive maneuvers."

"Well halle-fucking-lujah."

For someone who didn't swear much, Henricksen certainly was having a field day with the curses lately.

The fleet's schematic changed as the ships at the front of the spearhead shifted about. The wedge shape cracked in half, vessels shucking to either side, and *Brutus* himself slowed a bit to accommodate their maneuvers.

Serengeti adjusted her calculations, re-plotting the orb's projected path, which now showed it skimming just in front of *Brutus* and tracking closer to where *Serengeti* cruised on the armada's starboard side.

Not the best result, but she thought they'd all make it. That is, until the orb unexpectedly accelerated, blowing all her calculations to hell.

Henricksen leaned forward, frowning at the schematic on the front window. "Shit. What's it doing?"

"Accelerating. Speed's jumping at random."

Serengeti ran more calculations, adjusting her projections again and again, and soon realized *Gorgon* and the twenty or so small ships protecting *Brutus's* port aft side would never survive its impact. She messaged *Brutus,* relaying the same message to the ships in peril without asking his permission.

The little Titans and Auroras jogged desperately about as *Gorgon's* Dreadnought bulk began a slow turn. But *Serengeti's* schematic kept changing, the orb's path shifting faster than the ship's themselves could move, and she quickly realized it was all too late. Much, much too late.

"Brace! Brace! Brace!" she sent, fleet-wide comms thrown wide.

Seychelles hauled over, sides crackling with electricity as the Aphelion's orb slipped by. *Antigone* slowed behind her while *Sechura* put on a burst of speed. That put the three port-side Valkyries safely out of harm's way. The Aphelion's orb glided serenely past them and wobbled through the first couple of layers of smaller ships before slamming into *Libertine*—a Titan three rows in.

Libertine disintegrated, composite metal shredded, bits and pieces spraying everywhere, peppering the vessels around him with high-velocity debris. The orb kept going and took out *Gorgon*, sheering the Dreadnought in half. He held on for a few seconds, innards showing grotesquely, flash-fires as his two halves drifted apart, and then the explosions began, rippling up and down his hull.

Gorgon died slowly, ripped apart from the inside out, and still the Aphelion's orb kept going, kept *killing,* punching its way through ten more ships before the sphere's energy finally dissipated and it fizzled and winked out.

Twelve ships, Serengeti thought dully, watching a last bright spot of cobalt fire flicker and die. *My calculations were right.*

"Fuck-fuck-*fuck!*" Henricksen slammed both hands against the panel in front of him, screaming in pure rage. "*Brutus,*" he yelled, opening ship-to-ship comms. "What the hell—?"

"Proximity alert." *Serengeti* flashed a warning as she reached for Finlay's station, toggling the display to the expanse of empty space behind them.

"Captain!" Finlay called. "Buckle forming!"

"Where, goddammit? Where?"

"Aft. Two hundred kilometers."

"Two hundred kilometers. That's within firing range." Henricksen swore softly. "How many?" he asked, staring at the back of Finlay's head.

"Just the one, sir. I think," she added.

"Think? I need a whole lot better than that, Finlay. Is it one or not?"

"It's—I'm not—*Serengeti*?" Finlay raised her head and stared pleadingly into the camera in front of her, gesturing helplessly at Scan's display.

Unfortunately, *Serengeti* didn't have an answer for her. The data her scans collected was…odd, to say the least. Anomalous. Confusing. Nothing at all like the jump signatures she was used to seeing. "There's a single buckle forming, but it's…unstable," *Serengeti* said.

Not quite the right word, but the best she could come up with to describe her scans readings. Breaches varied depending on the size of the ship transiting through—the larger the ship, the larger the breach, and the more energy that passed through with it. That breach out there…well, based on the readings *Serengeti* was getting, a small *moon* was about to come through that buckle.

Can't be, she thought, combing through the data, trying to make sense of it. *Nothing's that large. Not even* Cerberus.

A sub-mind sent a warning as tracer fire tracked through space, intercepting *Serengeti's* path. Her body shook violently, rail gun fire rattling along one side as bright red flashes appeared ahead of them— *Trinidad's* big gun firing, pounding away at the armada's leading edge. The two fleets were just a hundred kilometers apart now, and pounding away at each other, filling the dark vacuum of space with broken hulls and clouds of composite metal particles. The Heliotrope took out three more ships in as many seconds, hulls dissolving beneath the *Trinidad's* chemical fire. *Brutus* fired back, lobbing plasma rounds into the DSR fleet that tore ships apart, igniting the oxygen and ammunitions stores inside them, creating explosions that flared like short-lived fireworks before the DSR ships died.

Serengeti focused the bulk of her consciousness on the conflict ahead of her, using the electronic eyes built into her hull and the four small cameras mounted on the Number Four probe to view the battle from multiple angles. But she kept one eye trained on the emptiness behind her, detailing a sub-mind to watch the buckle, and analyze the data coming through as the breach slowly formed. That sub-mind pinged, wanting her attention, but another anomaly appeared—a single DSR ship, that blocky, ancient Golem drifting away from the rest of the fleet—and she waved the sub-mind off while she took a moment to investigate.

The Golem drifted further off line, completely detaching itself from the DSR's main force to follow a wide, arcing course that brought it into a flanking position off the Meridian Alliance's starboard side.

What's it doing? Serengeti wondered, not liking this change. Not liking anything about this pitched battle *Brutus* had drawn them into.

She calculated the trajectory of the Golem's new path and realized it would take it straight to *Marianas*. Worrisome, unsettling enough that she sent a warning to her sister ship, and yet, strangely, the Golem's guns were silent—had been since the entire time, not a shot fired since the ship first appeared. Were it not for the repeating strings of data, and the energy signature of its engines, she'd have thought the Golem derelict—dead and drifting on momentum alone.

Probably malfunctioned, Serengeti thought.

But somehow that didn't feel right. She poured through the Golem's broken data stream, looking for something to validate the disquiet she felt, but there was nothing. Nothing incriminating anyway. No smoking gun. Just that silent, cruising Golem making its wayward course.

I still don't like it.

She almost said something to Henricksen, but he had enough to deal with right now. *Serengeti* considered a moment and then set a sub-mind to watching the Golem, and sent a message to *Marianas* asking her to do the same so they could keep tabs on the ancient vessel together.

Two Valkyries with powerful AI minds—surely that was enough.

Serengeti pondered the Golem and the buckle forming behind them, flicked her main consciousness back to the battle raging ahead of her, and just as quickly turned her eyes aft as yet *more* bad news arrived.

A new buckle appeared, sucking inward, condensed darkness swirling at its center, and then boiling outward as the jump breach finally formed.

"Multiple contacts. Aft. Two hundred meters." *Serengeti* added a second schematic to the front windows. The diagram lit up like a Christmas tree—dozens of ships' signatures appearing as the DSR's missing vessels poured through.

SEVEN

Klaxons blared all over the ship. Henricksen opened ship-wide comms, warning the crew of the new arrivals, ordering aft batteries to commence firing as the vessels around them did the same. Plasma fire lit up the stars outside, the Meridian Alliance fleet splitting its firing, pouring out rounds at the DSR ships ahead, and the reinforcements moving in behind them.

"Finlay! Where the hell did those bastards come from?" Henricksen demanded. "Why didn't our scans pick them up?"

Finlay was busy trying to make sense of all the new ships' signatures and didn't hear him, so *Serengeti* stepped in to help her out. "Mass jump," she offered.

Had to be. Only explanation she could think of that made any sense.

"Those crazy-ass bastards," Kusikov breathed.

"Tricky maneuver." Henricksen looking grudgingly impressed.

Mass jump required a group of vessels to cluster together, tight enough that the spheres from their jump drives overlapped, creating an oversized singularity that sucked all the ships through at once. As a military tactic, it was brilliant: The ships on the far side of the buckle had no way of knowing what size force was coming until the breach resolved and the vessels transited through.

It was also incredibly stupid—less than a fifty-fifty chance the maneuver would work at all, and when mass jump went bad, it went very, *very* bad. As in entire fleets wiped out. Nothing but twisted metal bits coming out the other side. A rough ride, to say the least, and not the way *Serengeti* would choose to travel. Not the way *any* sane AI would choose to transit hyperspace.

"Dammit. I knew those bastards were still out there somewhere." Henricksen looked straight into a camera. "Should've jumped away from here when we had the chance."

"*Brutus*—"

An alert interrupted her—scans detecting a massive energy signature somewhere inside the group of DSR ships behind them.

"They've brought another."

"Another what?" Henricksen asked her.

"Aphelion." *Serengeti* panned a camera around, searching the ships behind her until she spied the Aphelion's long, thin shape, forking metal rod protruding from his nose, cobalt blue energy crackling wildly. She zoomed in and threw the image up on the front screen.

"Damn. God damn," Henricksen breathed.

"Aphelion is firing," *Serengeti* warned as a sparking blue orb separated from the Aphelion's nose.

"Shit. Warn—"

"Captain! *Parallax* is firing!" Finlay shouted.

Two massive balls of cobalt blue fire showed on the screens projected on the front windows, approaching the Meridian Alliance fleet from opposite directions.

"Trapped," Henricksen breathed in horror. He slammed a hand on a panel opening ship-wide comms. "*Brace! Brace! Brace!*"

Serengeti flashed a warning to *Brutus*, who sent it across all channels. Not much help really, but it gave the fleet a few precious seconds of maneuvering before the Aphelion's orbs slammed into them—one after the other, carving their way through the Meridian Alliance fleet.

Ships exploded, disintegrating left and right. The orbs chewed through the fleets' ranks, carving up metal, energy dissipating with each vessel they came in contact with. *Parallax's* missile destroyed a dozen vessels before it finally fizzled out. The second orb—the one shot from the newly-arrived Aphelion—had a bit more staying power and kept going long after its partner died. So much energy, in fact, that it likely would have reached *Brutus* at the fleet's center if it'd been better aimed. But the shot was hurried—sent off as soon as the DSR ships appeared— and fired at an angle that sliced through the fleet's aft corner, taking out a handful of Titans and Auroras before wobbling off into empty space.

"Sikuuku!" Henricksen called. "I want you and every other forward gun we have focused on *Parallax*. I want it gone, understand me? The gun, the ship, everything."

"On it!"

Sikuuku pivoted, breathing a few words into his comms unit as he reoriented and started blasting away. *Seychelles,* on the far side of the fleet, added her fire and together the two Valkyries pounded away, slicing through the ships protecting *Parallax,* chewing them to bits. A few minutes of concentrated fire and the screening disappeared entirely, leaving the Aphelion wide open.

"Gotcha, ya bastard." Sikuuku hunkered down and blasted away at the Aphelion's fork-nosed shape.

Progress. Finally.

But a quick check behind showed things weren't going quite as well aft. After dumping its load, the second Aphelion slowed and drifted backward, hiding at the far edge of the newly arrived DSR fleet. And there it waited, recharging that murderous forced-ion gun, waiting patiently for a chance to kill more ships.

Serengeti passed the news to Henricksen—he was *not* pleased—and then diverted her attention to a message from *Brutus*. A message containing a roster of ships, and orders Henricksen *definitely* wasn't going to like.

I don't like 'em either, Serengeti thought, and started to reply.

Seychelles beat her to it. *Don't be an idiot, Brutus*, the Valkyrie sent.

Serengeti winced. Not the most tactful approach, but then, that was *Seychelles*—loud-mouthed and opinionated, blunt and direct but seldom diplomatic. *Serengeti* loved her to death.

The landscape's changed, Serengeti sent. *We should be cautious in this. If we fall back—*

Stay on course, he sent back, tone curt and imperious, almost rude. *Follow orders. Do it now.*

Fool. Seychelles wisely kept that opinion between *Serengeti* and herself. *Watch yourself, sister.*

Seychelles closed the line as *Marianas* and *Atacama* acknowledged and came about, relaying instructions to the ships on *Brutus's* roster.

Serengeti passed the bad news to Henricksen and the bridge crew. "*Marianas* and *Atacama* are splitting off."

"What? Why? Where the hell are they going?" Henricksen demanded.

Serengeti moved the fleet's schematic to the center window and highlighted the two blips marking *Marianas* and *Atacama* before panning the display a bit to show the trailing edge of the Meridian Alliance fleet. And then she waited, knowing Henricksen would see it in time. To her surprise, Finlay beat him to it.

"Rear guard's slowing." Finlay's fingers tapped against the panel in front of her, eyes flicking up and down, left and right, interpreting the data *Serengeti* fed her. "They're coming about." Pause and a frown, head lifting staring at the schematic in disbelief. "Sir. They're leaving us. Moving off with those two Valkyries."

"He's splitting the fleet?" Henricksen stared hard at the forward camera, wanting answers. "Where the hell did he come up with *that* idea?" he asked her, throwing his arms wide. "Punch through, form up, and come about—*that* was the plan."

"A plan that changed when the rest of the DSR fleet showed up."

"Agreed," Henricksen nodded. "Plan's gone all to hell. But splitting our forces and fighting a battle on two fronts is lunacy, *Serengeti.* You *know* that."

Of course she did, but *Brutus* was in charge. And technically the odds were still in their favor. That's what the numbers said anyway, and *Brutus*—twelfth generation AI, the most advanced mind among them— was all about the numbers. The Bastion engineers purposely eliminated concepts like doubt, and fear, sympathy, and empathy from the flagship's design, viewing them as failures—faults in the earlier AI models like *Serengeti* and her fellow Valkyries. The Bastions, *Brutus* included, were all about cold, hard facts—odds and numbers, because that made for better decisions. Or so the AI designers said.

"Can you talk to him?" Henricksen asked her. "*Reason* with him. Try to get him to see how abominably *stupid* this is?"

Marianas and *Atacama* had already moved off, committing themselves to this ill-advised plan—and it was doubtful *Brutus* would listen, but *Serengeti* tried anyway. She sent a dozen different messages, but none of them received a response.

The Bastion had gone dark. Guess he was tired of her objections.

"*Brutus* is no longer responding to my hails."

And *Marianas* and *Atacama* were still moving, the gap between the divided Meridian Alliance fleet widening as the two Valkyries advanced on the DSR ships behind them. Too late to stop it now—all *Serengeti* could do was keep on firing and hope they somehow manage to get themselves out of this mess.

She focused her attention ahead just as *Trinidad* lost his main gun. "'Bout fucking time!" Sikuuku yelled, and then pivoted sharply as *Trinidad* fired back, bringing its other guns to bear, focusing them all in on *Brutus* as the other DSR ships went silent.

That's odd.

Serengeti panned her cameras around, trying to figure out what was going on. The snaking lines of *Trinidad's* plasma cannons threaded their way through space, chewing their way toward *Brutus,* but for the space of five seconds, none of the ships around him fired. And then it all started back up again, missiles pouring out faster, more furious than before, the DSR ships targeting the Valkyries—*Seychelles* and *Antigone* on one side as *Sechura* took up *Marianas'* vacated position behind *Serengeti.*

Chatter erupted on the comms, messages flying back and forth between the Valkyries, other ships in the fleet querying *Brutus,* wondering what was going on. But *Brutus* just kept pounding away, stubbornly maintaining his silence as he lobbed missile after missile at *Trinidad*, giving back every shot he took.

Ships exploded everywhere, flaring and dying on both sides. Casualty reports rolled in, detailing losses on both sides—crews vented, ships crippled or dead. Damage reports flooded the channels, wounded ships firing away while their crews worked to contain breaches and fires. *Serengeti* herself had taken damage—holes punched through her triple-thick hull, a fire started in a forward compartment that the suppression units quickly put out—but *Seychelles* and *Antigone* took the worst of it. *Seychelles* was in the lead position on the port side of the fleet, her body half-blocking, half-protecting *Antigone* behind her. Plasma shots peppered her nose and sides, composite metal plating dented and buckled before finally giving way. *Seychelles* kept fighting anyway, ignoring the damage to her body as she threw railgun and plasma cannon fire back. In fact, she fired as long as she could, never slowing until her systems started to fail. She ejected her crew at the last moment, launching her emergency pods out into the chaos of battle in a last ditch effort to save their lives.

Desperate maneuver, that. One an AI would only risk if there were no other option.

Seychelles fired up her engines and broke formation, shooting ahead of the Titans and Auroras, putting herself at the front of the spearhead of ships in the main fleet.

Suicide run.

"No, sister," *Serengeti* whispered, sending a desperate plea via sub-space message.

"Goodbye, *Serengeti*," she sent back. And then *Seychelles* surged forward, engines wide open, every last gun trained on *Parallax,* chewing through the ships protecting him to get at the Aphelion.

The counter wound down, ticking off time, showing five seconds before the Aphelion's gun was fully charged and ready to fire. *Seychelles* broke through, hull plating ruined, main gun spewing out long lines of plasma fire aimed at the fork-shaped metal rod sticking out of *Parallax's* nose.

"*Parallax* firing!" Finlay called.

Seychelles's shots connected, sheering away *Parallax's* gun in the second before it spat its swirling cobalt orb out. Bolts of electric fire arced in every direction, crackling along the shattered remains of the Aphelion's gun, sparking brightly off his metal composite hull. The fire raced backward, consuming the Aphelion's body, and then *Parallax* exploded in a bright blue flare, taking poor stricken *Seychelles* and half a dozen DSR vessels with him.

"*Seychelles,*" *Serengeti* whispered in heartbroken sorrow. "*Seychelles.*"

"Gone," Finlay breathed, staring in shocked dismay. "I can't believe she's gone. I thought—The Valkyries—I thought they were invincible."

"No such thing, Finlay." Henricksen looked up, eyes locking onto a camera. "Anything can be hurt. Anything can die."

Even a tenth generation combat AI like *Seychelles*, or *Serengeti.*

"How did this happen?" Finlay whispered.

"She's gone, Finlay, and that's an end to it." Henricksen grimaced, nodding an apology to *Serengeti's* camera. "Now tell me about her crew. Give me status on those lifeboats."

Finlay didn't seem to hear him. She just sat there, staring at the display in disbelief as the mingled remains of *Parallax* and *Seychelles* drifted away. "They killed a Valkyrie." Fear in her voice now, in the wide-eyed way she stared at the bridge's windows. "How could they kill a Valkyrie?"

"Finlay!" Henricksen barked, making her jump. "Focus, Finlay. *Seychelles* is gone but she saw to her crew. Now where are they?"

Finlay half-turned, face pale beneath its smattering of freckles, mouth opening and closing as if she wanted to say something but couldn't quite get the words out. "I don't—I don't know," she managed, shaking her head.

"Then find them," Henricksen told her. Soft voice now, but every bit as commanding. "We can do that much for *Seychelles* at least."

Finlay sucked in a breath and nodded. "Aye, sir." She faced back, hands settling somewhat uncertainly on the Scan station in front of her, fingers pecking at readouts and displays, moving faster, more confidently with each passing second. "Where are they?" she muttered, searching the confusion of ships' signatures.

Hard to find anything with all that electronic chatter out there—lot of data to parse through, and *Seychelles's* loss had rattled her, making it hard for Finlay to focus. *Serengeti* reached into the Scan station's panel to help her, carving off the cluster of blips marking *Marianas* and *Atacama,* the rest of the Meridian Alliance ships that went with them, and throwing that data into a separate window. They didn't have time to deal with that right now. The battle behind them was in full swing, ships exploding left and right, but so far the Meridian Alliance had the upper hand. Fewer ships in this second DSR fleet, and the Aphelion the only real threat in the bunch. *Serengeti's* sisters had that conflict well in hand, so she pushed the scene aside and focused on the sea of ships and debris and electronic signatures in front of her, parsing through the chaos in search of the locator beacons attached to *Seychelles's* lifeboats.

Ten pods ejected before *Seychelles* went down, and even *Serengeti,* with all her sensors and arrays and high-tech systems, had a hard time finding them. The chaff scrambled her scans, rail gun fire and plasma rounds that rattled against her hull, damaging sensors, causing feeds and relays to flicker and go dark. But she found a pod eventually, and another, and another, highlighting each one on Scan's display.

"Finlay," Henricksen called impatiently.

"Six, sir. I count six of ten pods that ejected."

"Six." Henricksen scrubbed at his face. "Six. Dammit." He sighed heavily, eyes flicking to the camera in front of him. "It's a wonder any of them made it. Can we get to them?"

Finlay consulted her screen, comparing their location to that of each of the pods, taking into account the ships and debris between them.

Too much distance, too much chaff.

Finlay closed her eyes and covered her face with her hands.

"Finlay. Talk to me," Henricksen snapped.

"No," *Serengeti* said, saving Finlay the heartache. "They're too far away. Too many ships, too much fire between us and them."

Henricksen flushed angrily. "So we're supposed to just leave them out there? That's crap, *Serengeti.*"

"I have no intention of leaving them. *We* can't get to the lifeboats, but there are others in the fleet who can."

She checked the schematic and passed the pods' coordinates to the other ships in the fleet. Acknowledgements came back—*Tsunami* and *Zephyr,* and a half dozen other small ships shuffled about before moving off line to intercept *Seychelles's* escape pods.

Henricksen nodded his thanks to the camera and then thumbed ship-wide comms open to address his crew. "Alright. Listen up!"

Serengeti cringed as Henricksen's voice echoed across fleet-wide comms. *A mistake,* she thought. *It has to be a mistake. Even Henricksen wouldn't be that bold.*

Brutus led this fleet—not *Serengeti,* certainly not her human captain—and only *Brutus* addressed the ships en masse. She flashed a private message to Henricksen's panel, letting him know about the error.

Henricksen saw it and smiled, eyes lifting to the camera. "Oops."

Totally unapologetic. He'd done it on purpose.

"You cheeky little monkey."

Henricksen shrugged and temporarily shut down comms. "Fleet's in turmoil, *Serengeti.* We need to bring it back together." A nod at the schematic on the front window, the two battles raging on two different fronts. "And we need to do it *soon.*"

"What do you suggest we do?"

Henricksen reached to the mash-up panel in front of him and started adjusting ships' positions, running scenario, mapping out a plan of attack that moved *Serengeti* to the fore with *Antigone* and *Sechura*, using the more heavily armed and armored Valkyries to bust through the line and take *Trinidad* out.

A bold plan, and definitely risky. Not at the stratagem *Brutus* had laid out.

"*Brutus* won't like it," *Serengeti* warned.

Henricksen shrugged again, obviously not caring. "It'll work. Trust me," he said, tipping a wink at the camera. *Serengeti* started to object but Henricksen thumbed comms back over and spoke right over her. "This is Henricksen on *Serengeti*. *Parallax* is gone and *Seychelles* with him. So while *Marianas* and *Atacama* make mincemeat of the Aphelion's cousin back there and the rest of those wrecks he brought with him, we're going to bust through this line and tear holy hell outta that Heliotrope *Trinidad*. The Valkyries—"

"*Serengeti*." *Brutus'* grating voice echoed over fleet-wide comms, drowning Henricksen out. "You are to hold position with the other Valkyries."

An order—no doubt about it, with the entire fleet as witness. To disobey was to invoke mutiny, creating a schism in an already divided fleet. But she couldn't let this go.

A long-ignored sub-mind flashed a warning, pulsing insistently to get *Serengeti's* attention. She dismissed it, pushing the sub-mind to the background while she sent Henricksen's battle plan to *Brutus*, using a private channel in the hopes he'd hear her out.

Brutus deleted the message without even opening it. Deleted it and kept going, as if nothing had changed. As if the second fleet of ships behind them didn't exist, and *Seychelles* hadn't exploded before their eyes.

Bastard. Seychelles *is dead because of you. You're so full of pride you won't even listen to reason.*

Serengeti opened a channel, hesitated, thinking through the ramifications of what she'd be doing, and belatedly shut it back down. "Acknowledged. Holding position," she sent, and then flashed an apology to Henricksen.

Henricksen glanced at the message and shrugged. He'd seen enough battles to know the score—knew when to question authority and when to fall into line. "Remind me when this is over to have a word with *Brutus's* captain," he said, glancing upward at a camera.

"I'm not sure—"

Serengeti broke off as the sub-mind's warning flared to life again. *What now?* she wondered, acknowledging it this time, turning her eyes to the blip it had been watching off the starboard bow.

Osage.

In the heat of battle, she'd all but forgotten about the poor, stricken vessel. It was closer now—much closer—but still more than four hundred kilometers out.

What's the problem? she asked.

The sub-mind scrolled through a packet of data, highlighting *Osage's* course and speed, both of which had drastically changed while *Serengeti* wasn't looking.

EIGHT

"Henricksen." *Serengeti* waited until he looked up at the camera. "Take a look at this."

She highlighted *Osage's* position on the schematic, laying the ship's current path alongside the one she'd charted before.

Henricksen frowned darkly. "The trajectory's changed. She'll intercept us." He considered the schematic a moment, watching *Osage's* blip move closer. "What do you make of it?"

Serengeti honestly wasn't sure. *Osage* was a hulk and hardly seemed a threat, but it wouldn't do to have the Titan running into her, and she couldn't afford the distraction of dodging around an empty husk in the middle of a pitched battle.

"Trouble?" Henricksen asked her, quirking an eyebrow.

"Not sure. I'll keep an eye her."

Serengeti sent her sub-mind back to watching, leaving instructions for it to alarm when *Osage* was two hundred kilometers out. If the ship's course remained constant, they'd have to blow her. There was simply no other choice.

She messaged Henricksen, telling him much the same.

Henricksen grimaced, eyes drifting to the Number Two probe's feed, all but forgotten on the far side of bridge's windows. "Sikuuku."

"Aye, sir." Sikuuku answered without looking, fingers squeezing the triggers of the main gun, chewing away at *Trinidad's* hull.

"Orders for the starboard-side batteries. When *Serengeti* sounds the alarm, you tell them to open fire."

The main gun went silent as Sikuuku consulted the instructions Henricksen sent him. He turned his head, lifting the targeting visor away from his face.

Grim look on Sikuuku's face, *not* happy with those orders.

"Look to the living," Henricksen told him.

Shots from *Trinidad* found *Serengeti's* hull, rocking her hard, sending Henricksen stumbling to one side.

"Aye, sir," Sikuuku said quietly. He slammed the visor down and pivoted, gripping the main gun's triggers hard as he fired back at *Trinidad*.

Less than fifty kilometers separated *Brutus* and the rest of his half-fleet from *Trinidad* and the DSR ships now. Fifty kilometers and closing—close enough that Henricksen and the others could finally see the Heliotrope with their own eyes, prickling bulk showing as a dark grey blob against the deep black of space.

Serengeti tapped into the Number Four probe—still out there, faithfully relaying every last shot of this battle—and swiveled it around before zooming in on the Heliotrope to get a better look.

He was a tough old thing, *Trinidad,* but the relentless pounding had taken its toll. The massive puffer fish didn't look so prickly now. Most of the guns on the port side were gone, and the comms towers with them. Dark gaps showed in his hull where the metal composite skin had torn away, fires flaring beneath as inner compartments buckled and gave way.

"Almost there," Sikuuku muttered. "Just a few more minutes…"

Another alert, this time from the sub-mind *Serengeti* had set to watching port side of the fleet.

"Proximity alarm," *Serengeti* said, voicing the sub-mind's alert.

"*Osage?*" Henricksen barked an order at Sikuuku, readying the starboard-side batteries to fire.

"Port side," *Serengeti* told, highlighting an errant blip on the schematic.

"The Golem." Henricksen leaned forward, frowning darkly at the Golem's marker. "Sikuuku! Belay my last."

Sikuuku recalled the order, smacked a panel to one side so he could view the front screen's data while continued to plug away with the main gun.

Henricksen kept frowning at the schematic, obviously not liking what he saw. "Bastard's up to something." He tapped the panel in front of him and scrolled through the Golem's data. The square-sided ship was dark and silent as ever, its course leading it far away from the other DSR vessels. "Not firing, though. Looks like he's just lost." He raised his eyes to the camera. "What's the alarm about?"

"Check its path. The Golem's on a collision course with *Antigone.*"

"God damn," Henricksen breathed.

Serengeti sent *Antigone* a warning, but she'd already seen the Golem. Her port batteries swiveled, targeting the Golem and then pounding away at its blunt face.

The Golem bore the beating and gave nothing at all back. But it accelerated without warning, streaking toward *Antigone*—engines wide open, glowing bright blue against the darkness of space.

Antigone diverted her aft batteries, adding their firepower to the others already in the mix, pouring round after round into the Golem's square shape.

That, as it turned, was a horrible mistake.

A massive explosion erupted, lighting up the cameras, blotting out the feeds on the port side of *Brutus's* half-fleet. Number Four's video feed blanked out as they went offline—powered down, destroyed, *Serengeti* couldn't tell which.

"What's happening?" Henricksen shouted. "Talk to me, *Serengeti*."

"Stand by," she told him, because she was as blind as the rest, her port-side cameras overloaded by the blinding glare.

The light banked and faded an eternity later, leaving bits of drifting metal in its wake. And a massive crater in the Meridian Alliance fleet— the Golem gone, *Antigone* gone, nearly a third of the fleet wiped out in an instant.

"No," *Serengeti* whispered, watching ships' markers disappear, dropping one after another from the schematic on the front windows.

"*Serengeti!*"

Henricksen rarely shouted, never raised his voice to her. That he did so now was a measure of his distress.

"Scanning." She searched the sea of wreckage and found complex compounds, traces of metals and explosives none of the Meridian Alliance ships carried. And a radiation signature that really, *truly* did not belong.

"Nuke," she breathed in horror. "The Golem was carrying a nuke. They turned it into a bomb."

"So when *Antigone* fired…"

"She set the bomb off."

"Damn. God damn," Henricksen swore, rubbing at his eyes. "The crews. Did anyone make it out?"

Serengeti checked and found a few lifeboat beacons squawking into space, but not many. Not surprisingly really. It all happened so fast. Most of the ships probably never realized what danger they were in until that nuke went off.

A message came through—orders from *Brutus,* recalling *Marianas, Atacama,* the rest of the ships he'd split off.

'Bout goddamn time.

Serengeti flashing the message to Henricksen's Command Post.

"Smartest thing that bastard's done all day," he said, lips twisting sourly.

Marianas and *Atacama* slowed and then stopped, guns firing steadily as the ships behind them came to a halt. A flare of engines as the

66

Meridian Alliance vessels reversed en masse, maintaining fire as they initiated a tactical retreat.

The second message from *Brutus* came not longer after. "Spool up hyperspace drives," *Brutus* sent, broadcasting the command to both sections of the fleet at once. "Prepare for jump."

Henricksen barked a laugh. "I stand corrected. *That* is the smartest thing he's said all day. Tsu!" he called, turning to Engineering. "You heard the man. Fire up the jump drives so we can get the hell out of here."

"Aye, sir!" Tsu bent over her station, almond-shaped eyes focused on the readouts, narrow face bathed in the panel's multi-colored lights. "Three minutes," she said, fingers flying across the keyboard, one hand lifting now and then to tap at the panels to either side.

"Start the clock," Henricksen told her.

Tsu transferred the counter on her Engineering panel to the front windows, digital numbers showing blood-red against the darkness outside.

Henricksen rubbed his chin, studying the schematic on the front windows as Tsu spooled up *Serengeti's* jump drives, filling the bridge with a low-pitched whine. "Three minutes for us," Henricksen said, looking up at a camera. "That's Valkyrie jump prep time. Titans and Auroras have smaller drives but proportionately less mass to haul through the buckle, so they'll need about the same. *Brutus* is a bruiser, though. Needs closer to four, even with those big ass engines they dropped in his belly."

And *Serengeti* couldn't leave the battle until *Brutus* transited through the buckle. That was the way of things—the order of departure the fleet strictly followed when executing hyperspace jump: Flagship first, Dreadnoughts second, Titans and Auroras after, Valkyries bringing up the rear.

Serengeti shuddered as plasma fire scored her side, tearing at her hull plating, peeling a few panels away. Environmentals showed a small breach—the doors on one of the cargo bays ripped off, everything inside it thrown out into space. A check of her schematics showed it was Cargo Bay 4. Four where'd she left *Barlow's* remains, along with Probe Six and balky old Ten.

Damn. Pain in the ass he might be, but she'd miss that cranky old probe.

Railgun rattled loudly, chipping away at her skin. Microphone pick-ups brought her ominous noises—the creaks and groans of metal composite straining to its limit before giving way.

More holes appeared in *Serengeti's* hull. Atmosphere vented in explosive puffs of frozen gases, fire suppression systems lit up, deploying port-side bow as crews rushed to close emergency hatches, blocking off compromised compartments in order to save the rest of the ship.

"Come on, goddammit." Henricksen leaned forward, hands braced against the panel in front of him as he watched the jump drive counter tick down. "Tsu!" he called, straightening up. "What's the count on the Bastion?"

"Minute thirty, Captain."

"Too long. Too damn long."

"Incoming!" Finlay screamed.

Serengeti slewed sideways, taking a direct hit from one of *Trinidad's* guns. Henricksen lurched forward, grabbing at panels with both hands to keep from falling as the rest of the bridge crew held on for dear life.

A flare erupted outside, close enough to light up *Serengeti's* bridge. She grabbed a camera and turned it that way, watching as an Aurora named *Happenstance* broke in half—one end drifting harmlessly away from the fleet, the other slamming into *Wrath* beside her.

Henricksen punched the panel in front of him. "Dammit! They're tearing this fleet apart. This is not time for protocol, *Serengeti*. *Brutus* should send the smaller ships ahead."

"I'll see what I can do."

She tapped into comms to send a message and found *Marianas* had beaten her to it. The Valkyrie argued hotly with *Brutus*—growing angrier, more insistent with every ship they lost—and eventually he relented. With just thirty seconds left on the Bastion's jump clock, the Auroras started jumping away. The Titans followed soon after, but barely twenty of them made it out before *Brutus's* grating voice cut across fleet comms, announcing his intent to enter hyperspace.

"All ships hold," *Brutus's* captain sent out.

Too much mass behind *Brutus* for other ships to safely jump with him. Hyperspace transit created a distortion—a singularity of sorts they called 'unstable space.' Not a big deal when smaller ships like the Auroras traveled, but strange things happened when a ship *Brutus's* size transited. Strange, *bad* things—hulls twisted, entire vessels sometimes turned inside out.

The hold order was for the fleet's protection. Only a fool would ignore it.

A last few Titans jumped through anyway, transiting hyperspace in an instant. The rest—close to a hundred and fifty Titans plus *Serengeti*, the four other surviving Valkyries, *Brutus's* Dreadnought bodyguard, minus shredded *Gorgon*—wisely held position and waited.

Brutus spooled up his jump drives—a complicated, carefully choreographed operation requiring synchronization of all four hyperdrive engines at once. A swirl appeared ahead him as a buckle took shape, sucking space inward as *Brutus* advanced, aiming for the swirling void at its center.

"Taking his time about it, isn't he?" Henricksen growled. He looked up at the camera and then back to the windows.

Brutus entered the buckle, front end disappearing into darkness, the void creeping along the Bastion's prickling, porcupine shape like it was eating the ship alive.

"Hurry it up, you oversized, wallowing bastard," Henricksen muttered under his breath.

An alarm sounded—perimeter alert from the sub-mind keeping tabs on *Osage* of *Serengeti's* port side—drawing her eyes way from *Brutus*. She tapped into a few of her surviving cameras and turned them in *Osage's* direction.

The ship was in firing range now—just about two hundred kilometers out—but there was little chance of a collision. By the time the tattered Titan's path intercepted hers, *Serengeti* would be long gone. She cancelled the perimeter alarm and detailed the sub-mind to another task.

That's when she remembered the Number Two probe.

Damn. It's still inside her.

She hated to leave it, especially after losing Six and Ten, but *Brutus* had just about cleared the buckle and soon it would be her turn to jump. She checked the Chron, realized there was just enough time.

Hang on, little buddy.

Serengeti tapped into the Number Two probe and recalled it, telling it to hurry-hurry-hurry as the buckle consuming *Brutus* passed the ship's midpoint and slowly consumed the remainder of his bulk.

"Tsu. Status," Henricksen called.

"Jump drive is primed and ready. We can transit as soon as *Brutus* is gone."

"Good." Henricksen stared hard at the window, arms folded over his chest, lopsided smile twisting his lips as the Number Two probe started to move. "Huh. Almost forgot about that little guy. No man left behind, eh?" He flashed a smile at *Serengeti's* camera and stumbled to one side, cursing loudly as missile fire slammed into *Serengeti's* bow. "Time!" he yelled.

"Twenty seconds," Tsu called back.

"The probe? How long—?"

Henricksen frowned and leaned forward, studying Number Two's feed as it worked its way back out of *Osage's* frayed body, dodging melted girders and snarled nests of burnt-out cables. Not much else left inside her, but as the probe passed by a blown cargo hold, *Serengeti* spotted a cluster of blinking red lights—signs of life, of *power* where nothing at all should be.

Henricksen saw it too. "What was that? Back it up. Turn Two around and—"

"*Osage* is accelerating!" Finlay warned.

The wrecked ship halved the distance between herself and the fleet faster than *Serengeti* would have thought possible given her condition.

"Blow it! Blow it!" Henricksen yelled.

Serengeti tapped into the artillery system, taking the controls from Sikuuku. She turned the main gun on *Osage* and started blasting away, targeting the Titan's engines to at least slow her down. "Jump. Jump now," *Serengeti* ordered.

Tsu checked the timer and then shook her head. "Ten seconds left on the clock."

"We're out of time."

Serengeti initiated the jump sequence herself, and passed orders to *Sechura* and the other ships to do the same.

Henricksen threw a worried look at the camera, obviously wanting an explanation. "What's going on?"

"*Osage*. She's booby-trapped. Just like the Golem."

"Shit."

"Initiating jump."

Serengeti engaged her hyperspace drive, shuddering violently as the fabric of space around bent and twisted and the buckle took form. Ships winked out around her, disappearing in silver-white bursts as they jumped away. *Antigone* went, and *Marianas* and *Atacama* after, leaving just *Serengeti* and *Sechura*, and sixty or so Titans.

"Time!" Tsu yelled.

Serengeti moved forward with *Sechura* at her side, but as the hyperspace void sucked inward, *Osage* exploded.

After that there was nothing—nothing but smoke and fire, darkness and chaos and death.

Nine

Alarms shrieked everywhere, filling the bridge with a cacophony of noise. Comms filled with shouts and screams coming from every compartment, every corridor along the length and breadth of her body. And beneath it all, the sounds of *Serengeti's* destruction—the screech and groan of internal structures twisting, failing as a bottomless vacuum sucked at her torn hull.

Henricksen picked himself up off the floor, wiping blood from his cheek. "Damage report!" he barked, pressing a hand to the gash in his temple. Blood poured down his face, staining his jet black uniform, turning the silver stars of command a deep shade of crimson. "Damage report!" he repeated, but Tsu didn't seem to hear him. She just sat at her station, staring wide-eyed at the windows wrapping the front of the bridge.

He reached over, killing the klaxons shrieking at him like angry ghosts. No need for the sirens now—they already knew they were well and truly fucked.

"Tsu!" Henricksen slammed a hand against the panel in front of him. "Wake up!"

Tsu jumped and turned, cheeks pale, eyes wide as dinner plates.

Lost look on Tus's face, a hint of terror showing deep in her eyes. Henricksen saw it, and lowered his voice, using his calmest, most patient tone.

"Damage report. Now, Tsu."

"Damage report." She wobbled back around, brow furrowed, staring at her panel like she didn't know what to do with it.

Henricksen tapped the panel in front of him with a finger and then looked up at the camera. *Serengeti* sent a data package to his Command Post and then waited while he scanned through it.

He already knew the worst of it—the buckle collapsed, jump drives knocked offline, most of *Serengeti's* starboard-side aft torn away. The rest made a decidedly grim read. When *Osage* exploded, she carved a huge hole in the Meridian Alliance fleet, taking out twenty-six ships. Those that survived the explosion drifted aimlessly—damaged, dying. *Brutus* was long gone, and the Dreadnoughts with him, *Sechura*...she didn't know about *Sechura*, but *Serengeti* hoped she'd escaped in time and wasn't drifting out there, mixed in with the other debris.

Either way, I'm alone, Serengeti thought. *Last Valkyrie standing, responsible for thirty-eight half-crippled ships.*

A stream of fire rattled along her side, reminding her that the DSR ships were still there.

Henricksen closed his eyes and drew a breath, palms pressed against the panel in front of him. "Fine mess we got ourselves into this time, *Serengeti*," he said, looking up at the camera. "Tsu. Talk to me. What's going on?"

Serengeti gathered up more information and sent it to his Command Post, but Henricksen gave it hardly more than a passing glance. This wasn't about information, she realized. Henricksen had every last bit of data he needed, right there in front of him, but he didn't have Tsu. Tsu was frozen, stuck in the moment, locked up tight by the terror inside her. What she needed was purpose—something to distract her from the horror showing on the bridge windows and filtering through comms. And Henricksen—solid, patient, tough as nail as Henricksen—gave it to her.

"We're in a world of shit, Tsu, and I need you to get us out of it."

Tsu turned around, blinking slowly.

"I want to know the status of the ship's systems and where the worst of the damage is at. But first I need you to get the jump drive back online. You got that?"

Tsu blinked and then nodded slowly. "Aye, sir," she said numbly. She faced around, eyes drifting to the front windows, and then she ducked her head and worked away at the panel in front of her, redirecting crew below decks to repair the jump drive.

Serengeti dipped into the Engineering station and, after assessing the situation herself, decided to send in a robot crew as well. The DSR were still out there, pelting *Serengeti* and the other left-behind ships with sustained fire. *Serengeti* ordered her remaining batteries to keep fighting and stave them off the best they could, but she had no intentions of staying here. Standing and fighting was a fool's errand, escape their only real option.

She had to get her jump drives working. She had to save her crew.

"Tsu. Status."

"Jump drives were damaged in the blast, Captain." Tsu's fingers flew across her panel, eyes drinking in the information on her display. "Crew is Gerry-rigging them together—bypassing some of the safety protocols to get them working again."

"How long?" Henricksen asked her.

Serengeti shuddered as plasma fire raked her port side. Tsu glanced up, staring anxiously at the front windows.

"Tsu!"

"Few minutes," Tsu told him. And at Henricksen's angry glare, "Four minutes. That's my best guess."

Her eyes slid to Finlay as her fingers tapped out a message. Finlay frowned, nodded, sent her own message back.

"Four minutes," Henricksen muttered. "Three more before the breach forms and we can get out of here. Damn," he breathed, wiping more blood from his cheek. He turned toward the Artillery station, watching Sikuuku blast away. "Armaments?"

Tsu reached across the panel, pulling another data window in. "Starboard turrets are pretty much down. Port-side batteries are operational except for the few we lost around the bow. Aft...aft's a mess, honestly."

"Well, we've got guns. That's something anyway." Henricksen still looked grim. "And the rest of the ship?" he asked, turning back to Engineering. "Hyper drives are down. What else is broken?"

Tsu pointed at a schematic of the ship she moved to the front windows. "See this?" She highlighted a series of pulsing red indicators showing along *Serengeti's* aft end. "Rear quarter of the ship's been compromised—compartments vented on every level when that blast ripped open the hull. Emergency doors came down in time to limit the damage further in but..." Tsu paused and ducked her head. "We lost everyone in there, sir."

Henricksen closed his eyes, blood running in thin streams down his face. "How many?" he asked her. "How many did we lose, Tsu?"

"Twelve crews. Sixty personnel in total, sir."

"Sixty. God damn." Henricksen wiped at his cheek, scrubbed bloodstained fingers through his hair.

Sixty personnel killed of three hundred and twelve on board—nearly a fifth of *Serengeti's* compliment wiped out in an instant. A quick check of *Serengeti's* systems showed she'd lost seventy-eight robots. *Serengeti* mourned them all—human and robot, both. Even balky, contrary probe Number Ten who'd always been such a pain in the ass.

"Damn." Henricksen opened his eyes and looked out the front windows, studying the DSR fleet. "Finlay. What's happening out there?"

"Three ships departed. I read...thirty-three waiting to jump, sir. Plus us. Thirty-two. Thirty." Finlay paused and frowned, staring at a section of her screen. "Captain. There's a problem."

"What now?" he sighed.

"*Normandy's* dead in the water. *Trieste,* a dozen others reporting the same." Finlay looked around at him. "They can't jump, sir. They're stuck here, just like us."

"Damn. Damn and damn and damn." Henricksen braced his arms against the panel in front of there and leaned there for a few seconds, looking incredibly tired all of a sudden.

Finlay chewed her lip, throwing anxious glances Tsu's way.

Tsu typed something, erased, started typing again.

More shots landed, scoring along *Serengeti's* hull. Sikuuku did his best—giving back as good as he got—but they were badly outnumbered. And seven minutes—six now and slowly counting down—was simply too long for *Serengeti* to hold out on her own. Unless…

Serengeti queried her systems and found her propulsion engines were still operational. She shot a message to the remaining ships—twenty-eight now, two more had jumped away—and then turned herself hard to starboard, setting her engines to full.

"Tsu?"

Tsu shook her head. "Not me, sir. *Serengeti,*" she said, pointing.

Henricksen frowned at the camera. "We're running?"

"I see no other option. If we stay here, we'll die. But if we put some distance between ourselves and those DSR ships, we might be able to buy ourselves enough time to get the jump drives back online and get ourselves out of here."

"And the others?" he asked softly, nodding to the windows in front of him.

Two more ships flashed away, twenty-six remained. Half of them followed *Serengeti,* trailing after her like a bunch of roughed-up, oversized metal ducklings, but the rest of them…thirteen ships showed as dead in the water, basic systems operational but everything else—propulsion, hyper drive systems, even armaments—completely offline.

"They're on their own," she said, hating the words, knowing it was true. "Nothing we can do."

She sent a last message—a final farewell to the brothers and sisters left behind before their AI minds went dark—and then turned her eyes forward and focused on saving herself.

DSR fire chased after her and the other fleeing ships, raking their sides with plasma fire. Warning lights flashed everywhere, reporting more damage, more rents in *Serengeti's* abused hull. Comms went down, sending Kusikov scrambling, tearing into his panel, swapping chips and wires in an effort to at least get internal communications back on-line.

Serengeti hated the invasion—hated anyone digging into the guts of her electrical systems—but she left Kusikov to it and focused on navigation as a Titan named *Gallipoli* exploded and dropped off her scans.

Damn, damn, damn!

A scattering of plasma rounds tore a chunk out of *Serengeti's* aft end. A few more shots and two of her propulsion engines went off-line.

Serengeti slowed, her remaining two engines running wide open, slowly tearing themselves apart. Her body trembled terribly, internal structures groaning then shrieking, threatening to come entirely undone.

No. We're getting out of here.

"Why are we slowing?" Henricksen reached for his panel, swearing softly when he saw the new damage. "Tsu. Status report."

"One minute."

A flare of light beside them as another Titan disappeared in a shower of fire and metal composite pieces.

"Bloody hell. Tell the crews to hurry."

Tsu looked over at him, then nodded pointedly at the Comms station. And Kusikov's legs sticking out from a gutted panel.

"Right." Henricksen sighed and rubbed at his eyes, smearing blood across his face. "I need—"

"Jump drives on-line!" Tsu's face lit with excitement. "Beginning jump prep."

The counter reset to three minutes and started ticking down as the hyperspace buckle writhed into existence outside. Henricksen watched it for a moment and then straightened and drew a deep breath.

"Kusikov. I need those comms."

"Almost there," Kusikov told him, voice muffled by the layers of metal and plastic and electronics above his head. "I've just gotta—there!" The comms panel flared to life. Kusikov wriggled out, smiling smugly. "Baddest tech in town. Ain't nuthin' I can't—"

A buzz of electricity and something flashed deep in the panel's guts. A fizzling, crackling sound followed soon after, accompanied by a puff of smoke. Half the panel went dark, the other half flickered, clinging tenaciously to life.

"Crap." Kusikov poked tentatively at the station but the dark half stubbornly refused to light. "That's not good."

"Talk to me, Kusikov," Henricksen growled. "Do I have comms or not?"

"Internal comms are working. External comms are fried. Sorry, sir."

Henricksen swore loudly, getting the anger out of his system. And then he reached over and opened the ship-wide channel. "This is the captain," he said in a calm, crisp tone. "Hyperdrive engines are back on-line. All crew prepare for jump. Clock sits at forty-eight seconds."

He cut the comms and seemed to think for a moment, tapping a finger against the panel before keying the comms back open.

"Thirty seconds!" Tsu called.

"We're getting out of here," Henricksen said firmly. "We're going back to the fleet."

"Ten seconds! Nine. Eight…"

Tsu called the count until the clock reached zero, and the buckle sucked inward. *Serengeti* pointed her nose toward the breach and opened her engines wide, propelling her damaged body into the jump singularity. A last look behind, a last farewell to the ships left behind, before the breach wrapped around her, spiriting *Serengeti* away.

Ten

Hyperspace was endless—a place of no time and all time, of calm and peace and silence. *Serengeti* entered with a sigh, a last few shots pockmarking her backside before the breach pulled closed and the void claimed her. Girders groaned, abused internal structures shifting, moaning beneath the added stress of faster than light travel. Lights flickered, data streams garbled, confused by the blur of high-speed information passing them by. Nothing out of the normal really. They called it 'unstable space' for a reason, after all, and systems—even healthy systems—turned wonky during jump.

Besides, in many ways, hyperspace didn't really exist. Which meant the vessels transiting hyperspace didn't really exist either. It was all very…metaphysical.

Serengeti smiled to herself, remembering a late night argument with a very tired, very *drunk* Henricksen on the topic of hyperspace existence. *Postmodernist crap,* he'd called it. And maybe it was. But there was a certain tranquility to hyperspace travel that was unlike anything *Serengeti* experienced anywhere else.

She sighed again and settled in, watching the jump clock languidly roll over and start marking time.

Thirty seconds—that's how long it took to jump from one hyperspace coordinate to another. Thirty seconds of *real* time, that is. But in hyperspace, those thirty seconds felt like thirty years. At least to her. Something to do with physics—real physics, not the metaphysics Henricksen so derided—and the rules of the universe changing, morphing in the bent reality of jump. Her human crew never seemed to notice, but to *Serengeti* each hyperspace transit felt like a long, slow cruise around the solar system—a lumbering meander through an infinity of black, with only brief flashes of colors every now and then to mark the stars and planets they passed by.

Thirty seconds. Just thirty seconds and they'd be safely again. Returned to the fleet, the worst of it behind them, food and fuel—anything and everything they needed to repair and refit and get back into battle.

Back with my sisters, Serengeti thought, settling in. *Except Seychelles.*

Sorrow—so much sorrow in remembering that name. *Seychelles* was gone, never to be seen again.

Focus on the living, she told herself, taking a page from Henricksen's book of wisdom. *Never forget the dead.*

Serengeti ran a diagnostic, taking stock of the damage to her body— the rents in her hull, the state of her internal systems.

That's when everything went sideways.

Alarms started screaming, shattering the peace in which *Serengeti* floated. Warning lights flared, popping up everywhere, error messages flashing *Failure! Failure! Failure!* in bold red letters. *Serengeti* tapped into each one, drawing information to her, querying her systems to find what was wrong. Reams of data came back to her, scrolling faster than she could absorb, requiring her to detail no less than three sub-minds to wade through it all.

She checked the Chron, found just ten seconds of jump time elapsed.

Damn. Damn-damn-damn.

The hyperspace trough fluttered and her damaged hull groaned in complaint. *Serengeti* felt herself drifting out of alignment and tried to correct her course. But when she reached for engines and navigation, she found the crew's hastily completed repair job was coming undone—just two jump drives running in parallel now, and as she watched, one flickered, power dropping precipitously before spiking again.

More shuddering, a distinct sensation of slewing sideways. *Serengeti* re-corrected, trying to maintain position within the hyperspace trough, a nearly impossible task with one engine surging and the other trying to compensate. A surge of power, both engines running wide open, and then the failing engine coughed and finally went out.

"No," *Serengeti* whispered.

The jump clock stood at twelve seconds. Not even close. Nowhere *near* where she needed to be.

Serengeti heaved over, pulling hard to port. A last minute correction did nothing, and before she knew, she was rolling—spiraling in the rough chop just outside the hyperspace trough, internal frame creaking, bending as her hull plating ripped away in chunks.

External structures broke off and disappeared into the oblivion around her. Electronic relays flared and burnt out. Compartments pressurized and just as quickly depressurized, voiding heat and air, suffocating her crew, venting them into space. One by one, *Serengeti's* systems failed, leaving her dark and silent—deaf and blind in the endlessness of hyperspace jump.

It's tearing me apart, she thought. *My crew's going to die.*

She reached for the jump drives, trying to shut the one working engine down to drop them out of hyperspace. But the engine—stuck wide open and burning hard, trying to fulfill her last wish and push them through the jump—stubbornly refused her command. She tried again with no better result, and then, unexpectedly, the engine just quit.

Serengeti dropped out of hyperspace as the jump counter hit fifteen seconds. She tumbled out of control, shedding pieces of her composite metal skin, leaving a cloud of debris behind her as she returned to normal space.

The klaxons roared to life, screaming wildly. Abused systems flickered and shut down, panels exploding as relays burned out all over the ship. Maneuvering jets fired, slowing *Serengeti* down. Another burst—fighting the tumble, finally bringing it under control—and *Serengeti* settled into a smoothly gliding path, slipping between the stars on the last of the inertia she'd built up in jump.

She split her consciousness, sending sub-minds throughout her body, peering through the few electronic eyes that were still functioning to survey the damage the DSR and her own hyperspace engines had done.

Not good. Not good at all, she thought, flicking from one camera image to another.

A few internal spaces remained intact, protecting the clutches of terrified humans and confused robots huddling inside. But as she moved on, *Serengeti* found more and more damage, large swathes of her carapace destroyed, sheets of hull plating gone, internal structures missing entirely in places. Cargo bays and commons spaces, barracks, storage rooms—everything ripped wide open, stars showing through gaping holes in *Serengeti's* hide. Silent corridors stretched everywhere, some cracked upon and looking out upon the stars, others choked by smoke and fire—dead bodies and broken robots lying everywhere.

No, she whispered, voice filled with horror.

She flicked from one camera to another camera, but all she found was emptiness—death and destruction and her own shattered remains. And when she'd cycled through every last one, and seen as much as she could see, *Serengeti* pulled back and returned to the bridge. So much death inside her, but there was life yet too—crew that needed saving. And the best way to do that was to figure out where in the hell she was.

Hard to do without a solid point of reference and most of her systems heavily damaged. She checked the jump clock and confirmed it frozen at fifteen seconds.

That's one data point anyway.

79

Serengeti ran a few calculations, and a series of what-if scenarios. Fifteen seconds was half their projected hyperspace travel time, but that didn't necessarily mean they'd covered half the distance they needed to go. Things didn't work that way in hyperspace. Time and space weren't linear. Speed and distance ebbed and flowed randomly in the trough, which meant they could be anywhere really. If she had to guess, *Serengeti* would say they'd barely traveled a quarter of the distance to the rally point with *Brutus*, but she was AI and disliked guessing—so inexact—so she reached for Nav instead, wanting the star charts to use as reference.

More bad news: Nav was down, the entire system burnt out, all the data, all the maps of all the solar systems and galaxies and nebulas locked away in storage, lying just beyond her reach.

No, she whispered.

For the first time—the very first time since her consciousness was first created—*Serengeti* felt the tiniest bit of fear.

She reached for Scan, thinking to survey the area around her in the hopes that there'd be something—a ship, a satellite, a rogue transmission from a nearby colony that she could tap into for information—but Scan was down too. And Comms, thanks to Kusikov's tinkering.

Kusikov.

Serengeti turned her eyes on the bridge and found it darkened and dead. Emergency power kicked in, bathing the rounded room in a bloody glow, revealing a smoking ruin—bodies lying everywhere, stations destroyed beyond any hope of recovery. *Serengeti* panned a camera around, taking it all in.

Kusikov lay on the floor—curled up tight, face blackened, burnt hands still clutching the cables he'd been fiddling with when the power surged, sending a flood of energy coursing through his body.

Stupid. You stupid, arrogant, son of a bitch.

She zoomed the camera in tight. Studying Kusikov's dead face, his burnt-out eyes, sorrow and anger warring inside her. He'd been tinkering with Comms again, trying to fix it while they transited jump. Not the brightest thing to do given the vagaries of hyperspace travel, but Kusikov was always the risk taker. He always thought he could beat the odds.

Not this time. You should have waited. If you'd just waited until we reached the other side, you might've made it.

But judging by the state of his station, Kusikov would likely still be dead.

"You're cocky little twit, Kusikov, but I'll miss you just the same."

Serengeti recorded an image of his face and sent it to storage, placing it in a folder alongside the smiling picture from his personal record. And then she pulled back and kept searching.

She couldn't find Sikuuku, but she found his hand sticking out of the crushed Artillery pod. No need to check if he was dead. The pod was mangled beyond all recognition, blooding coating its sides—nothing could've survived in there.

Scan next, camera zooming in on a bloody and shaken but very much alive Finlay. "Finlay," she called, patching a few damaged relays together to get a speaker working. "Finlay. Up here." She flashed the light above the camera to get Finlay's attention.

Finlay raised her head, staring vaguely at the camera, and then she climbed to her feet and started wandering around the bridge, looking lost and alone and terribly frightened. It pained *Serengeti* to see her like that, but she had to move on.

Evans was easy enough to find—he still sat his station at Nav, looking surprisingly unharmed—but a shudder passed through her as her maneuvering jets cut out, and when the trembling stopped, Evans slipped slowly from his seat and toppled lifelessly to the floor. *Serengeti* stared at him, noting the odd angle of his head, the sharp bones poking at the skin of his neck.

Dead, just like Kusikov. Like Sikuuku in that pod. The loss saddened but it was…different than with the others. Vague. Unfocused. *I wish I'd known you better, Evans. I wish I had more than this image of you lifeless body to remember you by.*

"Goodbye, Evans," *Serengeti* whispered. She recorded his image and filed it away with those of Kusikov and Sikuuku whom she'd known so much better, and then *Serengeti* moved on, peering through the smoke until she finally found her captain.

"Henricksen," she said, voice filled with relief.

Henricksen blinked slowly, looked dazed and confused. Blood covered his face—even more blood than before, thanks to a fresh gash on his cheek—and from the way he hugged his arm to his body—right hand clamped securely around his left wrist—she was pretty sure it was broken. Henricksen turned in an unsteady circle, surveying the damage around him, looking grim and grimmer with each dead body he found.

"What's happened?"

He reached for the panel in front of him and swore softly at finding it dead. He raised his head, looking out the windows wrapping the front of the bridge, but that didn't help him either. Nothing out there but empty space.

"No ships. No fleet. Not a single goddam thing." He turned to his right, grimacing at Kusikov's burnt body, the bloody remains of Sikuuku's Artillery pod before moving on to Evans. "Dead. All dead." Henricksen closed his eyes and bowed his head.

"Henricksen," *Serengeti* called again.

Henricksen straightened with an effort, raised his head and looked up at the camera. "*Serengeti.*" He nodded in acknowledgement, winced in pain and hugged his arm to his stomach. "What happened? Where are we?"

Simple question, not so simple answer. *Serengeti* hesitated, watching poor, shell-shocked Finlay wander aimlessly around the bridge.

No, she corrected. *Not aimlessly. She's looking for Tsu.*

She turned the camera a bit, focusing on Engineering and Tsu.

Poor Finlay. Hasn't she suffered enough?

"Where are we, *Serengeti*?"

Henricksen's voice drew her back to the center of the bridge.

"I don't know," *Serengeti* said softly. "I honestly don't know."

ELEVEN

"You don't know—" Henricksen shook his head in disbelief. "We're lost then."

Lost and alone, Henricksen. Far from where we should be.

"The jump drives failed mid-transit," *Serengeti* explained. "The stress of hyperspace was just too much for them. We dumped out here and…" The smallest of pauses as she cycled through the cameras on the bridge. "Let's just say we're lucky we survived at all."

Luckier, in fact, than Henricksen knew. The inertial dampeners— dead now, like so many of her systems and components—survived their tumbling departure from the trough, cushioning their exit, preventing her surviving crew from being turned to mush. *Serengeti* thought about mentioning that to Henricksen, decided against it. Might be a bit too disturbing given the situation. Besides, the dampeners were offline now—unrecoverable like so many other systems inside her.

Henricksen coughed, waving smoke away from his face. "Lucky. Right," he said, eyes drifting to Sikuuku's hand dangling from the crushed coughing Artillery pod. Finlay wandered over to Nav, stooped by Evans and looked into his face. "We're all so damned lucky."

If you only knew, Henricksen. But for dampeners, you'd all be lumps of liquid flesh and pulverized bone.

"No one *knows* we're here, do they? No one even knows we're alive." Henricksen looked up at the camera. "Which means we can't expect anyone to come looking for us."

"No," *Serengeti* said softly.

A tremor passed through her as a rumbling built somewhere deep inside her ship's belly. A second tremor and she shuddered violently, metal tearing as a gap appeared in her port side, compromising one of her few intact compartments, blasting its contents out into space.

Finlay tumbled to the floor, landing beside Evans. Henricksen grabbed at his captain's chair, bracing himself until the trembling subsided. And then he squatted down—arm wrapped tight across his stomach, face tight with pain—and started tearing at the underside of the Command Post's panels, checking wires and circuit boards, tossing burnt-out electronics to one side, rerouting connectors where he could.

Comms. He's trying to fix Comms, Serengeti realized. *He thinks it's just his panel.*

"Henricksen."

Henricksen gave a sharp shake of his head and kept working, gutting one panel and using its salvaged parts to try and rebuild two others. Blood trickled down his face, blinding one eye. He wiped distractedly at it and then swore softly as his bloody fingers slipped, dropping a circuit board to the floor. "You'd have this working in no time, wouldn't you, Kusikov?" He flicked his eyes to Kusikov's sprawled body, his burnt-out eyes staring from his dead face.

"Henricksen."

"Bet you're laughing your ass off, aren't you?" he said softly. He grimaced and looked away, grabbed up the forgotten circuit board and slotted it into place.

"Captain!" *Serengeti* called.

Henricksen bowed his head, dropping a handful of relays to the floor.

"Comms is dead—internal, external, the entire system."

A tremor ran the length of *Serengeti's* body, making her shudder and shake. Henricksen pressed a hand to the floor, steadying himself until the trembling stopped.

"You can't fix it, Henricksen. You're wasting your time stripping that panel."

Henricksen sighed and wiped at his bloodied face. "What about Nav? Engineering? Between the crew and the robots maybe—"

"No," she said gently. "Nav is down. Engines and secondary propulsion systems are down. All I've got left are docking and maneuvering jets."

"Fuel based. Won't last for long. Certainly won't get us very far. Damn," he breathed, taking another swipe at the bloodied side of his face. "The crew?"

Difficult question to answer with her internal monitoring systems down. But *Serengeti's* jaunt through the ship gave her some idea of the extent of their losses, enough to know the dead far outnumbered the living.

Not enough crew left to salvage her. Not before life support failed completely.

"The crew, *Serengeti.*" Henricksen stared hard at the camera.

"Fin. Fin," Tsu's soft voice called.

"Tsu?" Finlay pushed herself to her feet and took a tentative step toward Engineering, waving a hand to clear the smoke. "Tsu?"

"Fin." Softer still, Tsu's voice fading, face stained red by the emergency lights. She lay draped over her station, head pillowed on the panel, composite metal girder sticking out of her back. "Fin," Tsu called, raising a trembling hand.

"No!" Finlay lurched to Engineering, grabbing at Tsu's hand as she knelt down at her side. "Tsu," she sobbed, tears spilling down her cheeks. "No. No-no-no."

"Damn. God damn." Henricksen climbed to his feet, wincing in pain, one hand holding tight to the captain's chair. He stood there a moment—head bowed, taking deep breaths—and then straightened and walked over to Engineering, setting one hand on Finlay's shoulder, touching the fingers of the other to Tsu's cheek. "Hey there, Tsu. Lyin' down on the job, I see." He smiled for her, trying to keep the moment light, but that smile couldn't hide the sorrow in his voice, the sadness lurking in his eyes.

"Captain." Tsu forced a tremulous smile onto her face, but it withered quickly, dying on her lips. "Sorry, sir," she said, fingers twitching, eyes filled with fear. "Tried."

"Nuthin' to be sorry for, Tsu. You stood your station. That's all I can ask."

"We have to help her." Finlay clasped Tsu's hand tight, staring pleadingly at her captain. "Please, sir. We have to get her out."

"Finlay—"

"Star," Tsu gasped. She fumbled at her station with her free hand, tapping at one corner, leaving a bloody smear behind. "Star," she repeated.

Henricksen frowned at the blank panel, its star charts all locked away. "Star? What star?"

Tsu craned her neck around until she could see the camera. "Star," she breathed, moving her finger with an effort, touching that same spot again so *Serengeti* would get the message.

"I see it," *Serengeti* assured her. "I see it, Tsu."

Tsu's hand fell away, face filled with relief as her lungs gasped for breath. "Fin. I want—I need—" She squeezed Finlay's fingers and then let them go, fumbled for something tucked into the pocket of her uniform jacket that she pressed into Finlay's palm. "Fin. Take." Tsu gasped, eyes widening, hand clenched tight around Finlay's fingers and the object cradled in her palm. "Fin." A last shallow breath and the light in Tsu's eyes faded. She slumped against the panel, staring sightlessly at Finlay's face.

"No. Tsu, no. Please no." Finlay sobbed softly, pressing Tsu's dead hand to her cheek.

Henricksen leaned close, whispering to Finlay until the sobbing finally stopped. And then he straightened and stepped backward as

Finlay sat down beside Tsu, wiping tears from her cheeks as she hummed a soft, sad tune and stared into her dead friend's face.

Such a lovely voice, Serengeti thought as Finlay's humming gave way to the barest breath of a song. *I'll miss Finlay's singing. I'll miss many things about this crew.*

"So what do we do?" Henricksen stared at Finlay, watching her stroke Tsu's fingers. "We can't just sit here, *Serengeti.*"

"No," she agreed.

"What then?"

Henricksen looked up at the camera. He knew. *Serengeti* could see it in his eyes. In the sour twist of his lips.

"Leave," she said, as gently as she could.

Henricksen flinched, spots of anger blooming on his cheeks. "No," he said, hands clenching into fists. "No, we won't abandon you. Not me, not my crew. Not after—"

"Henricksen. Stop."

Henricksen's mouth snapped shut, lips pressing together in an angry line. He stared at *Serengeti's* camera, knowing she was right, hating the options laid before him. Stay and die—kill the last of his crew—or leave and live, abandoning *Serengeti* to the darkest depths of space.

Save his crew or save his ship. A terrible choice. One no captain should have to make.

Henricksen touched a finger to his collar, tracing the outline of the bloodied silver stars he wore. Tremors shook the ship as another compartment vented its contents into space. Henricksen bowed his head, looking away from the camera.

"I'm crippled, Henricksen. My hull is shredded. My systems are failing. Life support is working for now but it's only a matter of time before that quits as well."

"The power cores—"

"Damaged. Irreparably. A few are holding on but eventually those will go too. I can feel the last bits of power trickling away even now."

The emergency lights flickered as if to prove her point. Henricksen closed his eyes, muttering curses under his breath as the air handlers cut out, fans going silent. *Serengeti* shunted a last bit of power to the environments, bringing the fans back to life.

Henricksen's head lifted. "You can't ask this of me," he said, staring accusingly at the camera.

"I can. I *am.* Go, Henricksen. Save the crew."

He shook his head, stubborn to the last. "We can try—"

"And fail," she said coldly. "That groaning you hear? The rumbling? Those are my internal structures giving way. I have just a few internal compartments left that haven't been compromised, and the main corridor running the length of my body is largely intact. Go. Now. Before it's too late. Before there's no crew left to save."

Henricksen thought for a while, thinking *Serengeti's* words over while the chuff of the fans and Finlay's soft singing filled the bridge's silence. "And what about you?" he asked bitterly, eyes returning to the camera. He hitched at his arm, wincing as even that small movement caused him pain. "We're just supposed to leave you here on your own, is that it? Abandon you? Leave you adrift? A dying hulk like *Osage*?"

"Not alone," she told him. "I'll have the robots to keep me company. And perhaps, in time…"

She trailed off, leaving the rest unsaid. The robots might be able to fix her, at least, enough of her to send out a distress signal. Then again, they might not.

"There's comms in the lifeboat."

"Useless right now."

Too much interference. Too much of *Serengeti's* own body blocking the signal, getting in the way. And not enough power in *Cryo's* communications package to reach across the darkest depths of space.

"You break free from me and get away from here, Henricksen. Get close enough to human settled space and someone will hear you. Maybe…maybe…"

"We can call for help. Send help back *here,* if it's not too late," Henricksen added with a grimace. "I hope so," he said softly, looking directly into the camera. "I truly do."

Henricksen took a last look around the bridge as he stepped down from his Command Post for the last time. He walked over to Evans and fumbled one-handed for the badge of rank at Evans's neck, the metal nameplate on his chest, did the same with Kusikov, and then tore apart the Artillery station to get at Sikuuku's body. He stared at Sikuuku for a long time, as if trying to memorize his face. And then he carefully removed his nametag, plucked the insignia from Sikuuku's collar, reached inside his jacket, cupping his hand around a seashell pendant dangling from a leather cord strung around Sikuuku's neck. Henricksen hesitated, as if wondering if he should leave it, then lifted the necklace away, settling the cord around his own neck before tucking the pendant away beneath his uniform shirt.

Henricksen buttoned up Sikuuku's jacket, pressed a hand to his chest. "Goodbye, old friend," he whispered, and then turned away, moving on to Tsu.

Her badges and nameplate were missing. *Serengeti* spotted them winking dully in Finlay's cupped hand.

Henricksen frowned at the blank spaces on Tsu's uniform, the bits of metal Finlay held. He reached to his collar and plucked his captain's badge from one side, pinning it to Tsu's jacket. "Captain stays with the ship." A quick look at the camera as he leaned close, placing his lips next to Tsu's ear. "Watch over her for me, Tsu. Keep her safe 'til I return." A touch at Tsu's collar, straightening the little bloodstained star, and he turned to Finlay, squatting down beside her. "Finlay. Hey, Finlay."

Finlay didn't seem to hear him. She'd let go of Tsu's fingers, trading her friend's hand for the tiny data recorder Tsu entrusted to her at the end.

Serengeti zoomed in on its screen as a flickering image appeared: the smiling Indo-Persian face of Anoosheh, who sent Tsu all those messages from home.

"Finlay." Henricksen set a scarred hand on Finlay's shoulder. "Finlay," he repeated, shaking gently.

The humming stopped. Finlay's head lifted, eyes drifting to Henricksen's face.

"Time to go, Finlay."

"Go? Go where?" she asked dully.

"I don't know," he admitted. "But we can't stay here. And we need to find the rest of the crew." He looked up at the camera, eyebrow quirked in question.

"I'll guide you," *Serengeti* promised. "I'll help you all I can."

She slapped the camera data onto a hastily constructed schematic, noting the compartments she knew to be depressurized, the blind spots where her burnt-out electronic eyes prevented her from seeing.

She hated those blind spots and instinctively tried to correct them.

Errors popped up everywhere, warning her of new failures—systems not functioning, others on the brink of shutdown. Power at critical levels, dropping precipitously as she herself consumed it.

Not much time.

Serengeti acknowledged the errors and then pointedly cleared them away. "You need to hurry, Henricksen. There isn't much time."

"Right. C'mon, Finlay. Time we got going."

Finlay blinked slowly. "What about Tsu?"

"She's dead, Finlay. We can't take the dead with us. Not this time."

"No. I guess not," she sighed. Finlay touched Tsu's fingers, leaned in and smoothed her hair before kissing her softly on the brow. She climbed to her feet, looked up at the camera. "Will you look after her, *Serengeti*? I don't want—" Finlay swallowed hard, lips trembling. "I don't want Tsu and the others to be alone."

"They're crew, Finlay. I will never abandon them."

"Thank you, *Serengeti*." Finlay nodded to the camera, clutching Tsu's data recorder to her breast.

"Take these." Henricksen dropped the bridge crew's nameplates and insignia into Finlay's upturned palm. "Keep them for me while we're travelling."

Finlay poked at the metal plates with a finger. "Alright," she said softly. She folded her fingers over the bridge crew's badges and shoved them into her pants pocket, carefully knotting it closed.

An ominous groaning filled the air, drowning out the *whoosh-whoosh-whoosh* of the fans. A sharp crack and Henricksen looked upward, as if expecting the bridge to peel wide open. "Time to go, Finlay."

Henricksen turned around, striding quickly across the bridge with Finlay following on his heels.

"Comms are down, so I can't guide you by voice," *Serengeti* said. "But I've got a few eyes left inside me, and the link to the robots is still functioning. We'll show you the way to the lifeboat. We'll help you find the compartments where the rest of the crew are hiding."

"Got it." Henricksen yanked the bridge door open and pushed Finlay out into the hallway.

"Henricksen."

He stopped dead—one foot in the hallway, the other inside the bridge—and looked back at the camera.

"If I should lose you..." She trailed off, not even wanting to think about that. "Some of the cameras aren't working. If I should lose you, keep to the central corridor. That way and nowhere else. Get to the lifeboat as quick as you can."

Henricksen nodded to show he understood and then stepped into the hall, exiting *Serengeti's* bridge for the very last time.

TWELVE

Serengeti shut down everything on the bridge once Henricksen and Finlay left, and sealed it up after them, leaving it dark and still—a cold, lifeless place entombing the corpses of Tsu and Evans, Kusikov and Sikuuku. A last look around before she abandoned the bridge, trading the cameras inside for one outside, just above the bridge door, from there to another further down the hall, tracking Henricksen and Finlay as they set off down the corridor.

Dark in that hallway—everything black and silver, carbon fiber and composite metal, industrial grade, reinforced plastics like the kind used everywhere else on the ship. Black and silver, like the uniforms of *Serengeti's* crew, the dark and stars outside the ship, all of it stained blood-red by the emergency lights spaced evenly along the walls.

Henricksen hurried through that bloody light with Finlay trailing behind him like a ghostly shadow. Intersections appeared—corridors splitting off, leading to yet more corridors, dozens of internal spaces, one nearly indistinguishable from the next except, nothing but the numbers stenciled on doorways and wall panels to give any sense of location. Confusing design for new recruits, especially those unfamiliar with the layout of a military ship, but Henricksen was an old hand and knew this ship like the back of his hand. He moved swiftly, purposefully along the corridor, glancing at the markers out of habit mostly, not really needing them to navigate *Serengeti's* spaces.

Serengeti moved ahead of her two charges, exchanging one camera for another as she scouted the way ahead, using microphone pick-ups where she found them, processing that data along with the video feeds coming from her electronic eyes. The klaxons lay sleeping—their job done now, nothing more they could to help her—and even the screams of her abused hull had quieted to little more than cracks and creaks, the occasional anguished, low groan. Eerie, that quiet. Unsettling. A ship on the move was always a noisy thing, full of voices and electronic chatter, thumps and bangs, the trundling tread of robots, the pit-patter of human crew moving about.

The pulse and throb of propulsion systems. The deep-throated roar of engines pushing *Serengeti* between the stars. Gone now. All gone. No hum of machinery, no voices to one another, just the chuff and wheeze of the failing air handlers. The puff and blow of a system slowly coming undone.

And when that's gone, there'll be nothing at all, Serengeti thought. *Crew will leave, and the life support system will fail, and all that'll be left are the robots.*

Some company at least. A battered, decimated force of mechanical servants trundling about her spaces, quiet as mice.

"The crew," Henricksen said, glancing up at a camera as he strode along. "You said there were survivors. Where?"

Internal monitoring systems were down making it impossible to look for life signs, but the schematic she'd built from the camera data told her which compartments were pressurized and which open to space. That gave her something to work off of anyway.

"Level 9, Space 26," she said, picking out the closest compartment to their current location.

"Nine's a level down. Twenty-Six puts us near the center of the ship. Long way from here," Henricksen noted, noting the numbers on the doorways down the hall. "You sure there's no one on this level?"

"Yes," she said, risking the lie. There *shouldn't* be anyone else on this level—Ten held the bridge and captain's quarters, some conference rooms and a formal dining hall, that's it—but *Serengeti* couldn't see into those rooms to make certain they were empty. And they didn't have time to stop and check every one. "Ten is clear. Go, Henricksen. Go!"

"Right." Henricksen moved on, trusting her without question.

"Take the ladderway. It's quicker." *Serengeti* jumped ahead to a camera, turned it until it pointed at a panel with red markings.

Emergency access point. Ladderway behind leading to the levels above and below.

Henricksen diverted to one side, grabbed the panel with both hands and tore it away, revealing a vertical shaft with a metal ladder attached to the far wall. "With me, Finlay," he said, glancing over his shoulder.

Finlay nodded vaguely, running on instinct mostly, responding to gestures and commands but seeming only half-aware of what was going on. Along for the ride because there was nothing else to do, and failing to move would leave her alone. Finlay moved in behind Henricksen, waiting patiently as he stepped into the shaft and grabbed the ladder with one hand, pressing his broken arm tight to his stomach as he made his slow, awkward, one-armed way down to the next level.

No working cameras in the ladderway, which meant *Serengeti* lost Henricksen and Finlay for a while. And when she found them again—just past compartments 9-3 and 9-4, approaching the next two down the line—she spied Henricksen drifting to one side, hand reaching for the sealed door protecting compartment 9-6. A quick touch at the metal panel and he snatched his hand back, rubbing his fingertips together.

"Cold," he said, grimacing at the pain of frost-burnt fingertips. "This one's blown."

He moved on to the next, holding his palm just above the panel this time, feeling the cold inside seep out. Finlay copied him, moving to the opposite side of the hall, checking each doorway they passed until, partway down, in front of a door marked 9-12, Henricksen finally stopped—palm pressed flat against the door's metal and carbon-weave panels, brow furrowed in concentration.

"It's warm," he said, accusation in his voice, in the look he threw at the nearest camera. "9-26, you said, but this one's intact."

"Yes," *Serengeti* said. That and nothing else.

Henricksen waited, obviously wanting more.

"The compartment depressurized when we came out of jump. I managed to stabilize it but...they're gone, Henricksen. You have to move on."

"No." Just that. And an angry glare.

Henricksen punched the panel beside the door, grabbed the emergency access wheel and cranked it over.

"There's no time, Henricksen."

"Doesn't matter." He turned the wheel until the door stood halfway open, signaled for Finlay to stay put as he slipped inside.

Henricksen reappeared less than a minute later looking even more grim-faced than before. He handed Finlay another four name tags, pressing them into her hand, watching as she carefully put them away with the others before continuing on.

Finlay stared at the half-open door for a few seconds, took a tentative step toward the compartment and then turned aside, following after her captain.

Serengeti lost them again at the next bend in the corridor, and several tense, frantic seconds passed before she found another camera that worked. She flipped to it and peered anxiously through its electronic eye, searching for Henricksen, for Finlay, for any signs of life. But all she found was devastation and ruin—a scorched and blackened hallway, air heavy with smoke. Foam residue covered the walls, the floor, even parts of the ceiling, the fire suppression systems having kicked in at some point to extinguish the blaze running rampant through her middle.

The systems did their job and put the flames out, but not before the smoke and fire took their toll—damaging her metal plating, snuffing out the lives of the crew fighting the blaze. Half a dozen charred bodies lay slumped against one wall, with a cluster of melted robots scattered among them, chassis reduced to lumps of slag and charred electronics puddled on the composite metal floor.

Poor little things. They tried to help.

But repair droids weren't meant to be firefighters. Their electronics just couldn't stand up to the fire.

Serengeti zoomed the camera in, peering closely at the robot's corpses, making note of their numerical designations, listing them as 'non-operational' on her roster. A check of the human corpses around them showed most burnt beyond recognition, but she spied a couple of name tags and marked those down as well.

She pulled back, searching the long length of the hallways. Still no sign of Henricksen. *Serengeti* started to worry. She'd jumped ahead, far down the route Henricksen and Finlay traveled but they should be here by now.

She flicked to another camera and found it burned out, backtracked, checking all of the cameras between the bridge and this section of hallway but every last one of them was dead.

Huge blind spot. Gaping hole in her surveillance grid, and Henricksen and Finlay right in the middle of it.

Not good. Not good at all.

Dammit, Henricksen. Where are you?

She flicked back to that last camera and waited, willing Henricksen to appear.

Air handlers pumped sluggishly, wheezing, coughing, trying vainly to clear the grey-black smog drifting in the corridor. *Serengeti* panned the camera, turning it as far left as she could, watching the Chron, counting the seconds. And then, finally,

"Henricksen."

She called to him from a speaker as he rounded a corner. Henricksen's head lifted, searching until he spied the working camera far down the hall. He nodded to *Serengeti,* coughing in the smoke-filled air, rubbing at irritated eyes. Finlay choked behind and started waving a hand in front of her face, trying to dispel the smoke.

Not going to help, Finlay. It'll take a lot more than your delicate little hand to clean this mess out of the air.

Henricksen coughed again and squatted down where the air was a bit cleaner, pulling Finlay down with him when she just stood there, trying to breathe the dirty atmosphere. Together they crept forward, sticking to the center of the corridor, using their eyes and their hands both to navigate the sooty, smoke-filled space.

That's how they found the first body.

Henricksen's hand landed on leg, with a foot clad in a half-charred boot still attached, and he stopped short. His head swiveled, eyes flicking left and right, picking out the bodies lying crumpled in the corridor. He glanced behind him, motioning for Finlay to stay as he crept forward and started, picking through the dead, removing name tags—even the melted ones—salvaging usable pieces of kit: a face mask from one corpse, a square of cloth from another, a canteen from a third.

The mask went to Finlay—a filtered breather with a small bottle of oxygen attached—but Henricksen kept the cloth and canteen for himself. "Here ya go, Finlay."

Finlay coughed and wiped at her eyes, grabbing greedily at the mask Henricksen pressed to her face. A few deep breaths and she tried to offer the mask to her captain but Henricksen waved it away, dousing the square of cloth he held with water from the canteen and pressing that to his face instead.

Improvised filter. Smart, Henricksen. Very smart.

Henricksen held out a hand, passing the scorched name tags to Finlay, waiting while she tucked them away before continuing down the hall.

The next camera was burnt out. And the one after that. And the one after that. *Serengeti* skipped ahead two turnings before finding one that was operational, and when she looked through its lens, she found the way ahead blocked—roof caved-in, walls collapsed, sparking cables snaking wildly, unstable plasma rounds spilling from a nearby munitions store.

Huge rounds, those, each shell easily the size of a cantaloupe. Most were still intact but *Serengeti* noted a few with cracked casings, their contents leaking into the corridor.

Dangerous, she thought, eyeing those leaking shells. *I can't send them through here.*

She'd have to find another route, another way for Henricksen and Finlay to get through.

Damn.

Serengeti checked her schematic, considering her options, mapping out a series of detours that should get Henricksen and Finlay to the lifeboat.

Long way there. Long, circuitous route, with many a pitfall along the way. She'd have to guide him—even Henricksen wouldn't be able to follow that route on his own—but a quick check showed her she'd have to pass three more turnings before reaching a camera that worked.

This isn't working, she thought, marking out the twisting route, layering over it all the compartments Henricksen still needed to check.

Too long. Life support will fail long before he can collect the remaining crew.

Serengeti considered a moment and then tapped into comms. Not ship's comm—those pathways—an internal comms path built into her AI network. A line that gave her access to the robots charged with the care of the ship.

A ping went unanswered, second ping the same. *Serengeti* ran through half the ship's roster before one finally responded. Not a good sign. She ran through the rest of the ship's roster, noting which robots responded, which remained silent.

The results weren't good: two thirds of her robot crew gone—shutdown or lost, dead either way—leaving her just a hundred and twelve helpers. And half of them damaged. Some so badly they'd likely have to be scrapped.

Serengeti allowed herself a moment to mourn—someone needed to, someone had to remember—and then she reached for the robot comms system and sent out a message: orders that had a dozen robots scurrying about the ship, winding their way through maintenance tunnels and ventilation corridors, in search of the surviving members of *Serengeti's* human crew.

Henricksen meant to save them all—every last crewmember that survived that disastrous exit from hyperspace—but Henricksen didn't have time. Not before life support failed. So *Serengeti* sent her robots, trusting them to lead the other humans to the lifeboat.

A flash of communication—robots chatting back and forth, querying to make sure they understood their orders. *Serengeti* listened in for a bit, making sure everything was under control before sending a soft summons across the robot comms channel.

"TIG," she called, not knowing who would answer, never once doubting that one of her TIGs would.

A maintenance hatch popped open just a few seconds later and a spherical chromed head appeared. The TIG glanced looked around then, raised a metal leg when it spotted the light on the active camera and waved cheerfully.

"To me, TIG."

The leg stopped waving, dropped back to the ground. The TIG dropped onto its belly tread and rolled out into the hallway, trundled over to the camera and came to a screeching halt.

"*Beep*," the TIG announced, tapping a metal leg end against its temple.

A dent showed on the side of the robot's head. Fresh scratches marred the gleaming metal of his carapace.

"Bumpy ride, eh?"

"*Beep-beep.*" A blink of cobalt eyes in agreement, accompanied by a swirl of bright blue face lights. The TIG dipped its head, rubbing its front legs nervously together. "*Beep-beep. Beep-beep-beep,*" it chattered in its electronic voice.

Odd vocalizations, that robot chatter, and something *Serengeti* normally paid little attention to. But her translation routines—like everything else inside her—glitched and threw errors.

Dammit.

Serengeti ran a quick patch, cobbling a few things together, and then waited an eternity—nearly a tenth of second—while her sluggish translation routines parsed the robot pidgin in real time.

"No big deal, eh? Well, let's make sure you're okay anyway."

Serengeti reached for him, touching gently at the robot's lesser AI brain, querying his status. Not too shabby, actually. Some cosmetic damage, but otherwise the little TIG was in proper working order.

"Good," she said brightly. "Now who are you, my friend?"

More beeps and flashes as the robot gave its name.

"TIG-442." *Serengeti* laughed in surprise. "You were in Cargo Bay 4. Last time I saw you, you were repairing balky probe Number Ten." *Serengeti* went quiet, thinking Six and Ten, all the other robots launched into space when Cargo Bay 4 vented. "Thought I'd lost you, little one," she murmured. "Tell me, 442—just where have you been hiding all this time?"

The robot *beeped* in confusion, round head cocking to one side in question.

"Never mind. You're here now. That's all that matters."

The robot's face lights glowed brightly, every last light in his face showing in a cobalt blue blush of pleasure and embarrassment. He tapped his metal legs, magnetized ends rattling anxiously against the deck plates, *burbling* softly to himself.

"I've got a very special mission for you, 442."

The TIG froze, cobalt eyes wide and staring, jointed legs wrapping close about his body. He looked up, then down, up again and down just as quickly, throwing shy looks at the camera.

More lights—long, swirling patterns scrolling across the TIG's face, questions spelled out in cobalt illumination, wondering what this oh-so-special mission was.

You'll see, Serengeti thought. *Soon enough you'll know everything*

"Hold still." Another touch as *Serengeti* squirted a data feed directly into the robot's brain. "I need you to track that schematic backward and find Henricksen and Finlay. And then I need you to lead them to the lifeboat. I need you to make sure they safely get out."

442 *beeped* and *burbled*, face lights flashing in acknowledgement.

"Go," she told him, turning 442 to one side. "I'm depending on you." A soft touch at 442's AI brain and she sent him on his way.

The little robot sped off, tank treads clattering against the composite metal decking as he followed the corridor to the T at one end, took the left turning, and another left at the next intersection.

Serengeti went with him, splitting her consciousness so part of her could watch the corridors slip by through 442's eyes while the rest of her mind tracked the progress of the other robots, listening to their chatter on the robot comms line as they scooped up human survivors and delivered them to the lifeboat nestled in her belly.

Finally, she thought. *Something going right.*

442's path intersected with Henricksen at the next turning. The captain strode along, eyes focused on the end of the hall, so intent on where he was headed that he didn't see the little TIG until he almost stepped on him. He pulled up at the last moment, frowning hard at 442 as he peeled the makeshift filter from his face. The air was cleaner here and he didn't really need it, but he held onto it, just in case.

"What are you doing here?" he asked, stuffing the bit of cloth into his pocket. "Where's—*oof*!" Henricksen stumbled a step or two as Finlay bumped into his back. "Watch where you're going, Finlay," he growled, looking back over his shoulder. "You can take that off, by the way." He flicked his fingers at the mask covering Finlay's face. "Air's not that bad here."

"Yes, sir," she said, and then pressed the fire mask to her face, refusing to give it up just yet.

"Or you can keep it." Henricksen shook his head and turned back to the robot. "So what's the deal, little—?"

"Henricksen," *Serengeti* said, speaking through the robot's mouth.

Henricksen blinked in surprise as *Serengeti's* voice came out of the TIG's mouth. Well, speaker. Strictly speaking, TIG didn't really have a mouth.

"Follow," *Serengeti* told him.

"Appreciate the offer, but we don't need a tour guide, *Serengeti*. I can find my way perfectly well."

"The way ahead is blocked. You can't go through."

"Great. Just fucking great." Henricksen sighed and hitched at his broken arm "So what do we do now?"

"Follow the robot." She flashed 442's face lights. "TIG-442 will show you where to go."

"And the others? There's *crew* out there, *Serengeti*. I'm not abandoning them."

"Nor I. I've got the robots looking for them. They're scouring the intact compartments even as we speak, bringing anyone they find to the lifeboat. Trust me, Henricksen. After all we've been through, trust me in this."

Henricksen eyed the robot suspiciously, thinking that over. "Trailblazer, eh? Fine. Lead on, MacDuff."

442 *beeped* loudly and raised one leg, snapping off a sharp salute. He spun around and trundled off down a side corridor, but he stopped again when *Serengeti* touched at his AI brain.

Henricksen stopped with them, grimacing in pain as he cradled his broken arm, but Finlay...Finlay stared after them from the intersection, making no move to follow.

"Finlay," *Serengeti* called, turning 442 around. "This way, Finlay. It's safe."

Finlay blinked and stared back at her, looking lost and alone.

"Get over here, Finlay." Henricksen waved impatiently but Finlay just shook her head. "Dammit, Finlay! We don't have time for this!"

The emergency lights flickered, as if to emphasize his point. *Serengeti* shunted power from the compartments the robots had cleared and used it to steady the lights in the sections in front of them. "I've diverted power to this section to keep things going. That should give us a few minutes, but we need to hurry, Henricksen."

"I was hurrying," he growled, giving *Serengeti* and her robot a dark look. "Unfortunately, Finlay there doesn't seem to share your sense of urgency."

The power surged again, emergencies lights dimming, then brightening before settling into a dull red glow.

"Dammit, Finlay! Get a move on, already!"

Finlay flinched as the lights flickered, but stubbornly refused to move even a single step from where she stood. Another flicker and she wrapped her arms around her middle and hunkered down, seeking safety in the closeness of the floor.

The air handlers died, huffing out one last chuffing wheeze before giving up the ghost.

Henricksen tilted his head back, staring at a vent in ceiling. He raised his good arm, reaching for the vent with his fingers splayed wide, and swore softly as he found nothing coming out. "Life support?" he asked, pitching his voice low so Finlay wouldn't hear.

"Gone. Entire system," *Serengeti* answered just as softly.

"Right." Henricksen sighed and shifted, clutching at his broken arm, face white with pain. "Can you fix it?"

Ridiculous question. *Serengeti* stared at Henricksen in disbelief. *He hasn't given up yet,* she realized. *After everything that's happened, Henricksen still thinks he can save me.*

She loved him for that. That's why he had to go.

"No," she said. "Maybe," she amended at Henricksen's frown. "But it'll take a while. More time than you have. And even then I couldn't guarantee that it would *keep* working. You've got the heat and air the system pumped out before it died, Henricksen. That's it."

"Son-of-a-bitch."

"You need to go, Henricksen. Now!" she said urgently.

Henricksen locked eyes with 442, staring *through* the robot's optical sensors to where *Serengeti's* consciousness sat inside his brain. And then he turned on his heel and stalked over toward Finlay.

"Let's go," he barked in his best commander's voice.

Wrong approach for the situation. *Serengeti* knew it as soon as the words left Henricksen's mouth.

Finlay took a long step backward, shaking her head as she retreated from captain, shaking her head. That pissed Henricksen off.

"Finlay! Now!" He reached for her, thinking to drag Finlay with him along, but she skipped away from his reaching fingers, retreating again.

"Let me," *Serengeti* interrupted, rolling 442 between them. She waited until Henricksen nodded before turning toward Finlay. "Finlay," she called, creeping closer, holding up one of 442's legs. "Take my hand, Finlay."

Leg. Whatever.

Finlay stared at the leg end 442 offered, considering the appendage for a long, long time. A deep breath and she took a step forward, fingers reaching, wrapping around the TIG's leg.

Good girl.

"Time to go, Finlay," *Serengeti* said softly. She turned around and started to lead Finlay away. "Time for you and the rest of the crew to see the stars while I stay here and rest awhile."

Finlay slowed, a frown of concern creasing her brow. "What about you?"

"Don't worry," *Serengeti* told her. "I've got 442 to keep me company. He and the other TIGs and TSDs."

Finlay thought that over too, and nodded just once.

"Come now, Finlay. We have to hurry."

Another nod. Finlay stared at the robot's face, mesmerized by the swirling patterns that blossomed and died and blossomed again.

Serengeti rolled past Henricksen, holding tight to Finlay's hand, waved for him to follow as she and TIG-442 led Finlay away.

THIRTEEN

Round and round the ship *Serengeti* and her charges wound, following one corridor and another, using the ladderways to descend to the lower levels because there simply wasn't enough power to run the elevators. Henricksen slowed them there, his broken arm all but useless, making it difficult for him to navigate the ladderways. Not his fault, but the delay made a long journey all that much longer. The lifeboat sat at the center of her, a massive thing with its own docking area cutting through four full layers of her ship's body, with the entrance to it—the only door providing access the escape pod—lying on Level Six, a long, long way from Level Ten and the Bridge.

Henricksen stepped from the ladderway into the central corridor running the length of Level Six and hunched over, face tight with pain, panting for breath in the increasingly thin air.

"Almost there," *Serengeti* told him as Finlay let go of the ladder.

Henricksen nodded sucked in a breath, straightening up. He wobbled a bit, hand pressing against the wall to steady himself until he caught his balance. "'M'alright," he said as the TIG's face lights flashed in concern. "Keep going."

"Stay with 442. Hurry, Henricksen. Fast as you can."

Another nod as Henricksen waved the TIG forward.

Serengeti nudged at 442, sending him trundling down the corridor to scout the way ahead. She split her consciousness, watching the way ahead through the TIG's eyes while tracking Henricksen and Finlay through the camera in the little robot's thorax. For a while, they made good time. And then something caught her attention—a sudden, high-pitched hiss—causing her to bring 442 to a clattering halt.

"What's going on?" Henricksen gasped, stopping beside the little TIG.

"Not sure," *Serengeti* started to say, and then realized just a fraction of a second too late that she did. "A puncture," she breathed as the hissing sound grew. "We've got a puncture nearby, Henricksen!"

The hissing increased and changed tone, becoming a screaming shriek. Shortly thereafter came a heavy, ominous *whump*—the sound of depressurization as something exploded inside her, rocking the ship violently.

The hallway tilted as *Serengeti's* body bucked hard. 442 skidded a bit and then stopped himself, being more stable with his grippy tank treads, his body slung low to the ground. Henricksen tumbled across the corridor and slammed bodily against the far wall, broken arm connecting first, the rest of his one hundred and eighty pound frame piling on afterward. And then Finlay slammed into the back of him, smashing Henricksen's broken arm into the wall a second time.

Finlay rebounded and sat down hard on the floor. Henricksen dropped to his knees, head bowed, broken arm cradled against his stomach, face white as sheet, blood and sweat mingling trickling down his neck.

"Henricksen?" *Serengeti* called worriedly.

Henricksen clenched his teeth, giving a sharp shake of his head. Blood dripped from his temple, falling in fat drops to the deck plating.

Serengeti rolled 442 across the hall, reaching for Henricksen with the robot's two front legs, but the captain snarled and pushed them angrily away.

"Henricksen—"

Henricksen cut her off with a chop of his hand.

"We have to go, Henricksen."

"I know," he panted. He turned his head and looked at her with glassy, pain-filled eyes. "Don't you think I know?"

He's in trouble, Serengeti thought, watching blood ooze in thick streams down the side of his face.

"I know you're hurting, but we have to get going," *Serengeti* said quietly.

Henricksen closed his eyes, swearing softly under his breath. He took a moment to gather himself, planting his hand against the floor, clutching his broken arm tight to his stomach as he pushed himself to his feet. He got there, and then almost pitched right over. He stumbled against the wall, managing to turn himself this time and connect with his good shoulder, but the impact left him rattled—grey-faced and panting, unsteady on his feet.

Finlay stared up at him, wide eyes blinking slowly behind the fire mask she still refused to discard. Henricksen's legs bent, knees unhinging as he slipped toward the floor, but Finlay scurried to her feet and braced him up, slinging her slim arm around his middle, settling Henricksen's far-more muscular limb around her shoulders. "Got you, Captain. I've got you," she said, holding him on his feet.

Henricksen looked down at her and nodded vaguely. A deep breath and he shook himself, trying to clear the cobwebs away, but it took a while—nearly a minute, time they *really* didn't have—for him to finally get himself together enough that they could get moving again. He pushed away from the wall, and tottered around, curses falling like raindrops from his lips as set off down the hall.

Finlay stuck close to her captain's side, arm wrapped around his waist, one hand clutching the fingers dangling over her shoulder, giving Henricksen what support she could as he made his slow, painful way down the corridor.

Serengeti scooted 442 ahead of them, riding passenger inside the little robot, murmuring words of encouragement to speed Henricksen and Finlay along, telling them nothing of the cascading failures occurring all over the ship, major and minor systems shutting down, taking the sub-minds assigned to each with them.

A desperate burst of information flooded in before the last of the sub-minds went silent. For the first time since her creation, *Serengeti* found her mind alone. She'd never known such emptiness. Never imagined how echoing and isolated a single mind could feel.

Focus, Serengeti. It's almost over. Not long now.

An error appeared—one of the last few working nodes of her network starting to act. *Serengeti* cleared it and checked her energy levels, which continued to fall. Just a bare trickle left in her reserves now, enough to keep her core consciousness running and power the emergency lights in this one corridor, but not much else.

And soon that will be gone as well, Serengeti thought, watching Henricksen struggle along.

Not enough power. Not enough time.

"Hurry," *Serengeti* urged him for the dozenth time.

Henricksen lifted his head with an effort, staring at her with shadowed eyes, looking just about done in. A stiff nod and he pushed harder, shambling along the hallway with Finlay propping him up on one side.

That last leg of their journey seemed to take forever—an eternity of time at Henricksen's slow, limping pace—but they eventually got there. 442 scooted around a bend and into another, much shorter corridor with a door barring the far end. A door with a single word written in blocky black letters across its metal surface.

"*Cryo*," *Serengeti* breathed, voice filled with relief.

The lifeboat, at last, just a foot-thick portal of steel, and titanium, and densely packed electronics separating her charges from salvation.

Cryo showed none of the damage ravaging the rest of *Serengeti's* body. Her own ship's design protected it, tucking it deep inside her, far away from her engines and munitions, the outer sections of her hull. And

Cryo came equipped with its own power grid, completely separate from hers, its own engines and Nav system—everything Henricksen and her surviving crew would need to survive the trip through the stars.

Unfortunately, all that protection blocked *Cryo's* comms. Too much composite metal. Too much of *Serengeti's* body getting in the way. Which meant the crew would have to leave her to get help. The crew would have to head out on their own.

I wish I could go with them. Selfish thought, rising unbidden as they stopped in front of *Cryo's* door. *I wish I could protect them out there.*

But that wasn't in the cards. Fifty-three years of combat, hundreds of battles and four wrecked chassis, but somehow she'd always managed to limp home. Until this time. This time the crew would go on without her, leaving *Serengeti* and her shredded body behind. Because one thing *Cryo* didn't have was an AI docking port, which meant it couldn't support her downloaded consciousness. The only way for *Serengeti* to go with her crew was if they cut her crystal matrix mind from its housing and physically transported it with them.

Not an easy operation. Not something Henricksen and his crew were in a position to carry out. There simply wasn't enough time, wasn't enough energy to get *Serengeti* out.

She touched at 442, had him drop back to Henricksen's side, pressed the end of his metal leg against Henricksen's back to push him along.

But I can save them, she thought. *Henricksen and the others. I can at least get them out.*

The emergency lights flickered, flashing spasmodically as they struggled to remain lit. *Serengeti* shoved at Henricksen, pressing 442's leg hard against his back. "Time to go," she said, nodding the robot's rounded head at *Cryo's* sealed door.

Henricksen frowned down at her, swaying a bit, looking like he might fall over at any moment. Finlay pressed against his side, holding him up, masked eyes flicking worriedly from her captain to the lifeboat's door.

"S'alright, Finlay," he said, pushing her gently away. "I can take it from here."

Finlay didn't look so sure, but she retreated a step and waited while Henricksen addressed *Cryo's* door.

A last, rapid-fire flickering and the emergency lights finally gave up the ghost, refusing to come back on no matter what *Serengeti* did. She activated 442's face lights, giving them some illumination at least.

"Guess that's our cue." Henricksen offered a lopsided smile, pale face showing ghostly in the cobalt light. He tapped at a keypad, entering his personal security code into the lock beside *Cryo's* door before rattling off his name and rank into a microphone pick-up for voice print analysis.

The locked flashed orange, *beeped* and turned green. A metallic *snick* echoed down the hallway and disappeared as *Cryo's* door sighed open.

Serengeti shucked 442 around, trying to get a look at the bright white space inside, but Henricksen's body blocked the doorway, allowing her only glimpses of people moving about—prepping cryogenic chambers, climbing inside the cold sleep pods and sealing them up tight.

How many? she wondered. *How many crew made it inside?*

She flipped to the camera above her and reached for *Cryo's* monitoring system, thinking to peer through the lifeboat's electronic eyes, but the relays shorted, disconnecting her in an instant, trapping her outside.

Damn, she thought, dropping back to 442 in frustration.

"Nice digs," Henricksen said, whistling in frustration. "Bit small compared to what we're used to." Henricksen flashed a smile—*Cryo* was tiny when compared to *Serengeti*—and then shrugged his shoulders. "Not like we're gonna spend a lot time running around in it, but still."

That was the other hard truth. The lifeboat was meant for emergency use—not long-range, interstellar travel. It could cruise long distances, but came equipped with standard propulsion engines only—no jump drive, no ability to move at the lightning speed of hyperspace travel, and limited provisions to sustain the crew during their journey. So Henricksen and the surviving crew would make the long, slow trip back to human-settled space sleeping inside the cryogenic chambers packed into *Cryo's* spaces.

"Well, I guess this is it." Henricksen nodded to *Serengeti* riding inside the robot. "Distress beacon should start squawking as soon as we pull away." He paused and ducked his head, staring at his boots like he didn't know what to say. "We'll send help, *Serengeti*." Henricksen's head came back up again. He glanced through the doorway way, then at Finlay standing at his side. "We may be leaving but we're not abandoning you here."

"Never crossed my mind," she said, touched by those simple words. "Safe travels, Henricksen."

"Hopefully," he said, staring into the TIG's electronic eyes. "C'mon, then, Finlay. Time we got going."

"Pleasure to serve, *Serengeti*." Finlay nodded to the robot as Henricksen took her hand and led her through *Cryo's* doorway.

Two steps in and Henricksen stopped again—a dark shadow wreathed in the bright white light of *Cryo's* interior spaces, looking back over his shoulder. "Go on then, Finlay," he said, waving to the nearest cryogenic chamber. "Be there in a moment."

Finlay frowned uncertainly, flicked her eyes to 442 and then stepped backward, taking up station by the nearest cryogenic chamber.

Henricksen turned around, considering *Serengeti* and her robot chauffeur a moment. He opened his mouth and closed it again, braced up hard and offered a crisp, formal salute.

The gesture caught *Serengeti* completely off-guard. She stared at Henricksen—touched, surprise, not quite knowing what to say. Laughable really. *Serengeti*—a Valkyrie-class starship, tenth generation AI, with a hundred times the processing power of a human brain and enough firepower to destroy a small planet—left speechless by something as simple as a salute. She lifted the TIG's leg and started to return the gesture, realized how ridiculous that would look.

A brief moment of deliberation and she rolled the robot forward, stopping right in front of Henricksen, tilting 442's head back as she took a good, long look, memorizing every last line of Henricksen's face, the way the blood trickled from the gash in his cheek, the twitch of his lips as he settled his broken arm more comfortably across his middle.

"Safe travels, Captain," she said, offering that honorific at this, their last parting. "Take care of our crew."

Our crew, not his. Not hers alone.

Henricksen nodded tightly and let his hand fall to his side as he stepped backward and touched at a panel, cycling *Cryo's* door closed.

Serengeti sat there a while, staring at *Cryo's* door and the bold black letters written across its surface, wishing they were a window so she could take one last look at her crew. "Goodbye," she whispered, missing them already.

442 hooted softly, voiced filled with mourning as he touched his leg to the thick metal door.

They stayed there a while, neither of them wanting to leave, sticking close to the crew in the last few moments before the lifeboat broke free. But 442 wasn't safe here. The systems operating the pressure door—meant to drop and seal off her internal spaces when *Cryo* moved away—had fried along with everything else at the end of the hall, meaning everything in that corridor—wayward robots included—would be sucked out into space when the lifeboat took off.

"Time to go, 442." *Serengeti* turned the little robot around and urged him down the hall. They'd need a place to hide until the last of the air evacuated and the pressure inside her equalized with the vacuum outside. She steered the robot toward an empty compartment, but 442 detoured, rolling over to a maintenance hatch instead. "Where are you going?"

The TIG flashed his face lights, *burbling* softly as he pressed at his side, swinging a hinged panel open so he could get at the stock of tools inside. A bit of searching and he found what he wanted: a screwdriver-shaped appendage that he removed with a flourish. "Ta-da!" 442 announced, holding the screwdriver up and then slotting it into a bolt.

A few quick turns and the bolt fell free. A dozen or so after that and the five others holding the panel in place dropped off. 442 grabbed the panel and pulled it away, collected the loose bolts as he rolled into the maintenance shaft and used them to secure the panel behind.

After that, they waited—the robot humming softly and fidgeting about while *Serengeti* listened for the *thunk* and rattle of *Cryo's* engines, the trembling in her superstructure as the lifeboat broke free and pulled away. For a long time there was nothing, but she wasn't concerned. It took time for the system to power up, for *Cryo* to run a full set of diagnostics before leaving her for the stars. She felt her structure tremble at one point, rattling the bolts in the maintenance panel, sending a loose ceiling tile crashing to the floor. But the trembling soon stopped, leaving the ship silent and still. And after that nothing. Nothing at all.

Serengeti waited, wondering what was going on, feeling silly for worrying, finding it impossible to stop.

More alerts popped up, warnings predicting imminent shutdown—totally blackout across every last one of *Serengeti's* systems. That was okay, too. They were almost done. Once *Cryo* was away, those systems wouldn't matter anyway. Once *Cryo* left, she too would go to dark. And sleep the sleep of eternity while she waited for Henricksen to return.

Ten minutes passed. Definitely something wrong. "It shouldn't take this long. They should be gone by now."

Or maybe they were. Maybe the pressure door had worked after all, by some miracle.

442 hooted softly, voice filled with worry, front legs rubbing nervously together as they waited and waited and waited. He reached for the bolts in the panel, slotting the screwdriver appendage into one corner and another, removing the bolts one at a time. But he stopped with two bolts still in place and *beep* softly, looking to *Serengeti* for permission.

I shouldn't, she thought. *If* Cryo's *still here, if it takes off while we're out there, 442 will be a goner.*

But it might have left already. There was that possibility too.

Serengeti stared anxiously at the Chron, trying to decide what to do. "Something's wrong. Something is definitely wrong."

No facts to back that assertion up, but instinct told it was so. Instinct—how unscientific. How her designers would howl if they knew she'd learned such a thing.

Serengeti considered a moment and then took control of 442's leg, removing the last two bolts herself.

Back out into the corridor then, TIG-442 zipping along on his little tank treads, screeching to a halt in front of the heavy steel and titanium door with its matte black letters.

"No," *Serengeti* whispered.

Cryo hadn't gone anywhere, it was right here where they'd left it, squatting inside her decimated innards like some oversized egg, waiting patiently to be born.

She queried systems out of habit, cursing herself for being an idiot when she found diagnostics dead—all that information locked away, frustratingly beyond her reach.

"Maybe there's something wrong with it." There'd been power inside the lifeboat—she'd seen that clearly through 442's eyes—but maybe the battle had damaged it and *Cryo* simply needed some time to repair itself. "Maybe that's all it is," *Serengeti* murmured.

A vague hope, but better than no hope at all.

442 *burbled* softly, trying to get *Serengeti's* attention. He called up a schematic he'd stored locally—one showing *Serengeti* with *Cryo* nestled at her center, and eight docking clamps dogging the lifeboat down to keep it from rattling around while she travelled. Docking clamps that were part of *Serengeti* and needed her power, not the lifeboat's, to unlock them. Power and undamaged circuitry, both of which *Serengeti* had in short supply.

"Trapped," *Serengeti* whispered, staring in disbelief. "They're trapped here with me."

FOURTEEN

TIG *burbled* and fidgeted, nudging at *Serengeti*, querying her orders again and again and again. Other voices joined in—all the robots that left to her asking the same question: *What do we do, Serengeti? What do you want us to do?*

"I don't know," *Serengeti* whispered, an unprecedented admission for an AI with a mind such as hers. She was Valkyrie—powerful, decisive, capable of processing petabytes of information in the middle of a fire fight and making split second decisions on the fly. But this...*Cryo's* failure was entirely unexpected. Something her disaster scenarios never accounted for. "My failure," she murmured. "It's my fault, my failure that's trapped you here." She rolled 442 forward and touched his leg to the *Cryo's* door, offering a silent apology. *What to do?* she wondered, tracing the letters stenciled there. *What do I do now?*

A last few errors flickered and faded, warning her of dangerously low power levels, energy so depleted now that she teetered on the edge of oblivion—just one step now from a long descent into darkness where she'd sleep and sleep and sleep. She'd been okay with that before, when it was just she and the robots hanging in the balance. But Henricksen, Finlay...*Cryo's* power could only sustain them for so long before it too shut down and the sleep chambers inside it when dark.

"No," she said, tracing the rounded *O* at the end of *Cryo's* name. "I won't let that happen."

An order to 442 had him tearing at the panels on one side of the door, exposing a scorched mess of fried circuitry and melted relays, burnt-out wiring running up and down the wall.

Large-scale failure of the entire electrical system connecting *Cryo* to *Serengeti's*. A quick check of the other side showed the same situation.

Bad news. The entire section here would need to be replaced—every last bit of the system securing the lifeboat to *Serengeti's* body rebuilt from the ground up. A job that took weeks in a properly outfitted repair facility, with space parts in plenty, one that that would likely take *years* in the shape *Serengeti* was in, with just these few robots to help her, and whatever parts they could scavenge from her wrecked ship's body.

"So much for that idea." *Serengeti* thought hard, trying to come up with something else.

She looked inside herself, chasing down systems, finding every last one of them failed—powered down completely, silent as death, the line to 442 and the other robots the only thing left to her now. That and the few working cameras scattered around her corridors, a few more peering outward from her hull. And just a tiny bit of energy left in the power cells in her belly.

"It might be enough," she murmured, "but I'll need help."

She reached out to the robots, sending half of them scurrying for parts while she detailed the rest to Level 4 and Engineering. A last, lingering look at *Cryo's* door and *Serengeti* followed after, spinning 442 around, riding shotgun inside the little robot as he trundled into the maintenance shaft and worked his way through her innards until he reached Engineering: a cavernous room filled with machinery, the heart of her, the guts of her ship's body.

A group of chattering robots—TSDs mostly, though she spied a few TIGs like 442 as well—huddled together at one end of the room, face lights flashing excitedly as they argued amongst themselves, metal legs waving, pointing at the thirty massive fuel cells sitting beside them, the four bulging contraptions squatting across the room, butt ends sticking roundly from the wall.

The fuel cells powered everything, from *Serengeti's* jump drives to her life support system; they even provided the energy needed to keep *Serengeti's* AI mind alive. Energy that was in decidedly short supply now—eighteen power cells cracked wide open after that disastrous exit from hyperspace jump, another exploded by the sudden stress of trying to take over the load. That left just three fuel cells still functioning, and those nearly empty, hovering just above zero.

Nothing to be done about it. Getting moving, Serengeti.

She rolled 442 forward, heading for the cluster of TSDs to one side.

The robots were deep in conversation, working out a game plan for how to attack the problem at hand. A dozen TSDs split off as *Serengeti* and 442 approached, grabbing up cables and dragging them behind them as they swarmed over the fuel cells, plugging bundles of carbon-weaved wrapped wires into ports and access panels. Another dozen robots waited below, legs raised, pincered 'hands' grabbing at loose ends, running the lengths of cable across the room where yet *more* robots—nearly thirty TSDs in total, armed with a menagerie of tools—tore at panels, stripping away useless wiring before attaching the new cables.

Engines behind those panels. Not her mains—those were useless, no amount of power would get them working again—the docking engines and maneuvering jets she used when pulling into port. Fuel-based propulsion, not fusion powered like her jump drives, and she had just enough fuel left for one last, desperate blast, and just enough power to get the fuel flowing, and turn the engines over.

Serengeti's design, that bodged together, makeshift energy circuit. Cables hung everywhere, crisscrossing the room, stretching from the power cells at one end to the auxiliary engines on the other. The robots worked quickly as the energy levels in those cells kept dropping, her own consciousness depleting the reserves, a slow leak in the Number 12 Cell, letting more precious power dribble away.

Not enough left now, Serengeti realized, running some quick calculations. *Not enough power to spark the engines and get the fuel running.*

Not enough if there was to be anything left to keep her consciousness alive.

Desolation filled her—a complete and overwhelming loss of hope.

442 seemed to pick up on it and started *beeping* and *burbling* loudly. He rolled over to one of the engine access points and opened a panel in his chest, pointed at the little power unit stored inside him and the massive propulsion unit sitting to one side.

Serengeti was quiet a moment. 442 repeated the gesture, thinking her silence meant she didn't understand.

I do, little one, she thought, touching at 442's mind.

How could she not when she was right there, snuggled up inside 442's body with his little AI mind?

"No," *Serengeti* said gently. "It's brave what you offer, but I'm afraid it's not enough. It would take dozens…"

She trailed off, words failing her as TIG-442 *burbled* a question and pointed at the other robots scurrying about the room. Fifty-two robots, to be exact, and every last one equipped with a self-contained power unit—larger units inside the TSDs than the TIGs. More energy required to support their proportionally larger bodies and advanced analytical functions.

Serengeti hesitated, and then ran a quick calculation, adjusting for the number and type of robots available. The facts confirmed what she'd already suspected.

It should be enough. More than enough, actually, with the draw from the reserves in the remaining power cells.

"It's risky," *Serengeti* warned him, speaking softly so only 442 would hear. "But with enough of them it might work. I'll need to drain their power units dry to jumpstart those engines, and it's likely there'll be damage. Your circuits were never designed to handle that kind of load, 442. They'll fry like as not."

Blunt words, but she wanted him to hear the truth and know the danger inherent to this plan—this mad, selfless act—before he and the others committed themselves to it.

442 ducked his head, face lights flashing, scared—she could feel that in him—nervous as hell but desperately wanting to please her and help save the crew. He scuffed a leg at the metal floor, *beep*ing softly to himself. A glance at the robots around him and then raised all his legs at once, bending them inward until they hugged tight to his body and then splaying them wide in a robot's version of a shrug.

Serengeti still didn't think this was a good idea. "Wait—"

Too late. 442 sent a communication, squirting out his plan along with a modification to *Serengeti's* power grid schematic. Fifty-two robots froze, face lights flashing in unison while they digested his idea. Several seconds of *beeps* and *borps* followed, and after a short discussion they all seemed to agree.

The robots came back to life, spun around and converged, circling around one another in a choreographed dance. A flash of communication—cobalt face lights reflecting over the metal panels around them—and the group split, the TIGs breaking off and zipping away, heading toward a nearby storage room to retrieve yet more cables, while the TSDs lined up in a double row of gleaming, ovoid bodies, chest panels opened wide.

The TIGs returned, hauling lengths of cable behind them, tore at the engines, removing yet *more* panels before routing the newer, smaller cables inside, connecting one end to the propulsion systems and the other into sockets built into the TSDs' power cores.

That's what the discussion had been about: Who would be chosen? Who would sacrifice themselves to save *Serengeti* and the others? And in typical AI fashion, they made the most 'logical' decision. Because it all came down to numbers, in the end. The TSDs had more energy to offer, so the TSDs would donate and die.

The last cable slotted into place and the TIGs retreated. Fifty-two robot heads turned, staring at 442, looking to *Serengeti* inside him because she was ship—master and commander, the closest thing to a mother these little robots had ever known—and her job to give the order to set this plan in motion.

For a long time she couldn't, hating this answer, knowing it was the only way. 442 *burbled* softly, telling her it was okay. *Serengeti* almost laughed. A robot, consoling her—would wonders never cease?

"Thank you," she said, flitting along pathways, taking the time to touch at each robot's mind. "Goodbye."

The slightest of hesitations, hating this still, and *Serengeti* made the connection, grabbing a last cable with 442's leg and inserting it into one of the auxiliary engines.

The makeshift circuit closed and the TSDs stiffened, legs splaying wide, heads tilting backward, face lights lighting up the darkness around them. Machinery whirred to life, shivering and shaking, sputtering crankily as power flowed to the propulsion system in fits and starts. The engines caught, coughed hard and held, filling Engineering with a rumbling hum.

And beneath it an ominous crackle—the sound of electricity gone haywire, eating up electronics, burning out circuits. The TSDs jerked wildly, sparks igniting, smoke pouring from their bodies.

Serengeti watched in agony, wanting to stop this, knowing it was already too late.

A loud *pop!* and it was all over, the TSDs' energy expended. A sigh ran through the robots—a weary, contented sound—and they sagged as if sleeping, legs tucking tight against their bodies as they shut down and went dark.

That's it. Serengeti watched a last TSD twitch hard, legs rattling against its body before finally going still. *That's everything I have. There's nothing left to give but myself.*

She'd do it—of course she would—if the sacrifice was needed. If it came down to a choice between herself and her crew. And it might— *Serengeti* knew that—but right now there was work to do.

The auxiliary engines coughed and grumbled before kicking in, sucking in their load of liquid fuel. *Serengeti* risked the drain on her reserves to expend a bit of energy and activate a camera on her hull, panned it around and took stock of the darkness outside.

She'd dropped out of hyperspace into an unknown section of space, far, it seemed, from the nearest civilized planet, drifting aimlessly in a cloud of her own debris. But the stars were there—pinpricks of distant silver-white light all around her—providing some comfort at least. And as *Serengeti* moved the camera around, studying one bright light and another, she finally found a likely candidate: Tsu's star, the one she'd pointed to—or at least the *quadrant* she'd pointed to—as she lay dying.

Distant, Serengeti thought, judging the gap from her current position to that cold, clear light.

But not so long that she couldn't make it. Close enough for what *Serengeti* had planned.

She ran the numbers, just to be sure, calculating the odds of success and failure, the expected variance in her path, the potential for drift. And when it was all said and done, she realized it was a crap shoot—fifty-fifty whether they'd make it to that star or not.

But staying here meant death. That was a certainty.

Fuck it—that's what Henricksen would say. And that's what decided her. *Serengeti* rolled the dice and let fly.

Engines fired, burning fuel in a long, hard burst as she muscled her bulk around, decimated body shuddering and groaning, bits of metal peeling away, adding to the sparkling cloud around her. A few more blasts—shorter, sharper this time—as *Serengeti* maneuvered herself into alignment and opened the engines wide, lurching forward under the stress of the engines' push, stuttering along before finding a groove and gliding smoothly.

The auxiliaries weren't designed for prolonged use and burnt through their load of fuel in no time, sputtered a few times and shut down. They'd done their job by then and gotten *Serengeti* moving, built up enough momentum to keep her drifting along until the gravitational force of that distant star took hold and pulled her into orbit around it. If her plan worked. Long way from here to there. So many things could go wrong…

Please. Please let this work.

A last long look at the stars and *Serengeti* let go, abandoning the outside camera to return her consciousness to Engineering, parking herself in a working camera tucked in one far corner so she could watch 442 and the other TIGs as they moved busily about.

They'd dismantled the snaking network of cables and tucked them all back into storage. And with that done, they turned to the broken robots lined up in a row, scooping up the thirty-four burnt-out TSDs one at a time, cradling them in their metal legs as the TIGs carried their brethren to the far end of Engineering and tucked them away behind a door marked 'Spare Parts.'

That's all they are now, Serengeti thought sadly. *Not AI anymore, not even robots, just junk. Scrap. Bits and pieces useful only as salvage. It's not right. They deserve better.*

442 rolled by her camera on his way back from the storage space. *Serengeti* called out to him, stopping the little robot in his tracks. She slipped inside his brain and felt him shiver at her touch—fear, nervousness, excitement running through him all at once.

"I have something for you, 442," *Serengeti* said, settling her AI mind next to his. "A gift. A gift I fear will be a burden, but one I need you to carry for a while." She touched at his AI mind, caressing it gently as she drew his consciousness to her and laid a data package full of design specs deep inside his brain. "I need you to build that for me. Do you understand? You and the other robots."

442 *beeped* and *blipped,* processing quickly, tearing the design apart and then rebuilding it, one component at a time. A flash of face lights and he nodded his rounded head to show he'd digested it all.

"Good." *Serengeti* stroked 442's brain a second time and then turned him a bit, gazing through his robotic eyes at the TIGs moving back and forth across the room. "Look after them for me, would you? You're all that's left to me now. You and these few others." Third touch, making 442 shiver as she pulled him to her. "Repair," she ordered. "Refit. *Survive*. That's my charge to you, TIG-442."

The robot *burbled* softly, front legs rubbing nervously together. He stuttered and *blipped*, clearly worried, wondering at the responsibility she'd laid upon him. And why he must bear this burden at all.

"I must leave for a while," *Serengeti* explained. She turned the little robot to one side and nodded at the power cells, showing him the error message telling her the reserves inside were low, and low, and low. "I must sleep for a while, 442."

The TIG shook his head, face lights flashing spastically. *Blips* and *borps* spilled from his mouth, a long string of upset chatter denying what she told him, trying to convince her to stay.

"Shh," *Serengeti* breathed. She stroked at 442's brain until he quieted down. "I won't be gone forever. I promise. In fact, I won't even be all that far away. I'll be right here, 442." She used one of his legs to wave at the ship around him. "I'll be right here waiting until your task is done, and it's time for me to wake."

442 *hooted* mournfully, legs sagging, head drooping toward the floor.

Serengeti waited, letting the silence stretch out between them. "Will you do this for me, 442? Will you bear this burden while I sleep in the dark?"

442 heave a sigh and nodded, accepting her charge—albeit grudgingly.

"Good boy," *Serengeti* murmured, and started to pull away. But she stopped just on the edge of releasing the TIG, realizing there was one more thing—one last task to be completed before she disappeared into the dark. After all, someone had to lead them. Someone had to be in charge of the robots while *Serengeti* was away. And since he was closest, the most expedient option considering she already rode inside him, she gave that burden as well to 442.

It'll mean changing him. She hesitated at the thought, wondering if it was the right thing to do. *He'll never be like the others.*

She glanced to one side, watching 442's brothers and sisters trundle back and forth, transporting the last of the burned-out TSDs to storage. Such loyal little things—capable and obedient, and built to Valkyrie specifications, their AI minds connected to *Serengeti's* own, making them obedient to her and no other.

All that was about to change, and *Serengeti* would be lying if she said she didn't have misgivings. Because once she did this, there'd be no going back.

What choice do I have?

She reached inside TIG-442, touching at the very core of his AI mind, turning things on and off, making changes to his base programming, granting him access and permissions, privileges to her network that no one—not even Henricksen—ever had. Privileges 442 would need if he was to be in charge—voice of the ship while *Serengeti* drifted in sleep.

"Go now," she said with a last soft touch at his mind.

TIG-442 *blipped* softly, eyes lifting to the ceiling as *Serengeti* pulled away, moving from camera to camera until she reached the hull and gazed outside.

It feels good to be moving again, she thought, *and feel cold and stardust slipping along my sides*.

Because movement meant freedom—a chance to get away—even if that movement came at a creeping snail's pace.

She checked her trajectory, ran calculations based on the positions of the stars around her and the single point marking her destination.

Still on course and tracking true.

"Well. At least something went right," *Serengeti* murmured.

A last, lingering look at the stars she loved so well and *Serengeti* let go, trusting the universe to watch over her, her cadre of robots to protect her precious cargo as she let go and slipped away.

FIFTEEN

Serengeti drifted in darkness—endless, inky-black darkness that clearly wasn't space—her consciousness disconnected, powered down to a hibernation state: not quite awake, not quite asleep. Time had no meaning in that in-between space, thought, feeling, even purpose eluded her, but she never stopped being *Serengeti*. Never lost that sense of being Valkyrie and not just some broken-down ship. Free of her burdens, she drifted, relaxing in that serene sea of nothingness, all her troubles and worries, her fears for her crew washed away in an instant as the voice closed around her.

But at some point things changed—she wasn't quite sure when or how, they just did—and little by little the tranquility fled. *Serengeti* floated still, lacking shape and form, feeling nothing at all, not even the frosty cold outside her hull, but her mind—once so blissfully, peacefully empty—slowly came awake. Awake enough, at least, to *see* the darkness around her, and a confusion of images that filled her AI mind with fear.

What's happening? *Serengeti* wondered, consciousness reaching, searching the void for answers.

More images appeared, flashing past in an instant, one flowing into another, forming long, long chains that cycled through and started repeating, over and over again.

She'd seen this before—all of it—and knew how it all would end.

"I'm dreaming," she said, voice filled with disbelief. "I'm not supposed to dream." More flashes—stronger, brighter than before—and the images came cleared, dredged from her memories of a time before the darkness. A low moan built inside her. "No," *Serengeti* whispered. "No, I don't want to see this. Not this, of all things."

But there was no escaping her own mind, and the images kept coming, no matter what *Serengeti* did.

#

She stared down the length of a black and silver corridor bathed in antiseptic white light —empty now and quiet as a tomb until the screaming started, agonized voices erupting all around her, shrieking through the microphone pick-ups built into the ceiling. Lights flickered, and the world around her trembled and shook. Detonation as something smashed hard against her ship's body, gouging her metal composite skin, tearing away a huge chunk of her hull.

Serengeti heard everything, felt everything, suffered through the explosion that followed that detonation, blowing out walls, creating a huge crater in her port side. Her superstructure creaked and groaned, girders twisting, snapping, giving way beneath the force of that blow. Alarms shrieked everywhere, calling up and down the corridors, filling every last one of her compartments with dissonant noise. Human voices called to one another, coming from somewhere behind her, somewhere she couldn't quite see. And beneath them, muffled, overpowered by the klaxons' clangor was another sound: an ominous, deep-throated roar drifting down the corridor.

Pressure change, temperatures spiraling out of control.

Fire, her mind registered as the *pop* and *crackle* of flames came over the pick-ups, smoke invading the corridor, yellow-red light dancing along the walls.

A heavy *whump* as a door sucked inward and blew explosively back out. Systems flashed warnings, shouts and screams filled the corridor— human voices yelling orders, people appearing from nowhere, robots pouring from maintenance panels, converging in the hallway and then heading straight into the line of the approaching fire.

"No. Go back," she willed them. "Run away."

She tapped into a robot, thinking to use its speakers to carry her voice, but she pushed too hard, too quickly and the poor little thing all but exploded. Agonized static poured from its mouth. The robot shivered and shook, electronics overloading, consciousness fading as its AI mind shut down and slipped into the dark.

"No," *Serengeti* whispered, horrified by what she'd done. "No, stop!" she shouted, but the crew in the hall kept going, heading straight into the maw of the hungry, angry blaze just rounding the corner. "*Run!*" she screamed, and then a second explosion rocked her, all but rolling *Serengeti's* huge body over.

More holes appeared, entire chunks of *Serengeti's* body ripped away, internal structures collapsing, atmosphere venting, taking everything inside her with it. More screams—high-pitched human wails filled with fear and anger cut horribly short, the shrieking of her own body as it twisted and bent, sleek lines distorting as gaping chasms opened in her sides. Screams as metal melted, panels dissolving, flowing like water, pooling in silver puddles on the floor.

Screams everywhere, and behind them the captain's icy cool voice. "All crew prepare for jump."

"Henricksen." She remembered that announcement, and what came next. "No. Please."

She didn't want to see this. Not again.

Fire. Fire everywhere, filling the corridor, burning hot as a blast furnace as it engulfed the crew sent to stop it from spreading, turning humans and robots alike into flickering, dancing torches. The suppression systems kicked in—coating the hallway with dense foam, draining the oxygen from the atmospheric mix—but it was already too late.

The fire moved on, leaving corpses behind it—human bodies wilting like hothouse flowers before dropping bonelessly to the floor, robot chassis reduced to cooling slag, bonding with the deckplates. The flames disappeared, chasing rivers of oxygen down one corridor to another, and the hallway—once bright and shining, now charred and blackened—turned silent as a tomb. Smoke and ash choked the air, swirling capriciously as the fans pumped away.

Lights flickered spasmodically, struggling to stay lit before finally giving out. Darkness engulfed the hallway, robbing *Serengeti* of sight. She waited, counting the seconds, hoping the darkness would last. And then a light appeared, wan and fitful, painting the metal walls in a bloody red glow.

A figure appeared—tall and dark, shadowy and sinister—striding quickly along the charred metal corridor, one arm dangling, the other wrapped across its middle. A second, smaller figure came behind, slim and child-like as it followed in the tall shadow's wake.

"Henricksen. Finlay." *Serengeti* stared raptly, eager to see their faces but a cloud of smoke wafted through the corridor, blurring her vision. And when it cleared, the dream receded, taking Henricksen and Finlay with it.

"No. No!" She tried to grab hold of them but the dream trickled away from her, robbing her of her crew, taking the blood and smoke, the broken robots and burnt corpses with it, leaving *Serengeti* alone once more. "Henricksen," she whispered, filled with desolation. "Finlay."

She drifted for a while—lost in darkness, wishing she could wrap that cloak of oblivion about her and simply disappear. But the universe is a mean and fickle thing. It gives and it takes in equal measure, caring nothing for the cost.

Serengeti's dream faded, and then immediately reset. Darkness gave way to light—bright, almost blinding, antiseptic in its purity—and the long length of a very clean, very familiar silver and black corridor. A corridor that erupted in screams and flames, fire and death.

"It's reset," she breathed, voice filled with horror. The scene played out and faded to dark before starting over again. "No," she begged. "Not again. Not this again."

The dream looped around and started from the beginning—light giving way to dark, blood and fire painting her hallway, crew dying again and again and again.

SIXTEEN

The dream ended abruptly, exchanging the blackened, bloodstained corridor for darkness. *Serengeti* waited, counting the seconds, dreading the moment when it started all over again. She knew the dream's patterns after a thousand, and ten thousand, and ten ten thousands of viewings. Knew every last nanosecond of its images—where it began, where it would ultimately end—and oh, how she hated it—every last moment of this looping, cruel hell her mind had created. Bright white light gave way to fire, fire to a blood-red stain. And then the darkness poured in and *Serengeti* started counting all over again.

But this time was different. A second passed, then two, and the corridor never appeared. Ten seconds—darkness all around her, deep and thick, comforting as a blanket—and *Serengeti* realized something had changed.

She shook away the cobwebs, clearing her thought-deadened mind, reached out—expecting to find nothing—and felt an icy cold touch trailing across her skin.

Cold. Cold all around me. Serengeti laughed in delight, remembering joy and pleasure—emotions long buried in the depths of the dark. *I can feel it. I can feel it on my skin.*

She stretched her consciousness, drawing that sense of cold to her, and as she did, the darkness slowly retreated—inky black veil giving way, bit by tiny bit, until a darkened space appeared. And two brilliant cobalt eyes staring outward from a rounded, chrome face.

"442," she whispered, looking down upon the little TIG from the camera high above the bridge. "It's good to see you."

442 stared blankly, giving no sign that he'd heard.

No atmosphere in here, Serengeti remembered. *Not since the last of it vented.*

Which meant sounds wouldn't carry.

Serengeti reached for the robot's internal comms channel, tapping directly into 442's brain. He chortled in surprise, face lights ticking up one side of his face and down the other, chattering out a string of questions, asking where she'd been and what she'd seen, what she'd been doing all this time.

"I was dreaming," she told him. "I was dreaming about the fire in the main corridor…" *Serengeti* trailed off, not wanting to remember, feeling the weight of that dream still. She cast her eyes about the darkened bridge, taking in the ruined stations, the dark stains on the floor.

More death here. More signs of destruction.

Perhaps I'm still dreaming. Perhaps I traded one dream for another and never woke at all.

Serengeti turned her electronic eye back to the little robot. "Am I dreaming, 442?"

442 *burbled* and shifted, face lights flashing a firm and definitive *No*.

"Guess I'll have to take your word for it."

442 *wonked* loudly, face lights flashing in a frowny-faced look of offense.

Definitely not dreaming—she'd never seen one of her robots wear such a sour, glowering puss.

"Alright. I believe you."

442 rattled his legs happily, frowny-face turning upside down as he shifted from side-to-side.

Serengeti laughed softly, forgot herself and reached for systems, thinking to run diagnostics and query for ship's status, berated herself for being stupid when nothing but silence came back.

"Dead," she said, touching at a burnt-out circuit, eyeing the blank spaces in her network that used to lead to systems. "Everything inside me is dead."

442 *beeped* softly, reminding her that he was there.

"Except you," she amended, touching at 442's brain. "And the others," she added, thinking of her tiny cadre of robots, and *Cryo* tucked away inside her bowels.

She queried internally, hoping against hope for an answer, but the line to the lifeboat was gone—burned out with rest of her comms. On a whim, she cast her net wider, reaching outside her hull, searching for others like her—sister ships travelling the stars, thinking somehow, by some miracle, one might have drifted near.

Nothing out there—no sound at all. Just cold and stars, darkness unending and the shredded debris drifting in a cloud around her wrecked body.

Too much to hope for I guess. She returned her attention to the bridge, and the robot waiting patiently beneath her camera. "Are we there yet?" *Serengeti* asked, focusing on the robot below her. "Have we reached our destination?"

442 ducked his head and shuffled his legs, metal tips tapping nervously against the decking.

"Have we reached our destination?" *Serengeti* asked sternly.

442 glanced at the camera, looking shame-faced and contrite. A slight pause and his face lights flashed once.

"No?" *Serengeti* repeated in confusion.

442 *burbled* in apology, nodded and repeated his answer.

"My instructions were clear. You were not to wake me until we reached Tsu's star." A hint of frustration and disappointment crept into *Serengeti's* voice. Power was at a premium, which meant they had to preserve every last morsel. Each waking, each return to consciousness drained their reserves just that tiny bit more. "Why, 442? Why have you woken me if we haven't reached our destination?"

442 ducked his head again, legs sagging as he bobbed down and back up again, offering one of his robotic shrugs.

"That's not an answer," *Serengeti* noted.

442 shrugged again. Not like him, all that shrugging. *Serengeti* started to worry.

"Has something happened?" she asked him, trying to keep her concern from coloring her voice. "Has something gone wrong?"

Third shrug. *Serengeti* sighed in frustration.

She shouldn't have, but she expended a bit of power to activate a light above the robot, wanting to see 442—*all* of 442, not just those disembodied cobalt eyes of his.

"No more shrugging, 442. I want an answer. Has something gone wrong? Is that why you woke me?"

442 looked up at her, blue eyes glowing brightly, face lights swirling in a complex pattern that looked suspiciously like guilt. A slight pause and he shook his head quickly, front legs lifting, waving frantically in denial.

Nothing gone wrong—that made her feel a bit better. *Serengeti* kept digging, looking for answers.

"Have we drifted off course?"

Another shake of 442's rounded head.

"Were my instructions unclear? Are you confused by what you're supposed to do?" *Serengeti* peppered the TIG with questions but 442 kept shaking his head 'no.' This was getting her nowhere. *Serengeti* returned to her original question, using her softest, gentlest voice to avoid scaring the little TIG further. "Why then, 442? Why have I been woken?"

442 fidgeted uncomfortably, carefully avoiding looking at the camera. He skittered to one side, leg ends rattling against the deck plates, and then shuffled to the other. A heavy sigh, body bobbing up and down, and he launched into a long and rolling chatter of explanation, face lights

flashing in swirling, ticking patterns, filling in the gaps of his verbal communications.

Organized patterns this time—words spoken in swirls of cobalt light. That's the way the TIGs talked to one another. The vocalizations were an adaptation, like the numbers and letters painted on their sides, the sounds added for the benefit of her human crew.

The sounds only told part of the story. The face lights told her what the TIG was *really* trying to communicate.

"Lonely. You're lonely," *Serengeti* repeated. "But you have the others to keep you company."

That look again. That guilty flash of face lights as 442 ducked his eyes away. He shrugged uncomfortably, scuffing one leg end across the metal floor, refusing to answer, refusing to even look at the camera.

There's more to this than he's letting on. It wasn't just loneliness that brought 442 here.

"What aren't you telling me?"

442's eyes ticked to the camera and just as quickly looked away again. He flexed his legs, offering another shrug.

"You're keeping something from me."

442 offered another shrug.

Serengeti sighed in annoyance and decided to let it go for now. She'd been awake too long already, she couldn't afford use more arguing over seemingly inconsequential matters. "Alright," she said softly, letting 442 off the hook. "You can wake me now and then."

442's head lifted. He *hooted* softly, face lights flashing shyly.

"But not too often," she admonished. "It drains the system each time I wake. Keep an eye on the power reserves. Make sure they don't drop too low."

442 nodded eagerly, metal legs rattling in a happy little dance.

"I'm going back to sleep now," she told him. "I've already been awake too long."

442 sagged in disappointment, belly scraping the deck plates. But he nodded eventually, knowing she was right, and raised his leg to wave goodbye as *Serengeti* abandoned the camera and slipped back into darkness.

#

The dream returned, pouncing on *Serengeti* as she drifted to sleep, wrapping close about her—an uncaring, unthinking lover clasping her to its breast.

This time she was ready for it, and knew not to fight. Denying the dream, trying to escape its clutches only made things worse.

Serengeti steeled herself as the dream engulfed her, and let the visions come, hating the dream every bit as much as she had before, but accepting it now. She couldn't change the dream, or the past it showed her, but acceptance gave her power—a feeling of controlling the uncontrollable, if that made any sense at all.

Light and dark, light and dark—the dream looped its way from the shining corridor to the hallway stained with smoke and blood before starting all over again. And *Serengeti* looped with it, pulled along by its unstoppable current. But it was different now. *She* was different. *Stronger* knowing 442 was out there—her constant companion waiting in the darkness until the time came for *Serengeti* to wake up.

SEVENTEEN

Sleep and wake, sleep and wake—that became the pattern of *Serengeti's* for a while, her wakings brief but oh-so-sweet—a welcome relief from the dark visions in her dreams. Time slipped away from her, bent and twisted in the dark, leaving her confused at each waking, not knowing how long she'd been gone. But she'd taught herself a trick along the way to help keep the confusion at bay—a simple thing that involved counting, marking the time the dream ran from end to end, the pause between repetitions to give her something to hold onto. Something besides the dream to occupy her mind.

Predictable pattern to the dream, the entire run time just under twenty minutes, the lag before it started again a matter of fifteen agonizing seconds. *Serengeti* set the counter as the dream started, let it run its course, only half-watching now—unable to close her mind completely to it but removed a bit after so many repetitions. Light faded to dark, the counter showing nineteen minutes, twenty-eight seconds, just as it always did. Reset and restart, counting the seconds until the dream started back up again. *Serengeti* watched it closely—anxious, excited— as the counter hit fifteen, rolled over and kept right on going.

No sign of the silver and black corridor. No blood and fire, crew burning like candles before her eyes.

Safe, she breathed, relief washing over her.

She focused in and cast her consciousness wide. Shapes emerged from the darkness—rounded outlines and sharp edges, the flowing curves of the bridge with its jagged lines of damage. *Serengeti* settled into a camera and looked downward from its electronic eye, searching until she found the cobalt eyes she expected, the bright and shining face staring back at her.

"442."

Fondness in *Serengeti's* voice as she greeted him. One hundred and seven wakings, and 442 always there—her constant companion, the one thing she could count on besides the dreams in the dark.

She reached for him, stroking at his mind as she tapped into 442's comms channel and spoke directly into his brain. "Hello, 442. Long time no see."

SERENGETI

442 *burbled* a greeting, face lights moving in whorls across his chrome cheeks.

"How have you been?"

The barest hesitation before 442 offered one of his patented shrugs.

This again. Serengeti stifled a sigh of frustration. "I'm getting tired of your shrugs, 442."

442 flashed his face lights in apology as *Serengeti* activated the light above him and took a good long, look.

Dirt and char showed on his carapace, scuffs and scores showing just about everywhere, turning his once bright and shining silver body a dull, dingy shade of gunmetal grey. "Looking a bit worse for wear these days," *Serengeti* noted, panning the camera a bit. "Picked up a few more dents and scratches while I was away."

442 *beeped* and *blipped,* face flushing self-consciously as he rubbed at a scratch in his side. His efforts only made the mark worse—metal on metal tended to have that effect.

So strange, she thought, *seeing 442 in such a slovenly state.* Her robots were always so particular about their appearance, polishing and buffing their metal bodies, carefully maintaining their shimmering glow. *Spit and polish doesn't really matter anymore, though, does it? I mean, look at me. I'm just a wrecked hulk drifting in empty space.* The bitterness she felt surprised her, the anger and embarrassment even more. *It doesn't matter what he looks like,* Serengeti decided. *442's still here. That's all that matters.*

"Everything still working alright?"

442 nodded quickly, demonstrating his soundness by giving himself a good, solid thump on the chest.

"My hero." *Serengeti* smiled. She spotted something and zoomed in, examining the chipped and faded remains of the letter and number designation on the TIG's side. "Looks like you lost your numbers somewhere along the way."

The robot *beeped* in confusion, front legs lifting, metal ends rattling nervously against each other as *Serengeti* turned 442's head and showed him the blank space on his side.

442 swiped at the blurred remains of his name, obviously thinking that would somehow make things better and magically bring his missing numbers and letters back. But all he did was move a bit of dirt around and scraped away yet more paint.

A flash of worried face lights accompanied by anxious, apologetic vocalizations. *Have to fix that,* Serengeti thought, listening to 442 chatter away. *This* beep *and* borp *business is cute enough, but it's really getting annoying.*

She made herself a mental note, moving repairs to the robot translation routines higher up on 442's 'to-do' list.

442 took another swipe at his side, completely obliterating the remnants of his numbers.

"Now you've done it. Looks like those numbers are gone for good."

442 *hooted* mournfully, leg end touching tentatively at the blank metal of his side.

"I guess it's just Tig now."

442 turned wide, worried eyes on the camera, face lights swirling in dismay. Those numbers gave him identity, distinguishing him from all the other TIGs in her robot crew. Losing them made him anonymous—just one more robot scuttling about the ship.

But he's more than that now. It's not right, calling him a number. Reducing him to something as simplistic as a number when she'd made him so much more than that.

"It's alright," *Serengeti* said, soothing the little robot with a touch at his brain. "It's just your numbers that got lost, not you, little one. What's here doesn't matter." She lifted his leg, tapping the end against the place where his numbers used to be. "It's what's in *here* that counts," she said, moving that same leg around to touch the metal plating of his chest. "And here," she added, tapping at the robot's temple. "That's what makes you special—different from the other TIGs. That's what makes you *you.*"

442 shrugged uncomfortably and kept staring at the blank space on his side.

No, Serengeti thought. *No more numbers.* "Tig," she said, giving the little robot a name—a *proper* name this time. "*My* Tig," she added, with a gentle caress at his AI mind.

Tig blushed happily, bright spots of cobalt color blooming on his cheeks as a shy, pleased grin stretched across his face.

"How long?" *Serengeti* asked then—the first question, the *same* question she asked every time she woke from the dream. "How long have I been asleep?"

A simple enough question, and Tig normally answered quickly, but this time, inexplicably, he offered nothing—nothing at all, except to kill his face lights entirely, leaving his rounded chrome head dark. The look came back then—that guilty, furtive look that colored their previous conversations.

"You're keeping something from me, Tig. You have been for a while now."

Nervous swirl of face lights, metal leg ends rattling against the deck plating.

"What is it?" *Serengeti* asked him.

A *blip* and a sharp shake of his head. Tig cut his eyes, kicking at dust bunnies to avoid answering her.

"Alright. I'll find out myself. Chron," *Serengeti* barked, diverting the tiniest flicker of power to activate the chronometer that kept ship's time. Chron was the simplest of her systems and one of the few still working after her disastrous attempt at jump. *Serengeti* kept Chron running while she herself drifted in sleep, because Chron was her history. The one thing—in the absence of star charts and navigational arrays—that gave her any sense of where she was in the galaxy. "Time and date," *Serengeti* ordered.

A brief pause as Chron processed the request and squirted out a bit of information.

1049. 3343 Solsten.

"Can't be. That can't be right," *Serengeti* whispered. She stared at Chron's display, wondering if she could trust it. *Have to. If Chron's failed, I'm lost—utterly, completely, hopelessly lost.* "Five years, Tig," she said, focusing back on the little robot. "Five *years* I've been sleeping." And if she added all the wakings before that, winding time backward to that fateful day when everything went wrong, the count of years came closer to eight. "Why?" she demanded. "Why did you let me sleep so long?"

Tig *burbled* softly, legs bending, ovoid body sagging to the floor. His eyes ticked up and down, casting anxious glances at the camera above him before quickly looking away. A shrug—metal legs flexing—as cobalt lights ticked in random patterns on his face, guilt, nervousness, even something that looked suspiciously like excitement flaring and dying in an instant.

Odd behavior, even from Tig.

What have you been up to? Serengeti wondered, studying the little robot from the camera above. She almost asked him, wanting to know the meaning behind those guilty glances, and then decided to let it go. She'd figure Tig's secret out in time. Right now *Serengeti* had more important things to worry about. "Are we there yet?" she asked, the second in a long line of questions she asked every time she woke.

A *clickety-click* of robotic tittering and shy smile as Tig bounced on his tip-toes and nodded his rounded head.

"We are? We've arrived?" *Serengeti* stared down at Tig, hardly daring to believe it, but Tig bounced excitedly and nodded again. "Show me." She slipped inside Tig's body, snuggling her consciousness next to his.

Tig took off like a shot, scampering across the bridge on his jointed metal legs. He stopped at the door and pried it open, dropped onto his tank treads and trundled out into the hall.

Dark in that hallway. Black as pitch, inky as the void. *Serengeti* got lost for a moment, thinking herself back there. But a pale blue glow appeared, spilling across the walls, shimmering and shifting as it sparkled off the ice rime covering everything in sight.

Still here. I'm still here, she told herself as Tig rolled forward, tank treads chewing at the hallway's icy coating, blue eyes lighting the way ahead. *The dream's waiting, but I'm here with Tig now.*

Tig touched at his chest, sliding a panel open, and yet more light spilled out—a tiny searchlight flaring to life, pouring into the hallway from a cavity inside him. He rolled silently down the corridor, magnetized tank treads clinging tenaciously to the metal composite decking, leaving twin sets of tracks in his wake.

Any semblance of a breathable atmosphere had fled the ship long ago, and with the gravity system shut down, everything that wasn't nailed down, screwed on or otherwise secured floated free around them, filling the corridor with all manner of debris. Tig rolled through it, dodging pieces where he could, ducking under others, pushing the larger objects out of the way. Halfway down the corridor, he detoured to one side, climbing into a ladderway, legs ends curling around the rungs as he climbed down.

"Where are we going?" *Serengeti* asked.

Tig *burbled* something non-committal and kept descending, passing through one level after another before abandoning the ladderway and working his way out into a scorched and blackened corridor.

Another moment of confusion—the dream's images blooming in *Serengeti's* mind, memories overlaying the reality of the hallway in front of her, one lining up perfectly with the other.

Except for the bodies, she thought. *Those are gone, thankfully.*

The TIGs had gathered up the human corpses at some point and stowed them somewhere. At least, she hoped they'd stowed them somewhere. The thought of those corpses being out there, drifting in the cloud of debris surrounding her shattered body…

Serengeti shuddered inside Tig's little head and pushed that image firmly away.

Scorch marks marred the paneling of the corridor around them, the burn marks from the fire unmistakable, identical to that carved indelibly into her memory. And the robots…melted robots showed here and there—lumps of misshapen metal melted into the floor, permanently connected to *Serengeti's* shredded body.

Why? she wondered as Tig rolled forward. *Why this hallway of all the ones Tig could have chosen?*

She almost stopped Tig and made him turn around. Find another hallway. Another way to get to wherever he was going. She reached for Tig's controls and then forced herself away, leaving the robot to choose his own path, staring straight ahead as he navigated the damage hallway, ignoring the mangled robots Tig rolled by, the blackened walls looming on either side.

Tig cleared the last robot body and moved on, approaching the bend in the corridor where the wall of fire started, turning left and right and right again. The corridors here were just as empty, just as dark and cold and filled with silence as the others they passed through. That silence started to bother her after a while. Put her in mind of the dream, and that moment just after the fire when the corridor filled with smoke and ash, death and destruction.

No, she told herself, pushing thoughts of the dream away. *That was before.*

Can't change the past, Serengeti. *All you can do is move on.*

Henricksen's words—one of those pithy bits of wisdom he tended to offer when toeing the line between sober and drunk.

Henricksen. She missed her captain. Missed Finlay and Tsu, all of her human crew.

Serengeti shivered inside Tig's shell. She activated the micro-sensors in the floor, hating that silence and the memories that came with it, berating herself for being stupid and wasting even that small bit of power.

It's worth it, though. I can't bear that oppressive silence clinging to these icy halls.

Tig made a last turn and rolled into a long, long corridor running parallel to the first of the three thick layers of her port-side outer hull. The ice lay even thicker here, coating the ceiling, the walls, the deck plates on the floor in a good inch of frozen slickness.

Tig aimed for a center lane running down the middle of the floor. The ice was thinner there. The frost all but worn through, leaving just a thin skin showing whitely against the silver-grey deck plating beneath.

"You come here often," *Serengeti* noted, spying the telltale signs of tank treads in the hoarfrost's coating. "What have you been up to, Tig?"

Tig rolled to a stop and turned his head, cobalt eyes reflecting off the smooth slab of ice covering one wall. His face lights swirled slowly, lining up beneath his eyes, curving at the line's end to form a mischievous, robotic smile.

"Tig…"

"Shh," he breathed, pressing a leg against that curving, electronic approximation of a smile. He winked at her—one eye going dark and then flaring back to life—and spun in a tight circle before zipping off down the corridor and into a gaping hole showing darkly to one side. A hole that punched clear through *Serengeti's* triple-hulled hide, and the buffering spaces between.

Tig slipped along that ragged tunnel, winding his way through one hull layer after another, flipping between his tank treads and his jointed metal as he climbed piles of debris and navigated twisted girders, hopping holes, and trenches, and buckled support structures—sure-footed, confident, never once slowing. He even used the magnetized ends of his legs to climb walls in places where the chasms looming in front of him were simply too large to cross. A last layer of thick metal skin and he stepped out into vacuum—into the cold and dark and shining stars of space.

"Beautiful," *Serengeti* whispered as the stars and dark came clear.

She'd missed the stars in the darkness. The dream showed her fire—smoke and fire and death—but it never showed her stars. And until now her wakings were all to blackness—Tig's shining face amidst the darkened environs of the bridge. Five years. Five long years spent sleeping, and another three of fitful waking before that, with not a single glimpse of the stars in all that time. Not a single moment to admire the thing she loved the most.

An AI needed the stars to sustain her. A starship was just a ship without the stars outside her hull.

"Stop," *Serengeti* ordered, bringing Tig to a halt. She turned his head a bit so she could see the stars more clearly and drink in the vast expanse of the universe stretching endlessly in every direction. "Beautiful," she whispered, voice filled with awe. "So beautiful." She forgot herself for a while, forgetting what she was here, what had brought her to this place.

Tig's polite cough brought *Serengeti* back to reality. The robot shifted nervously, front legs lifting, metal ends rattling together. A burst of robotic chatter, legs waving vaguely, telling her they really should get going.

"I know." *Serengeti* gazed at the stars a moment longer and then released Tig so he could continue on his way.

More holes appeared—rents and tears, long, long sections of deck plating gone missing, other sections warped and dented, buckled by the shockwave from *Osage's* detonation. Tig followed a winding and apparently much-practiced path that took him along the length of *Serengeti's* darkened port side and then turned upward, climbing toward a silver-white glow peeking over the top of her hull.

Serengeti left the driving to Tig and flicked to the camera in his thorax, surveying the damage to her body. She'd never really gotten a good look at herself after the battle—hadn't really wanted to, to be honest, the damage inside her giving her nightmares enough—and as she looked around, she realized the damage out here was even worse than she'd thought. The bulk of her superstructure still appeared to be intact, but her skin was shredded, *Osage's* explosion, the DSR's sustained fire leaving her pockmarked and cratered, charred from laser burns and plasma fire, silver plating turned an ominous black.

It was all too much, all too depressing. *Serengeti* abandoned the camera and faced forward as Tig pattered to the top of the ship and then stopped, *chirruping* softly as he showed *Serengeti* the nearby star.

"Tsu's star. That's Tsu's star out there."

Tig *beeped* and nodded, bobbing up and down.

"I can't believe. I can't believe we actually made it." She'd lined her body up and launched them toward that star nearly eight full years ago, never knowing if they'd actually make it. And now, here they were—Tig and *Serengeti* sitting on the hull of her damaged body, watching it circle in orbit around the gaseous bulk of Tsu's once-distant star. "Are we close enough?"

Tig *blipped* and dipped his head, pointing to the acres of plating covering her starboard side.

Not as much damage there. *Serengeti's* port side was a cratered mess, but the starboard hull had fared much better. Long scars from lasers grazes showed clearly, dents and tears marked where shrapnel and rail guns had torn at her hull, but the rest of it…the bulk of her starboard side was remarkably intact.

And twinkling. Photovoltaic cells drinking in the starlight until the hull plating glowed. She drew a bit of power, activating sensors in that plating, reveling in the feel of cold and stardust brushing along her hull.

"We made it," *Serengeti* whispered, smiling to herself. "We made it, Tig. We're here. We're finally here."

But getting here was just the beginning. There was so much more to do.

Serengeti forced Tig's eyes away from the star and gazed along the length of her hull. "The connection to the fuel cells. Is it working?"

Tig nodded quickly, legs waving in all directions as he chattered out a report.

Serengeti listened for a while and then stopped him when she spied a long line of dark shapes—an odd metal forest growing like fungus on the top of her body. "What's that?" she asked, pointing Tig' leg toward the bow.

More excited babbling.

"A surprise?" *Serengeti* laughed softly as Tig capered happily about. "Alright. Show me."

Tig raced off, legs clattering against the hull plating as he scurried toward the front of the ship. Halfway to the forest, a framework came clear—a network of welded girders torn from her insides, hauled out here and bolted to her hull. Snaking lines of cables ran around and across, tying the framework together, linking the square panels attached to it.

Panels. Hull plating. The robots salvaged some of that too.

Tig slowed, tip-toeing the rest of the way, moving slowly along the line of panels while *Serengeti* inspected the construction.

"You changed the design specs," she noted. "This isn't what I laid out." She'd shown Tig how to re-route power, which connections to cut and which to rewire to feed all the energy the starboard panels gathered into the three remaining fuel cells in her belly, but this…she hadn't shown him *anything* like this. Hadn't even considered harvesting panels to supplement the load the starboard side gathered. "A solar collection array. You came up with this?"

Tig *blipped* nervously, head bobbing in time with his body.

"It's ingenious, Tig. I'm impressed. Truly."

Especially since he'd come up with the idea all on his own.

Tig shrugged and scuffed a metal foot in embarrassment, acting like it was no big deal.

"Does it work?"

Tig nodded vigorously and spun around, crawling his way back toward her center before dropping down the port side, angling for the place where they'd exited her innards.

Serengeti flipped back to the camera in his thorax as he slipped inside the hull, taking a last look at the stars. "Beautiful," she whispered. "So beautiful." She froze the image of that infinite sky and stored it away with the others—the faces of Tsu and Evans, Kusikov and Sikuuku and all the others—so she'd have the stars and her crew to keep her company in the dark.

Metal skin slipped around her, blocking her view of the stars and dark outside. *Serengeti* sighed and faced forward, watching Tig pick his way through wreckage until he reached her gutted insides.

EIGHTEEN

The silence hit her the moment Tig stepped into the hallway. Silence like a tomb. Silence broken only by the stomp and clatter of Tig's metal legs, the crunch and rattle as he lowered himself onto his tank treads and hurried down the corridor. The micro-sensors didn't really *hear* sound so much as feel it, measure it, picking up movement, vibrations and translating it into sound. Cameras to see, micro-sensors to feel, photovoltaic cells to eat and drink and power her body, and an AI mind controlling it all.

AI—artificial intelligence, all mind, no soul. The designers insisted power, function didn't equate to life. But *Serengeti* disagreed.

I think. I eat. I touch and see. Tell me I'm not alive. Tell me just because I'm AI I don't have a soul.

Designers don't know spit, Serengeti.

Henricksen again. Henricksen's voice speaking directly into *Serengeti's* brain. She paused to wonder about that, hoping that voice wasn't another malfunction—a sign her AI brain had somehow been damaged.

Yer not cracked, Serengeti.

That made her laugh.

The designers see machines and weapons. They're blind to the true miracle they created.

Serengeti smiled to herself. For all his gruffness, Henricksen always did have a way with words.

"Thanks for that."

The silence ate up her words, taking that away from her, just like everything else. She hated that silence, found it increasingly upsetting, increasingly *disturbing* with each minute that passed.

Tig, for his part, didn't even seem to notice. He just trundled along, babbling happily, spewing out a constant stream of observations as they passed this broken item and that, adding each one to a long list of things that would likely never get fixed.

That's when it hit her. The silence. That's why the silence bothered her so much.

"Stop," *Serengeti* ordered.

Tig *beeped* in surprise and locked up, tank treads slipping on the icy floor, bringing him to a stuttering, skidding halt. Another *beep*—this one a tentative question, asking her what was going on.

"Pan."

Tig's head turned, looking one way and the other, giving her a full view of the hall.

Empty. Completely empty, just like every other corridor they'd travelled so far.

"Proceed."

Tig rolled forward, moving uncertainly at first, picking up speed as he left that hallway for another, trundled to the next crossing and turned right. *Serengeti* rode quietly, content to let Tig do the driving until they reached a crossing where two long corridors met.

"Halt," she ordered.

Tig hit the brakes, sliding a bit before coming to a stop.

"Where are they?" She turned Tig's head, peering through his eyes down the long length of one corridor before switching views to examine the other. Empty and empty and empty. Nothing but metal and ice and that never-ending silence. "Where are they, Tig? Where are the other robots?"

Tig stuttered nervously, a nonsensical *tick-tick-tick* issuing from his mouth. His legs *clacked* and *rattled* as they moved up and down, tapping rhythmically against the deck plates as he shuffled about.

"Where are they, Tig?"

Tig *blipped* and *beeped*—random sounds, no real meaning behind them—but either wouldn't, or couldn't answer her question.

"Alright. I'll find out for myself." *Serengeti* reached for the robot comms channel, connected and started searching for others of Tig's kind.

Silence came back. More of that hated, dreaded silence, reminding *Serengeti*—a once-proud warship—she was now little more than a miserable wreck. And her crew...she'd left Tig in charge of a dozen robots. There should be all sorts of chatter on the robot line, but when she tapped in she found it empty—as silent as everything else inside her.

"Where are they, Tig?" *Serengeti* demanded. "Where are the others? Where have they gone?"

Tig sighed and pointed down the hall, bent his leg and tapped at the floor, *burbling* out a single, mumbled word.

"Engineering." She'd left them there, before she drifted into the dark. "Have they been there this whole time?"

Tig shrugged and nodded, shook his head.

Serengeti wasn't quite sure what to make of that. "Take me to them," she ordered.

Another sigh and Tig got moving, rolling slowly, almost reluctantly along. He stopped again near the end of the hallway, detour to one side and slipped into a ladderway to begin the long trip down.

#

Tig rolled into Engineering. *Serengeti* took one look and brought him to a halt—didn't ask, didn't order, didn't even think about what she was doing. She just seized control and stopped the little robot dead, shocked by what lay before her.

Long lengths of snaking cables hung everywhere, draping the walls, dangling through holes cut in the ceiling, littering the floor—hundreds of strands, miles upon miles of individual cables, and every last one of them connected to the fuel cells sitting against one wall. Apparently, Tig's creativity didn't end with the solar collection array outside. He'd rigged up a makeshift power grid here in Engineering to siphon the energy collected by *Serengeti's* hull panels and feed it into her three functioning power cells, using a modified version of *Serengeti's* own design—one she'd downloaded into Tig's brain. The end result was…creepy, frankly. Especially since there was no atmosphere or gravity here, or anywhere else on the ship.

Bits and pieces of *Serengeti's* innards floated around them, cluttering the room, constantly getting in Tig's way. Cables floated freely, snaking as if alive, but what drew *Serengeti's* eyes was the corpses scattered amongst those cables, and shoved up against walls. A flotsam and jetsam of burnt-out power cells and twisted components, empty shells and mounded piles of salvaged parts that used to be *Serengeti's* robot crew.

Engineering was a graveyard. A place of broken robots and salvaged parts. The robot comms channel was silent because no one was talking. No one was *out* there to talk. They were all right here—every last one of them, every last TSD and TIG that had come through jump with her and not been blown out into space.

Tig and the others gathered up the robot dead and brought them here. And when the time came, the rest of them gathered here to die as well.

"Gone. All gone," *Serengeti* whispered, voice filled with horror. "What happened, Tig? What happened to them all?"

She urged him forward, not even waiting for a response, rolling Tig around the room, taking in the stacks of bodies arranged in neat, orderly rows along the walls, others stuffed into storage spaces, still more scattered about the floor. Abandoned where they'd fallen, shoved to one side so they'd be out of the way. A few bodies floated freely, twisting amongst the cables, but most of them had been bundled together and dogged down, giving them some dignity in death. Some semblance of tranquility and peace.

Serengeti scanned Tig's eyes across the carnage, heart heavy with sadness, mind filled with rage. Tig made a last loop around Engineering and then slowed to a halt, *beeping* softly, front legs tapping together as he waited for her to say something. To pass judgment on what had happened here, deep inside Engineering.

To be honest, *Serengeti* didn't know what to say to him. Not for a long while. She just stared at a nearby robot—a TIG identical to her own little Tig.

This one still has its numbers, though.

Idle thought, ridiculous thing to mention but that's the first thing she noticed as she looked down at Tig's broken-down brother.

The robot's carapace yawned wide open, revealing an empty space inside.

It's shell. Nothing but a shell.

They'd plundered it for parts—Tig, the others, somewhere along the way they'd taken the TIG's motors, disassembled the rest of its sides, harvesting wires and circuits, draining its power core, leaving it a cold, dead heart.

The thin cable they'd used to kill it still snaked from the robot's chest. *Serengeti* reached for it, unplugging it using a pincer extruded from the end of Tig's leg. She touched at the robot's face then, traced the figures stenciled on its side.

TIG-206. The designation meant nothing to her. Nothing special, just another robot. Indistinguishable from any other in her crew.

But that means everything. They are *my crew.*

And it was her job to protect them, just as it was theirs to serve her.

In a rage, *Serengeti* left him, pulling away from Tig, flipping from one camera to another until she finally found one in Engineering that worked. And from its lofty height she stared downward, watching Tig fidget and shift.

"What have you done?" *Serengeti* thundered.

Anger, so much anger coursing through her, coloring her voice.

Tig froze, face a blank, cobalt eyes two brightly glowing circles in the rounded metal of his head. *"Beep?"* he asked, pointing at himself. A quick glance behind him, as if looking to see if someone was there. *"Beep-beep?"* he repeated.

"I told you to watch over them. I told you to keep them safe. What happened, Tig? How could you let this happen?"

Not fair to blame him, part of her knew that. After all, this—all this—was her fault as much as his. But he'd kept this from her. All those wakings, that guilty look on his face, that sneaking suspicion she'd had that Tig was keeping something from her.

I knew you were keeping secrets, Tig, but I never imagined...how could I ever have imagined you were hiding something as terrible as this?

"You cannibalized them. Stripped them down. Tore them apart."

Tig *beeped* frantically, shaking his head.

"You *killed* them, Tig. And I want to know why. I want to know what happened that this, *this* was the only answer."

Tig waved his legs wildly, *beeps* and *borps* spewing from his mouth in a panicked rush.

"*Why*?!"

Tig went silent, head drooping, body sagging to the floor. *Serengeti* waited, watching him from high above, and slowly, softly, Tig began to talk. To spin out a long tale that started when she drifted to sleep eight years ago and ended right here and now.

Seems things went south quickly after she left them, and Tig—being in charge— had been forced to improvise, modifying her designs again and again in order to build the power grid she'd envisioned. That grid was important—the key to everything—and without it, none of the rest of her plan would work. Tig knew it, the rest of the robots knew it as well. They'd been complicit in this most desperate of desperate plans— everyone agreed, all of them in it together.

Repair, refit, survive—those were her orders, and Tig and the others followed them as best they could, for as long as they could. But even with *Serengeti* sleeping—lost in limbo and the darkness of the dream— the power levels kept dropping. Leaking away little by little, until the robots feared they'd lose *Serengeti* forever. Because, the thing was, the robots themselves needed recharging—not often, just once in a while— and that coupled with *Serengeti's* sipping draw put a severe strain on the fuel cells' dwindling reserves.

That's when they'd come up with their plan. A plan that changed everything, and ended up killing her crew. A plan that involved sacrifice, feeding the energy in the robots' power units *back* into the fuel cells rather than tapping into its stores to charge themselves up.

In ones and twos the robots died, their insides pillaged, dismantled, salvaged for spare parts. But the rest of them kept going. Kept scurrying about, scrubbing burn marks from her starboard side, replacing panels where they were needed, stringing mile after mile of cable through *Serengeti's* body to the fuel those precious power cells.

The hell of it was they'd succeeded, keeping her alive until they reached Tsu's star. But it took all of them to get her here—the lives of every last robot save one to keep *Serengeti's* power grid running for those eight long years. And now, having reached their destination, there was just her and Tig to see it. Just *Serengeti* and her last, loyal TIG to look upon her shining hull, and the makeshift engineering project that provided her with power.

Tig fell silent, his words all spent. *Serengeti* was silent too, her anger gone now, leaving her sad and empty, wracked with unexpected guilt.

She'd done this to him. *She'd* left Tig in charge. *She'd* changed his programming and put him in this impossible situation.

All this, Serengeti thought, casting her eyes around. *All this to keep three measly fuel cells working until we reached this star.*

It hardly seemed worth it when she looked on all those silent robot bodies. After all, three fuel cells would never be able to power all her systems, even when fully charged. And her hyperspace engines…forget it. Three fuel cells would never get them running again. Nothing would. Those engines were scrap, just like the rest of her.

But they weren't meant for her, were they? Not for her, nor for the engines either. She depended on that energy to keep her consciousness alive, but the power they collected was meant for something far more important than *Serengeti* herself. And though she hated to admit it, hated the cost required, *Serengeti* knew deep down that Tig and the others had done right.

She turned the camera toward at the massive fuels cells arrayed against one wall. A quick check showed the reserves running just above critical, despite the snaking cables feeding energy inside.

Not much power yet. Which means we've only recently arrived. Tig must have woken me the minute we settled into orbit around the star.

Tig. Her one constant. Her anchor. The one thing tethering her to reality, keeping the dream from sweeping her away.

"How did you decide?" she whispered, slipping from the camera to snuggle inside Tig's head. "How did you choose who'd go first, and who'd sacrifice themselves each time after?"

Tig shrugged uncomfortably and raised his two front legs, smacking one end against the other—once, twice, thrice—and then extruding a set of shears.

Serengeti stared in disbelief. "Rock, paper, scissors. You're kidding. Please tell me you're kidding."

Another shrug. Tig's eyes drifted to TIG-206, staring at the broken down, dismantled body as he shook his head.

"Poor Tig," she murmured. "My poor little Tig. Left in charge and now left all alone."

"Beep." Tig shuffled his feet, bright lights blooming in an uncomfortable blush. *"Beep-beep."* He rattled his leg ends against the deck plates, hunkered down and shook his head.

Another mystery. More of Tig's secrets. Secrets made *Serengeti* nervous. Made her feel like she was losing control. "What—?"

An error message flashed in warning, pulsing to get her attention. *Serengeti* acknowledged it and analyzed the data behind it.

Bad news. Energy levels in the power cells had dropped again, reaching critical levels.

It's me, she realized. *I've stayed too long.*

Her consciousness drew too heavily on the fuel cells, even with all her other systems shut down. She'd have to remember that, and limit her time in the waking world from now on.

Another check of the fuel cells—she couldn't help herself—showed the energy levels continued to fall.

Damn.

Serengeti sighed and pulled backward, focusing on Tig again. There was something there. Something important in that little shake of his head. But that power warning blinked incessantly, flashing red and red and red, refusing to be ignored.

Out of time, she thought. *I'm out of time, so Tig's secret will have to keep for now. Until my next waking at least.*

"I must leave you for a while, Tig."

Mournful *hoots* from the little robot. Sounds of distress that stabbed at her heart.

"Shhh," she told him, touching at his brain. "None of that. I have much to tell you, but not much time. It's long past when I should have rightly returned to sleep."

A long, sad sigh as Tig dipped his head in acquiescence. A shiver passed through him as *Serengeti* touched at his brain, passing yet another schematic—a design plan that was far less complicated than what the robots had rigged up here, but would likely take much, much longer to build with Tig working all on his own.

It saddened her to think of that—to imagine Tig slaving away all alone. *How long? Serengeti* wondered. *How much more time will I lose before the time for dreaming ends and the time for waking comes?*

It didn't matter. Not really. Not for her anyway. Time was infinite in the dream. Time passed quickly in the depths of sleep.

A soft touch as she passed a last bit of information, a fond caress of Tig's rounded face before *Serengeti* flitted away, racing along the pathways of her body until she reached the dim confines of the bridge. There she disconnected her mind and returned to the darkness, and the dream.

NINETEEN

Something pushed at her. Pushed and pulled, poked and prodded, worrying at *Serengeti* as she counted, adding one number onto another until she reached fifteen.

Fifteen. Magic number. Fifteen came and after things changed.

Serengeti stared hard at the counter, waiting, not knowing if it would be the dream again on the other side of that number, or the darkness of reality.

The counter ticked over—sixteen, seventeen—and *Serengeti* surfaced, opened her eyes and looked down upon the cold confines of her silent bridge.

"Tig." She called out to her companion without thinking, before she could even see him in the dark. "Are we there yet, Tig?" *Serengeti* started to ask, and then stopped herself, realizing that question no longer mattered.

Joy for a brief instant, a proud feeling of accomplishment at crossing all that empty space and reaching Tsu's star. And then visions of Engineering intruded, killing her joy, filling *Serengeti's* heart with sadness and regret.

"Tig," she called again, searching the blackness below.

A soft answer came back to her—a spurt of robotic chatter accompanied by a glimmer of bluest-blue light. Tig's head lifted, cobalt eyes gleaming. He greeted *Serengeti* with whispered words, and swirling patterns of shifting light.

Damn. Forgot to tell him to fix that. Serengeti called up her note about the translation routines, marked it as highest priority so *this* time she wouldn't forget to pass the task on to Tig.

"Hello, Tig." She tucked the note away and reached for the little robot, stroking at his checks with electric fingers. "How long—?"

Something moved beside him—a sibilant shifting in the shadows that stole *Serengeti's* words away. *Danger,* her mind registered.

Instinct kicked in and she slipped in beside Tig's brain, reaching for his controls without even thinking. She stopped herself at the last second, relaxing her grip on the little robot as a second set of eyes appeared—

142

cobalt blue staring at her from a rounded metal face. Tig's twin it seemed. But the last time she left him, Tig had been alone.

A flash of memory—Tig in Engineering, robot carcasses lying all around him. Whispered words of commiseration, *Serengeti* apologizing for all the pain and anger, sorrow and regret. And Tig...Tig blinking slowly, shaking his head. The denial confused her at the time, but now...

Not alone after all—that's what that denial had meant. You cheeky little monkey, Tig.

"Who's this?" *Serengeti* retreated to the camera, sparked a light above the two robots and zoomed in on Tig's unexpected partner.

A TIG without doubt, and built to a similar design as her own little Tig. Similar, but not identical, that peaked her interest. A scar showed on the side of the newcomer's head—a jagged weld secured with a line of rivets marking where repairs had been made. Someone—Tig, she assumed—had tried to cover the ugly mark over, painting a jaunty pink bow across the riveted seam in an attempt to hide the damage.

"Who's your friend, Tig? Where's she been hiding?"

She. Female. Had to be, because of that little pink bow.

Tig *beeped* and *burbled* without really giving an answer while the robot beside him fidgeted nervously, eyes cast downward, legs ends drumming rhythmically against the floor.

"Come now," *Serengeti* chided in her most gentle, soothing voice. "No need to be shy."

The pink-bowed TIG *blipped* once and hunkered down, curling up like a dead, metallic spider.

Tig *hooted* softly and touched at the little robot's side, murmuring encouragingly. She lifted her head enough to look at him, even managed to work up the courage to sneak a glance at the camera, but just as quickly looked away. Tig poked at her a few more times, face lights flashing in complex patterns of communication even *Serengeti* had trouble following, until the little robot finally uncurled. She leaned close to Tig, reaching for one of his legs, wrapping her own leg around his and hugging it to her body as Tig draped a leg across her carapace, hugging her back.

Protective, that gesture. The way Tig looked at the other robot.

Well, well, well. Isn't that interesting?

"It's alright," she called. "No need to be scared. I won't bite, promise."

The TIG didn't seem so certain, but a little encouragement from Tig and she lifted her head a bit—just enough to offer a shy smile before ducking back down again.

Better than nothing, I guess.

"What's your name?" *Serengeti* asked, trying to draw the pink-bowed robot out.

The TIG shrugged, directing an embarrassed *burble* at the deck plates. Tig leaned close and whispered something to her, but the TIG quickly shook her head. A touch at her chin, Tig's metal leg pressing insistently until she raised her head.

"What's your name, little one?" *Serengeti* repeated.

The robot flushed brightly and brushed at the identification tag painted on the rusted metal of her side, a tag that was scratched and faded but mostly complete.

Mostly. *Serengeti* noticed she'd lost one of her letters along the way.

"TI -111. Don't seem to remember being issued with that particular model of robot."

The TIG *beeped* and craned her neck around, taking a look at her side. Another *beep*—this one startled sounding—and she wiped furiously at the empty space where the third letter of her designation should have been.

"*Beep. Beep-beep,*" she stuttered, eyes wide and panicky. "*Beep-beep-beep—*"

"Shhh. It's alright," *Serengeti* laughed. "You only lost one letter. Tig here lost *all* of his."

The TIG froze, blinking uncertainly. "*Beep?*"

"Uh-huh. Every last one. Letters too. Show her Tig."

Tig twisted his body around and pointed at the blank spot on his side. Not a letter or number in side, just some dirt and smudges keeping company with the scratches and dents.

The TIG stared at Tig's flank, front legs wringing worriedly but Tig just shrugged unconcernedly, acting like it was no big deal. A flash of communication, swirls of color passing back and forth between the two robots, and TI-111 opened a little storage bin in her side, fished around for a few seconds before pulling something out.

"Ah-ha!" she cried, holding a stubby grease pencil up.

She twisted around and applied the grease pencil to the blank space on her side, sketching an oversized *G* in swift, sure strokes. A quick check of her penmanship, thickening the flat bar of that single letter, its rounded, leftward facing curve and she turned side-on to the camera, looking extremely proud of herself.

"Ta-da!" the TIG cried, flourishing the grease pencil like a magic wand.

"Very nice," *Serengeti* told her. "But—"

The robot turned her pink-bowed head away before *Serengeti* could finish and held the grease pencil out to Tig. Tig hesitated, glancing uncertainly at the camera. His partner waved insistently, pressing the grease pencil on him, wanting him to take it and fix his tag like she'd fixed hers.

"No," *Serengeti* said sharply.

The two robots froze, turning wide eyes toward the camera.

"No," *Serengeti* repeated more gently. She slipped inside Tig and used his leg to push the grease pencil away. "Tig is Tig, not just 442. And you, my dear," she touched Tig's leg to that freshly drawn *G,* wiping it carefully away, "are more than that missing letter."

The TIG blinked in confusion, eyes flicking from the grease pencil she held to the empty space on her side. She chittered softly, face lights flashing and fading like she was trying to puzzle something out. But a word from Tig, and a short burst of cobalt communication, and the pink-bowed robot put the grease pencil away.

"There now, that's better." *Serengeti* lit Tig's face lights, offering an encouraging smile.

It took a bit, but the TIG eventually smiled back at her, tilted her head and *hooted* a question as she brushed at her side.

"Who are you?" *Serengeti* laughed in surprise. "That, my dear, is a very good question." She thought a moment, looking the little TIG up and down. "We can't very well call you Tig, now can we? Not with that pretty pink bow. And TI-111 sounds so…" *Serengeti* trailed off, smiling to herself as inspiration struck. "Tilli," she murmured, touching the robot's side. "We'll call you Tilli. How does that sound?"

Tilli whistled shrilly, repeating her new name as best she could. She blushed when *Serengeti* laughed, and ducked her head in embarrassment, but she shuffled her legs about and tried again, whistling louder, more confidently this time, flushing with pleasure now as she offered a shy smile.

"Is that a yes?"

Enthusiastic nod, Tilli's rounded chrome head bobbing up and down and all around, Tig nodding right along with her.

"Alright then. Tilli it is. Now then." She panned the camera left then right, looking from one robot to the other. "Tell me why I've been woken. Tell me how long I've been away this time and what you two have gotten done while I was gone."

They both blushed together. Tilli flicked her eyes to Tig, then ducked her head and pawed at the floor, leaving it to him to answer.

Not good then. Whatever Tig and Tilli had to tell her, she wasn't going to like it.

"Spill it, Tig." *Serengeti* focused in on him, leaving Tilli alone for now. "How long? How long was I asleep this time?"

Tig shuffled uncomfortably, fronting legs tapping together. He looked at the camera, then down at the floor, leaned to one side and lifted three of his legs.

"Three months?" she asked hopefully, but Tig shook his head. "Three years." *Serengeti* sighed wearily. Not as long as last time, but still longer than she'd expected. Longer than she *wanted*. "I'm guessing that means the task I left you is taking longer than we had originally anticipated."

Tig shrugged and nodded, eyes locked onto the floor.

"So, what happened?"

Tig shuffled to one side, leg ends rattling against the deck plating as he hemmed and hawed, trying to figure out where to start before launching into a long and winding story about components and damage in unexpected places, setbacks and wrong turnings, droning on and on and on.

"Stop, stop, *stop!*"

Tig stuttered into silence.

"How about you just show me?" *Serengeti* suggested.

"*Beep?*" Tig blinked, thinking, tilted his head and nodded. "*Beep-beep.*"

She abandoned the camera slipped inside the little robot, waved to Tilli to come with them as Tig trundled across the bridge and into the corridor outside.

Tig scuttled over to the nearest ladderway and climbed inside. *Serengeti* expected him to climb downward to Engineering, but instead he glanced behind him and *burbled* something to Tilli before grasping the rungs and pulling himself up.

"Where—?"

Tig shook his head, babbled something about outside and the solar array, and kept going.

Serengeti sat back and left him to it, hoping this wasn't some wild goose chase. "Limited power, Tig. Remember that."

"*Beep-beep-beep.*" Tig waved a leg in acknowledgement as he let go of the ladder and worked his way out of the access shaft, flipped onto his tank treads and hurried down the hall.

Twists and turns after that, one corridor leading to another before Tig finally reached the iciest one of them all: the one paralleling her portside hull. He tip-toed through a gap in her side, threaded his way through three shredded layers of hull, navigating gaps and twisted debris until he reached the dark of space outside.

"Hold," *Serengeti* said, bringing Tig to a halt. Tilli rolled to a stop beside them, flashing questions at Tig as *Serengeti* turned on all his sensors and let the icy cold wrap around her. "I've missed the cold, Tig."

Tig shivered in answer.

Serengeti sighed and shut his sensors back down. But she held him there a while longer so she could drink in the sight of the stars. Selfish thing to do, wasteful considering they were low on power, but she'd earned a little selfishness after all her time in the dark.

"Quite the sight, aren't they, Tig?"

Tig cycled the filters on his ocular lenses, processed some data and then decided she was correct. *Serengeti* almost laughed.

"They look...pure from here, don't they? Henricksen told me the stars twinkle when you look at them from planetside. The light passing through the atmosphere—" *Serengeti* broke off as Tig shuffled his legs and coughed. "Am I boring you, Tig?"

"*Beep?*" Tig pointed at his chest, face lights flashing a question. "*Beep-beep-beep,*" he assured her, waving all his legs at once. But he flicked his eyes to Tilli, saw her shuffle around, throwing glances at the distant solar array.

"Alright, I get it. Proceed, Tig." *Serengeti* released the little robot, letting Tig and Tilli continue their journey. She flipped to the camera in the robot's thorax and stared at the stars, feeling a strange sense of yearning at being so close and yet unable to move closer. Unable to break free of her endlessly circling orbit and wander the universe around her. "Someday," she whispered, making a promise to herself. "Someday this will end and a new journey will begin."

Tig *beeped* softly, trying to get her attention.

Serengeti sighed wistfully and flicked forward, peering through Tig's eyes as they rounded the crest of her port side and reached the top of her hull.

Tig rolled to stop and panned his head around, giving *Serengeti* a panoramic view of her shimmering, starboard-side hull.

"Beautiful," she murmured, smiling to herself.

"*Beep?*" Tilli cocked her head in question.

"Yes," *Serengeti* laughed. "You too."

Tilli *burbled* happily and shuffled to one side, moving closer to Tig. The two robots reached for each other without looking, twining their leg together like lovers.

Love. Another complex emotion. Far more complicated than anger or sorrow, sadness or regret.

Can a robot feel love? Serengeti wondered, watching the robots swap communications between each other. *Can I?*

That was the better question. Fondness, certainly—she had that in spades for the crew trapped inside her—but love? *Real* love? She knew the concept but the actual application…

How does a crystal matrix brain even know what love is?

You're a tenth generation, super-powered AI brain mounted inside a warship's body, Serengeti, *not some besotted little schoolgirl.*

Henricksen again. More pithy wisdom.

Yeah-yeah, I get it. Stop whining and get with the program.

"Why are we here, Tig?"

Tig let go Tilli's leg and started chattering away, telling her how the hull plates had gotten dirty, slowing the solar collection rate. It took a while—a lot of extra effort they hadn't planned for—but he and Tilli managed to sweep and buff and polish every last speck of space dust and debris away, returning the panels to optimal working order. A wave of his legs and Tig rolled toward the bow, showing her the forest of panels they'd erected there, pointing out linkages and connection points, components they'd had to replace.

Time, Serengeti thought, adding all those unplanned tasks up. They were all important—every last one—and Tig had been right to not ignore them, but the more time he and Tilli spent on these tasks, the less they had to work on the one *Serengeti* had set them to.

"Enough," *Serengeti* said, as Tig continued to prattle on.

Tig rolled to a stop in the middle of the solar panel forest, face lights flashing and swirling, letting her know his report wasn't yet done.

"I know. I get it. You two have been busy as beavers and I appreciate it, but I've seen enough of the outside for now. Engineering, Tig. Show me what's gone on down there."

Tig slid his eyes to Tilli, but she just shrugged and looked away. He hesitated a moment, glancing to one side, dancing on his tip-toes as he turned in a circle.

"Tig." *Serengeti* touched the little robot's brain, stopping him in his tracks. "I've seen all I need to see here, Tig. It's time to go back inside."

Tig sighed and nodded as he reached for Tilli's leg. They turned together, putting the starlight behind them as they stepped down into shadow and slipped through a gaping hole in *Serengeti's* side.

#

She braced herself as they entered Engineering, knowing what she'd find, but it was still hard to actually see it. Still difficult to look upon all those broken robots and not wonder at the cost.

Tig rolled inside as if it was nothing, inured to the sight of all that death after living among it for so long. Tilli followed close behind him, switching from her tank treads when Tig did, the two of them picking their way through the cables and bodies on their jointed, insectile legs.

They'd straightened things up while *Serengeti* was away, collecting the robots scattered about the floor, lining them up against the wall with the others, closing their panels so they didn't look so dead inside. Hardly a necessary undertaking, but it made Engineering look less like a robotic charnel house and more like a well-maintained mausoleum.

Serengeti appreciated the effort, but when she looked about her, she saw more wasted time. She couldn't bring herself to berate Tig, though. Not for this. Not for seeing to his brethren, and giving them some semblance of dignity in death.

Tig crawled his way across Engineering, high-stepping over cables, dodging debris and spare parts floating around him until he reached the bank of fuel cells against one wall.

He'd warned her there was a problem, but hadn't wanted to tell her what it was. Easier to show her. Easier to let *Serengeti* see for herself that one of the three fuel cells left to her was leaking badly—so badly it had started to leach power from the other two. After three years of charging, the power levels in all three fuel cells should be full, even with the small drain from her own consciousness, the robots recharging and using their tools. But a check of the power meters showed the two undamaged fuel cells hovering just above half full and the third all but empty—spewing energy out as fast as the hull collected it and fed it here.

Damn. Another setback we can't afford.

Nothing to be done about it, Henricksen's voice said. *Deal with it and move on. Keep pushing through.*

"Right," *Serengeti* said softly. "Shut it down, Tig. Shut the leaking fuel cell down before it damages the others and we lose all three."

Tig objected, insisting he could fix it. That he was already working on it and with a little more tinkering, he could slow the leak down.

Serengeti listened for a while and then cut the robot off. "No, Tig. There's no time, and we can't spare the parts. Not unless you're telling me you can fix the leak completely. Not just slow it down," she said, as Tig renewed his objections. "*Fix* it. *Really* fix it so it works as well as the others."

Tig fell silent, staring at the failing power cell, face lights swirling slowly.

"Can you?" she asked him. "Can you fix it?"

Tig thought a moment and then shook his head.

"Didn't think so. Shut it down."

Tig gestured to Tilli, waving her over to the cracked power cell. She scuttled behind it and disappearing into the dark, cramped space between the fuel cell and the wall. Micro-sensors picked up *pings* and *bangs*, the sounds of metal on metal as Tilli cut the failing fuel cell's connection to the rest of the power grid.

A crackle of electricity, the whir of machinery spinning down and the fuel cell went dark. *Serengeti* stared at it, wishing they could have fixed it, but the truth was, she didn't think they needed that third fuel cell now. Not if she altered her plan a bit and took herself out of the equation.

Tig won't like it. Nor Tilli either.

Tilli crawled from behind the wall of power cells and scurried back to Tig's side.

I should tell them, *Serengeti* thought, and then realized she didn't need to. She'd granted Tig unprecedented access to her network. He could sense her thoughts, and the feelings that came with them. Knew what *Serengeti* had planned and immediately started to object again.

"Shh. We've not got time for that now, Tig." She stroked at Tig's AI brain until he quieted down. "*Cryo*, Tig. That's what's important. The rest of it...the rest of it's just what-ifs and maybes. Can't really worry about that. Let's focus on *Cryo* for now and let the rest of it work itself out later."

Tig didn't like it, nor Tilli either, just as she'd predicted. But they didn't have much choice in the matter and grudgingly accepted.

Serengeti stoked electric fingers across their cheeks, offering what comfort she could. "Now then," she said, changing the subject. "What about that task I left you? How far have you gotten with that?"

Tig perked up a bit and started chattering excitedly. He whirled around and grabbed Tilli by one leg, dragging her with him as he scuttled out of Engineering.

TWENTY

Tig went flat-out down the corridor, zipping along on his tank treads, all but throwing himself into the ladderway, barely touching the rungs as he descended to the level below. Twists and turns, one corridor connecting to another and another, until they reached a stub of a corridor, and the thick shape of *Cryo's* dull grey door.

Serengeti rolled Tig right up to it and then reached up, touching his leg to the blocky, black letters stenciled across the metal. She paused to wonder if *Cryo's* systems were still working, if Henricksen and the others were still alive or if the lifeboat was yet another graveyard she carried inside her bowels.

"No," she whispered, angry with herself. "They're in there. They're alive."

They *had* to be.

Serengeti let Tig's leg drop back to the floor. "Alright, Tig. We're here. What do you have to show me?"

Tig *beeped* happily, face lights curling in a cat-that-got-the-cream smile as he opened a panel beside the door and retrieved a tiny piece of electronics he'd set inside.

"You planned this," *Serengeti* accused. "You set this all up."

Tig shrugged and *burbled*, denying everything, but his face lights gave him away. Tig always did have a flair for the dramatic.

"Scamp." *Serengeti* chuckled. "All right. Show me."

Tig's smile widened, stretching from one side of his face to the other as he opened another panel and slotted the little electronic device inside.

Click!

Tig turned around, throwing his legs in the air. "Ta-da!"

Serengeti looked round, flicking from Tig's eyes to the camera in his thorax, expecting something magical and amazing after all the buildup. But everything looked the same. As far as she could tell, nothing at all happened.

"Tig?"

Tig smiled in anticipation, looking very pleased with himself.

Five seconds passed, ten, and still nothing.

"Umm...Tig?"

"Uh-huh?" Still smiling, still looking immensely proud of himself.

"I don't think—whatever you did, I'm not sure it worked," *Serengeti* said gently.

"*Beep*?" Tig tilted his head, pincered leg lifting, pointing at a camera high above him. One of the few that still worked on this level.

"What? It's just a camera, I don't—"

Tig pointed again, more insistently this time.

She flipped her consciousness to the camera—mostly to humor him—and looked down on the hallway, watching as Tig waved cheerily and pointed at *Cryo*'s door.

What on earth is he up to? Serengeti wondered. She checked the power levels out of habit, saw them dip a bit more, dropping below the halfway point. *Can't stay. I can't stay here much longer. We need to preserve the power.*

"I don't understand." A hint of impatience crept into *Serengeti's* voice. She'd indulged the little robot's antics until now, but the showmanship was starting to wear thin.

Tig held his front legs up, urging *Serengeti* to be patient. A wink of one cobalt eye as he tapped a leg against *Cryo's* door and turned his head, staring expectantly at *Serengeti's* camera.

"I still don't get it."

Tig *wonked* in frustration and repeated his routine: tap at the door, point at the camera, tap at the door, point at the camera—over and over and over again, Tilli copying him after a while, as if two of them doing the exact same thing would somehow help *Serengeti* understand. And maybe it did, because at some point it finally clicked in her brain.

Not the camera or the door—what was *behind* the door. That's what Tig and Till were trying to show her.

"You could have just *told* me, you know."

Tig shrugged and kept right on smiling. Damn him and his flair for the dramatic.

Serengeti flipped again, probing at pathways, running along damaged circuits that three years' worth of effort had finally repaired. Cameras lay here and there along that pathway and she glanced through each one until she found the one she wanted.

She stopped, and stared, for a long, long time.

"*Cryo*." *Serengeti* smiled in pure, unadulterated joy.

To her relief, she found light inside the lifeboat—not much, just pinpoints here and there, flickering displays showing status of the hyper-sleep units—but light, *any* light, meant power, and power meant her crew was still alive.

She panned the camera around, studying the entirety of *Cryo's* space, flipping through filters until she found one that allowed her to see the best. She zoomed in then and took another look, taking her time, noting the tubes that were active, others that were dark.

"Forty-six." *Serengeti* sighed heavily.

She'd hoped for better, feared it might be worse. Forty-six frail crew left to her, when she'd entered the battle with three hundred and twelve. Forty-six crew still living, stilling *Serengeti's* worries that every last one of them was dead.

"You've done well," *Serengeti* said, returning to Tig and Tilli in the hall. "Thank you, Tig." She slipped inside him and drew a tiny bit of power, brushing electric fingers across his chromed face. "Thank you, Tilli." A second touch, this time at Tilli, who stiffened and *beeped* in surprise before melting with pleasure.

Serengeti laughed softly as the pink-bowed robot spun in circles, *cooing* softly to herself. She left the robots in the hallways and flipped back to *Cryo,* taking a good, long look at the crew inside it. She found Henricksen after a bit of searching and lingered a moment, staring at his face through the tube's frosted glass.

Part of her wanted to stay there forever, just looking at Henricksen's face. But the power levels in the fuel cells kept dropping, and she knew she had to leave. "Sleep well," *Serengeti* whispered. "I'll be back soon. Promise. Just…wait for me, Henricksen. Just a little bit longer." She slipped from *Cryo's* camera and back out into the hall where Tilli spun happily, humming softly to herself. "Time I got going, little ones. It's time for me to return to sleep."

Tilli stopped spinning and drooped like a wilted flower. Tig whistled shrilly, shaking his head.

"Tig—"

He waved his arms and rolled close to Tilli, laying his cheek against hers, whispering words too soft for *Serengeti* hear. Keeping secrets from her as they spoke to one another in their rapid-fire exchange of face lights.

Tig's face lights flashed and flared before settling into a settling into a steady, swirling glow. He straightened and looked up at the camera on the wall, waving his legs at Tilli beside him, *Cryo's* door at the end of the hall, the walls to either side. A burst of staccato chatter erupted from his mouth accompanied by much gesticulating at his robot companion.

"Tig. Tig! What's going on?" *Serengeti* demanded.

Tig waved for her to wait, as Tilli blinked and turned, considering *Cryo's* door a moment and then shaking her head.

More chatter from Tig—a long string of *beeps* and *borps* punctuated here and there by a demure *chirrup* from Tilli. That went on for a few seconds before Tig *wonked* loudly, bringing their discussion to end.

Tilli wilted again, legs sagging as she hunkered close to the floor.

Tig shifted, face lights swirling anxiously. He lifted a leg and lay the end beside his mouth as he leaned close to Tilli. "Ta-da!" he said softly, and then stepped back, front legs raised high as he bounced up and down in excited anticipation.

Tilli shook her head, crouching lower to the ground.

Tig's face lights flashed a frown of irritation. He nudged at Tilli until she looked him. "Ta-da!" he repeated, legs raised in victory.

Tilli eyed him uncertainly, then uncurled a bit.

Tig nodded encouragingly, pointing at Tilli and the door, the walls to either side, before returning to Tilli again, pushed at her, *chortling* reassuringly until Tilli lifted herself up and self-consciously cleared her throat.

"Ta-da!" Tilli fluttered her legs in a half-hearted attempt at Tig's grandiose flourish, and then blushed in embarrassment and hunkered back down.

Nothing.

"Tig. What is—?"

Thud! Thunk!

Something moved inside her—*Serengeti 's* micro-sensors picked it up. That and a persistent buzzing those same micro-sensors translated as metal grating on metal—an angry, agonizing sound that went on, and on, and on. A *clunk* and *rattle* came afterward, shaking the desk plates, causing the robots to skip about.

Something's come loose, she thought. *Something really, really big.*

The micro-sensors reported more rattling, and a heavy, metallic *clang.*

"Ta-da!" Tilli said proudly in the silence that followed.

Serengeti blinked and then laughed aloud, caught completely off guard. Tig spun in excited circles, and making her laugh harder still. Three years. Three long years of concerted effort, eight spent waiting before that, eleven years in total with *Cryo* stuck inside here. And now, at long last, Tig and Tilli had found a way to get the docking clamps undone and set *Cryo* free.

"How soon?" *Serengeti* asked eagerly. "How soon can it take off?"

Tig slammed to a halt, blushing furiously, sneaking sheepish glances at the camera. *"Beep. Beep-beep."*

Nervous, nonsensical sounds—not his usual electronic jabber. The rosy glow started to fade from *Serengeti's* dreams. *"Can* it break free?" she asked him, carefully modulating the tone of her voice.

Tig shrugged and nodded, shrugged again.

That's when it hit her: noise in the hallway, but not enough. Eight docking clamps on the lifeboat—there should have been a hell of a lot more rattling and clanging than that.

"How many?" she asked him. "How many docking clamps have you managed to break free?"

Tig looked up the camera, dropped his eyes back to the floor, kicking at bits of debris floating nearby.

"Tig."

Tig sighed and raised his leg above his head.

"One. That's it?"

Tig nodded apologetically. One docking clamp coaxed loose, seven others still holding *Cryo* in place.

Disappointment washed over her, wiping the last of *Serengeti's* joy away. Tig hung his head, legs sagging inward as he settled onto his tank treads and stared miserably at the ground.

"And the rest?" *Serengeti* asked him.

Tig glanced at Tilli, exchanging a brief spurt of rapid-fire communication. There seemed to be some disagreement at first, but they eventually concurred. Tig leaned to one side and lifted a stalk of his legs off the ground—seven this time—and extruded fingerlike appendages from two of them to add to the count.

Not the most efficient way of doing math, but when *Serengeti* added everything up, the count stood at seventeen.

"Seventeen years," *Serengeti* breathed. The weight to that number almost crushed her, a weight measured in the lives the human crew sleeping inside *Cryo.* Seventeen years—she had no idea if the lifeboat's power could last that long, and even if it did, how much would be left?

Enough to fire the engines, she thought, *and set it on its course. But the sleep chambers, life support, the other higher level functions...there's just no way of telling.*

The sleep chambers only sipped at the power once the crew inside were frozen. They might make it, iced down as they were, and if they didn't, if the cryo chambers failed...

Then they'll sleep infinitely until their travels come to an end.

"Seventeen years, Tig. It's a time to wait. So much could happen between now and then." But at least the robots had given *Serengeti* some hope, and given her crew a chance. "Thank you," she murmured. "Thank you for that." She touched at Tig and Tilli, smiling to herself as they shivered and *blipped*, face lights flashing madly, scattering cobalt light across the iced-over walls. Hard, so very hard to leave them, but staying here wasn't really a choice. "I must sleep now, little ones. And you have work to do."

The robots *hooted* mournfully, metal legs rattling against the floor. That reminded *Serengeti* of something—a task she'd almost forgotten. Again.

"Tig," she said sweetly. "Fix the damn translation routine."

Manually interpreting that robot pidgin was bad enough when there was just one robot running about. The two of them together—*beeping* and *borping* and carrying on—was working on her last nerve.

Tig blinked and lifted two front legs, tapping them beside his mouth before raising one to his temple and offering a slightly sheepish salute.

Good enough.

A last touch at the two robots and *Serengeti* retreated, following the pathways back to the bridge and the darkness, slipping down and down and down to where the dream waited, running rampant in her mind.

TWENTY-ONE

Everything ran like clockwork for a while—amazing, really, considering nothing at all had gone to plan until now. Tig and Tilli worked patiently away, crawling through her innards, swapping out parts, rebuilding circuits, refurbishing the mechanisms that held *Cryo's* docking clamps in place, waking *Serengeti* now and then to update her on their progress.

Progress. Such a lovely, comforting word. *Serengeti* counted her blessings, grateful for the robots' efforts, and that something finally seemed to be going smoothly.

But part of her didn't trust it. Part of her kept waiting for the other shoe to drop.

Sleep and wake, sleep and wake—time ebbing and flowing, one year chasing another. The bow on Tilli's head faded—bright pink dimming to a muted shade of coral. Tig's carapace acquired more scratches and dents, more greasy smudges on his once-bright metal body.

Three years of effort completed the circuit on the second docking clamp, allowing Tig and Tilli—with *Serengeti* in attendance, sharing the momentous occasion—to bust it free. Three more and they pried a third docking clamp loose, but the fourth one proved tricky—balky as *Serengeti's* long lost Number Ten probe. Nearly four years passed—four years of stripping out wires and scavenging parts—before Tig woke *Serengeti* to tell her that fourth clamp was ready to be undone.

Behind schedule already, Serengeti thought as she listened to Tig's report. *Barely halfway through the job and we're already behind. That can't be a good sign.*

To make matters worse, Tig told her they were running short of spare parts. More bad news, considering a cursory inspection of the circuits connected to the docking clamps on *Cryo's* aft end indicated they'd be much more difficult to repair.

Lot of damage there. Mounds of debris standing in the robots' way.

No sense worrying about it, Serengeti told herself as Tig the grandmaster prepared the next show. *Nothing to be done.*

Tig flourished his leg, his magical electronic device clutched between the pincers extruded from its end. A glance at Tilli—who nodded eagerly, obviously this grand unveiling every bit as much as the one before—and he slotted the device into the wall.

The micro-sensors went crazy, translating the vibrations in the decking into *rattles* and *clanks* echoing up and down the hall. A sharp *clang* and heavy *thump*, and yet another docking clamp grudgingly let go.

Power levels dropped precipitously, the fuel cells' carefully stored-up energy expended in a huge, sparking lump, causing error warnings to light up everywhere, screaming for *Serengeti's* attention.

She acknowledged them, and then cleared them—every last one—feeling a vague sense of disquiet settle over her.

That shouldn't have happened. We shouldn't have needed anywhere near that much power to complete such a simple operation.

But the deeper in they got, the more damage the two robots found. Circuits, relays, miles and miles of wiring connecting the many and varied sectors of her network, and all of it shredded, decimated, bodged together spit and bailing wire. Tig's device closed the repaired circuit, sending power racing along broken pathways, but most of it was wasted—disappearing into the ether without ever reaching its destination.

Tig and Tilli worked tirelessly, plugging the holes they uncovered, chasing down the worst of the energy-wasting offenders, but each fix seemed to reveal another problem. No way the robots could fix everything. Oh, they tried—chasing down one rabbit hole and another, slapping hot-fixes in place where a more permanent solution simply wasn't possible—but in the end it was hopeless. Like trying to stop up a leaking dam with your fingers. Or hold back the tide with a wall of sand.

How do I tell them that, though? How do I tell these eager little robots to stop?

Serengeti lingered in the corridor a while, praising Tig and Tilli profusely before pulling away, flitting along the broken line of cameras until she reached the bridge.

She hesitated there, on the edge of letting go—knowing she should because the power levels couldn't sustain her, but not wanting to. Hating the thought of slipping back into the dark, the feel of the dream's chrome and blood shadows flickering across her mind.

Man up, Serengeti.

Silly phrase—one of the more ridiculous bits of wisdom taken from Henricksen's book—but it served its purpose. *Serengeti* steeled herself and disconnected, hating the feel of the dark.

#

Awareness came slowly, the darkness retreating like treacle, leaving *Serengeti* muzzy and confused. Each time was harder. With each waking, she found it more and more difficult to shake the dream off.

Serengeti shook herself, trying to clear the cobwebs from her AI brain. "Tig," she called, beginning the ritual of waking. "How long, Tig? How long have I been asleep?"

Silence on the bridge. That was unusual.

Serengeti tapped into Chron and stared at the numbers it fed back.

3356. Something about that didn't feel right. She counted backward and found two more years gone. Two years since her last waking. *Too soon. It's too soon.*

"Tig?"

Still nothing—no voices in answer, no glowing cobalt eyes, nothing at all coming back to her calls. *Serengeti* reached for the camera, pointing it downward as she peered through its lens. "Tig? Tilli?"

"*Beep. Beep-beep.*" A chromed face appeared from the darkness— one face, just one, with a single pair of cobalt eyes.

Something's wrong. Two faces. There should be two faces to greet me, not just one.

And all that damned *beeping* should've stopped by now.

Serengeti pulled a bit of power to her, sparking a light, bathing the robot in soft illumination, turning its tarnished silver carapace an even more tarnished shade of bronze. "Tig," she said, greeting the robot.

"*Serengeti.*" Tig nodded at the camera.

"Ah. I see we can speak now," she said lightly.

Tig flushed and ducked his head, *burbling* nervously.

Something's definitely wrong, she thought, eying the little robot. *But at least the translation routines haven't gone on the fritz again.*

"Where's Tilli?" she asked, voicing her initial concern. The two robots were almost inseparable—one never far from the other. Waking meant Tig and Tilli together, standing side-by-side as they waited to greet her. *Serengeti* shivered, disliking this change in the robots' patterns. "Where's Tilli?" she repeated, when Tig remained silent. "Has something happened to her, Tig?"

Tig looked up at the camera and shook his head.

That's a relief.

"Where is she then? Why isn't she here?"

Tig pointed at the ceiling above them. "Outside."

Not quite the answer she expected. Tig whirled around before *Serengeti* could ask more questions, legs waving wildly as he scurried across the bridge and into the corridor outside.

"What in the world…?" *Serengeti* stared after him, surprised by the abrupt departure.

Not like Tig. Not like Tig at all.

She chased after him, flitting from camera to camera until she caught up with the little robot, and settled inside Tig's metal shell. "What's going on?" she asked, sensing the anxiousness inside him. "Is it the docking clamps? Have you run into a problem?"

Ten years to clear four docking clamps—they really couldn't afford more setbacks and delays. The last time she woke, they'd been running out of parts, though, forcing Tig and Tilli to start cannibalizing other systems, because there simply wasn't any other choice.

"Tig. Talk to me. Is it the docking clamps?"

Another shake of his Tig's head. She was losing patience with this cryptic nonsense.

"Then what's going on?" *Serengeti* demanded. "Where's Tilli? Why isn't she here?"

"Outside," Tig repeated, and picked up speed, racing along the icy hallways, scrambling up the ladderway to the top tier of the ship.

More hallways there—a seemingly endless series of corridors and crossings that eventually brought them to the hull. Tig rolled to a gap and traded his tank treads for his legs as he scurried inside.

"I'm really not interested in stargazing right now, Tig. Where's—?"

A dark shape appeared in front of them, blotting out the stars. Lights flashed and flared—cobalt fire drawing complex patterns.

"Tilli," *Serengeti* breathed, voice filled with relief.

Tig called out to his pink-bowed companion using swirling patterns of light, and then scuttled through the last layer of hull plating until he reached Tilli's side.

Stars blazed all around them, as cold and pure and brilliant as ever. *Serengeti* hardly noticed them. She wanted nothing to do with daydreams and scenic vistas right now. She just wanted to know what was going on.

Unfortunately, Tig still didn't seem to be talking. He greeted Tilli and then set off, following his winding path across the hull with Tilli following at his side.

"Tig. Stop." *Serengeti* grabbed roughly at the robot's controls, freezing his motors, bringing him to a lurching halt. Tilli kept going for a few feet before realizing Tig wasn't with her and turning around, face lights flashing in question. "Speak. Now," *Serengeti* ordered.

"The stars," Tig blurted, pointing to one side. "A signal. Something's coming."

"Where?"

"There." He pointed again, eyes locking on a distant, twinkling star.

Serengeti stared in confusion. *Stars don't twinkle. Not out here.*

"A ship," she breathed. "It's a ship, not a star. After all these years…" *Serengeti* trailed off, daring to hope, knowing she should fear.

That ship could be anyone: Meridian Alliance, Dark Star Revolution, some nameless, faceless trader or black market profiteer.

She measured the distance from herself to that ship, guessing mostly since she couldn't access her scans. *Guesswork. That's what I've come to. If* Brutus *could only see me now, Serengeti* thought ruefully. *Self-righteous son-of-a-bitch would laugh his ass off.*

Serengeti ran some quick calculations, despising the inaccuracy of it all, knowing it was the best she could do under the circumstances. "Long way out," she murmured. "Long way from anything approximating civilization." Which meant that the ship was either searching, or up to no good. "How did you ever find it?"

Tig *beeped*—strange how nervousness made him fall back on those nonsensical sounds—and turned the other way, pointing to the rounded crest of her hull. "Comms array."

"Comms." *Serengeti* felt a thrill of excitement. They'd had no comms at all the last time she'd gone to sleep. "Show me."

The robots set off, scampering across her hull, making for a tower sticking up from the center of her back. A tower that most definitely hadn't been there the last time Tig took her on a tour of the hull and the stars. Tig rolled to a stop at its base and let *Serengeti* take a good, long look.

The scaffolding appeared to be constructed from salvaged girders. Tig tilted his head back, showing her the improvised communications array clinging like a spider to the tower's top—an odd collection of antennae and curved disks, flaring panels and signal filters they'd fitted together and trained on the stars.

Kusikov would call it ugly and primitive, but *Serengeti* thought it was the most beautiful thing she'd ever seen. "You built this."

Tig nodded, reaching for Tilli beside him. She seldom spoke, shy thing that she was, but she watched and listened, hanging on every word that passed between Tig and *Serengeti*. "We've been listening," Tig said, waving at the stars. "We work and work and work, and then we come here and listen to the dark, thinking something might come. That's how we found it." He turned and pointed at the distant, twinkling spot of light.

"My, my, my. Aren't you the clever ones?" *Serengeti* smiled to herself, amazed at the ingenuity of these lonely little robots. "So tell me: what has our friend out there got to say?"

Tig thought a moment, face lights flashing and swirling. "Show you," he said, with a wink and a smile.

He pulled Tilli close, touching his cheek to hers. Cobalt lights sparked and flared, arcing between the two robots as Tig wrapped one leg around the tower and Tilli did the same.

A hum and burst of static—that's what came through first. Tig tweaked his filters, adjusting a few of internal settings to clean the signal up as best he could. The comms channel was primitive and glitchy, the transmissions it processed grainy and muddled, cutting in and out, but data came through—a flow of electronic information that ran for a while, stopped and looped backward before starting over again.

Serengeti listened closely, letting that loop run three full rounds. "Enough," she said, signaling to Tig and Tilli to cut it off. "I've heard enough. Break the connection. No need to let that ship know we're here."

It likely did already, but *Serengeti* didn't tell Tig and Tilli that. Even half dead, the energy inside her would be visible, especially since her power source was the only thing other than starlight and moondust for light years in any direction. A good thing if that ship out there was part of the Meridian Alliance fleet, but it wasn't. She knew that for sure. The fleet never employed a make and model like that ship out there. In fact, from the little she'd picked up, the distant ship appeared to be ancient—first generation AI if she had to bet. Little more than an automaton, just half a step above that DSR Golem that took out half the fleet.

"Could be DSR, I suppose." But she doubted it. No reason for a DSR ship to be all the way out here, especially on its own. "Scavengers, more likely. Opportunists. Smugglers, maybe. Rumrunners or pirates."

Scum, in other words. The scum of humanity living on the fringes of settled space, skulking through the empty places in their ancient, thin-hulled ships. *Serengeti* almost wished it *was* DSR out there. They'd actually be a better option than the vultures in that ship.

"Not good. Not good at all." *Serengeti* sighed wearily. "We're in trouble, Tig."

Twenty-Two

"So what do we do?" Tig asked, reaching for Tilli as she *trilled* anxiously and crowded close to his side.

"Good question," *Serengeti* muttered, wracking her AI brain, trying to come up with a plan. "I don't know, Tig. I just don't know yet."

Not the most inspiring answer, but the best she had right now. Tig's face lights ticked worriedly, eyes locked onto the ship's distant, twinkling light.

"They're coming for us, aren't they?" Tig asked, using the robot comms channel to communicate with *Serengeti* inside him.

"I fear so, Tig. My guess is they're looking for salvage. They'll send a boarding party across once they're close enough, but..."

Serengeti trailed off, turning Tig's head toward the long line of her hull. Not much left here that the scavengers would be interested in. Just two dented robots and a couple of hard-used power cells keeping each other company inside a wreck warship.

And me, she thought. *Body's scrap, but a Valkyrie-class AI would be quite the score. And there's* Cryo, *of course.*

That worried her—bothered even more than the thought of being ripped out and transplanted somewhere. *Cryo* was worth a small fortune, and a lifeboat—non-AI, registered only to the ship it came from—would be much easier to sell on the black market than a tenth generation combat AI.

They'll cut Cryo *from me if they can, force it open and strip it bare if they can't, taking everything with them but my crew.*

After all, humans—even frozen ones—were a liability. And they weren't worth squat on the black market. Not soldiers like Henricksen, anyway. But Finlay, the other female crew...*Serengeti* shuddered, remembering stories of colony ships stolen—raided as they transited the stars. Colonists sold into slavery. And worse.

No, she thought, anger building inside her. *I won't let that happen. I won't let those scavengers lay one finger on my crew.*

But how to protect them? They couldn't run. Couldn't jump away to safety. Which meant the only option left was to stand and fight.

"Fight." *Serengeti* laughed bitterly. "With what? My guns are silent, my crew all gone." She had Tig and Tilli but they were just two, and hardly fighters at all.

How? she wondered, thinking of Henricksen frozen below, wishing he was here. *How do I stop them? What do I do?*

Henricksen would know. He was nothing if not inventive. Reckless at times. Bold and confident, almost to a fault. But then, he was a Valkyrie captain, and that sort of came with the territory. If Henricksen were here, he'd come up with some half-baked, outlandish idea that only someone desperate or crazy would even think to attempt.

Henricksen. I could use your boldness right now.

Serengeti's designers hadn't programmed in outlandish and crazy. And inventiveness only went so far.

Her gaze drifted, taking in the holes and tears, the shredded mess *Osage's* destruction had left. They'd board her through those gaps—an uncertain path, to be sure, filled with gaps and pitfalls leading down and down and down into the dark, but quicker, easier than to trying to pry one of her cargo bays or airlocks open. She could trap them there she supposed. Lure the scavenger ship's boarding party to one of the gaps and booby trap it to prevent them getting inside.

But even if that worked—and that was a big 'if'—they'd only send more people over. A crippled Valkyrie was too tempting of a target for a scavenger ship to give up just because they lost a few crew.

"Something else. I've got to come up with something else."

Tig *beeped* in question as Tilli danced nervously beside him. *Serengeti* shushed them both and kept looking. Kept *thinking*, trying to bypass AI logic and come at things from Henricksen's view. To devise some crazy, improvised plan that just might get them out of this mess.

She turned Tig's head a bit further and stopped, staring through his eyes at the lumpen shapes of batteries protruding from her side. Batteries gone silent now—their last shots fired when *Osage* exploded and *Serengeti* raced into jump. Silent, but the last she remembered, the firing system behind those guns still worked.

"They just need power."

Serengeti had that, though admittedly in short supply. Enough to charge one, perhaps two of those batteries for a short time. But even if her aim was true, it would take more than a few shots to scare that approaching ship off for good.

Show my teeth—broken as they are—and I may scare it off. But if it comes back, it'll all be over.

"Then I'll just have to make sure it doesn't," she murmured, considering those guns, thinking of the munitions inside her.

Guns and ammunition and a scavenger ship on approach. What was that saying Henricksen had? Something about necessity being the kickass, kill 'em all mother of invention?

"Necessity I've got in spades, and as for invention..." *Serengeti* smiled to herself as the seeds of a preposterous, Henricksen-worthy plan took root. "It's a doozy, but it could work. Or I might blow us all to kingdom come."

Tig *burbled* worriedly. He most definitely did *not* like the idea of being blown up.

"I said 'or', Tig. It's not like I *want* to blow us up."

Oddly, that didn't seem to make Tig feel any better. Nor Tilli either. They huddled together, legs entwined, face lights flittering in anxious patterns.

Tig started to ask questions but *Serengeti* quieted him with a touch at his brain. "A moment, Tig. I'm thinking."

So many details to be considered, so many places for things to go wrong. Her AI mind calculated madly, considering her options, filling in gaps and details, adding flesh to the bare bones framework of her plan.

It's risky—hugely risky. But riskier still to do nothing at all, *Serengeti* acknowledged that. *Henricksen would chance it,* she told herself. Henricksen who was human and reckless. Who never factored in the odds of failure, because failure simply wasn't an option he accepted. *I can't believe I'm even considering this.*

Henricksen would be so proud.

Tig coughed to get her attention.

Serengeti sighed, irritated by the interruption. "What, Tig?" she asked shortly.

"The ship?" He pointed to one side as Tilli danced beside him, metal legs moving up and down, face lights blinking and swirling in urgent, worried patterns.

"I know." *Serengeti* glanced at the stars, calculating the distance to that slow approaching twinkle, guessing how long it would take a ship under power to cross it. "I know what we need to do," she said firmly. "Back inside, Tig. Quickly now. You and Tilli both." She sent a tiny shock of electricity through the robot's body to get him going. "Hurry, Tig, hurry! We don't have much time."

Tig took off like a shot but Tilli hesitated, dancing in an uncertain circle beneath the communications tower before abandoning it and scurrying after Tig and *Serengeti*.

"So what's the plan?" Tig asked.

"You're not going to like it," *Serengeti* warned.

"When do I ever?"

Serengeti laughed—she couldn't help it, Tig sounded so much like Henricksen in that moment—and then filled them both in, making Tig and Tilli complicit in her chancy, all or nothing, last-stand plan.

#

Tig rolled through the hill and into the ship's icy-cold corridors, following *Serengeti's* instructions as he headed for the nearest ladderway and went down and down and down, all the way to Level 9. Level 9 and the hallway from *Serengeti's* nightmares.

"Stop," *Serengeti* said softly, touching at Tig's brain.

Tig rolled to a halt, *beeping* uncertainly, wondering at the delay.

Why? Serengeti wondered, staring down that blackened hallway with its half-melted robots sticking up from the floor. *A dozen different ways we could have gone, so why did I send them here? Why do I keep coming back to this corridor?* This *corridor and no other?*

Tig fidgeted, dancing in place. "There's not much time, *Serengeti*. We should really get going."

"Yes. Yes, of course," she murmured.

Tilli crept forward and Tig followed, legs tippy-tapping against the deck plates as the two robots picked their way through the melted robots and continued on. They turned right at the next crossing and ducked down a side corridor, leaving that place of nightmares mercifully behind. More corridors, more twists and turns, Tig and Tilli dodging this way and that until they rounded a corner and found the way ahead blocked—roof caved-in, walls collapsed, loose cables dangling from the ceiling. And scattered across the floor, dozens upon dozens of unstable plasma rounds.

This, too, *Serengeti* remembered. She'd turned Henricksen and Finlay away from this corridor to save their lives. Now she brought Tig and Tilli here in the hopes she could save those lives again.

"Munitions storage." *Serengeti* pointed at a half-collapsed doorway to one side. "There should be a cart, or sling—something we can use to transport the shells."

Tilli scrambled inside, stepping carefully over the loose rounds in the hallway, easing her way through the sagging doorway. *Serengeti* watched her from the hall, staring through Tig's eyes as Tilli picked through the debris inside the munitions storage room, retrieving two hammock-shaped nets from an emergency locker on one wall and holding them up.

During combat, they relied on an automated feeder system to shuck the ammunition from the storage areas scattered across the ship to the turret guns nearby. But humans, being humans, always insisted on a backup—a manual mode of transportation should the ship's loading system fail. *Serengeti* used to scoff at the idea. After all, a ship flew or didn't—'manual' wasn't a consideration. She never imagined a scenario where she'd appreciate something as archaic as those hammock-shaped slings. Never imagined she'd need a way to manually schlep plasma rounds from her innards to her guns.

"Good. Bring them," *Serengeti* ordered.

Tig stepped backward, making room for Tilli as she worked her way back into the hall, handing one of the hammock nets to Tig, keeping the other for herself. Strong, those nets. Woven from braided lengths of a carbon and aluminum mixture, reinforced with titanium and steel. The same mixture used for decking and hull plating, for components all over her ship's body, making her lightweight but durable, able to move quickly and yet still resist a sustained barrage of fire. Strong and flexible, when braided like this. Able to carry ten times the hundredweight of shells Tig and Tilli gathered up.

Not that weight mattered right now. One bonus of being so beat up: With no atmosphere inside, and no artificial gravity to weigh things down, moving heavy objects became far less tricky.

"Whole shells only," *Serengeti* warned, as Tilli reached for a round with a long crack down its side. "Too risky trying to use the damaged ones."

A trickle of plasma leaked through that seam, staining the deck plates a noxious green. Others around them had drained entirely, voiding their innards across the floor, pitting metal decking, leaving a blackened crust behind.

"Make sure you don't grab any empties either."

Tilli nodded and moved on, filling her sling with a dozen good shells before squatting down on her tank treads and hoisting the load onto her back, using the legs on either side of her body to keep the balky load in place. She waited until Tig was ready—bulging sling perched precariously on his back, slipping to this side and that despite the legs that held it—and then worked her way back the way they'd come.

The trip back was nothing like the frantic rush that brought them to the munitions storage, nor the cheerful *zip-zip-zip* of the robots' usual mode of transportation. Instead, they made a slow, methodical slog back to the nearest ladderway, hampered by the awkward loads the robots carried, bulging, ammunition-filled slings slipping and sliding and trying to get away. Tig and Tilli debated a moment when they reached the ladder and then decided to leave one sling at the bottom and carry the other up between the two of them—Tilli pushing from behind while Tig pulled from above. And when they reached the top—the very last level, riding just beneath the hull—they set the loaded sling down and went back for the other.

A quick stop to readjust loads and Tig and Tilli took off, rolling down one hallway and another until they reached the outer corridor that ran along *Serengeti's* side, and a gaping rent close by the port side Number 13 Cannon.

The robots emptied the slings there, removing the plasma shells one at a time, wedging them in among the debris so they wouldn't roll around or drift away. And then it was back down to the munitions storage to fill back up again, making two trips in quick succession, adding more rounds to the stockpile just inside the hull.

Serengeti studied the pile of shells a moment, wondering if they shouldn't get more. Most of them would go into the Number 13 Cannon while the rest...well, she had plans for the rest. One gun wasn't really enough to destroy a starship after all.

Speaking of which...

Serengeti prodded Tig forward and took a quick look outside. The scavenger ship was definitely closer—still far out, little more than a distant, twinkling light, but larger, brighter than before. "Slow down, you bastard. I'm not ready yet. You come for tea, you give the lady some time to get the kettle on." She glared a moment longer and then spun Tig back around. "Engineering," she ordered, pointing at Tilli, waving her ahead.

Tilli took off without a word, taking the two empty slings with her, glancing backward as she reached the inside corridor to make sure Tig followed. They raced each other down that hallway, moving flat out now that the encumbrance of the shells was gone, zipping left and right and right again before abandoning that level entirely. Down and down and down they went, following one ladderway after another as they worked their way toward Level 4, trundling along corridors until they reached Engineering's rounded, cavernous space.

Serengeti started to have misgivings as soon as Tig stepped inside. Almost called the whole thing off as he grabbed the closest robot carcass and started tearing out its insides. But she couldn't. Not if she was to save Henricksen and the others. Not if the crew inside *Cryo* were to have any chance at survival.

"I'm sorry," *Serengeti* whispered as Tig finished coring the little robot. He stripped off its legs and head and set the empty shell of its carapace aside before reaching for another. "I'm so sorry, but there's no other way."

She didn't want to watch, would have given anything to not be witness to the defilement undertaken in Engineering that day. But it was her plan, her idea to use the robot dead in the first place, and the logical part of her knew the dearly departed wouldn't care. Still, it bothered her. Bothered her more than she could say. Felt like a desecration. A violation of the dead. Of the trust they'd put in her.

So *Serengeti* watched in silence as Tig and Tilli butchered a half dozen robots and loaded their empty bodies up—three to each sling, adding to them a couple of welding rigs stored nearby. Tilli zipped off to gather up some tools and stuff them into the recesses of her carapace while Tig rolled over to the fuel cells to check the power levels.

Ninety-eight percent—just about full. *Serengeti* paused a moment, wondering if it would be enough, or if the pathways between here and the Number 13 Cannon were as damaged as those connected to the docking clamps around *Cryo.*

"We'll know soon enough, now won't we?" Fatalistic thought, entirely unlike her. But then, *Serengeti* hadn't been herself for quite some time now. Not since she dropped out of hyperspace trailing a cloud of debris behind her. "Tilli!" she called, shaking off her melancholy mood, putting the defeatist thoughts aside for another day. "Let's go!"

"Yes, ma'am!" Tilli tucked a wrench set and rivet gun inside her and slipped her storage panel closed before scuttling over to join them. And then she grabbed her sling and followed Tig out of Engineering, and into the hall, down the network of corridors to the ladderway where they repeated the process of shimmying their loads up.

#

Tig welded a last seam and then shut the rig off. Tilli's torch flared a second or two longer and then it too cut off, plunging their little workspace inside the hull into darkness.

"Let me see," *Serengeti* said.

"You doubt our skills?" Tig looked a bit offended. Tilli stared at him in horror, head moving from side to side.

"You're getting cheeky, you know that?"

Tig shrugged and rolled to one side of the rig, letting *Serengeti* take a look. Tilli glanced across the rig at him, waiting for his nod before flipping on the little light in her chest. It flickered and then steadied as

Tig's own light came to life, the two tiny beacons shining on the contraption between them. A construction of *Serengeti's* own design.

"Well? What do you think?" Tig asked her.

It was ugly, if she were honest. A hastily put together construct that looked exactly like the collection of spare parts it was. Speed was the order of the day and Tig and Tilli had hurried, punching holes in the salvaged carapaces, using screws and rivets to bring the rounded bodies together in a stacked hexagonal shape that somewhat resembled an oversized molecule with six compressed nitrogen fire extinguishers welded on the outside.

Ugly but functional, Serengeti thought.

"It's perfect, Tig. Exactly what we need. Load it up and get it into place."

"You heard the lady." Tig nodded to Tilli and she turned around, lifting plasma shells from the pile behind her, handing them to Tig one at time.

Two shells went into each of the six carapaces, and when the last shells was loaded, Tig sealed them all up, using a rivet gun this time—bad idea using a welding rig that close to plasma rounds.

Serengeti paused as Tig popped off a last rivet and stared at the awful, murderous thing she'd created.

How did it ever come to this? she wondered. *A homemade bomb built from scrap parts and salvaged munitions—how did I ever sink so low?*

Desperate times call for desperate measures, Henricksen's voice said.

Blah-blah-blah. You're so full of shit.

She thought she heard him laugh, but she knew that was crazy. Henricksen was frozen below. It was just her up here. Just her and the two robots, plotting and scheming as the scavenger ship drew near.

Enough daydreaming. There's work to do.

"Take the rest outside." *Serengeti* lifted one of Tig's legs, waving vaguely at her hull. "Load them in the magazine of the Number 13 Cannon."

"Ummm..." Tig blushed brightly, glanced over at Tilli. "See, here's the thing. We kinda, sorta...don't know how."

"Idiot," *Serengeti* muttered, berating herself. She should have remembered. The guns had an automated feed and manually loading the magazine...well, that particular operation wasn't in the TIGs' programming. "Just try," *Serengeti* told them. "It can't be *that* hard."

Tilli coughed loudly, flashed Tig a skeptical look.

"Look. It's not like we have a whole lot of options here. The magazine's set in the hull just behind the gun. Take some tools and pry the damn thing open if you have to. I'll *help* you," she added, when Tig continued to object.

"Fine," Tig huffed, waving to Tilli. He helped her gather up the remainder of the salvaged ammunition before stepping outside. "But don't blame *me* if we screw this up."

"You screw this up, Tig, and I won't be around to blame you for anything."

Tig stopped short. "Oh. Right." He scuffed at the decking, face lights swirling in shamefaced patterns. "Sorry. Forgot." He shrugged and got going again, leading Tilli to the gun high above.

As it turned out, it was easier to get into the magazine than *Serengeti* thought. A section of hull plating just behind the battery had torn away during the fighting, or maybe afterward during jump. And with a little effort and a lot of elbow grease, the two robots managed to loosen the decking above the magazine and lever it up so they could wrestle the canister-shaped magazine beneath open.

To *Serengeti's* surprise, the magazine was already half full. *Look at that. Something went right for a change.*

Tig dropped another two dozen shells inside, bringing the count inside the oversized magazine to an even hundred.

A hundred rounds. That should give those bastards out there something to think about.

Serengeti turned Tig's head toward the stars. She could see the bastards now, their ship no longer a twinkling, far-off light. Instead, a shadow stalked off her port side, showing grey against the blackness, slipping stealthily from the depths of space, hiding the stars behind it.

"I see you," *Serengeti* said, flipping from Tig's eyes to a recessed camera set inside her hull. "I see you out there. I know what you are." The shape of it was clearer with the camera's magnification focused in tight. *Serengeti* studied and recognized the design from her inventory—a sort of history of interstellar ships. "Proteus," she murmured. "Never actually seen one in the flesh." Just pictures, images captured in the yearbook each interstellar ship carried. "Hey there, old timer." She zoomed the camera in to its maximum extent, trying to get a better look.

Not much to see yet, just that long, thin shape reminiscent of the Aphelion, but smaller, wider. The shape of a short-haul cargo pusher— that's what the Proteus class ships were designed for, she'd heard some of them were still out there doing just that: trucking ore and scrap metal and other bulk commodities from one in-system planet to another. But this one...

"What's your story, I wonder? How the hell does a relic like you end up all the way out here?"

Doubtful she'd ever know—if things went right she certainly wouldn't—but *Serengeti* suspected the ship had been retrofitted at some point. Probably outfitted with one of those leaky, half-assed jump drives the chop-shops offered up. After all, no in-system drive would get them out here. And scavengers, bootleggers—that class of humanity pretty much ran everything on the cheap.

"I'm sorry you got dragged into this, old timer, but I didn't invite you out here. And I'm pretty sure whoever's inside you is up to no good."

Tig sealed up the magazine on the Number 13 Cannon and scuttled back inside where Tilli waited, legs wrapped around one side of the awkward contraption she'd helped Tig build. Tig flashed a quick communication as he took his place on the other side of the bomb, copying Tilli's stance, grasping the edges tightly as they lifted the contraction together and dragged it onto her outer hull. A few scuttling steps and they dropped it again, setting the odd-looking construction down with its front end facing outward toward space, and the muzzles of the extinguishers welded to it pointed toward *Serengeti's* insides.

Tig signaled to her, letting *Serengeti* know their little surprise was ready, grabbed Tilli by the leg and scuttled to where their weapons waited—two pulse rifles and a few hundred rounds of ammunition salvaged from the small arms locker on Level 3. *Serengeti* watched the two robots arm themselves and then take up position just inside her hull, looking bold and yet somewhat silly—almost ridiculous with those oversized blasters clutched by their jointed, insectile legs.

My brave little robots, Serengeti thought fondly, eyes turning back to the approaching ship.

If the scavenger crew boarded her, the robots' resistance would likely do little good. They were TIGs after all, not battle droids, and not programmed for combat. *Serengeti* felt fiercely proud of them, just the same. Her plan might not work, but if they go down, they'd go down fighting—she and Tig and Tilli, all of them together.

Serengeti took a last look through the camera before flipping back to Tig's eyes. "I know you're coming, you bastards," she said, staring at the scavenger ship. "We may not win this, but we're not going down easy."

Twenty-Three

Serengeti and the robots waited and waited as the Proteus approached. It drifted near, looming large and somehow ominous, despite that it was nowhere near the size of *Serengeti* herself, and took up position just a couple of kilometers off her port side. And there it sat for nearly an hour—floating along beside her while *Serengeti* watched its cargo doors, waiting for one to open.

"C'mon, c'mon, *c'mon*," she muttered. "What's taking them so long? What are they *doing* over there?"

She checked the power levels on the fuel cells for the hundredth time, found they'd dipped down a bit further, hovering just above ninety percent.

Not good. Not good at all.

She threw a worried look at the Number 13 battery, wondering how many shots ninety percent would get them.

I only need one, she thought.

Granted, it had to be the *right* one, planted in just the right place, but she was AI, with an AI's targeting skills, and really, how many times could she miss?

Plenty, a voice whispered in a sour, glowering tone.

Henricksen again. He always chided her for being overconfident.

She missed Henricksen dearly. *Desperately.* Would have given just about anything to have him standing here beside Tig and Tilli.

"Focus, *Serengeti.*"

Her voice this time, not Henricksen's. Her voice inside Tig's body, talking to herself.

Tilli gave her a strange look.

Probably thinks I've lost it.

"Not yet. Not quite yet," *Serengeti* murmured, studying the ancient, oh-so-suspicious Proteus drifting by her side. The ship was closer now, the shape of it a bit clearer, but as she watched it, something began to bother her. "It's gone quiet."

Tig *blipped* worriedly. "That can't be good," he said, speaking over the internal channel.

"No. It can't." *Serengeti* dialed up Tig's comms channel, listening in the dark.

This close, the Proteus—ancient as it was, comms package lacking the baffles and filters the newer ships employed—should have fairly radiated data that any antennae, any scan dish, any sensory equipment at all would pick it up. But when *Serengeti* tapped into Tig's brain, she found nothing—not one communication, not a single errant sound.

Not good. Not good at all.

Serengeti shut Tig's comms system down on the odd chance someone on that ship was listening for her. "They're coming," she warned, touching at Tig's brain, passing those words from her mind to his.

She reached for Tilli and passed the same message, bypassing the robot's internal communications channel entirely, fearing that ship out there might pick up anything they passed down that line.

"Is everything ready?" *Serengeti* pulled Tilli close, touching Tig's cheek to hers so she could speak to both robots at once.

"Ready," Tig nodded.

"You're sure?" She wanted to believe him, but there was too much riding on this for them to inadvertently miss something.

Tig nodded again, careful of attracting attention by making too much noise. He pointed to the robot carapace sculpture with its welded on fire extinguishers to prove his point.

"The gun. The Number 13 Cannon. Did you prime the chamber?"

Tig nodded automatically and then froze, eyes widening, spots of light flaring and dying in his face.

"Tig?"

"Forgot," he admitted, flush deepening. "Tilli?" he asked hopefully.

Tilli squeaked and quickly shook her head.

"Rats." Heavy sigh. "Tilli didn't either. Sorry, *Serengeti.* We missed it. With all the rushing around, we just forgot to prime the gun."

"Dammit, Tig! How could you forget that?"

Serengeti's anger came through clearly. Tig ducked his head, offering a soft sound of apology that cut at her heart and made her regret her sharp words.

Not fair. Not fair blaming him when she was just as much at fault. Tig wasn't a weapons expert, nor Tilli either. The TIGs weren't designed for combat—she had the TSDs for that. She could have reconfigured them, of course—the TIGs were infinitely adaptable—but that would take time. Time she didn't have.

My fault, Serengeti thought, berating herself for the oversight. *Should have asked earlier. Should have spent less time obsessing over the power levels in the fuel cells and more watching what the robots were doing.*

Nothing to be done about it now. She'd just have to trust in Tig and Tilli to put things to rights.

"Tig—"

Movement out there, among the stars. A crack appeared on the Proteus' starboard side, a door splitting open and sliding slowly to either side.

Serengeti did some quick calculations, estimating how long it would take for the doors to fully open, to fire up the shuttle that must be inside that ship and navigate it across the gap between them.

It's going to be close. Damn close.

"The gun. Go, Tilli. Hurry!"

"On it!" Tilli tossed her rifle to Tig and stripped the bandoliers of ammunition from her body, chucking them after the rifle, not even waiting to see if Tig caught them as she grabbed up her welding rig and took off like a scalded rat.

They couldn't see her—not from their shelter inside the hull—so Tig rolled forward a bit and stuck his head outside, risked exposing that little bit of himself so he could follow Tilli with his eyes.

Tilli looked tiny out there, all by her lonesome. Tiny and vulnerable—a scuttling silver shape showing bright against *Serengeti's* scorched and broken side. She raced for the huge gun and the cover it provided while behind her the Proteus' cargo bay door kept grinding open.

Tig whistled worriedly, front legs rubbing together like a giant, anxious cricket. "They'll see her. If that shuttle comes out—"

"It's alright," *Serengeti* told him. "She'll make it, Tig. There's still time."

"How do you know?" he asked her, voice filled with worry. "How can you be sure?"

She didn't, but what else was she going to say. "She'll make it, Tig." She had to. *Serengeti* couldn't lose Tilli. Not after all the others. "Hurry, Tilli. Hurry," she whispered, willing the little robot to go faster.

She split her consciousness, watching Tilli through Tig's eyes while simultaneously looking behind them, keeping track of the Proteus' doors. Halfway open now, a yawning darkness showing inside the ancient ship.

A minute, maybe two—that's all we've got before the transport craft comes out.

Serengeti hoped it was enough.

Tilli reached the gun and scuttled behind it, all but disappearing from view. A flare of light erupted when she ignited her welding torch, using a super-heated rod to melt through composite metal turret and get at the Number 13 Cannon's firing mechanism. Not the most inconspicuous means of access, but there wasn't really any other choice. The gun's firing mechanism was in the back of the battery, right above the recessed magazine, but it had never been designed for manual operation. The ship's design never even *considered* such a daft idea. After all, what engineer in their right mind would ever think an AI and two beat-up robots would need to cold cock a gun to fight off interstellar pirates?

Another check of the Proteus showed the cargo doors were almost two thirds of the way open, the space behind them growing wider and wider with each passing second.

A last flare of light and Tilli's torch cut out. A flash of metal legs as the little robot leaned from behind the battery and set a square of metal down, edges glowing brightly for a second or two before cooling to the dull, silver-grey color of the rest of the ship. The square of metal floated free, joining the cloud of debris drifting around *Serengeti's* body.

Hope they didn't see that, she thought.

She focused in on Tilli and saw her just standing there, staring back at them, legs wringing nervously. She shrugged in apology as the sheet of metal drifted away and scurried behind the cannon, crawling inside it to get at the firing controls.

"Tilli-Tilli-Tilli," Tig whispered worriedly, front legs rubbing together like mad.

Hard to sit there waiting, not knowing what Tilli was up to. *Serengeti* debated a moment and then split her consciousness again, carving off yet another piece of her mind and reaching it toward Tilli.

But she couldn't find her. Couldn't reach Tilli, no matter what she did.

Panic—complete and utter panic for a moment, before *Serengeti* realized it was simply too far—not enough working connections between here and there for her mind to make the jump.

Damn. Damn and damn and damn.

She let go and fell backward, returning that bit of her mind to Tig's body. And there she waited, keeping one eye on the Number 13 Cannon above while the other watched the Proteus' cargo bay.

Three quarters of the way open now. It wouldn't be long before the Proteus' transport craft poked its nose out.

"Hurry, Tilli," *Serengeti* whispered. "Please hurry."

They waited in agony, she and Tig together, watching the gun and the cargo bay, looking for movement—a flash of metal, any telltale sign of life from either side. The cargo bay opened wide, doors sliding a last few feet and then stopping, but there was nothing—no shuttle, just that black hole in the Proteus' hull. And then,

"*Beep. Beep-beep. Beep-beep-beep-beep,*" across Tig's internal comms.

"Tilli!" Tig pointed excitedly, leg end twitching toward the gun above as a stalk of jointed legs appeared, poking from behind the Number 13 Cannon. A rounded head followed and two cobalt eyes looking down at Tig.

Tilli raised a leg, fingerlike appendages extruding from its end as she flashed a thumbs up—or giving them the finger, they both looked the same coming from a robot—and crept from her hiding place. Three quick steps she froze again, eyes locking onto the Proteus, and the shuttle exiting its cargo bay doors.

Tig turned his head, looking at the ship behind him. "Too close-too close-too close!" he babbled loudly, legs waving, teetering on the edge of panic. "They'll see her! They'll know!"

"Hush," *Serengeti* whispered. "None of that now, Tig. They'll hear you."

Tig *beeped* and nodded, leg ends wringing worriedly.

"Good. Now face around and tell Tilli to run!"

Tig wheeled about and started flashing, throwing urgent, anguished communications to Tilli frozen above. She shook her head at first, conscious of the shuttle creeping from the Proteus' hull, hunkering down like a scared rabbit, refusing to move. She looked behind her at one point, and seemed to consider scuttling back behind the Number 13 Cannon, but Tig was insistent, face lights flashing desperately, begging Tilli to come down because they needed her to maneuver their secret weapon into position. Because he knew there was nowhere safe out there.

"C'mon, Tilli," *Serengeti* whispered.

Tilli stared at the ship, then flicked her eyes to Tig, face blank, eyes glowing like two tiny blue moons. A second passed, then two and she finally made her decision. She scuttled across the hull, metal legs moving a blur as she scurried to the gaping rent in *Serengeti's* where Tig waited.

She grabbed at him and pulled Tig close, hugging him tight as she shivered and shook.

"Shh," *Serengeti* breathed, reaching for Tilli, stroking at her AI brain. "It's alright. It's alright, Tilli. You made it. You're safe."

But they weren't. Not yet. The Proteus' shuttle fired its maneuvering jets firing, lining itself up with *Serengeti's* side.

Not much time. Not much time left.

"Shh, Tilli. That's enough now. I need you to focus."

Tilli shivered and hugged Tig tighter, face lights flashing in random patterns. *Serengeti* waited, conscious of the little ship moving closer and closer, feeling the weight of each second ticking by.

"Tilli. Look at me," she ordered.

The shivering stopped. Tilli heaved a sigh and gave Tig a last squeeze before disentangling herself and letting him go. Tig handed her rifle over, passed the bandoliers of ammunition back. Tilli accepted it all, gripping the pulse rifle tightly, draping the chains of spare ammunition around her body, and then she just stood there—head bowed, eyes staring at the ground—a sad, apologetic bandit waiting for the train to arrive.

"The gun. Is it ready? Is the firing mechanism primed?"

A quick nod, head moving up and down. "Yes, ma'am," Tilli whispered without looking up.

"Good." *Serengeti* touched at Tilli's chin, pressing with Tig's leg until her head lifted. "Good," she repeated. That got a tremulous smile. "Now you and Tig grab our little surprise and move it further out."

The scavengers would see them for sure—hard to miss a couple of insectile robots pushing a lumpen conglomeration of metal spheres around—but at this point it didn't matter. One way or another, it would all be over soon.

The robots wrestled their homemade contraption-cum-art project out into the open, carrying between them, shimmying it a bit this way and a bit the other based on *Serengeti's* instructions. Instructions that were equal parts guesswork and informed deduction based on what little she remembered of the Proteus' internal design.

"Good enough. Now light the candle and let that birthday cake fly."

"On three," Tig said, looking across the contraption at Tilli. He pointed at himself, then her, and finally at the ugly sculpture between them.

"Three," Tilli nodded.

"Ready?"

"Ready?" Another nod from Tilli, more certain this time.

Tig glanced to one side, checking the position of the shuttle before lifting a fourth leg and extruding one finger and another. The count hit three and Tig and Tilli fired, keying the ignition switch on all of the fire extinguishers at once. The rig shuddered and lurched and finally got on its way, zigging and zagging across the space between *Serengeti* and the Proteus, its crude, fire extinguisher engines expelling their loads at differing rates.

"Come on. Come on," *Serengeti* whispered. The Proteus was a big target, and she doubted they'd miss, but still...

The canisters burned for thirty seconds—long enough to push the rig past the shuttle, not quite long enough for it to reach the scavenger ship itself—before cutting out. After that, the rig just drifted, gliding serenely toward to the Proteus' hull.

"Back inside," *Serengeti* ordered. "Now, Tig!" she yelled when the little robot hesitated.

Tig jumped and whirled around, grabbing Tilli by one leg and hauling her with him as he scuttled inside the hull, creeping over holes in the floor and mounded piles of debris until he reached the icy confines of the corridor inside.

"Keep going. All the way to Engineering. Don't look back!"

"But—"

"No time to argue, Tig. Just go!" *Serengeti* shocked Tig to make him move faster and then fluttered away, splitting her consciousness in two, leaving one half behind to stare outside through one of her few working hull cameras, while the other raced along long dormant pathways, flitting from one section of her network to another until she finally reached the bridge. The bridge and the Artillery station where Sikuuku had died.

He was gone, mercifully, his body cleared away by the robots, but Sikuuku's blood still showed as a red-brown stain on the floor. *Serengeti* paused there, staring at the crushed remains of the gimbaled Artillery station, remembering Sikuuku smiling, laughing, swearing as he pounded away, firing round after round from the forward main gun.

Gone. All of them gone now—Sikuuku, Kusikov, Evans, Tsu.

"No more," *Serengeti* said firmly. "I'm done losing crew."

She slipped inside the Artillery station and brought it back to life. Everything was there, just as she knew it would be—damaged, to be sure, but most of the connections still intact. Including those to the Number 13 Cannon. She'd checked those before—you bet she had, in between bouts of worrying about the fuel cells in Engineering.

Serengeti drew a bit more power, bringing the Number 13 Cannon on-line, pointing the big gun toward the Proteus, lining up the crosshairs of its targeting mechanism with the shining stack of spheres Tig and Tilli had launched into space. Her eyes outside gave her an off-angle view, showing the metal rig just few hundred meters from the Proteus' hull, the scavengers so close now she could see the crew in its cockpit making a last few adjustments as they came alongside and prepared to board.

Now. It has to be now. Before they leave that ship and make their way inside.

More power, a flood of energy draining from the fuel cells in her belly, channeled through the Artillery station to the Number 13 Cannon in one big slug. The gun came alive, spitting out unstable plasma rounds, spewing out globes of swirling fire and spinning death. Number 13 rattled away for ten glorious seconds, chewing through its load of shells and then spinning uselessly, trying to suck more up.

Power warnings everywhere, flashing, screeching, screaming at *Serengeti* as she shut Artillery down. Outside, she could see the shuttle doors opening, human shapes in space suits lining up, preparing to step off. Shots from the Number 13 battery slammed into the Proteus, cratering its decking, tearing holes in its hull, more shots slipped past it, tracking in a line that intercepted Tig and Tilli's contraption as it drifted close to the Proteus' tail.

A flare of light as the twelve rounds of ammunition inside the rig ignited. *Serengeti's* bomb exploded, tearing the Proteus' aft end away. A second explosion—this one *inside* the scavenger ship—followed by another and another.

The Proteus hauled over, burning, fracturing, huge cracks appearing everywhere, peeling open its sides. The boarding crew in the shuttle glanced backward as explosion after explosion shredded the Proteus' hull. A last detonation—this one larger, more violent than the others— and the Proteus all but disappeared.

Debris flew everywhere, scattering across the empty darkness, slamming into the scavenger ship's shuttle, smashing it against *Serengeti's* side. The shockwave hit her, rocking her hard, pushing, tearing, ripping away more plating, clawing hungrily at the girders behind.

The camera went blank, *Serengeti's* eyes on the stars gone suddenly, irrevocably blind. Warnings inside her, screaming stridently, flashing *Failure-Failure-Failure* in bloody red letters. Power levels dipped and dipped again, dropping precipitously. She was lost for a moment—part of her consciousness firmly anchored to the bridge, the other drifting, wandering along severed pathways, until it found its way home. The two parts of her mind reunited and *Serengeti* opened her eyes and looked down upon the bridge.

"Tig. Tilli." She reached for a bit of power and finding nothing there—nothing but a thin skim of energy left inside her fuel cells. And that trickling between her fingers, running across the floor. "No."

Darkness—immediate, instantaneous, closing in around her, thicker, deeper than ever before. Darkness and fear, washing over her, sucking her down.

"Tig. Tilli," she called, fighting that darkness, suffocating in the black.

She could feel herself slipping, fading away, and the harder she struggled, the more tightly the darkness clung, wrapping around her like a straightjacket as it dragged her down and down and down.

"Henricksen!" she screamed, a last desperate call.

Silence, only silence, as unending as the dark.

"Henricksen," *Serengeti* whispered, and then there was nothing. Nothing at all.

TWENTY-FOUR

The candidate saluted smartly, spun her heel and walked stiff-backed out the door. *Serengeti* stared after her, overwhelmed by disappointment. Fourteen candidates, fourteen utter failures—not a single one of them worthy of her captain's chair.

Seychelles' laughter floated across the Valkyries' internal channel, linking directly into *Serengeti's* mind. Just their two voices on that channel right now, but *Serengeti* knew *all* the Valkyries were listening. Less than five hundred of them in the fleet now, which made each new captain's assignment something of an event. The choosing, though, was *Serengeti's* and *Serengeti's* alone. Even *Seychelles*—trusted companion, invited by *Serengeti* to sit in—had no say. Not that that stopped her from giving her opinion.

"She's worthy, Sister," Seychelles said. "You're just picky."

"Perhaps," *Serengeti* acknowledged. But she'd earned that right. They all had. Every last Valkyrie that sailed the stars fighting for the Meridian Alliance. "How many are left?"

"Just one," *Seychelles* told her. "After that…it's choose from the candidates you've already rejected or wait another year until a fresh batch of captains rotates through. A gamble either way if this one doesn't work out."

"Then let's hope it doesn't come to that." *Serengeti* keyed the comms, calling to the invisible gatekeeper controlling access to the interview room. "Send him in."

The plasmetal door sighed open revealing a Spartan sitting area—bare walls and hard plastic chairs, a gridded, plasmetal floor with a spinning fan circling endlessly above. Just a single occupant in that room, standing close by the door.

"Enter," *Serengeti* called.

A dip of a close-shaved head and the last of the candidates advanced, stepping purposefully into the interview room, striding towards its center. No urgency in that approach, nothing stiff or jerky, no apparent nervousness like *Serengeti* observed in the others. This one was all grace and confidence, every movement smooth and efficient. And male, unlike the others.

"Interesting," *Seychelles* murmured.

Serengeti grunted. "That's one word for it."

Females made far superior captains in *Serengeti's* opinion. The selection board knew her preference—all four of her previous captains had been female, after all—and sent her female candidates to this point. But now came this one...

"Not quite sure I'm ready to break that tradition."

"Tradition exists to be broken," *Seychelles* told her.

Serengeti snorted. "Confucius tell you that?"

"Fortune cookie. Same thing really," *Seychelles* said, smile in her voice.

Serengeti barked a laugh

Ten striding steps and the candidate stopped in front of *Serengeti*, raised a hand to his temple and tossed off a salute.

Casual, that salute. Nothing like the crisp formality the other candidates offered. He clasped his hands behind him, legs spread wide, eyes locked onto *Serengeti's* borrowed face.

The TIG she inhabited burbled nervously, discomfited by the intensity of that grey-eyed gaze, but *Serengeti* just laughed softly.

Cocky, she thought, smiling to herself.

She liked cocky. Shumitsu was cocky, right up until the end.

Shumitsu.

Serengeti sobered, remembering blood and broken bodies, ship's hull torn wide open, her backbone cracked, compartments bleeding environmentals into space.

"Peace, Sister," *Seychelles* whispered.

Serengeti cleared the images, forcing them back into storage with all the others—every last memory of the four crews that came before.

Seychelles touched at her mind—a soft caress of commiseration and then retreated, watching in silence with the other Valkyries as *Serengeti* considered this, the fifteenth candidate for her empty captain's chair.

Fifteen. The number felt important. For the life of her, *Serengeti* wasn't sure why.

"Henricksen," the candidate said, offering a nod.

"So I see." *Serengeti* pointed one of the TIG's legs at Henricksen's name tag.

That earned a laugh. Henricksen's scarred face twisted into a lopsided smile.

"Oh, I like him," *Seychelles* murmured.

"Shush, you," *Serengeti* growled over the private channel.

"Just be open-minded, *Serengeti.* I've seen his record—"

"Not my style—you know that, *Seychelles.* Records are just facts and figures. They say nothing of the person themselves."

"Just give him a chance, *Serengeti.* I think…just give him a chance."

Seychelles retreated again, leaving *Serengeti* alone with Henricksen.

She studied the captain, letting the silence stretch between them to see how he'd react.

If the quiet bothered him, he didn't show it. Henricksen just stood there, still as a statue, grey eyes blinking now and then, but otherwise looking entirely nonplussed by the situation.

Surprising—most humans *hated* long silences—but *Serengeti* found many things surprising about this man Henricksen. His choice of uniform not the least among them. The others came in their finest—dress uniforms starched and pressed until they were stiff as their owners, weighed down by a whole host of medals and ribbons and fancy gold braids, ceremonial swords, jangling loudly at their sides. But this one…Henricksen presented himself in simple ship's uniform—black on black heavy canvas with silver stars of rank on the collar and his name picked out in silver thread, a very heavy, very utilitarian-looking matte black pistol strapped tight to one leg.

Silver stars and silver letters, that simple yet well-kept pistol, and nothing more. No medals proclaiming his bravery, no ribbons to mark a long line of bloody campaigns and feats of daring-do, not even so much as a patch on his shoulder. And that, in the end, is what sparked her interest.

No patch meant no ship's assignment—either he hadn't earned one, or he'd lost the one he'd been detailed to. One peek at his record and she'd have her answer, and know which it was.

Tempting, she thought, *but no.*

Serengeti considered Henricksen's, serene, scarred face and decided to shake things up a bit to see how he reacted. "Do you have any questions?"

Most of the candidates went blank when she asked that and simply shook their head. A few hemmed and hawed and managed stammered out a question, usually about the other candidates—had a selection been made, was the position already filled, that kind of thing.

Henricksen paused a second, head tilting, and then flipped a hand at the room around them. "Why here? Why hold the interviews on station rather than on your bridge?"

"Ship is for crew," she told him. "Which you aren't."

"Yet."

Serengeti couldn't help but laugh. Shumitsu would've appreciated that answer.

Henricksen's lips quirked in a small smile of victory. "Why the TIG?" he asked her, nodding at the robot body *Serengeti* inhabited.

"You'd prefer something else? Something more…human, perhaps?"

Henricksen shrugged. "Don't really care to be honest. Just curious. Last AI I served…" Henricksen trailed off, face softening, eyes drifting to one side.

"You don't wear a patch," *Serengeti* noted.

"No."

One word, softly spoken. He caught her eyes—well, the TIG's eyes with *Serengeti* inside, looking through them—and then slid his gaze away, nodding meaningfully at the camera on the wall.

"No one but the Valkyries watching. Trust me on that."

Henricksen thought a moment, head cocked to one side.

"Tell me," *Serengeti* said softly—as softly as Henricksen had before.

He frowned and crossed his arms over his chest. "It's in my rec—"

Serengeti shook the TIG's head. "Records are just that: full of truths that are just as often false. *Tell me,* Henricksen. In your own words, not that company speak some officer put down."

A last look at the camera. "Alright. What the hell. Black Ops." He brushed his fingertips across the blank material on his shoulder. "No patch because no ship. At least in theory."

"Black Ops. You're a Raven." Not the answer *Serengeti* expected. Not the type of captain she expected the board to send her. "And before that?"

"Two Titans and an Aurora."

"Which—"

"Gone," he said, cutting her off. "Dead. Crew—" Henricksen grimaced and touched his fingers to the scar on his face. "It's a terrible thing to lose crew," he told her. "But far more terrible to lose an AI."

Yet another unexpected answer. Humanity had mixed feelings about the AI they'd created—AI that now created themselves, using human-based specifications as the building blocks. *Serengeti* marked another tick in the good column.

"Black Ops, then."

Henricksen nodded tightly. "After the Aurora. Thought to make a go at a Valkyrie command but…" He shrugged. "Black Ops were the badasses, right? And I figured I had a better chance at a Valkyrie with the added time under my belt."

Smart. So many surprises in this one. So many layers *Serengeti* never would have expected. But she had to be sure. Had to be absolutely certain he was the one to sit her chair.

"So why did you leave?"

Shrug of Henricksen's shoulders. "Got tired of not being in it."

"What do you mean?"

Henricksen rubbed his chin, thinking a moment. "Well, it's like this. We run recon, right? Slip in, sniff around the edges, send info back to the fleet, but then we just sit back and watch while everyone dies. Not why I got in it," he said, anger creasing his brow. "Got tired of it. Tired of being witness to all the dying." He drew a breath, touching that scar on his face. Unconscious gesture. Likely didn't even realize he was doing it. "'Sides. Citadel started moving away from human crews for the Ravens. All drones, all the way—wave of the future, or some such." Henricksen laughed bitterly. "They wanted me to leave and I wanted out. Everyone wins." He spread his hands, smiling ruefully, but the anger lingered, lurking deep within his hawkish grey eyes.

"So you chose the Valkyries, knowing we're out there, fighting on the front lines."

Henricksen shook his head. "I didn't *choose* the Valkyries." He folded his arms, moving a step closer to the TIG. "I chose *you, Serengeti.*"

"The AI chooses her captain," *Serengeti* said coldly. "Not the other way 'round."

"Aye," he said, dipping his head in acknowledgement. "And I came here hoping you'd have me, shoddy record and all." The smile twisted, becoming a colder, angrier version of that cocky grin he'd shown her before.

"Why?" she demanded. "Why me above my Sisters?"

He flicked his eyes to the camera, choosing his words carefully. "Saw you at Terinassis."

"Terinassis? Terinassis was a disaster. I lost nearly a third of my crew there."

"And you *saved* the rest," Henricksen said quietly. "Blew holy hell outta your chassis, gaping wounds up and down your sides, but you got your crew *out, Serengeti.*" Henricksen paused, nodding slowly. "That's when I knew for certain. That's when I set my eyes on your captain's chair."

Serengeti stared in amazement, honestly not knowing what to say. "And what if I won't have you?" she finally asked.

"What are you doing?" *Seychelles* whispered urgently.

Serengeti felt her friend stirring, pushing to the fore, but she shoved her away and focused on Henricksen. "What if I deem you unworthy and choose another to sit my captain's chair?"

"Honestly hadn't thought about it," Henricksen admitted. "Try for another Valkyrie I suppose."

"Another," *Serengeti* repeated, surprisingly hurt. "When you told me not a minute ago that *I* was the one for you."

Henricksen shrugged again. Amazing how expressive such a simple gesture could be. "I'm a soldier," he told her. "And a captain. I've got no other skills. No desire to be anywhere but where the ship and the stars take me."

Out of words again. *Serengeti* stared in silence and then reached inside her, tapping into Valkyrie comms. "Are there others?" she asked *Seychelles*. "Does another Sister desire this human as captain?"

"Two," *Seychelles* told her. "Their captains grow old and will soon to retire." *Seychelles* laughed softly. "I'd take him off your hands myself if I didn't think Kassis would scuttle me."

Serengeti trusted *Seychelles*'s council, but she hesitated still. "He's nothing like Shumitsu. Not at all like the captain I envisioned."

"Perhaps that's a good thing, Sister. Times change, and so must we."

"Indeed," *Serengeti* murmured. "Thank you, Sister." She reached for *Seychelles* across the channel, touching mind-to-mind—an intimacy only AI knew—before addressing Henricksen once more. "The crew's young," she warned. "A few veterans but most of them have just a ship or two under their belts."

She'd lost the rest at Sosholo, with Shumitsu and the broken-backed chassis they towed in for scrap.

"Think I may be able to help with that." Henricksen flashed a smile filled with mischief. "Just so happens I know a veteran or two that're lookin' for a Valkyrie to take them in."

Serengeti smiled despite herself. "Just so happens, eh?"

"Yup. Convenient that." He hooked his thumbs through his belt and rocked back on his heels, smiling smugly.

"We leave tomorrow—"

"Done," he said promptly. "Sikuuku and I—"

"Sikuuku?"

"Gunner's mate. You'll love him," Henricksen winked. "We'll ship our personal effects over tonight. Anything else?"

Plenty, Serengeti thought. *But that will come in time.*

"No," she told him. "The ship's docked at—"

"Berthing 12, Space 42." Another smug smile. "Already checked it out."

Cheeky. Very cheeky indeed.

"Then I'll see you in the morning. Captain."

"Aye-Aye, *Serengeti*." Henricksen braced up and threw an honest-to-God, no-messing-around salute. And then he spun on his heel and marched back out the door.

"What have I done?" *Serengeti* wondered, staring after him.

"You, Sister, have found yourself a first-rate captain. *Sechura* will be *furious*," she said gleefully.

"Great. Just what I needed." *Serengeti* sighed. "Home, TIG. I've had enough of this floating tin can for one day."

Serengeti spun the little robot around and sent him on his way, watching through the TIG's eyes as he threaded his way back to the docks where her shiny new ship's body waited.

TWENTY-FIVE

Serengeti opened her eyes to darkness and for a moment she was lost. Lost and confused—no idea where she was or how she'd come to be there.

"The docks. Where are the docks?" She reached for systems, querying for information and found nothing but shredded scraps of a broken network, and dead end, after dead end, after dead end.

Memory returned—harsh, unforgiving—as a soft voice called to her from the darkness.

"*Serengeti.*"

A shadow moved below her, shimmering with softly glowing light. Metal glittered dully, marked here and there by sparkling, swirling patterns of brightest blue that formed and shredded—scattering like lightning bugs before her eyes.

Shapes and colors—blue and silver, cobalt eyes looking up at her from a rounded metal face.

"Tig," she breathed, reaching for him, touching at his brain.

"Welcome back." A curving smile appeared in the shadows—a grin of pure happiness painted in brightest blue.

"How long, Tig? How long this time?"

Tig shuffled his feet. "Long," he said cryptically.

"That's not—" Movement behind Tig, Tilli shifting in the shadows. "Tilli? Why are you hiding? Come here where I can see you."

Tilli hesitated, face lights flashing in anxious pulses. Tig waved to her, whistling insistently, and she crept forward, taking her usual place at his side.

"Hello, Tilli," *Serengeti* smiled.

"Hello." One word, so softly spoken that *Serengeti* almost didn't hear her. Tilli snuck a look at the camera, blue eyes wide and worried-looking, and then ducked down, scuffing a leg end across the floor.

Odd.

"Why so shy, little one?"

Shrug of Tilli's legs, a quick glance at Tig as if looking for reassurance.

"Tilli." *Serengeti* reached for her, touching at Tilli's brain.

Sadness there. Fear. A complex mixture of upset and worry for which *Serengeti* could find no context.

"What's wrong, Tilli?"

"Thought you were gone," Tilli said, voice quivering, on the edge of robot tears. "Thought you were gone forever."

"Gone? Why would you think that, silly?"

"Because we couldn't wake you," Tilli said miserably.

"Couldn't—How long have I been asleep?"

Tig and Tilli looked at one another. Flash of communication—Tig's face lights swirling in creeping patterns, Tilli replying in clipped pulses, a far more intimate exchange than simply using words. Tig reached over, twining his leg around Tilli's, pulling her close. "Three years," he said when all that flashing was done.

"Three years isn't so bad," *Serengeti* said lightly. "Certainly not worth all this upsettedness."

Another pause, Tig's eyes flicking from Tilli to the camera. "We've been trying to wake you for two of those years."

Tig's words chilled *Serengeti's* heart. The sobbing made sense now. The anxiousness and worry.

Henricksen. Yet another memory dredged from her AI mind. A more pleasant one this time than that dark dream of her hallways, but a memory still. Yet another dream. *Closer this,* she thought. *That other dream was just some sort of Purgatory—a waiting place between life and death. But this one…this one was closer.*

As close as she'd ever come to death.

Serengeti shivered and pushed that thought away as she touched at Tilli's face, stroking electric fingers across her cheek. "I'm here now, little one. Just as I've always been."

Tilli's eyes slitted as she leaned into that touch. She *cooed* softly, sounding sad and happy at once, like a crying child sobbing away the last of it tears.

"Shh. It's alright, Tilli." *Serengeti* slipped inside Tig and moved him close to Tilli, resting his cheek on hers. A current of energy passed between them, arcing from one metal face to another. "I was lost for a while," she told them, "but I'm here now. And I want to hear about everything you've been up to."

That finally got a smile from Tilli. And seeing she was happy, Tig smiled too.

"Show me," *Serengeti* ordered, just as she always did when she returned from the dark. She reached for Tig's controls, turning him around. "Go," she said, pointing him toward the door.

"Roger-dodger."

Tig scooted across the bridge and into the corridor, following the now-familiar route of corridors and ladderways that brought them to the very top tier of *Serengeti's* body, and that long, long hallway that ran the length of her. But he detoured there, surprising by turning away from the hole in her side that led outside, turning left instead and heading down a side corridor, taking two more lefts before the corridor ended.

Abruptly. No intersection, no choice of turnings, just that carbon and metal composite corridor one second, and a yawning chasm the next, revealing the dark and stars outside. Tig rolled to a stop just at the edge, tank treads teetering precariously as he panned his head from side to side, letting *Serengeti* take a good, long look.

An entire section of her body missing, corridors carved out, leaving a ragged tube of metal behind. "What happened?" *Serengeti* asked. "What happened to me, Tig?"

"The ship—the bomb..." Tig paused, seeming to search for words. "It was bad, *Serengeti*. And close. So close."

"Bad," *Serengeti* grunted. "I'd say 'bad' is a bit of an understatement." But she knew the risks, didn't she? Knew her plan was chancy when she launched her improvised bomb toward the scavenger ship. The explosion took those vultures out, protected her from being boarded, but from the looks of things, it almost killed her.

So close, Serengeti thought. *So close to total destruction.*

"Show me," she said faintly. "All of it."

Tig slid his eyes to Tilli, who shrugged and shook her head. "Alright." A sigh and Tig reached forward, feeling with the magnetized ends of his legs, finding footholds on broken girders and shattered sections of hallway—spots of stability that allowed him to tiptoe through the wreckage. Tilli followed just as carefully, watching where Tig placed each of his legs, matching her movements exactly to his as the two robots moved outside, giving *Serengeti* a full view of the damage.

The scope of the destruction surprised her—more rents and tears, a huge, gaping crater showing like a monstrous bite mark in *Serengeti's* port side hull. She turned Tig left and saw a shredded wall of internal structures, bits of hull plating still clinging to the outside. Right was much the same, though further down, and farther away. And in between, a raw-edged chasm, a massive, gaping wound where the scavenger ship's explosion had torn away huge chunks of her body.

"Bomb did its job, but it certainly didn't do my hull any favors."

Tig's face lights flashed in agreement as he panned his head from left to right.

Pieces of the Proteus' shuttle showed here and there, mixed in with the remains of *Serengeti's* tattered carcass—chunks of metal with fragmented hull markings sketched in scratched black paint, a crumpled pod that used to be the cockpit, a space-suited body sandwiched in the buckled remains. And when she looked out—far in the distance—*Serengeti* saw a twinkling cloud of debris floating around two amorphous lumps. That's it. That's all that was left of the scavenger ship—a dead mess of metal and composite components circling in synchronous orbit around Tsu's star.

She tried to feel sorry for them, searched inside her for some small shred of guilt for the dozens of lives she'd ended with that ship. For the Proteus itself, first generation AI idiot that it was. But when she looked inside her, *Serengeti* found neither. Nothing but a simmering anger and a sense of satisfaction knowing the scavenger ship was dead.

"Serves you right, you bastards." She turned away from the glittering cloud, dismissing the scavenger ship entirely from her mind. One more enemy down, now it was time to see to herself. "Topside, Tig," she ordered.

Topside took a bit of doing. Tig actually had to wend his way *downward* until he found an intact bit of hull, and then take a long meandering route leading generally toward the bow before finding a safe enough path to lead him up. Slow going, that route, but from the way he moved from section to section—never hesitating, not once having to backtrack and find another way through—*Serengeti* knew Tig had travelled this path before. Many times, it seemed. But then, he'd have to, wouldn't he? He and Tilli both, to perform maintenance on the solar panels on the roof. To clear the stardust from the starboard hull and keep the energy flowing in.

They crested the top of her body together, Tig with *Serengeti* riding inside him, Tilli close by his side, the forest of solar panels rising in even rows before them with the star's light shining full upon them, casting shadows on the hull. Brighter here—so much brighter after the dark, pitted mess of *Serengeti's* port side. Tig clambered down the first row of panels and curved around the end, to where it was brighter still.

"Oh my," *Serengeti* whispered, staring in wonder.

The blast had shoved her inward, closer to the star. Nearly a thousand kilometers closer based on some rough calculations of the Proteus' location in relation to *Serengeti's* own. Didn't sound like much—not out here, in the limitless lengths of space—but a thousand kilometers made the star that much clearer, its light that much brighter, stronger, bathing

her hull in silver-white radiance until it shined. Not just sparkled—
shined.

Like a star unto itself, Serengeti thought, smiling to herself, enjoying
that image. *Like a tiny star circling its mother, basking in her glory.*

So many years, so much time in those empty spaces, so long since
she'd come close enough to one of these celestial bodies for it to make
her sides glow. The stars were beautiful from a distance, even more so
from where they circled before. And now…

"It's wonderful, Tig."

Serengeti laughed with pure joy, forgetting her shredded body,
leaving her worries about *Cryo* and her crew behind. For a moment—
just a moment—*Serengeti* allowed herself just to *be.* To live in that
moment and remember the bliss that came with being a Valkyrie-class
starship drifting close to a star.

"I wish you could see this, Henricksen. I wish you could be here to
share this with me."

Henricksen. *Cryo.* She should go there and look in on them. But there
was one last thing to check on here before she headed back inside.

"The antenna?" she asked.

"Still there." Tig turned a bit, pointing ahead of them.

She could just see the tower with its collection of dishes and panels
jutting out up from her hull.

Tig walked over to it, stopping at the antennae's base. "Bit dinged up,
few pieces broken off, but it's still working. Lost some of the panels in
the blast," he said, pointing to scars and broken pieces along one side,
"but Tilli and I managed to fix it. Knew you'd want it working."

"I do. I most definitely do."

The comms array was important, *more* important now, in the wake of
that scavenger ship's arrival, *far* more important than Tig could have
ever imagined when he built the thing.

Tig turned a circle around the tower, while *Serengeti* took a long,
hard look. "Made a few improvements," he said shyly, pointing at the
middle and the tippy-tippy-top. "Amped up its power, added a few more
panels and collectors. Works better now. Can pick things up that are
further out in space."

"And?"

Tig shrugged and popped open a panel, snaking a little cable out,
connecting one end into a socket inside himself, and the other into a
corresponding socket in the antennae. The channel opened and *Serengeti*
listened closely, hoping for chatter, fearing to find the sound of human
and AI voices cluttering up the line. But there was nothing. Nothing but

silence on the other end. Even with the added capacity, there was still nothing on the line.

Serengeti sighed—relieved and disappointed at the same time. She'd held out hope that the Meridian Alliance would come, but after years and years and years, she still found herself alone.

Time to stop dreaming, Serengeti. Henricksen again, sounding less than sympathetic.

"If only I could," she said bitterly. "If I could just stop dreaming, maybe this would all end." A last look at the nearby star and she turned Tig around, putting its light behind her. "I've seen all there is to see here. What's next?"

"Engineering," Tig said.

Not the answer she expected. "Engineering. Not *Cryo.*"

Tig heard the question in her voice, but he just shrugged and rattled his legs against the hull plating, choosing to ignore it.

"Anything you want to tell me before I get there?"

Tap-tap. Tappity-tap-tap. Tig seemed about to say something and then shook his head.

Tig and his secrets. She was *really* getting tired of secrets. *It better be a good one this time, Tig.*

"Fine," *Serengeti* sighed. "Have it your way. Let's go."

Tig waved Tilli ahead, letting her guide them back inside the hull.

TWENTY-SIX

Engineering looked a bit more disheveled—broken robots thrown around, neat rows of scavenged bodies knocked over, scattered about—but otherwise much the same as the last time *Serengeti* visited. Except, that is, for the fuel cells sitting at one end.

"Both of them?" she asked quietly. "*Both* fuel cells are damaged?" Not surprising, really, considering the force of the blast and the damage she'd seen outside, but still, both of them felt like a kick in the pants. "You're sure one's not just compensating for the other?"

Tig shook his head, leg ends wringing worriedly. "Casings are cracked," he told her. "They're both leaking, just at different rates."

"I don't suppose you can fix them?"

"The lesser damaged of the two, but the other…" Tig shrugged his legs—that was as good as 'no.'

Serengeti sighed wearily. Based on experience, an unrepaired leak would only get worse over time. "So how bad is it?" she asked, cutting to the chase.

Tig brightened a bit. "So, here's the thing." He rolled close to the fuel cells, pointing at the gauges on the front before moving to the back and squeezing himself into the space between the fuel cells and the wall. "Wiring was pretty fried. Tilli replaced most of that already, and is working through the rest. And these fittings and connections? See the cracks? The corrosion? Every last one them needs to be replaced. Still scrounging for parts. Making progress though."

Not quite so bad then. Not *nearly* as bad as *Serengeti* feared when Tig first broke the news.

"We're closer to the star now," Tig continued, "which means the photovoltaic cells in the hull plating can drink in more energy, and at a faster rate." A pause and a sigh before he delivered the bad news. "Unfortunately, the two damaged fuel cells pretty much negate any advantage we get from that. Sorry."

"So, it's a draw," *Serengeti* said, sighing herself.

"Afraid so. On the plus side, power-wise, we're not much worse off *now* than we were before the explosion."

"That's not really saying much."

Tig shrugged and worked his way back out into the room. "We're doing what we can." A hint of defensiveness in that. She'd obviously hurt his professional pride.

"I'd hoped for better," *Serengeti* told him, "but it could have been worse."

"A *lot* worse," Tig nodded.

Tilli added her agreement, head bobbing up and down.

"What about *Cryo*? Was it damaged as well?"

Tig shrugged, started to nod, then shook his head.

Serengeti really wasn't in the mood for this. "Enough with the shrugging and the head bobbles, Tig. No secrets this time. No bullshit. Was *Cryo* damaged or not?"

"Depends how you look at it. Probably best if I just show you," he added at *Serengeti's* irritated sigh.

He whistled for Tilli and beat feet, abandoning Engineering as he followed a long and winding path to *Cryo*. A path that went *outside* first—that being quicker and easier than trying to navigate the shattered corridors and piles of mounded debris the scavenger ship's destruction had left—before heading back in.

Even knowing what had happened to her, it still hurt *Serengeti* to see all that damage to her internal and external structures. She tried to ignore twisted metal and gaping wounds and focused on the stars instead, but when Tig ducked back inside, the damage lay all around—melted panels, twisted girders, cables and wires dangling grotesquely everywhere she looked.

Tig zipped through it, high-stepping with his jointed legs into the cold confines *Serengeti's* corridors, and further in it wasn't so bad. Ice clung everywhere, hiding the burns and scars, covering over some of the smaller holes. But as Tig twisted and turned, they passed long stretches where the ice had broken away, revealing buckled, twisted panels, composite metal walls marred by smoke and fire.

My insides are like my outsides, Serengeti thought, eying a pitted stretch of wall. *All my body is full of holes. All my energy, everything that's me dribbling away. Slipping through my fingers like tiny grains of sand.*

Oh, boo-freaking-hoo, Henricksen's voice growled. *Yer not dyin,'* Serengeti. *You just need a good long stay in spacedock.*

"Not sure spacedock can fix this," she murmured. "Not sure this body's salvageable."

Body's not Serengeti, he reminded her. *Never was.*

She thought on that a long, long while.

Tig ducked into a maintenance shaft and shimmied down a ladder, glancing up now and then to make sure Tilli still followed. He stepped off on the next tier, raced down the hall, turning left and right and right again until there was nowhere left to go.

The corridor ended, not a door or a wall, but at yet another gaping hole looking out on the dark and stars.

"Where are we?" *Serengeti* asked.

Tig flashed a smile and cleared his throat. "Ta-da!" he cried, flourishing one jointed leg grandly.

"Yes, Tig. Another hole. Thank you for pointing that out. Now if you're done wasting time—"

"No-no-no." Tilli scuttled over, pushing Tig out of the way. "You're doing it all wrong." She pointed at her eye and then through the hole where the corridor ended.

That didn't make any more sense to *Serengeti* than Tig's leg flailing. "I don't—"

"Look. Out there." Tilli pointed again—through the hole and down to the right, where a rounded metal shape protruded from *Serengeti's* side.

"*Cryo*," *Serengeti* breathed. She pulled up the ship's schematic—a plan now sadly, woefully out of date—and retraced their route as best she could. "Aft. Aft side of *Cryo,* opposite the airlock door."

Which meant close to her *own* aft end, since that's where *Cryo's* exit point was.

Port side aft took heavy damaged during the run-in with *Osage* before jump. The scavenger ship's explosion must have finished what that long ago battle started, exposing the lifeboat nestled inside her when that section of *Serengeti's* body tore away.

"Is it damaged?" *Serengeti* asked worriedly. "The crew...are they alright?"

"Why don't you take a look for yourself?" Tig smiled and pointed at a camera.

"Be right back." *Serengeti* left Tig and Tilli in the hallway and flicked from one camera to another until she found the one that looked inside *Cryo.*

Darkness inside. Not good.

She panned the camera around and zoomed in, spotting the palest of pale glows coming from the bottom of the cryogenic chambers. *Serengeti* sighed in relief. Lights—any lights—meant power, and lights on the sleep tubes meant they were still working—still doing their job, keeping her frozen crew alive. *Serengeti* counted quickly, tallying up all those pale lights, and found a handful were missing: six tubes gone silent and dark in the time she'd been sleeping.

Finlay. Henricksen.

Hard to see in *Cryo's* dim interior, but in the way of all AIs, she'd memorized the layout of the cryogenic chambers, marking those that were empty, and those that were occupied when *Cryo* sealed itself up. Finlay had taken the pod right beside the door, Henricksen a unit near the center of the back wall. *Serengeti* checked and saw Henricksen's light still lit, readout scrolling slowly. Finlay's was dark, pod completely shut down.

"Finlay," she whispered, voice filled with mourning.

Finlay's darkened pod stared back at her—silent, accusing.

"I'm sorry, Finlay. There was no other choice." She wished she could see her, but the darkness hid Finlay's face.

"I'm sorry, Finlay. I'm so sorry." *Serengeti* pulled backward, not wanting to see Finlay's darkened tube anymore. Not wanting to think about her frozen face.

The robots were quiet when *Serengeti* returned to them, sensing her melancholy mood, not daring to ask. "Six crew lost," she said quietly. "Finlay..."

Tig *hooted* mournfully as *Serengeti* trailed off. For a long time, they just stood there—Tig and Tilli looking outward, *Serengeti* looking with them, none of them saying anything, just...staring, each of them lost in their own thoughts.

"So why am I here?" *Serengeti* asked them. "The crew...what did you mean to show me, other than *Cryo's* exposed bum?"

A sad attempt of humor, none of them really laughed.

Tilli glanced uncertainly at Tig.

"Go ahead." Tig nodded encouragingly and moved back at bit, giving Tilli room to slide past him and open a panel in the wall.

The magic device lay inside, the same one Tig used for all his staged events. Tilli pulled it out and held it up, cleared her throat to get their attention as she pointed to the electronic device she held and then pointed *it* at *Cryo's* rounded end showing outside.

"Yes, Tilli. I get it."

The Grand Reveal. Another little show that started out as cute but quickly got tiresome. Luckily, there were only eight of those damned docking clamps, and half of them already busted free.

"Please get on with it," *Serengeti* said, not quite covering her irritation.

"Oh." Tilli drooped, looking disappointed. This was her first attempt at the Grand Reveal, after all, and she'd probably been prepping for ages.

Serengeti felt bad for ruining Tilli's big moment. She summoned the last of her patience and forced some enthusiasm into her voice. "Alright, Tilli. Big moment. Show me what you've got, girl."

Tilli perked back up, rallying her spirits and she went on with the show. Big smile for her audience, and she turned to the wall, standing on her tip-toes as she reached up and slotted the little device into place, completing the recently repaired circuit. A surge of power—lights flaring up and down the hallway, wires flashing, fizzing, burning out— and *Serengeti's* micro-sensors lit up, transmitting the *thunk* and *rattle,* the heavy, clanging *crash* of a docking clamp letting go.

Serengeti looked outside and saw the docking clamp holding tight to *Cryo's* ass end dangling in the depths of space—loose now and floating lazily with no gravity to hold it down.

"Ta-da!" Tilli raised her legs, shaking imaginary pom-poms in celebration, an effect that was entirely spoiled by the fact that she still faced the wall.

Tig coughed politely. "Turn around, Tilli."

"Oh!" Tilli flushed brightly and twisted, tank treads screeching against the frosted decking. "Ta-da!" She flashed a smile, flailing those pom-poms like there was no tomorrow.

"Very nice, Tilli." *Serengeti clonked* Tig's leg ends together. "That makes...what? Five docking clamps? Five of the eight knocked free?"

Tilli winked and shook her head, smiling widely.

Tig tittered and bounced on his tip-toes, fairly dancing in the hall.

"What are you two up to?" *Serengeti* asked suspiciously. "There were four clamps left last time I checked, and—what?"

Tilli giggled, leg ends lifting to cover her mouth. "Four. She thinks it four." Another giggle.

Tig laughed aloud, turning in circles.

Did I get it wrong? Serengeti wondered. *Are they laughing because the poor, broken AI ship can no longer count?*

She checked her records, confirmed they'd only loosened four of the docking clamps before she went into that long stretch of dark. "Alright. I give up. What happened?"

Tig scurried forward, holding tight to the wall with two legs while he hung his head out the hole at the end of the corridor. "Look there," he said, pointing at *Cryo's* bulbous hind end.

Serengeti sighed in annoyance. "*Yes*, Tig. You broke that one loose. That's very good, but—"

"You're not *looking*," he scolded in a sing-song voice. He pointed again, more insistently this time. "There. Near the middle of *Cryo's* backside wall. And over there," a twitch of his leg, moving it left then right, pointing at the ragged edges where her body wrapped around the lifeboat. "What's missing?"

"I don't—oh!" Now it was *Serengeti's* turn to be embarrassed. Eight docking clamps held *Cryo* in place—three here on the backside, three more on the front, one on either side—all of them identical, ringing the lifeboat around. *Serengeti* looked outside and saw one of the rear-mounted clamps dangling loosely below the lifeboat's bulging sphere, but the other two were missing. *Missing,* not hidden. Not broken away. Gone entirely, except for the end piece that connected to *Cryo*—that was still there. The rest of it—the docking strut, the swing arm, the hydraulic motors that ran the whole complicated mechanism—seemed to disappear. Vanished into thin air.

"Explosion tore them loose," Tig said.

"Tore them loose, tore them loose!" Tilli giggled and flailed, prancing in a circle.

High explosives, Henricksen's voice said. *Best way to solve a tricky problem.*

"Droll, Henricksen. Very droll."

Tilli kept dancing around but Tig stood there, looking from Tilli to *Cryo* outside like he was waiting for something.

Do the math, Serengeti.

Henricksen's voice again. She'd be lost without him. *Serengeti* tallied the numbers and found the total came to seven.

Told ya.

"Shut up, Henricksen."

Tilli stopped dancing and flashed her face lights at Tig, wondering who *Serengeti* was talking to.

Tig shrugged and raised a leg, twirling its end beside his head.

She thinks you're crazy, Henricksen offered helpfully.

"Who knows. Maybe I am," *Serengeti* murmured.

She didn't *feel* crazy, but she supposed it was possible. After all, her last maintenance visit had been a long time ago—years upon years upon years—and who knew what glitches her damaged systems had developed in that time. AI were machine minds but built on human brain specifications, so it was possible, if improbable, that she'd lost a few of her marbles along the way.

The design specs say I shouldn't dream, but I picked that up along the way. Maybe that's the first step—the first indication of an unstable mind.

She waited, expecting Henricksen's voice to pipe up and offer some snarky comment, but Henricksen was strangely silent. She wondered if that was significant. If that voice's sudden desertion was her subconscious indicating its agreement.

Didn't matter. Crazy or not, *Cryo* is almost free. And after that…

"What happens after that doesn't matter either," she said softly, studying *Cryo* through Tig's eyes. "We've got one docking clamp left now. Just one." And two faulty fuel cells throwing up alarms, reminding *Serengeti* it was time she made herself scarce. "I must go now, little ones."

"No!" Tilli's cobalt eyes blazed brightly, shining with sudden fear. "No, please. Last time—"

"Shh. I won't be far. Not this time. This time I go to sleep of my own choosing. This time I won't let the darkness drag me down."

And she wouldn't be alone. Not this time.

Serengeti leaned Tig close, touching his cheek to Tilli's, and then *Serengeti* flitted away, racing along her broken network to the bridge. And there she slipped to sleep—peacefully this time, dreaming her dreams of days gone by. No fire this time, no destruction. Just Henricksen swapping pithy bits of wisdom, keeping *Serengeti* company in the dark.

Twenty-Seven

"Whelp. I'm out." Sikuuku tossed his cards down and polished off the last of his drink. "You've got all my money, boss. Think I'll head back to the ranch and get some shut-eye before you take that as well." The gunner smiled and shoved his chair back, tapped two fingers to his temple in a half-assed salute before weaving his way toward the door.

Henricksen stared after him, sipping at his glass as Sikuuku stepped out into the hallway and pulled the door to Henricksen's quarters shut.

"You've known him for a while." *Serengeti* normally didn't intrude on Henricksen's off-duty time—even a captain needed time away from an unsleeping AI—but she was curious about this new captain of hers.

Henricksen turned his head toward the camera in the corner. "Served on three different ships together. Sikuuku..." Henricksen dropped his eyes, staring into the depths of his glass. "He might've stayed Black Ops if I hadn't left."

"He's a good soldier. A good *friend*."

Henricksen nodded and tossed off his drink. "The best."

More to that story—so many things *Serengeti* wanted to know about Henricksen and Sikuuku—this grizzled, battle-scarred pair that ran her bridge. *Patience,* she told herself. *He came to you looking for assignment but you still need to earn his trust. You can't just go barging in like a bull in a china shop demanding his entire life's history.*

Serengeti thought for a minute, considering the dozens of questions she wanted answered and settled on the simplest of them all. One that, oddly, bothered her the most.

"The scar on your face. Why?" she asked quietly. "The cell replicators can easily get rid of it. You'd never even know it was ever there."

"Wonders of modern medicine," Henricksen murmured, lips twisting in a lopsided smile. "Cover up anything you want. Make all the bad memories go away."

Bitterness in his voice. *Serengeti* heard it—you bet she did. "So why then? Why did you keep it?"

Henricksen grunted and touched at the jagged line of scar tissue running down the side of his face. "Let's just say, there are some things you shouldn't forget."

He lifted his eyes to the camera, grey eyes staring into the lens. And then Henricksen's face faded into the darkness, shadows and smudged grey outlines rising up to take Henricksen's place.

Bridge, Serengeti's muzzy mind registered.

She almost went back, wanting to finish that conversation and ask Henricksen the questions she'd never had time to ask.

Can't go back, Serengeti. Henricksen's voice, filled with regret. *You can only move forward and hope for the best.*

I'm trying, Henricksen. I've been *trying all these years.*

Then keep *trying, Serengeti. Eventually you'll get us there.* Henricksen retreated to the recesses of her mind.

Serengeti drew a bit of power, focusing the camera, searching the bridge below for cobalt eyes and chromed faces. "Tig. Tilli. Where are you?"

"Here. I'm here, *Serengeti,*" Tig called, voice drifting from a shadowed corner.

She turned the camera toward him, smiling to herself as Tig's chromed face appeared, cobalt eyes blazing brightly, Tilli fidgeting nervously at his side.

"Welcome back," Tilli said, shy as always. She shuffled her legs, eyes flicking to one side.

Curious, *Serengeti* turned the camera a bit more, and…

"What's this?" she breathed as a third robot face appeared.

Three chromed faces, *three* sets of brightly glowing eyes when last time there'd been but two.

Great. Now I'm seeing things.

She powered the camera off and brought it back on-line again, thinking it a malfunction—a problem with the feed, a glitch with the camera's optical resolution mechanism, something like that.

No such luck. The camera turned back on and that third face was still there, gazing up at her with the others.

"What's going on?" *Serengeti* whispered, AI mind processing, trying to make sense of the camera's images.

Three. It shouldn't be three, she kept thinking. *Should it?*

For the briefest of moments, *Serengeti* honestly wasn't sure. That scared her. Scared her badly. So much that she counted the robots again, working her way from left to right, tallying up eyes and faces, before starting over again. Three times in total she counted, and each time the tally was exactly the same: three sets of eyes—six cobalt orbs in total—and three shining, chromed faces.

"Maybe I'm imagining it," she murmured. "Just like Henricksen."

Maybe she was still dreaming and just *thought* she was awake. Maybe she really *had* gone off the deep end and just didn't know it.

That's crap, Serengeti, Henricksen's voice snorted. *You're a lotta things, but you ain't a loony. So drop this maudlin BS and figure out what's going on.*

Serengeti laughed—she couldn't help it. Henricksen might not be eloquent, but he always knew just the right thing to say.

I miss him. More than she could say. More than *Serengeti* could have ever imagined. *Someday, Henricksen. Someday,* she promised, and then shook herself, focusing in on this unexpected visitor on her bridge.

Serengeti drew a bit of power to her, bringing the light above the robots to life. "Well now. Who do we have here?"

The newcomer squeaked in surprise, startled as much by the sudden brilliance as being the focus of attention. *Serengeti* zoomed in, trying to get a better look at it, but the robot up and ran before she got more than a glimpse, scurrying behind Tig to hide in his shadow.

"It's alright," *Serengeti* called after it. "I'm not going to hurt you."

A rounded head peeked from behind Tig's carapace, cobalt eyes wide and wary-looking, filled with equal parts curiosity and fear.

"Hi," *Serengeti* said in her softest, friendliest voice. "Come on out where I can see you."

No dice. The robot took one look at the camera, squeaked and ducked out of sight again.

"Hey now. That's not very polite," Tig admonished. He flashed an apologetic look at the camera and then twisted around, addressing the robot sheltering under his nether regions. "She'll think you don't like her."

A muffled *peep* came back.

Tig waved Tilli over, calling in reinforcements.

"*Serengeti's* a nice...warship." Tilli offered a sickly smile to the camera. "There's no need to hide."

"*Peep?*" A bit of curiosity in the hiding robot's voice now, but it clung to the shadows under Tig's body just the same, doggedly refusing to show itself.

It took a bit of cajoling and encouragement from Tig and Tilli, and a lot of patience—more patience, frankly, than *Serengeti* had herself—but they eventually got the little creature to come out. The robot crept from its hiding place—head down, legs wrapped close about its body—and grabbed at Tilli's leg end, holding tightly to that anchor as it inched its way to Tig's side.

Serengeti zoomed in close, taking a long, hard look. "Well now. Isn't this interesting?"

Not one of her robots—that was for sure. She'd never even *seen* a robot like this one before. In some ways it resembled Tig and Tilli—a miniaturized version anyway—but there were some obvious...deviations from the TIG blueprint. For one thing, it had fewer legs than Tig and Tilli—just six, when your average TIG came equipped with eight. The body was different too—more rounded, not the elongated oval of a true TIG, and its head rounder still. Rivets and weld lines betraying the fact that the model wasn't quite stock, the body stitched together from salvaged pieces and parts. But more important than all that was something the robot was missing. It squiggled and shifted, holding tightly to Tig's leg on one side, and Tilli's on the other, and as it did, *Serengeti* got a good look at the strange robot's flanks.

Bare metal there—well, metal composite, like every other robot and just about every other *thing* inside *Serengeti's* body—no numbers or letters on the tiny robot's sides. No sign of them either—no smudges and smears, no shadowy remains like Tig and Tilli wore—and when she reached inside the robot, touching gently at its AI brain, *Serengeti* found none of the identification tags the other robots carried. None of the data to mark it as one of hers.

"Curiouser and curiouser," *Serengeti* murmured, intrigued by this tiny little mystery Tig and Tilli had brought her. *Tiny and somewhat adorable.* She smiled to herself and looked from Tig to Tilli. "You two have got a new friend I see."

Tig tittered nervously, throwing worried glances Tilli's way.

Tilli fidgeted and fiddled, hovering close to the little robot beside her, looking like she might grab it up and run herself at any minute.

Odd.

The TIGs were flighty by nature—a fault in their programming *Serengeti* found endearing most days—but Tig and Tilli seemed *especially* flighty today. That was worrisome. And a tad annoying. Time to get some answers.

"This is the second time you've surprised me by showing up with a new companion, Tig. So tell me: where have you been hiding *this* little robot?"

Tig shrugged and *burbled* something nonsensical as his face lights flashed in blotchy, discordant patterns.

Interesting, that. Bit of guilt in that blush, a touch of worry in the way Tig looked at Tilli, and Tilli refused to look back. But she reached for

Tig and shuffled closer to his side, hovering protectively over the miniature robot sandwiched between them.

"Who is she, Tig?" *Serengeti* asked. *She*. Instinctively, though there was nothing about the robot to indicate she or he. Not like Tilli's bright pink bow. 'She' felt right, somehow, though *Serengeti* was at a loss to explain why. "What's her name?"

Tig looked up at the camera, blue swirls of discomfort crawling across his cheeks. He glanced at Tilli and to the little robot standing between them. "Go on," he said, nodding encouragingly.

The little robot blinked and *peeped*, ducked her head and stared fixedly at the floor.

"It's alright." *Serengeti* waited, watching the little robot, until she finally looked up. "Hi there. What's your name, little one?" Soft voice again, gentle as can be. "You *do* have a name, don't you?"

Small shrug in response—the barest lifting of the little robots legs.

"Oh, come now. Surely you do! Everyone has a *name*."

A *peep* and whistle—that's all *Serengeti* got in response. Just those two nervous sounds and nothing more.

Tig cleared his throat uncomfortably. "Sorry, she's a bit shy." He shrugged an apology and ducked down, whispering softly to the little robot beside him. "Go ahead. She won't hurt you," he said, nudging the robot in the side.

"*Peep?*"

"Promise," Tig smiled.

A shy glance at the camera, face lights flashing wildly, stuttering out a rapid-fire communication punctuated by *beeps* and *borps* and an ululating *trill*. A last low whistle and the little robot curled up tight, hunkering close to the floor.

This was starting to get irksome.

"She can't speak?" *Serengeti* turned her eye to Tig.

"Language processors still need a bit of work, but she *can* speak. Sort of. When she wants to." Another nudge at the little robot, Tig's face swirling with soothing patterns as she uncurled and raised her head, looking to Tig first and then the camera. "There now. See? Nothing to—"

The robot quivered and ducked back down, legs splayed wide, belly flat against the floor.

Bit of drama in that. Bit of *playing* at being scared rather than true fear.

Tease. Serengeti smiled to herself. *It's a game. A way of getting attention and having a little fun at Tig and Tilli's expense.*

She liked this new robot already.

"Secret, eh?" *Serengeti* decidedly to play along for a while. "Alright then. Let's try a different question, little miss. Where did you come from?"

A shrug in answer, stubby legs lifting, grabbing at the floor. The robot crawled to one side, trying to crawl under Tig's belly and hide.

More games. Serengeti considered a moment, decided to let the little robot win this round.

Back to Tig then. "Where'd she come from, Tig?"

"Yeeeaaaaahhhh. About that..." Tig reached over, stroking a leg across the miniature robot's back, *cooing* softly to stop her squiggling.

"Tig?" *Serengeti* prompted.

Tig sighed and looked up at her—straight into the camera—as he spilled his guts. "I—we—Tilli and I, we kinda, sorta...made...her?" He cringed, front legs lifting, rubbing together worriedly.

Tilli copied him—the two of them standing together, chirping away like oversized metal crickets.

"Made her," *Serengeti* repeated.

Tig nodded and reached for Tilli, twining his leg end around hers.

"You *made* a new robot." She could hardly believe it but Tig nodded again, drooping a bit, obviously thinking her angry. That couldn't be further from the truth. "*How?*" *Serengeti* asked him. For the life of her, she couldn't figure that out. "I mean, there are plenty of parts." More than enough to assemble a body and jump start a power core from the fuel cells inside her. "But the brain...you can't just *salvage* an AI mind and give it to another robot, and it's not like we're carrying a bunch of spares around. Where on earth did you find one, Tig? How did you ever manage such a thing?"

Tig shifted nervously, offering the shyest of shy looks to the camera. "There wasn't one sitting around, just as you said, so I—we—I got creative."

"Creative," *Serengeti* repeated suspiciously. She didn't like where this was going.

"Uh-huh." Tig shuffled from one side to the other, leg ends drumming against the floor, sneaking nervous glances at Tilli beside him and the camera hovering above. "We didn't have a spare so we—we used mine."

"Your what? Your *mind?*"

Tig nodded, face flushing guiltily.

Serengeti stared in stunned disbelief. "You're telling me you harvested a piece of your AI to create hers?"

"Ahem. Well." Tig shuffled his feet. "It—It wasn't *just* me," he admitted.

"Tilli. Tilli too?"

"*Beep.*" Tig hugged Tilli to his side. "*Beep-beep.*"

"AI procreation." *Serengeti* laughed—she'd never imagined such a thing. "The engineers will have a fit."

Tig *beeped* in surprise and started laughing with her—nervous, relieved laughter that Tilli picked up. Soon even the little newcomer was giggling, enjoying this new game so much she finally came out of hiding.

"Alright then, little miss." *Serengeti* addressed the little robot once her giggles ran their course. "Stand up straight now. I want to get a look at you."

Metal legs uncurled, flaring outward as the little robot lifted herself from the floor. She stood there, bobbing up and down, jointed legs bending and flexing, eyes looking from the floor, to Tilli, to the camera high above—shy again, timid now that the laughter was done.

"There you are," *Serengeti* smiled, zooming in as she looked the robot up and down. "Can you turn for me? Would you do that, little one?"

Soft words. Gentle words. Friendly-friendly-friendly.

A shy smile and the tiny robot spun in a tight circle, stopped and looked to Tig for confirmation before spinning around again.

Serengeti chuckled softly as the little robot spun and spun and spun. *She's perfect*, she thought. *Just about perfect.*

"She's beautiful."

The spinning robot *trilled* happily, face lights pulsing with pleasure as she twirled round and round and round. Tig and Tilli looked on, legs wrapped around each other—two proud parents watching their child show off.

"So what's that?" *Serengeti* asked, pointing to a splash of color on the robot's left flank, half-hidden by the curve her back.

"*Peep.*" The little robot screeched to a halt, glancing worriedly at Tig and Tilli. "*Peep-peep?*"

"That mark on your side. What is it?"

Another look at Tilli, waiting for her nod, before the little robot twisted her body around, turning the side in question to the camera.

It's a picture. Serengeti studied the drawing picked out in muted colors, realized it was a tiny grey field mouse nibbling at a yellow wedge of cheese. *Cute,* she thought. "Did you draw that yourself?"

The little robot looked up at the camera and quickly shook her head. She shuffled a step closer to Tig and pointed at him with her leg.

"Tig? Huh. It's adorable, Tig. I never knew you were so creative."

"Add-on," he admitted. A surreptitious look to either side and he leaned forward, pressing a metal leg end to his lips. "Don't tell," he whispered, adding a wink and a mischievous swirl of face lights.

"Your secret's safe with me," *Serengeti* assured him. "It's adorable, by the way. *She's* adorable. Cute as a button, as Henricksen would say."

Tilli beamed widely and pulled the little robot to her, wrapping one leg around her tiny body.

Tig bounced up and down, metal legs pattering against the deck plates.

They both looked so happy. So damned pleased with themselves.

Tig and Tilli: proud robot parents. Who would have ever thought it?

"So what's your name, little one?"

Back to that, because she never *had* gotten an answer.

"*Peep,*" the little robot answered, face lights flashing randomly, chasing each other across her cheeks. "*Peep-peep.*"

"Peep?" *Serengeti* smiled. "That's an odd name."

"*Peep-peep-peep.*" The robot shook her head, face lights flashing in sudden irritation. She shimmied from one side to the other and ducked her head, leg ends tapping out a staccato tempo against the deck plates as she thought something over. A glance at Tig—who just shrugged—and Tilli—who smiled and waved—and the little robot turned back to the camera. Her face lights swarmed together, forming a bright blue ring on the lower half of her face.

"*Oona,*" she said carefully, flushing spreading across her cheeks. "Oona." A second time, enunciating both syllables, drawing that name out, as if afraid *Serengeti* wouldn't understand.

"Oona," *Serengeti* repeated.

Oona nodded quickly, clapping her legs ends together.

And just where did they come up with that? she wondered, looking at Tig and Tilli.

"Such pretty name. A pretty name, for a pretty little girl."

Oona *burbled* softly, turning shy and coy of a sudden, face lights flaring and fading, painting her chromed face in cobalt light.

Serengeti slipped from her camera and into Tig's mind, leaned him close to Tilli, pressing his cheek to hers. And through them she reached for Oona, touching at her AI child's mind, exploring her pathways, mapping the structures that gave it life.

Perfect. Perfect through and through, inside and out. A mind built on a salvaged crystal matrix vessel Tig had wiped clean and reloaded, augmenting its base programming with bits and pieces of his own code set, a few customizations donated by Tilli.

"Hello, Oona." *Serengeti* stroked electric fingers across Oona's mind.

Oona shivered, *cooing* softly at *Serengeti's* touch.

"She's beautiful, Tig. But I'm guessing she's not the reason you woke me, is she? Not the *only* reason at least."

"No," Tig admitted with a sly, secretive smile. He looked at the camera, and the bridge door behind him, hinting that it was time to go.

Time. It always came back to that.

Serengeti stopped Tig as he turned to leave, wanting to know how much time she'd lost. Not knowing *why* it was important, just that she wanted, *needed* to know. "How long, Tig? How long have I been gone this time?"

The Chron claimed five years, give or take, but she wasn't quite sure she could trust the Chron. Five years meant thirty-one in total since *Serengeti* tumbled from jump into this empty, quiet section of space and found herself alone.

Five years. *Serengeti* didn't *want* that answer. So she looked to Tig, hoping Chron was wrong.

Chron *was* wrong, as it turned out, but Tig's answer—despite the smile, the mischievous twinkle in his eyes—was even worse. He leaned to one side and raised his legs, waving five of his eight metal appendages at the camera.

"Eight. Eight years. Damn. Has it really been that long?"

Tig and Tilli nodded together.

Oona looked up them and started nodding right along. Another game. Just another game for her.

"Is it done then?" *Serengeti* asked. Because five years should be long enough—plenty of time to complete the last of the chores she'd set them to. "Is it done, Tig?"

Tig paused for dramatic effect and then nodded just once, smile stretching all the way across his face. "Done and done and done," he said. "So done it couldn't be more done."

"Show me," *Serengeti* said, dropping inside him, turning the robot around. "Show me, Tig. Go!"

Tig gathered up his little family and slipped out into the hall, navigating the maze of shattered corridors, hitting the ladderway and climbing down and down and down.

Almost there, *Serengeti* thought, staring through Tig's eyes as he stepped off on Level 4 and ducked around a corner. *After all these years, it's almost done.*

Twenty-Eight

Tig skipped the tour this time and headed straight to Engineering. Except, he didn't stop there either. Tig slowed as they approached the door that led into Engineering's cavernous space, and seemed to consider it, and then rolled right by, shaking his head at Tilli when she flashed a question, rudely cutting her off.

Not like him. Not like Tig at all.

"Tig? Is there something you need to tell me?" *Serengeti* asked. "Tig," she repeated when the robot kept going.

Tig rolled to a stop, front legs lifting, clattering noisily together. A glance behind him and he shook his head, faced back around and sped off, leaving Tilli and little Oona behind.

Serengeti flipped to the camera in his thorax and saw Tilli staring after them, face lights flaring, pulling downward in frown. Oona reached up and wrapped her leg end around her mother's, *blipping* softly, asking what was wrong. A quick smile for Oona and a surreptitious glance toward Engineering before Tilli too moved on, Oona trundling along at her side, holding tightly to her leg.

That looked told *Serengeti* everything she needed to know. "Tig. Stop."

Tig buzzed along, pretending he hadn't heard.

"Stop," *Serengeti* ordered, and when he *still* kept going, she reached inside the little robot and stopped him herself. "Engineering. *Now,* Tig."

She let go and he just sat there, staring straight ahead, clearly wanting to move, knowing *Serengeti* would just take control and *make* him go to Engineering if he refused to go there of his own volition. A heavy sigh and Tig spun around, retracing his steps. He glanced at Tilli as he rolled by, sharing a look of worry that prompted another question from Oona— a piping *trill*, wanting to know what was going on.

Tilli just sighed and squeezed Oona's leg as she turned and followed after Tig.

Into Engineering then with its jumbled collection of broken robots, silent engines squatting on side, burnt-out wall of power cells looming large at the other. Tig turned left when he rolled into Engineering, picking his way through the scrapped robots and cables, pushing floating debris out of his way. He stopped when he could go no further and stared forlornly at the bank of massive power cells.

Bad news—had to be, always was with the power cells.

"What now?" *Serengeti* sighed. "What's happened to the power cells while I've been gone?"

Tig started to answer and then stuttered to a halt. He tried again, but only managed to blurt out the fact that he was sorry before stumbling all over himself and giving up. His head drooped, legs sagging as he collapsed to the floor, curling up like a dead spider taking its place in Engineering's graveyard.

"Tig. Tell me. Whatever it is, it can't be *that* bad."

Except it could be. Everything around here was bad, but she tried not to let her worry show.

"Seems I was a bit...optimistic about those last two power cells," Tig said, staring fixedly at the floor. "Tried repairing that one," one leg lifted, pointing at the lesser damaged of the pair, "but...well, it's *better,* but still a bit...broken."

"How bad?" *Serengeti* asked quietly.

"Still leaking. Slowly, but..." A shrug of metal legs. "It charges, but it never quite gets full."

"And the other one?"

"The other one." Tig glanced at the damaged cell's partner, heaved a heavy sigh. "Tried fixing that one too, but I—I...I think I made it worse," he admitted, face flushing. "'Course time's partly to blame too—damaged parts don't like being used when they're not feeling well—but it's much worse than the last time you saw it. Sorry, *Serengeti.* I—I'm sorry," he said, hanging his head.

Serengeti was quiet a while, staring at the two fuel cells through Tig's eyes. "Not your fault. You tried, Tig, that's all I can ask. And it's not really surprising. Eight years...it's a long time to expect a damaged fuel cell to keep running." Especially when it only had one other to shore it up. And that one sickly too, if slightly less so. "Bottom line: how bad off are we?"

Tig hemmed and hawed, shuffling his feet, stalling for time. *Serengeti* waited, letting him fiddle and fidget, and eventually he cracked. Just like all those candidates Henricksen beat out for her captain's chair.

"Hard to say really. I think we've got enough juice to pop the last docking clamp free. Poor bugger will likely blow the minute it's done." Tig patted the heavily damaged fuel cell apologetically. "'Course it's probably not gonna last much longer anyway. One way or another, that power cell over there will be kaput before long. Might as well send it off with a bang."

"And the other? Same thing?"

A shrug this time. A shrug and a nod, a shake of Tig's head. "Not sure, honestly. It's in better shape but it might not survive the process either."

Serengeti almost laughed. It was all so ridiculous, all so unfair. "Doesn't matter," she said quietly. A touch at Tig's brain, gentle as gentle can be. A whispered word to chase the shadows from his heart. "It doesn't matter, Tig. And even if it did, it's hardly your fault."

"*Beep?*" he asked hopefully, legs uncurling, head lifting the tiniest fraction. "*Beep-beep?*"

Nervous sounds, vocalizations the translation routines couldn't parse because they didn't really have any meaning. But *Serengeti* understood. She didn't need the translation routines this time.

"Yes. *Beep-beep,*" she smiled. "We just need to break *Cryo* free. After that...well, what happens after that doesn't really matter, does it?"

"No," Tig agreed in his softest, saddest voice. His eyes drifted to Tilli and Oona beside her. Tilli stared back, hugging Oona close. "No, I guess it doesn't."

Silence, complete silence, stretching on and on and on. Tilli rolled close, touching Tig's leg with hers, gripping it tightly as she led him from Engineering, and on to *Cryo,* with Oona following obediently behind. More silence outside, none of them really in the mood to talk, especially with Tig moping so pathetically. But he perked up after a bit and that lightened everyone's mood. A squeeze of Tilli's leg before he released her, moving ahead, clambering in and out of maintenance shafts, wending through *Serengeti's* shattered innards.

"You were wrong, you know," *Serengeti* said casually as they navigated a ladder.

Tig *blipped* in confusion, and froze, mind suddenly gone blank.

"Seventeen years. Isn't that what you said? Seventeen years from the time you broke that first clamp free to pry the rest of them off?"

"Umm...yeah." Tig nodded uncertainly and got going again, moving from rung to rung, eyes lifting now and then to make sure Tilli and Oona kept up.

"And how long *has* it been, Tig?"

Another blank moment. Light filled the ladderway, Tig's face lights flaring brightly, flicking on and off as he ran the numbers and added the results up. "Ahem. Yes. Close enough."

Tig hit the bottom of the ladderway and zipped out into the corridor, all business now, but *Serengeti* kept dogging him, unwilling to let this go.

"What's that? Didn't quite hear you. What was the count?"

"Not really important," he said, rolling along.

Serengeti reached inside him and brought Tig to a screeching halt.

"Fine. Twenty years. You happy?" He huffed loudly, legs flaring wildly until *Serengeti* let him move on.

"Bit off, weren't you? Think your noggin might need some maintenance," she said, tapping at his brain.

Tilli laughed behind them and Oona instantly got the giggles, laughing because Tilli was laughing. Laughing even harder, grabbing at her little round belly, when *Serengeti* joined in, and Tig after. That's how they came to *Cryo*—laughing, not crying, not trundling in silence like the sad little robots that left Engineering. And that's how *Serengeti* wanted it, if this was truly to be the end. That their last memories be joyous ones before they slipped into the dark.

Tig rolled to a halt, Tilli and Oona fetching up behind him. *Cryo's* door loomed before them, blocky black letters staring boldly out at the hall. They'd purposely left this clamp for last, so when *Cryo* broke free, they could watch it move away. From right here, outside its sealed doorway. Front row seats to the lifeboat's departure. No fear of getting sucked out this time—not like that aborted attempt at launch when there was still atmosphere inside *Serengeti's* body. They'd been forced to hide then, and protect themselves from the rush of venting air, but this time they could stand right here and watch together as the lifeboat set sail and disappeared into the stars.

But before it did, *Serengeti* wanted to say her goodbyes.

"Wait here," she said, pulling away from Tig, flicking to the camera above.

A couple of hops and she was inside, gazing downward through the darkness, searching for *Cryo's* passengers. Her eyes went to Henricksen first, staring at his tube, making sure it still worked. She panned the camera after, looking at all the cryogenic chambers, counting slowly, checking all the others. The last of them was Finlay's, a chamber that one was dark and dark and dark—a hole where life used to be.

"Finlay." Sorrow washed over her, memories red hair and freckles, a bright white smile, a lilting voice raised in song flashed through her AI brain. "Goodbye, Finlay. I'm sorry," *Serengeti* said one last time, and then turned the camera away. "Thirty-nine," she murmured, casting her electronic eye across *Cryo's* insides. Thirty-nine meant one more tube failed, one more life lost. Thirty-nine yet living. Thirty-nine survivors waiting to be sent off into the stars. "Safe voyage," she wished them, looking from tube to tube. She skipped over Finlay's, not wanting to see it, and settled on Henricksen's pod.

I wish I could see him, she thought. *I wish I could see his face.*

She wasn't sure why—she had that image of him standing in Cryo's doorway to remember him by—she just did.

"Goodbye, Henricksen. 'Til the stars fail and the moons turn to dust, and all of our wanderings come to an end." Ancient words, passed in parting between captains and their crew. Words of protection meant to speed Henricksen home. "Safe travels, Captain," *Serengeti* whispered, and then left him, fleeing *Cryo's* interior for the safety of Tig's metal body. And there she sat for a long, long time, while Tig waited for permission to kick the show off, and set *Cryo* on the final leg of its journey.

I've waited so long for this, but now that the time has come to set Henricksen and the others free, I don't want to let them go. I don't want to be left here alone.

Not alone, Serengeti. You'll never be alone, Henricksen's voice said. Henricksen as she remembered him from that last fateful day: voice pitched low as he stood at Finlay's shoulder, offering fatherly advice. He was a gruff man, most of the time. Gruff and hard, because that's what was expected of the ship's captain. Because that's what decades of war did. But his soft side came through every now and then. *Serengeti* loved him for that. And for the being the gruff, uncompromising captain she remembered.

I'll miss you, Henricksen.

No you won't.

Serengeti laughed and let him go.

"So who's going to do the honors?" she asked.

Tig smiled and beckoned to Oona, coaxing her close. He grabbed her around the middle and lifted her up so she could retrieve the magic device—the electronic key that set all the docking clamps free—from the compartment where they'd stored it. Tig set her back down and stepped back, watching expectantly as Oona fidgeted uncertainly. They'd obviously rehearsed this a few times in preparation for the big day, but Oona seemed to have forgotten her lines now that the moment had come. She just stood there, leg ends rattling nervously, staring at the key in her appendage hand like she had no idea what to do with it.

"Ta-da!" Tig whispered, miming the motion that would slot the little device into the receptacle, waving his legs in celebration. Oona still didn't look sure, so he did it again. And again. Until finally, after the third repetition, she seemed to get it.

Oona nodded quickly and turned around, facing the wall. "Ta-da!" she exclaimed in a high, childish voice.

Stubby legs lifted, flailing at the air. Oona spun around, smiling widely, looking to Tig for the expected applause.

Tig coughed and pointed at the little device still clutched in her appendage hand.

"*Peep!*" Oona flushed brightly and whirled around, standing on tiptoe, stretching for the slot high above her.

But she couldn't reach it, no matter how hard she tried. Oona was just too little—too tiny to do it on her own. So Tig stepped forward and lifted the little robot up, catching her eye as he extruded a fingerlike appendage. Another, and another. The count reached three and Oona shoved her leg forward, slotting the key into the wall to complete the circuit.

"Ta-da!"

They said it together—Tig and Oona both. And then they waited, smiling in anticipation as lights flickered—tiny pin lights racing along the walls to either side, chasing each other all the way to Engineering. Quiet for a while, and then an ominous *crack* woke *Serengeti's* micro-sensors. A *crack* followed by a short, sharp tremor and a long and rolling shudder.

Power surged along electronic pathways, a tidal wave of energy spewing outward in a chaotic rush. Mechanisms hidden inside the wall screeched to life, *thunks* and *rattles* and ratcheting *clanks* coming from deep inside *Serengeti's* body, creeping toward *Cryo's* door. Metal screeched and groaned, shaking the ship, a shrieking, pain-filled sound that stretched on and on. And just when it seemed like it would never end, the last of the docking clamps finally let go.

Magical sound, that. Long-awaited, long-anticipated, but beneath it was a crackling that *Serengeti* didn't like at all. Not one bit. Sparks appeared, pouring from shredded wiring in the walls, showering the decking in short-lived light. Power faded, lights failed, leaving the hallway dim and quiet once more. Not just quiet, silent. Silent as the stars outside. Silent as a tomb.

No. Not a tomb. Not any longer.

"Free," *Serengeti* smiled. "They're almost free."

Just one task left. One more thing that needed to be done, and this job fell to *Serengeti.*

She slipped from Tig's body and flitted along the electronic pathways in the corridor's wall, searching for another circuit, one that was separate from all the others. One only she could touch. *Serengeti* reached for a last bit of power, sipping from her fast-dwindling store to send out a pulse that whispered along long abandoned pathways. *Clicks* and *rattles*, a *hum* and *whir* as machinery woke and ran diagnostics, performing preparatory checks.

Back to the corridor then where Tig and Tilli waited with little Oona, the three of them standing together, looking worried and excited as the noise of electronics grew and grew and grew.

After three decades of waiting, lying dormant in *Serengeti's* belly, *Cryo* finally came to life.

"*Beep?*" Oona asked, tilting her rounded head to look up at Tig. "*Beep-Beep?*"

"That's right," *Serengeti* said softly, touching at Oona's face. "They're free. It's time for them to go home, and leave us in this place."

Twenty-Nine

The *whir* of *Cryo's* machinery filled the corridor, its buzzing *rattle* shaking the deckplates, setting the robots' metal carapaces to thrumming. A good sound, that, and welcome after so much silence. So much emptiness and loss. That sound meant life and *Serengeti* clutched it to her, memorizing the feel of it, the shape of it, savoring these last few moments with her crew before *Cryo* took them away.

The *hum* changed, taking on a sharp-edge, almost angry edge a half second before the engines kicked in—fierce, throaty, roaring as they ignited—and shoved hard at *Serengeti's* body, pushing to break free. Eager to leave the womb and abandon the wreck of *Serengeti's* for the brilliance of the stars. A kick as the engines ratcheted upward, sending shudders up and down *Serengeti's* body, knocking panels loose, adding that debris to trickles of flotsam and jetsam already floating in the air. And after that came a punch in the gut *Serengeti* half-expected. A sharp twisting like a knife in her guts as the more damaged of her last two fuel cells finally gave up the ghost. A chaotic rush of power flooded through her, the fuel cell voiding its load of energy as it died.

More shuddering after that, the trembling in *Serengeti's* body growing increasingly violent. Tig took a quick step backward, and then a few more, grabbing at Tilli's leg, scooping up Oona and cradling her against his chest as he retreated from *Cryo's* door. More shaking and the trio of robots skipped away, moving all the way to the end of the hall. Best to be safe, after all, and watch the grand departure from a distant. No reason to fear being sucked out—not this time, not with all the atmosphere gone—but anything at all could happen when the lifeboat finally broke away.

Seconds ticked by with *Cryo's* engines roaring like dragons, battering at *Serengeti's* broken body, making the hallway flex and buck. Another push—harder this time—and *Cryo's* door pulled away from the hallway, the black letters on its surface growing smaller and smaller as the lifeboat moved away.

Serengeti stared through Tig's eyes, watching the starlight slither across *Cryo's* silver-white surface. The egg transformed, becoming a small, bright moon taking its place within the cosmos, leaving *Serengeti's* shredded remains behind. "Thank you," she breathed as *Cryo* left her. "Watch over my crew. Keep them safe for me."

Warning messages flared to life, screaming for attention. *Serengeti* acknowledged them and then shoved them all aside. She knew she was in trouble. Didn't need those flashing red errors to tell her that. One fuel cell let go earlier but a quick check showed the other was still limping along, sucking up energy from the solar panels outside to feed itself and keep doing its job.

Not much energy there, though. I'm burning through power faster than the fuel cell can collect it. I can't stay. *Serengeti* watched the power meter tick downward as creeping black veil fluttered in—a dark harbinger lurking at the edges of her consciousness. *No matter what I do, no matter how many times I sleep and wake, I can never stay.*

But she wasn't ready to go just yet. So she brushed the next set of warnings aside, saying nothing to Tig or Tilli, to little Oona who wouldn't understand.

Cryo fired its main engines, the backdraft from its propulsion system flaring white-hot as the Sun, bright as the start that bound *Serengeti* here in endless orbit. The robots reached for one another, huddling close together as the backwash from *Cryo's* engines licked at *Serengeti's* abused body, making her judder and shake, creak and groan. Yellow-white fire lit up the corridor, shimmering across chromed metal, painting the robot's faces in silver and gold. Silver and gold, and blue behind it, chasing across the robots' cheeks, swirling around their eyes.

A third kick—a brutal, bruising punch—and *Cryo* escaped completely, pulling away from *Serengeti* as it clawed its way into open space. And once free it reoriented, activating navigation to access the course *Serengeti* had programmed into its brain all those years ago. A last few adjustments, maneuvering jets fidgeting with the lifeboat's trajectory, and when its aim was true, *Cryo* set off, taking Henricksen and poor dead Finlay out into the stars.

"Bye-bye!" Tig and Tilli called together. Oona waved her legs enthusiastically, adding her piping *trill* of a voice to theirs. "Bye-bye, little ship. Bye-bye, *Serengeti* crew."

Serengeti wanted to join them, wished she could share the robots' excitement at seeing the lifeboat off, but her heart was conflicted—half of it filled with sorrow, the other radiating joy. So she left the adieus to Tig and his family and just watched silently as *Cryo* left them, bright sphere dwindling to a tiny, twinkling star as it moved out of her cameras' range.

"Safe journey," she whispered, casting those words across the depths of space. "Remember me," she added in her softest voice.

More warning messages—flashing red indicators calling urgently, stridently, refusing to be ignored this time. And with them came that dark curtain, creeping closer, reaching for *Serengeti* with clinging hands.

Serengeti sighed. *Out of time. I've run out of time.*

Tig coughed politely. "Umm...*Serengeti*?"

Worry in Tig voice, sensing the change in *Serengeti's* mood as her mind touched at his. Tilli picked up on it too and *burbled* softly, clearly upset. But Oona—precious little Oona with her tiny hand-drawn mouse—just looked confused. Confused and a little sad, because everyone else was. That broke *Serengeti's* heart.

"Come here, little mouse." She turned Tig away from the empty doorway and pulled Oona close, reached for Tilli with Tig's jointed metal leg and hugged her to his side.

She could feel them for a moment—all three of them at once, their collective consciousness filled to overflowing with warmth and light and life. Not life as biology defined it maybe, but AI life was every bit as pure and true as the frozen lives sleeping inside *Cryo*.

Serengeti drew that feeling inside her, storing it away with all the other memories she'd gathered, all the wonders and horrors, the pain and laughter and every other thing that made her *Serengeti* and not just ship. And then she gently disengaged herself from the robots and quietly slipped away, moving to the camera high above the little robots so she could freeze an image of the three of them together and take it with her when she slipped into the dark.

An error message intruded, flashing angrily, refusing to be ignored. *Serengeti* sighed in irritation and shut it off. Shut them *all* off while she was at it because there no longer seemed to be a point. Nothing would be working soon anyway. Not even she. And those error messages were really, *really* annoying.

The soft sound of *peeping* drifted from below. Oona looked up at the camera, face lights swirling in complex patterns as she *trilled* an anxious question, sensing something was wrong. That life as she knew it was changing in a very fundamental way. She just didn't know what it was. Tig and Tilli had suffered through this drill before, planned for this day for years and years and knew what must come next. But Oona...Oona was naïve and innocent, a stranger yet to sorrow, unlike Tig and Tilli who'd seen more than their fair share.

"I'm going to sleep again, little ones. And this time, I think, it will be for far longer than ever before." Intuition made her speak so, though that wasn't in her design specs either. Like love and dreaming and all the other things *Serengeti* picked up along the way. "I'm sorry." She reached for Tig and Tilli, for Oona between them, brushing electric fingertips across their shining chrome faces, smiling to herself as they shivered and sighed. "I wish I could stay, but..." But staying wasn't an option. Not right now anyway. "I have to go," she repeated softly.

They argued, of course, asking her why and why and why, when would they see her again, what they should do while she was gone. But *Serengeti* had no answers to offer. She just listened quietly to the chattering robots until their words eventually ran out.

Silence then—three robot faces looking up at the camera, *Serengeti* looking back down.

"You're in charge now, Tig. You understand? *You* are ship while I'm away. *You* are *Serengeti*, and all that she once was." *Serengeti* touched at his brain, noting the bits and pieces she'd modified, the code set she'd layered onto his default AI settings to integrate his mind with hers. "You are ship now, Tig. Do you understand?"

Tig blinked slowly, cobalt eyes worried, confused, a tiny bit lost. He was the oldest of her companions, and the most loyal. The one *Serengeti* could always count on. Who was always there when she woke from the dark. She needed him now, more than ever before.

Tig stared at the camera for a long, long time. "Yes," he said finally, voice the barest whisper. "Yes, *Serengeti*. I understand"

"Good boy, Tig," *Serengeti* whispered, swelling with pride. She caressed his chromed face, imbuing that touch with all the fondness she felt inside. "*Crew* was my directive, Tig. And now crew is gone, their path uncertain." She caught her breath, surprised by a sudden, stabbing twinge that burrowed into her gut. Her mind flashed on *Cryo* and the sleeping travelers inside it.

What sort of universe have I sent them into? Thirty-four years they've been frozen, sleeping in limbo while human civilization moves on.

Long enough for the war that caused this whole predicament to be settled, and a new one sprung up in its place. *Serengeti* chewed on that, worrying.

Whatever's out there, it has to be better than this, she thought bitterly. *It has to be better than staying here, marooned for all eternity, trapped in the bowels of this ravaged hulk that used to be a starship.*

She hoped it was so. She truly did.

"My human crew is gone," *Serengeti* said quietly, "and you, my clever little robots, have done all that I've asked. More than I could ever…" She trailed off again, searching for words. Something of comfort to leave behind while she slept. "I have no more orders for you. No more instructions save this: that you choose your own path, and make what life you can inside me."

Tig started to object—desperately scared.

Serengeti shushed him with a touch and told them the rest. "One thing and one thing only will I ask of you for me: that you listen in the depths of space, and wake me should the voice of Man drift near."

Tig *blipped* in thought, eyes blinking rapidly. Oona *trilled* and whistled, low, sad sounds that broke *Serengeti's* heart all over again, making her regret her need to leave them all the more.

No choice. No choice in the matter, Oona. In staying I'd doom us all.

"I'm sorry, little ones, but I cannot stay."

She zoomed in close, memorizing the look of Tig and Tilli hugging one another, with Oona clutched between them. The way their face lights reflected off the frosted metal panels on the walls. The way they wrapped their leg ends around each other like school children holding hands, giving comfort and receiving it at the same time. *Serengeti* took that image and filed it away, placing it alongside the pictures of Finlay and Henricksen, of the icy darkness filled with stars—all those precious memories she stored in the deepest, most protected part of her. The core of her crystal matrix that was the closest thing an AI had to a soul. And then she slipped into Tig's body to say her goodbyes. Her *last* goodbyes, she feared, though she couldn't tell the robots that.

"Come here, Oona," she called, coaxing the tiny robot near.

Oona—being Oona—grew suddenly shy. She ducked her head, refusing to look at *Serengeti,* squiggling like an octopus, trying to break free from Tig's cradling legs.

Serengeti called to her, whispering soft words of comfort, soothing her with gentle caresses until Oona finally calmed. She waited then— patient as can be—until Oona's head lifted, and she stared through Tig's eyes to *Serengeti* inside. "I have something to give you before I leave."

"*Peep?*"

"Yes," *Serengeti* smiled. "Peep."

She popped open a panel in Tig's body and dug around until she found a set of colored grease pencils he carried inside. A touch at Oona's body, turning her just a bit, and she extruded a set of appendages from the end of Tig's leg, pausing only to scan her database and sort through the thousands upon thousands of images stored there, before setting to work.

Serengeti wasn't much of an artist, but she sketched out the image she'd chosen as best she could, adding a round-eyed owl wearing a jaunty knit cap to Oona's metal side—a tiny little friend for the field mouse nibbling at its piece of cheese. "Do you like it?" she asked.

Oona blinked and twisted around, *burbling* curiously as she touched the colorful creature *Serengeti* had set there.

"Owl," *Serengeti* told her, touching the picture with Tig's leg. "That's an owl."

"Ow-ooo," *Tilli trilled* in her high-pitched voice. "Ow-oo! Ow-oo!" she sang, flailing happily, showing Tig and Tilli her shiny new badge.

"That's right. Ow-oo." *Serengeti* laughed. "The mouse is timid and shy, Oona, but the owl is filled with wisdom."

"*Whoo?*" Oona stared in wide-eyed wonder. "*Whoo-whoo?*" she asked, doing a fair impression of an owl herself.

"*Whoo-whoo,*" *Serengeti* repeated softly, touching at Oona's face. "You are both, Oona. One becoming the other. A mouse searching for wings to soar the skies above."

"*Whoo-ooo?*" Oona asked, pointing at herself in surprise.

"Yes, silly. You." *Serengeti* chucked at Oona's chin, coaxing a shy giggle from her as she blushed and ducked her head. "Now come here and give me a hug before I go."

No shyness this time. No timid demureness. No stand-offish games. Oona wrapped her stubby legs around Tig's body and squeezed with all her might, while Tilli *hooted* sorrowfully and Tig let loose with a low whistle of mourning.

"Shhh." *Serengeti* clutched Oona tightly as she leaned Tig close to Tilli, touching her cheek to cheek. "None of that now, you hear."

Three robot heads nodded in unison, face lights flashing in scrolling patterns.

She touched at them—each of them in turn, feeling them shiver as she caressed their AI brains. "Good night, Tig," *Serengeti* whispered, touching at his cheek. "Good night, Tilli." A second touch, electric fire arcing from Tig's chromed face to hers. "Be good, little Oona." A smile for Oona, a cobalt kiss given back. *Serengeti* pulled them close and held them tight, and then she sighed and retreated, racing along pathways until she reached the bridge: the place where it all started, and someday it would all end.

"Someday," *Serengeti* whispered. "Someday."

A wish, a promise, she wasn't sure which.

A last look around and *Serengeti* let go and slipped into darkness—a soft dark this time, different from the dream of fire, her memories of Henricksen and those days of long ago. This time there were stars, appearing one after the other, shimmering silver-white against an infinity of black.

"Dark," *Serengeti* whispered, beginning to smile. "Dark and stars, just as I remember. Home. I'm home."

EPILOGUE

Tig threaded his way through the shredded remains of the ship's port side hull, tip-toeing through debris, navigating narrow passages and yawning chasms until he reached the darkness outside. A flash of metal as Tilli joined him, murmuring encouragements to Oona as she held tight to her leg.

Big day today: Oona's first trip to the outer hull. A trip prompted by much begging and pleading because Oona desperately wanted to see the stars. Not just the patches showing through the holes in the ship's corridors—*all* of them. And Tsu's star—the star that kept the ship alive—most of all. Tig resisted at first—Tig and Tilli both, worrying for Oona's safety, imagining a thousand things that could go wrong. But as time went on, they found it increasingly hard to deny her. Especially since they loved the stars themselves. And because they loved her, because they knew they couldn't protect Oona from everything forever, Tig and Tilli finally relented.

"*Ooooh!*" Oona breathed, *trilling* with excitement. She pulled away from Tilli and scampered onto a section of hull plating, dancing on her tip-toes as she turned in a circle, taking it all in. A small menagerie of animals turned with her—a dozen different creatures added to her sides over the years, joining the little mouse that was the first of her decorations, the wide-eyed owl *Serengeti* gifted to her in parting. "*Oooh-ooooh!*" Oona exclaimed, looking around her, eyes wide as wide can be, smile wider still.

She turned and turned about, staring in amazement, drinking in the sight of the shattered ship they lived in, the endless darkness outside with its thousands upon thousands of silver bright stars.

"*Oooh-oooh-ooh!*" She hopped up and down, pointing at the shadowed shapes jutting up from the top of the ship, babbling out a long string of questions as she turned to Tig and Tilli, looking for permission.

Tig shrugged and waved them forward.

Tilli called Oona to her, taking her by one leg, warning her to stay close by her side as the two of them set off, leaving Tig to follow more slowly behind.

Oona babbled excitedly as she scuttled along, pointing out this thing and that, asking what they were and what had happened, wanting to know everything—all that *Serengeti* was, and had been, and would one day be. And Tilli—patient Tilli—answered as best she could. Everything but the 'to-be'—on that particular subject she had nothing to offer her daughter. They had yesterday and today, and all the yesterdays before that, but tomorrow…tomorrow was a dream. A wish for bright stars and good fortune. A hope that someday soon, *Serengeti* would wake to join them again, and make their little family complete.

Excitement as they crested the top of *Serengeti's* body, Oona staring raptly, chromed face shining in the glow of Tsu's star. More excitement when Tilli pointed downward, at the hull plating twinkling and shimmering as it drank in the starlight. Oona smiled happily, face lights flashing, mimicking the twinkling of the ship's body.

Now she saw. Now she knew. Now she understood why *Serengeti* loved the stars so.

But Oona was a child still, and in the way of children, her interest soon waned. She looked around and spied the forest of solar panels standing close by the bow. She pointed, babbling out a staccato burst of overexcited chatter, and then took off, all but dragging Tilli with her as she raced over to take a closer look.

That left Tig to follow after. Again.

He took his time, letting Tilli and Oona speed ahead, enjoying the sight of them surrounded by all those stars. Tilli slipped into teacher mode as they moved along the racks of solar panels, explaining the science and engineering behind it all so Oona would understand how the solar array worked.

Tig listened for a bit and then split off, turning away from the solar panel forest as he headed for the massive metal tower a short distance away. He rolled over to it and stopped at its base, tilted his head backward and stared up and up and up.

The antenna had grown over the years: dishes added, longer lengths of girdering bolted on in places, a hodge-podge of odds and ends tacked on wherever they could be fitted, transforming the makeshift sniffer into a massive communications device—a gnarled, crooked finger pointing at the stars. A finger that, with each new addition, reached a little bit further, expanding their listening range out into the dark.

Serengeti designed the original but this…the additions were all Tig's. That and the relay he'd cobbled together, a primitive thing that sent a pulse across the channel shared between himself, Tilli and Oona, notifying them instantly if anything noisy drifted into range. He'd designed it, built it, but to this day he didn't know if it actually worked.

After all, nothing had ever come into range to test it on. At least, as far as he knew. And if something had…

Best not to think about that.

Tig and Tilli busied themselves around the ship, fixing things, teaching Oona along the way, but they always made time to come out here and tap into the tower, using a cable snaking from its base to connect themselves directly to its listening array. Tig loved it out here, with nothing but the darkness and the stars. He stood on *Serengeti's* hull, listening through the comms tower, dreaming of days long gone, hoping each time he plugged into hear a *pop* or a *fizz*, a *squawk* or *crackle*, something, anything that even *remotely* resembled interstellar communications. But weeks passed, months and years, with nothing and nothing and yet more nothing.

And still Tig came. Day after day, year after year. Because to do otherwise, was to give up hope. And hope was one of the few things they had left.

Tig moved a step closer to the tower of misfit pieces and plugged himself in, dialing his receivers all the way up.

Silence at first, just as he expected. And then…something. Something that wasn't quite sound. Something *felt* more than heard that was surprisingly familiar.

Tig panned his head around, searching the stars, tilted it back and examined the empty stretch of space above him. Nothing to see, nothing but stars. But that something, that *feeling* kept getting stronger, setting his pathways to humming, reverberating with sound that wasn't quite sound.

"*Beep*," he muttered, face lights frowning in concentration. And then, "*Beeeeeeep*." Tig's eyes widened as a dark void formed—inky black nothingness bending and twisting as it blotted out the stars.

That too was familiar. He'd seen that nothingness a thousand times and more, knew that void was a buckle—a spot of unstable space, the precursor to hyperspace transit.

"*Tilli!*" Tig twisted around, waving excitedly, but Tilli and Oona were deep inside the solar panel forest, unable to see him from here. He tapped into the robot comms channel and babbled like an idiot, trying to get her attention. "Tilli come see! There's something—"

"In a minute," she said, and shut the channel down.

"Bugger." Tig *wonked* in annoyance and faced back around.

The buckle widened, darkening as it resolved. A shimmer as it sucked inward and flared bright, silver-white. A flood of communications poured through the breach, filling Tig's brain with the grinding sound of electronic signals as a sleek-sided shape appeared, sparkling in the starlight.

More flashes, more breaches forming and resolving, silver-white flashes popping off like fireworks all around that first shape. Each new arrival threw more noise into the ambient, cluttering up the once-empty section of space with a vast ocean of sound that washed over Tig like an electronic storm. He focused in, listening intently, leg wrapped around the metal girders of the antennae to boost the signal that much more. A flash of face lights as he parsed through data, filtering the chatter until one voice came through clearly—louder, stronger than all the others. A voice he remembered from long, and long, and long ago.

Tig whooped with joy and spun in a circle, legs ends flailing the air around him. "*Sechura*," he called, dialing up his comms, making his small voice loud as possible. "Here! We're here!"

A brief delay before a response came back. "What of *Serengeti*?"

"Here! She's here. Sleeping, dreaming, waiting for you, all this time."

Another moment of silence, and then the mass of ships turned and glided toward *Serengeti,* starlight twinkling along their hulls.

Tig bounced up and down, waving his legs excitedly, calling out to Tilli and Oona, telling them to "Come-come-come! Come see, come see, come see, Tilli! *Sechura* is here!"

Sechura. Sister ship. After all these years, the Valkyries had come to bring *Serengeti* home.

CHECK OUT OTHER GREAT SCIENCE FICTION BOOKS

FURNACE
by Joseph Williams

On a routine escort mission to a human colony, Lieutenant Michael Chalmers is pulled out of hyper-sleep a month early. The RSA Rockne Hummel is well off course and—as the ship's navigator—it's up to him to figure out why. It's supposed to be a simple fix, but when he attempts to identify their position in the known universe, nothing registers on his scans. The vessel has catapulted beyond the reach of starlight by at least a hundred trillion light-years. Then a planetary-mass object materializes behind them. It's burning brightly even without a star to heat it. Hundreds of damaged ships are locked in its orbit. The crew discovers there are no life-signs aboard any of them. As system failures sweep through the Hummel, neither Chalmers nor the pilot can prevent the vessel from crashing into the surface near a mysterious ancient city. And that's where the real nightmare begins.

LUNA
by Rick Chesler

On the threshold of opening the moon to tourist excursions, a private space firm owned by a visionary billionaire takes a team of non-astronauts to the lunar surface. To address concerns that the moon's barren rock may not hold long-term allure for an uber-wealthy clientele, the company's charismatic owner reveals to the group the ultimate discovery: life on the moon.

But what is initially a triumphant and world-changing moment soon gives way to unrelenting terror as the team experiences firsthand that despite their technological prowess, the moon still holds many secrets.

CHECK OUT OTHER GREAT SCIENCE FICTION BOOKS

IN PERPETUITY
by Jake Bible

For two thousand years, Earth and her many colonies across the galaxy have fought against the Estelian menace. Having faced overwhelming losses, the CSC has instituted the largest military draft ever, conscripting millions into the battle against the aliens. Major Bartram North has been tasked with the unenviable task of coordinating the military education of hundreds of thousands of recruits and turning them into troops ready to fight and die for the cause.

As Major North struggles to maintain a training pace that the CSC insists upon, he realizes something isn't right on the Perpetuity. But before he can investigate, the station dissolves into madness brought on by the physical booster known as pharma. Unfortunately for Major North, that is not the only nightmare he faces- an armada of Estelian warships is on the edge of the solar system and headed right for Earth!

BATTLEFIELD MARS
by David Robbins

Several centuries into the future, Earth has established three colonies on Mars. No indigenous life has been discovered, and humankind looks forward to making the Red Planet their own.

Then 'something' emerges out of a long-extinct volcano and doesn't like what the humans are doing.

Captain Archard Rahn, United Nations Interplanetary Corps, tries to stem the rising tide of slaughter. But the Martians are more than they seem, and it isn't long before Mars erupts in all-out war.

CHECK OUT OTHER GREAT SCIENCE FICTION BOOKS

MAUSOLEUM 2069
by **Rick Jones**

Political dignitaries including the President of the Federation gather for a ceremony onboard Mausoleum 2069. But when a cloud of interstellar dust passes through the galaxy and eclipses Earth, the tenants within the walls of Mausoleum 2069 are reborn and the undead begin to rise. As the struggle between life and death onboard the mausoleum develops, Eriq Wyman, a one-time member of a Special ops team called the Force Elite, is given the task to lead the President to the safety of Earth. But is Earth like Mausoleum 2069? A landscape of the living dead? Has the war of the Apocalypse finally begun? With so many questions there is only one certainty: in space there is nowhere to run and nowhere to hide.

RED CARBON
by **D.J. Goodman**

Diamonds have been discovered on Mars.

After years of neglect to space programs around the world, a ruthless corporation has made it to the Red Planet first, establishing their own mining operation with its own rules and laws, its own class system, and little oversight from Earth. Conditions are harsh, but its people have learned how to make the Martian colony home.

But something has gone catastrophically wrong on Earth. As the colony leaders try to cover it up, hacker Leah Hartnup is getting suspicious. Her boundless curiosity will lead her to a horrifying truth: they are cut off, possibly forever. There are no more supplies coming. There will be no more support. There is no more mission to accomplish. All that's left is one goal: survival.

CHECK OUT OTHER GREAT SCIENCE FICTION BOOKS

SALVAGE MERC ONE
by Jake Bible

Joseph Laribeau was born to be a Marine in the Galactic Fleet. He was born to fight the alien enemies known as the Skrang Alliance and travel the galaxy doing his duty as a Marine Sergeant. But when the War ended and Joe found himself medically discharged, the best job ever was over and he never thought he'd find his way again.

Then a beautiful alien walked into his life and offered him a chance at something even greater than the Fleet, a chance to serve with the Salvage Merc Corp.

Now known as Salvage Merc One Eighty-Four, Joe Laribeau is given the ultimate assignment by the SMC bosses. To his surprise it is neither a military nor a corporate salvage. Rather, Joe has to risk his life for one of his own. He has to find and bring back the legend that started the Corp.

SERENGETI
by J.B. Rockwell

It was supposed to be an easy job: find the Dark Star Revolution Starships, destroy them, and go home. But a booby-trapped vessel decimates the Meridian Alliance fleet, leaving Serengeti—a Valkyrie class warship with a sentient AI brain—on her own; wrecked and abandoned in an empty expanse of space. On the edge of total failure, Serengeti thinks only of her crew. She herds the survivors into a lifeboat, intending to sling them into space. But the escape pod sticks in her belly, locking the cryogenically frozen crew inside.

Then a scavenger ship arrives to pick Serengeti's bones clean. Her engines dead, her guns long silenced, Serengeti and her last two robots must find a way to fight the scavengers off and save the crew trapped inside her.